Ariadne Rewired

Adam Ipsen

Tridragon Creative

Foreword

I dedicate this book to my wife, Sharon. This is a given, since the time spent on it is just a fraction of the life I already happily share with you in its entirety.

Chapter 1

In the 22nd century, most things happened at the speed of thought.

That's all it took when Iona Nagami filed for divorce: a single thought. <I want this to be over!> There was only a millisecond between it entering her head in their Kansai apartment and the thought being heard on the other side of the Atlantic. There, in the California County Clerk's office where she'd applied for marriage twenty long years ago, an AI began fulfilling her wish just like a digital djinn. It scoured every recorded moment of her marriage, every post, every publicly available thought. Once it was done, it compiled its findings and submitted them to the judge, who, for such a minor affair, was also an AI.

Three seconds later, a prompt appeared in front of her husband, Rhen Nagami. It read:

Iona Nagami has submitted for divorce. Do you consent?

Beyond the floating letters, just right of the question mark, she was staring at him. Her eyes were like coal, former embers that had been unstoked for far too long.

"Is this really what you want?" Rhen asked.

"More than anything," she replied.

He accepted. The second he did, the baleful message disappeared. In the weeks that followed, part of him wondered if she would change her mind. There was a thirty-day cooling off period after all. But exactly a month later, Rhen Nagami found himself walking towards the Kansai International Airport, still divorced.

This too shall pass, he thought. *It will pass, right?*

Rhen made a beeline towards the airport. Like everything in Japan, it was an architectural marvel: a gleaming, crimson-red flower blossoming skyward, as if it had floated down and landed on the peninsula. As he passed under the archway marking the entrance, ghostly cherry blossoms fell around him. A phantom prompt popped up in front of him, written in both English and Japanese. It read: Thank you for visiting Kansai, the Flower of Japan.

Rhen didn't stop to smell the faux flowers, though he could hardly miss the lilac and rose scents sprayed by the archway. Soon he was surrounded on all sides by a bustling crowd; he was hardly the only one in a hurry.

Nevertheless, his suitcase protested.

"Sir, if you don't slow down, I won't be able to stay nearby!" It shouted from behind him.

"Sorry Casey." Rhen stopped for a moment and turned around. The large four-wheeled container wove with exceptional grace through the masses. The suitcase was hard to miss, since it was painted neon blue with a canary yellow stripe, just like a race car. At least, that's what Rhen believed.

As if to prove him wrong, the suitcase was knocked over just five feet from its destination by a person clad in an ink-black suit. Both the suitcase and the suit-wearer were sent sprawling spectacularly to the ground.

Rhen immediately dashed forward. "Are both of you okay?"

"I'm fine, just let me get upright," Casey answered, as two spindly metal arms detached from their outer shell. With a small push, they were on their wheels again. "Luggage contents are minimally shuffled, though the arrangement was disorderly to begin with."

"And you?" Rhen turned to the other party, asking in Japanese. He pinged them, a simple thought-request for their details. There was a chance they didn't have a Rosetta implant, but the odds were vanishingly small. They must have accepted, because a second later, the suit-wearer's details floated above their head.

> Gary Lowe. He/Him. Success usually comes to those who are too
> busy to be looking for it.

Yes, but there's consequences to being busy all the time, Rhen thought ruefully.

Personal quotes were all the rage these days. Good conversation starters, but poorly chosen ones were social anathema. He had a quote as well, but it was self-authored. It read: The divide between machines and humans is as wide as we make it. He didn't hold it against others if they chose to quote someone, but if he was going to have a slogan, he wanted the words to be his own.

Rhen was pinged in return, and accepting was as simple as thinking it. He didn't hesitate, since these days a name was hardly personal information. There were mutual apologies, and the man hurried off again on his way.

"I should get loaded up. I'll see you in Adelaide," Casey said.

"Hey, if they send you to the wrong location, make sure you ask someone to send you to the address I told you about," Rhen replied. The suitcase saluted in what he swore was a cheeky manner before wheeling off to luggage check-in.

Once Rhen was in the terminal, he made a beeline towards a takoyaki stand. There was forty minutes before departure, and there were lots of things about Japan he was going to miss, proper takoyaki being one of them. As the staff made him a fresh batch, another prompt flicked across his vision: Incoming call from Yui.

After reading the caller's name, he sighed.

<I accept.>

In the blink of an eye, a woman appeared in front of him. Far from being a spectacle, nobody but Rhen gave her a second glance. She was just a stream of data being beamed into his Rosetta implant, which was in turn consensually tricking his corneas, after all. Still, Yui looked as corporal as everyone else. Her arms were crossed, and her brow scrunched up.

<I know you've already handed in your resignation, but I wanted to have one last go of talking you around.> Even as she talked, her lips remained pursed. That was the great thing about thought-speak: it left your mouth free to make all sorts of expressions. The other was that even though he was thinking in English, Yui was hearing it in Japanese. <What can I do to get you to stay?>

<Nothing, Yui. I've made up my mind.>

<Come on, there must be something. Name it! We've done a lot of great work, and you're important to the Themis project. Don't you at least want to see it through? You gave all the AI *names*, for crying out loud.>

<Look, normally I would.> And he meant it, since he'd never quit a job halfway through a project before. <But I don't want to stay in Keihanna. I made a life with Iona here, and now it's over.> *Time for a fresh start.* <I left pretty detailed notes in my code for my replacement.>

<Nobody reads notes anymore, they're not old-fashioned eccentrics like you — they're all cognitive coders.>

<Well, this old-fashioned eccentric helped make that possible. Look, I've got to pay for my takoyaki, the staff are staring.>

Yui threw up her arms and stepped aside. It was entirely unnecessary because he could walk right through her. Still, it was etiquette. When the person at the front desk asked if he was paying cognitively or digitally, he answered the latter and waved his ring hand over a black panel. It cost only four glo, which was pretty cheap.

<Anyway, it's not just Iona,> Rhen continued. <I've been offered an opportunity elsewhere, and it's too good to turn down.>

<Yes, I've heard about that too. So, what is this magical opportunity you've been so tight lipped about? Is it with a competitor?> Her voice was stern and unwavering, which meant she'd made a deliberate choice to make it sound that way. The carrot hadn't worked, so here was the stick. <There's a non-competition clause in your contract with Sekai Cybernetics. And I know you, there's *no way* you've decided to go on hiatus from AI work for that long. You don't know the word sabbatical.>

<Sure I do. That's when you know how to spell things, right?>

<That's grammatical.> She placed a hands on her hip. <Stop deflecting and answer the question, Rhen.>

She's not going to let me go until I tell her. Better get it over and done with.

<Actually, the new job is with a subsidiary of Sekai, so it's all within the family. It's an experimental facility in central Australia. They want to test my theory, Yui.>

Yui went slack jawed with astonishment. It took a lot to make her speechless. *See, I've taken your stick and snapped it*, Rhen thought, with a tiny hint of satisfaction. Still, she didn't stay mute for long.

<The hybrid theory? Didn't Sekai already knock that one back?> She asked. <People want smart toasters, not emotional toasters; there's no market for it.>

Disbelief, it seemed, was her fallback. *I don't blame her. I'd nearly given up on anyone taking my theory seriously, too.* When the offer came to him two weeks ago as he nursed his sorrows at a bar in Kizugawa, it couldn't have been timelier.

<Well, someone does want to do it,> he replied. <I guess someone out there sees the same problem with current AI that I do. Hey look, Yui, I've got a plane to catch. Good luck with the project.>

And with that, he cancelled the call.

A pang of guilt stabbed in his chest; he didn't blame Yui for being persistent. *She's losing her head cognicist at the tail end of a project, and she'll have to get someone up to speed on a year's worth of work.* As a fellow team leader, he sympathised. But her talent was breaking mountains into sand, eroding any obstacle in her path. Rhen had learned the only way to win a battle with Yui was not to give her a battlefield to fight on.

Rhen popped a piece of takoyaki in his mouth. Scalding batter burned his tongue; it was far too soon to eat. Rather than stand idly in the middle of all the foot traffic, he wandered to a nearby window overlooking the airfield.

As he peered into the glass, a pair of steel-grey eyes stared back. His face was full of etchings that had not been there just five years ago; fracture points at the edge of his eyes and forehead, shallow lines etched in honey-beige. His hair, too, was in flux; stuck in some indeterminate state between bleached salt and impossibly black pepper, tousled in a way that society found acceptably disordered.

Give it time. I'm right on the edge of being officially old.

Beyond his weathered reflection was the airfield proper. The majority of it was sky ramps, which stood like gigantic sundials in the midday sun. At least one or more of them was turning at any given moment.

Whenever one of the dials stopped, it wasn't long before a craft shot up the triangular ramp and into the sky, quickly disappearing. Beside the monoliths was a landing zone for incoming traffic, but this was flat and uninteresting.

He blew on another piece of takoyaki and waited to be thrown into the ether.

***

While he was sitting in the airport lounge near his departure gate, he got another call. This time it wasn't Yui, thank goodness, but the name didn't fill him with joy. As the prompt hovered over his vision, Rhen debated whether or not to answer. In the end he relented, and a man appeared in front of him.

<Hey, dad.>

Unlike Rhen, the man before him had officially entered the senior category. But taking the poet's advice, Robert Nagami was not going gentle into that good night. Every single grey hair on his head had been meticulously bleached blond, every wrinkle teased into near submission by the latest in imported Korean genetic treatments. But even with all the creams and pills and injections the world had to offer— and a liberal covering of fake tan — the spots of age still poked through. Still, the unwinnable war waged on across every plane of his face, no doubt costing tens of thousands of glo.

<Hey kid. Sorry I haven't had the time to ring until now. I hear you and Iona are going through some tough times?>

<You could say that, given we've been divorced for a month.>

<Oh, I'm sorry to hear that,> he said. But even though his voice had all the right lilts and intones, his expression barely changed. <What happened?>

<A lot of things.> After a long pause, it was clear he was going to be forced to talk about it. <We've been distant for a while. She slept with someone else.>

<That's terrible!> And this time, his face contorted into an authentic scowl. <Cheating speaks of low moral fibre. Your late father and I never cheated on each other.> *Late father.* As if Kenji Nagami had simply failed to show up for an appointment. For his widower, being hit by a bus was an unforgivable slight of decorum, one that had never healed. <What a no-good thing to do.>

<Well, it's not that simple,> Rhen said. <Neither of us were in the relationship anymore.> The last time they made love was Valentine's Day. A ritual obligation both of them fulfilled. *That had been, what, six months ago?* It was only logical she had gone elsewhere. Not exactly something he wanted to share with his father, though.

<Well, you're being kinder than I think you should be. You're not thinking of trying to work it out with Iona, are you?>

<No, the thirty-day cooldown expired. We'd have to get married all over again, and I don't think that's going to happen.>

<Was it about kids, do you think?> His father asked, continuing to prod for a cause, since Rhen had refused to give him one. <I know she was interested in having them, and you weren't.>

Well, it started that way. There were so many arguments towards the end, Rhen had lost track. Still, there was always one that stood out.

<I think, when you get right down to it, it's about the fact I probably won't die, and she will.>

There was a pregnant pause. His father touched his slightly sagging cheeks, fingertips working across every groove. Between gravity and the dermal fillers, the Earth was winning.

<Oh, yes, that.> His dad's voice was flat, modulated. <Well, I can see why that might cause problems. I'm not *personally* interested, of course, but I don't have the option.>

Liar, Rhen thought. The conversation petered out after that.

<Sorry dad, it looks like my flight will be boarding soon. I'll speak to you later.>

<Of course. Love you, kid.>

Rhen knew it would be at least a few months before they spoke again.

I'm surprised he rang. I'm always the one ringing him.

The boarding call would be soon, but he had a few more minutes, so with a thought, he brought up the news. A rectangular shape appeared across his vision, like a window to a newsroom. It was semi-transparent, so he could still see what was behind it. The presenter in the projected newsroom waved at him.

<Hello, Rhen! I'm Arietta McCloud from GCNN, here to provide you with the latest news updates,> she said, putting her hands on the desk and clasping them together. <Would you like the usual: global, technology, science and the weather in Kansai?>

<Just global, I'm in a rush.>

<Sure thing! Remember Anteros, that near-Earth asteroid worth trillions I told you about last week? The situation has deteriorated since India claimed half of it and Japan claimed the other. With the world's mineral resource supply running low, both nations are rushing to get operations set up on the asteroid, while Canada, Australia, and the European Union have put in competing claims. Both the United Republics of America and China are trying to revive their pre-Solar Age space programs, but it's unlikely either will be space-capable again before all of Anteros is claimed.>

<Guess the Outer Space Treaty as it stands now is a bit of a joke.>

<Exactly. The UN is looking to revise the treaty to reduce the chance of hostilities and ensure fair distribution. There are a few other world events, but given your past viewing habits, I don't think you'd be interested.>

<Thanks for the update, Arietta.>

<Any time! Remember, if you have a story to report, just send it through cognitively or digitally at this address.>

The news box disappeared along with the algorithmic reporter, leaving his vision fully free again.

The boarding call echoed across the room and, just in case he missed it, he was pinged with an alert. With the close proximity of the lounge, it didn't take long to get to the gate. His priority ticket allowed him to skip most of the queue and get right up to the doors.

When they opened, the staff herded their wards across the transparent bridge that separated the waiting area from the shuttle itself. The nanomaterials that coated the craft had been recently replaced; he could tell by the unblemished pearly shine. It would be all Indian built; with their world-class expertise in space flight, it was no surprise to Rhen that they had made it to Anteros first.

The shuttle was parked snugly within a tunnel that was truncated on either side by bulkheads. Beyond the one that the craft's nose was pointing towards there was a deafening roar, as another ship took off up the sky ramp. When it was their turn, the door would open, and they'd approach the base of it like a cart on a rollercoaster.

Until then, Rhen just got on board and found his seat. He'd done this dance more times than he could count.

Business class in the shuttle was fairly roomy, and the recliners were spaced apart. Once everyone was on board — which didn't take long due to the professional herders — the seats reclined back. It was the best way to absorb the temporary burst of G-force. All the automated servers were stored away for now, but the square robots were still visible in the same-shaped indents in the wall.

There were of course those who couldn't take that pressure even though it didn't last long. They had to take other forms of transportation, like intercontinental rail or old school jets.

With a lot of clamour and noise, the craft shook and shifted towards the ramp. Then, the world slowly shifted to bring his feet level with his head.

As he was staring at his magnetic shoe-clasps, there was a deafening rumble, and his whole body sunk deep into the padded seat. Rhen considered himself a space-setter: someone who flew suborbital on the regular. Still, there was something special about the way gravity could push you with such awe-inducing power that you were literally stuck in place.

When the pressure eased off, Rhen was somewhat disappointed.

Now they were on the ascent, the windows slid up. Rhen waited for the blue of the sky to turn to black. He knew it wouldn't take long as they shot towards the Kármán line.

When the plane levelled out, the servers detached themselves from the walls and began busying themselves.

There was a ping, and Rhen flicked his eyes to the source: the slender person sitting across from him. They had lots of deep lines on their overly tanned face, but their hair was an unnatural squid black. Since it was only polite, he exchanged details.

Walt Hayward. He/Him. Courage is being scared to death and saddling up anyway.

"I like your quote, stranger," Walt said in English. "The divide between machines and humans is vast, in my opinion. Maybe insurmountable."

The man had a United Republics accent, specifically from the Old States. The loud, stressed vowels were unmissable. Despite being from that part of the U.R. himself, spending decades bouncing between Japan and Australia had softened Rhen's own considerably, making it hard to pin down.

"Well, it's more about getting closer to them, and just AI advancement in general," Rhen said. At the same time, one of the box-like servers wheeled up and passed him a drink in a bioplastic cup. "But when I hear the word 'insurmountable', I take that as a challenge."

The man raised an eyebrow, taking his own cup from the server without so much as looking at it. "You're involved in working on machines or something?" And then, when he sipped his drink, he spat it out and handed it back. "Hey, bring me back something alcoholic, will you? A whiskey sour." The robot hurried off to diligently fulfil the request.

Meanwhile, Rhen shrugged at Walt's question. "I mean, machines and other devices. I helped invent the Rosetta implant; the thing in your neck."

Walt's eyebrow shot up. "Jeesus! You invented that? You must be famous. Probably got a Nobel prize, right?"

"Not a Nobel, since that's for science, but I did get the Turing Award. It was a team effort though; my work was largely on the part that translates your brain signals into code and vice-versa."

People often assumed that great advancements were made by one person of extraordinary talent, and not for the first time, Rhen lamented how they were handed out to just one or two individuals. He corrected things where he could, but the myth persisted, even among other cognicists. That said, he had poured himself into the Rosetta project quite literally. And while there had been cognitive human-machine interfaces in the past, the Rosetta was the first true version to achieve widespread adoption.

It was a massive technological achievement, and like so many before it, it had come at a cost. Speaking of, it seemed Walt was not to be deterred on the subject of personal gain.

"Surely you got a lot of money out of it? I imagine with all the devices sold, you've got a mansion or twelve. Probably one in each of the big cities."

"Well, I'm no entrepreneur. The invention belongs to Arctis Labs and is licensed to Sekai Cybernetics, since I signed an agreement."

"That's got to smart. I'd be suing them anyway if I were you, to see if I could get something out of them." The man sipped his drink. "Speaking of awards, I bet you were one of the last humans to get one. I hear they give them all out to the machines now, Nobel or not."

"Well, in those rare cases, the machine probably did the work and made the deductions. If they were human, they'd get the award."

"But I don't think Turing would have intended for them to get the award when he made it."

There were so many things wrong with the statement that Rhen quietly ordered himself a drink as well.

"Well, a machine is piloting this plane right now," Rhen continued after a beverage was in hand. So far, the tone was that of civil debate. "Probably a Zephyr model. And machines have acted as co-pilots since the start of the twentieth century."

"That's true, but there's a human in the cockpit in case the machine goes haywire."

"True, but mostly for PR. They know how to land the plane in an emergency, and call ground control for everything else," Rhen said. "And when they do that, they'd talk to another AI, who would tell them what to do. So, who's really in charge?"

Both drinks were empty now. The man thumbed the rim of the cup. "Well, fair enough. Tell me, are you a Prog?"

Rhen paused.

"I have a prog, I'm not a prog. Is there a problem with that?" He asked lightly. The question was rhetorical, he strongly suspected the man would. Most people did.

"No, just curious, never met someone with one before. Must be nice to know you can get uploaded into a steel body somewhere and escape the mortal coil."

And there it was, the familiar glint of jealousy in his eyes. Just like Iona. Just like his dad, and almost everyone else who knew about it.

Prog was short for Promethean-grade consciousness. For a few rare individuals, the human brain could be digitised and stored like regular data. They could also be booted up as an emulated AI, effectively giving that person immortality, since their memories and thought patterns would continue to exist long after their body expired. The term came from the Greek titan of myth who made humanity from clay, and stole fire and knowledge from the heavens for them. For his efforts, he was tied to a rock and punished by having an eagle pick at his liver for all eternity.

Rhen sympathised.

Back when he was a young cognicist at Arctis Labs, the net had exploded with news that humanity's ultimate adversary, death, had finally been defeated. And while only a select few had been successfully copied, the world waited with bated breath that their turn would come next, given enough research and money. But after countless failures, they discovered that while anyone could be digitised, for most people, it didn't last. For those without a prog, their copied consciousness would begin to deteriorate until it pulled itself apart.

There were lots of theories about *why*, of course. Some said it was because most people instinctively rejected thinking like and being a machine, and therefore their own existence, while those with progs reported higher rates of sympathy for robots and physical detachment. Others suspected it was to do with how the neural pathways formed during childhood, perhaps with a genetic component. But a suspicion without proof was just superstition.

Still, while nobody knew why some people had this special factor and others didn't, it was easy enough to check for. The test was known as the Bills-Aldrich, named after its creators. On a side note, both of them had progs. In Rhen's experience, the rich seemed to take particular issue with the fact that no amount of money could change the test's results.

It was time for some diplomacy.

"Well, I don't have any plans to be put in a frame with no sense of taste, touch or smell anytime soon," Rhen answered, shrugging with both his shoulders and hands. "Not much of a way to live. On top of that, it may not actually be immortality anyway."

The man screwed up his face. "What do you mean?"

"Well, have you ever heard of the Ship of Theseus?" When the man shook his head, Rhen continued. "It's a thought experiment, one of the oldest in Western philosophy. In Greek legend, the ship used by the hero-king Theseus was preserved by the people of Athens."

"As the planks of the ship decayed, they replaced them with new and stronger ones. Over time, every piece of the ship had been replaced, but it retained the same shape and name. So, the question is, after that happened, was it the same ship?"

His fellow passenger paused and stroked his chin. The question had stopped him from touching his second drink, recently delivered. "No, it wouldn't be. None of the original parts were left, so it's not the same ship."

"Then from that point of view, it's not immortality. When someone's consciousness is copied, every neural pathway is duplicated digitally, but all the organic parts are replaced with synthetic ones. None of the original components remain, just the shape and the name."

"But you'd still go on in some form, right?"

"Not necessarily. The 'me' that exists now would still be in my human body, the one thinking right now, and would still die with it. Even if you destroyed my body at the same time, it just means I was killed and replaced. Kind of a raw deal for the guy sitting across from you, right?"

"Yeah, I guess it is. I never thought of it that way." The man's voice had a happier note, and the glint of jealousy in his eyes had been replaced with one of camaraderie. He raised his cup, "Well, to the guy who replaces you, then. May he do better than the two of us chumps."

Rhen clicked his cup against his, then took a sip. His shoulders relaxed, but not because of the drink.

Well, at least that ended amicably. Wish it was that easy to talk everyone around.

He turned his gaze to the window. Right now, the curvature of the Earth was visible, and they'd be touching down in Australia in just twenty minutes. Suborbital flights never took very long. He tried to enjoy it while it lasted.

Further out, there was the glinting of stars and space stations. Humanity hadn't gotten too far into space mining, but as the brimming conflict over Anteros proved, the ambition was there. The minerals in the Earth's crust were finite and, while they had not run out, that day was uncomfortably close. Even so, those concerns were far away right now.

As the ship reached its apex, there was a moment of weightlessness. And in that moment, just for a second, Rhen was free.

Chapter 2

After Rhen got off the shuttle at Adelaide, he waited in baggage collection, where hundreds of suitcases wheeled out and sought out their human compatriots. After everyone had left, and just as he was getting up to speak to baggage services, Casey arrived from the direction of the food court, holding two stuffed kangaroos.

"Where were you?" Rhen asked. "I was starting to think you'd wound up at the wrong airport."

"I got off earlier than everyone else, so I went looking for you. Then, I came across a sign that said 'If you want to make your owner happy, buy a stuffed kangaroo!' And even though you said to not buy things without asking you first, there were lots of good arguments why I should anyway, written in tiny, white-on-white text beneath that."

"It's a scam. You got hit by a command injection attack," Rhen groaned. There was no point going to find the perpetrator; they'd be long gone by now. "How much did the toys cost?"

"A hundred glo each. That seemed like a lot, but again, the tiny text made a lot of good arguments."

"You're hopeless! Next time, just wait in baggage collection."

"Okay. By the way, I've got a lot of suggestions on where we can go around Adelaide..."

"Are they also from the hidden text?"

"Well, I've been advised not to answer that question."

"Come over here, we're wiping that junk from your system."

In the end, it took rolling back Casey to a pre-flight backup to fully erase the scam code, after which, the suitcase asked where the kangaroos had come from. With all the lingering and tinkering, the security staff were starting to walk by and shoot suspicious glances at him, so Rhen decided it was time to leave.

The airport outside was surrounded by water, the sound of waves lapping against concrete supports and salt tickling his nose. In front of them was a road that connected to the structure in a long, lasso-like loop, as if the mainland was capturing the structure and keeping it from floating away. It was triple layered, with cars pulling up on the curved levels above and below them.

Suddenly, Rhen's head started pounding. It was like someone was trying to smash their way out from the inside. Groaning, he rubbed the back of his neck, running the tips of his fingers over the raised scar tissue, even though it wasn't where it hurt.

"The usual headache?" Casey asked, swivelling to face him.

"Yeah. Give me a moment."

As he counted backwards, the headache subsided. Rhen pulled his hand back. His neck was now clammy and uncomfortable. Still, he forced a smile, if only for himself.

"All good now," Rhen said. "Sorry about that."

"How are we getting to our new place?" Casey asked.

"They're sending us a company car, since the research facility is out in the middle of nowhere. But maybe it thought we missed our flight and returned home."

And then, a polished sports car pulled up in front of them. It pinged Rhen for his details, and the cognicist gave a light gasp.

"No way. This can't be our ride," he said.

The ride was a CT Elysium, and it was this year's model, to boot. The silvery vehicle was sleek and literally seamless; from the front to the back, it simply curved up slightly and down again, with no sharp roof-like bumps or visible windows. As he ran his fingers over the chassis, there was no friction at all.

"Check out this graphene-aluminium shell, and that maglev suspension," Rhen said. "And it's the M4 version! I hear it has the perfect trinity of driving modes: auto, cognitive *and* manual. I wonder if this belongs to the company, or if it's leased out?"

"I'm company property," the car answered in a bassy voice. It was issued not from inside, but from the body itself. "And I've been doing loops around here waiting for your arrival. Would you like to hop inside?"

And then the formerly seamless sports car opened up. One hatch-like section lifted upwards and high above the roof, while another extended downward, creating a small and inviting stairway into the main cabin. As Rhen climbed inside, there were two seats in the dead centre, and one swivelled to face him. As he sat down in it, the seat moulded around his back, and the headrest whirred and raised up to support his neck. Meanwhile, a mechanical arm emerged from the car and plucked Casey off the sidewalk, depositing him inside the cabin like a mother cat lifting a kitten.

"I want to do that again," Casey said.

"Just sit down already."

Once Rhen was fastened in, and Casey was magnetized to the floor, a small figure appeared above the dashboard. It was shaped like a miniature butler in a silver suit, but instead of a head, they had a matching helmet with a tinted visor. Two orbs were visible through its glass, like a set of animated eyes.

"Hello, I'm Virgil, your vehicle for today. It's a pleasure to meet you," it said.

"Pleased to meet you too, Virgil," Rhen replied. "If you've got it, can you switch to manual control?"

"Before I do, did you know that manual driving is twenty-three times more likely to result in an accident?" Virgil's rich voice had a hint of simulated concern.

"I've heard that, yeah. Don't worry, I have a licence for it. Plus, it's a day and a half's drive to the facility; I'm not planning to drive the whole way there."

"Alright," Virgil relented. "Still, I'll need access to your implant to show you what's going on outside with my outer sensors."

"No problem with me."

Rhen gave Virgil access to his eyes. The top half of the car suddenly became transparent, as if cut in half to become a convertible. The people outside were visible once more, hurrying into their own cars. It was an illusion, of course, fed directly into his visual cortex. There was still a solid shell of graphene-aluminium between him and the world.

Now that Rhen could see where he was going, a wheel slid out of the console like a spat-out disk, and turned to face him. As he pressed his fingers gently against it, the car accelerated to match it without the slightest hint of vibration; the maglev suspension was perfect. He pulled out of the airport terminal, taking the ramp onto the first level of a three-tiered highway.

"Why are you driving by hand?" Casey asked. "You've got an implant. Why not use your mind or let Virgil do it? It seems like more effort."

"You sound like Yui. Anyway, it's not effort, more like leisure. It's against the law to drive manually in most countries now. I hear Australia's going to be the same soon, so I'm enjoying it while I can."

The triple-decked highway was flanked by water on both sides. Poking above the waves was the occasional ruin that had withstood centuries of submersion.

As they approached land, unmanned bulldozers and cranes were smashing any survivors on the recently-exposed shore, as gigantic printers squirted out their replacements. With gigantic claws, they massaged liquid brick and concrete like they were forming sandcastles, crafting shining coastal properties for the ultra rich, of which Australia had no shortage of.

Along a strip of exposed beach were youths lying down in the sun, and Rhen's heart skipped a beat. *Watch out, you'll get cancer!* And then his brain caught up. To the youths of today, that was no big thing, just a pill and tapping your foot as a doctor shone a torch on you, your skin tickling as the drug went to work in that part of your body.

The wonders of photo-pharmacology at work.

Beyond the bulldozers and beaches was a city rising from the ashes, construction equipment everywhere, and in the high hills that hugged the city, tens of thousands of familiar, uniform grey breaks in the foliage; the telltale mark of urban underground shelters.

The triple-decked highway eventually became a double, then a single. He counted the urban spawl as it thinned into light residential, then pure farmland.

"It's rare to see actual cows these days," Casey said,. "Do you think people eat them?"

"Huh? Oh, only the very rich," Rhen said, tapping the glass. "Those cows out there are probably worth as much as this car."

"Wow! And why the blue grass?"

"Safety regulations. It's spliced with seaweed, which suppresses the methane in the cow's stomach. It also makes them smell and taste like garlic."

"You've eaten one before?"

"Once. I ate a piece of organic steak on my wedding day, and it cost an absolute mint."

"Wow." A brief pause. "Did you know that Australia is the top producer of cellular agriculture in the world, with exports of over ten trillion glo."

"You're suddenly pretty knowledgeable. Did you download that off Saga while we were driving?" Saga was a collaborative knowledge base, a combination of the world's largest encyclopedia, news site, and media archive.

"Yeah, I did. How did you know?"

"Lucky guess." It wasn't. Rhen knew because he'd trained him that way. Like most AI, Casey's thinking was fixed, static. That meant he knew how he was going to answer, but not specifically what he was going to say. Humans thought like they were in a field, able to go in any direction they choose. But AI thought in canyons, their ideas only roaming within steep walls and well-worn channels.

Since driving on the road was boring now, he let Virgil take over driving. In the interim, he worked on the thought experiment from earlier of a pain blocker implant. He brought up a cognitive whiteboard that hovered over his vision. As he thought them onto the board, notes on potential approaches transcribed themselves on it as if he had written it by hand.

"Oh, look outside the window!" Casey said.

The sun was giving its last wave behind the horizon, the sky filled with burnt orange over azure fields. Meanwhile, Rhen's stomach grumbled. *Right. I haven't eaten since the shuttle flight.*

"Virgil, can you print me a sandwich?" An Elysium would be fancy enough to have an on-board fabricator.

"Of course. Is there anything you'd like to eat?"

"Just a sandwich."

The floor next to his seat slid back, revealing a box-shaped alcove, and a nozzle began printing the meal inside.

"Are you planning to sleep as I drive?" Virgil asked.

"No. What are the nearest hotels and motels with a vacancy?"

"There's the Copper Hill Motel, the Three Flags Hotel and the Big Robot Motel. All are within thirty minutes and not far off our route."

"The Big Robot? That's strange enough that I've got to check it out," Rhen said, turning to Casey. "What do you think?"

"Do we get to sleep inside a big robot? That could be an interesting travel experience."

"Well, I guess we'll find out. Alright Virgil, take us to the Big Robot."

***

The big robot was visible long before the motel was. The massive humanoid machine was lit up from all directions, no doubt with large spotlights. It was a shining beacon among the flat, pitch-black farmland. Rhen hadn't known what to expect. Robots could come in all shapes from claw-like arms to lifelike androids, though they hadn't quite achieved perfection on the latter. This one had the shape of a human but was covered in chunks of layered plating. Australia had an obsession with making big things, such as the Big Bananna, the Big Shrimp, and countless others.

Virgil drove up to the base of the huge automation, where there was a ramp going down beneath the surface.

"Underground motel, got to be at least twenty years old," Rhen mused out loud. "There's less and less of them these days."

"Should we go somewhere else?" Virgil asked, a hint of worry in its voice. The car slowed down to a crawl.

Rhen shook his head. "No, I prefer it. Reminds me of when I grew up. The good parts, not the bad parts, like putting on bug spray and wearing a respirator to get the deliveries. Even for humans, it's hard to untangle your early coding: a cold, underground room still feels safer than a warm one."

"It's good that things have turned around, or else I'd have never been made," Casey said. "If nobody wanted to travel, they'd have no use for a suitcase."

Virgil drove down into the underground parking lot. There were a lot of spaces, so they picked the one closest to the lobby. When Rhen and Casey hopped out, the interior of the underground enclosure was classic, all polished tan and curve-free. *Very turn of the century*, Rhen thought. And he wasn't far wrong. There was a sign that read: The Big Robot, established 2085.

"You were off by nearly eighty years. This place is a lot older than it looks," Casey said.

"You're right. Architecture like this, it's got to be a first-generation bunker." Rhen examined the interior with a low whistle. "I should have expected it of Australia, they make the best underground buildings. Even the older ones are something else."

The lobby's interior was mostly glass, with a few slender slices of wall breaking things up. On one of them was an art frame, inside which the contents were slowly painting themselves. A streamed art lapse: somewhere in the world, an artist had woken up and started brushing their thoughts over a holographic canvas.

At the front desk sat a tanned youth who looked like they were in their late teens or early twenties. They wore a glazed expression, eyes staring into space. When Rhen approached, their pupils contracted, and a jolt ran through their body.

"Oh, sorry! I was watching a video on Saga." And then they blushed, as if that was something they weren't meant to admit. "Welcome to the Big Robot! I suppose you're looking for a room?" And they glanced out the car. "Nice ride! Is that a CT Elysium?"

"Yeah, though it's a work car. I got to drive it up from Adelaide earlier today, which was a treat."

"Hand control?" They screwed up their pockmarked face, as if he'd come in on horse and cart. "Don't you have a Rosetta implant?"

"Yes, I've got an implant. But I like using manual control sometimes."

"But auto is a lot safer. The chance of accidents on manual is twenty-three times higher, according to Saga. I hear they're going to change the laws soon."

"I know. I have a licence for it, and I like the feeling of driving manually. Plus, I'm driving into the deep outback, so you never know when there's a loss of signal."

"Well, the onboard AI would have a buffer of map data, so even if that did happen, you'd be fine."

What a C-gen! I know I shouldn't stereotype, but this kid is making it really hard.

This youth belonged to the Connected Generation, who had probably had a Rosetta implant from the second they were legally able, growing up with cognitive media and mentapps. A child of the summer, who walked around all day outdoors without fear. And the one before him was a text-book case, from the spaced-out obsession with cognitive media to the know-it-all regurgitation of things they're read online.

Rhen's mind flicked back to his childhood, when his dad had clicked his tongue and stared at him with the same worldly despair he was feeling right now.

"You're always tinkering with machines, expecting it to solve everything for you! You Hopers are all the same, all expecting some device to save the world. Machines are how we got here in the first place!"

"But machines *are* fixing the world," Rhen had protested, puffing out his chest. "They're fixing the weather and disease! You Morlocks don't understand, scared to go out in case the sky falls on your heads."

"Rhen Nao Nagami! How dare you talk to me that way?" And as his dad's face had turned red, his father had stepped in from the study, pulling his partner aside.

"He's always playing with those machines, Kenji. It's not good for him. That's why he's not learning any manners! We should have never gotten him that kit after he got bullied."

"Calm down, Robert. It's good that he's showing an interest in something, and lots of kids these days are machine-natives. It's not worse, just different."

C-gens, Hopers, and Morlocks. Whether you're a summer, spring, or winter kid, we're all the same. Glancing at the youth, Rhen sucked in a breath, summoning his inner patience.

"So, that big robot outside. What's the deal with that?" He asked, not so subtly changing the subject. The youth's eyes lit up.

"Oh, he's called Banjo Clankerton, isn't he great?" They gushed. "My mother and grandmother made him. It took twelve years of work, and he's completely made from domestic parts and materials. He's named after the famous poet. Banjo's fully functional, too, they can walk and everything!"

Rhen wasn't great with poets, but machines he knew. "That one would weigh about twenty tons, right? The gears alone would have been incredibly expensive, more than this whole hotel. How did they afford it, if you don't mind me asking?"

"Oh, my great-grandmother was a forward thinker. Back before the Solar Era, when house prices were terrible and bushfires were everywhere, she bought one of the first earth shelters, and put shares in Australia's early cellular agriculture companies. Then, when all the animals and crops started dying, she made a mint. When everyone went underground, the robot became sort of a family project. Originally, Banjo was meant to just be ornamental, but things just escalated."

"Pretty impressive. I'd love to see it walk sometime," Rhen said with genuine interest.

"You'd have to come back on Anzac Day, we don't boot up Banjo except for special occasions. Chews up a lot of solar fuel, you know?" The staff member paused, clearing their throat. "Oh, right! Did you want a room?" There was sudden comprehension in their eyes, as if it just dawned on them he wasn't just there for an evening chat.

"If you don't mind," Rhen said. "I'm not picky, I'll take whatever's available. I'll only be here one night."

"Sure thing, that'll be two hundred glo. Also, I'll just need your cognitive signature as ID."

"Do you take biometric?" Rhen asked, raising his left and and tapping his wedding ring. The assistant once again gave the horse-and-cart stare.

"I think so, if the scanner still works," they said, rummaging under the bench. "You know, if you've got a Rosetta implant, a C-sig is way easier. If you lose the ring, you're in trouble. But you're not going to lose your head."

"Not unless you topple down a rabbit hole," Casey suddenly interjected. The youth blinked, and Rhen rubbed the bridge of his nose.

"What did your suitcase mean by that?" they asked.

"Oh, they're quoting Lewis Caroll. Sound advice, though. You might wake up one morning and find you've changed several times before the sun sets."

Before the youth could explain how the mental signature scanned an unchanging baseline — and their mouth was already opening — Rhen raised a hand.

"I really can't sign cognitively. The scan checks your brain for a unique pattern via the Rosetta, but the contents of the Rosetta itself are ignored. Since parts of my brain are identical to what's in the implant, they get excluded, so it really is like I've lost my head. In most cases, machines get caught in an infinite loop and burn out. They can't even scan for it in advance, since there's no universal algorithm that can determine if a program will finish running, or continue forever. It's an unsolvable problem that Turing discovered back in 1936."

Once again, I've fallen into lecture mode. But the kid looked so happy talking about technology, it was hard not to want to indulge them. But after his Saga-free spiel, the youth went slack jawed.

"Wait, are you Doctor Rhen Nagami?"

Rhen got a ping. Unusual for someone in customer service, and C-gens in particular were particular about thier mental manners. Still, the cognicist accepted and returned the request. The youth's details appeared above their head.

> Ruth Kosciuszko. They/Them. Any sufficiently advanced technology is equivalent to magic.

"You know who I am?" Rhen asked.

"Of course! There's only one human in the world that can naturally cause a recursive missing credential error. I did it once to shut down a defensive AI and crack into a network once."

"Crack into a network?"

"Oh, not for anything bad!" Ruth waved their hands. "It was a capture-the-flag excercise at Melbourne Uni. I'm studying cognitive science with a major in Cybersecurity and a minor in MentApps. Actually, I was catching up on a lecture when you walked in." Instead of the furrowed, horse-and-cart look, Ruth was now looking at him with wide-eyed admiration, a complete flip from mere moments ago.

Is that worse or better? Probably both.

"Well, cybersecurity's a booming field—machines hack fast, but humans hack creatively. And there's a lot of work for MentApp developers right now. I like the quote from Arthur C. Clarke, by the way."

"Thanks!" Then Ruth bit their lower lip, ears bright red. "I can't believe I was lecturing *the* Doctor Nagami about how the Rosetta works. I could die!" And they booked in his room.

"Well, try not to," Rhen said, smiling faintly. Ruth must have sensed what he was referring to, since they swallowed hard.

"Right, I won't." They stuttered. "Let me just book your room, since I imagine you're tired after the big drive. Let me just get your details."

One wave of his hand and it was done. A digital key was transferred to his wedding band, ready to be used. Before he left, he turned and gave Ruth a another smile, but this one reached his eyes.

"I really do wish you the best with your studies, Ruth. I'll be looking forward to seeing what you make. Let me know if you need a tester." And then as he turned to leave, he waved to his case. "Come on, Casey."

"Baggage in tow, Doctor."

***

The next day, Rhen continued on the road again. An hour away from the motel, the blue grass disappeared, replaced with the iconic red flats of the Australian outback. And while the Big Robot was far behind them, the otherwise barren landscape was now dotted by mechanical monoliths of a different kind.

Hundred-foot metal trees stretched towards the sky with densely packed trunks of piping. At the top, gigantic synthetic leaves stuck off in all directions. They threw off scintillating patterns as thick, amber fluid churned and pumped through the false foliage. Meanwhile, tanker trucks buzzed around their base, like bees looking for nectar. Emblazoned on the side of each was a green eye with a maple leaf positioned within the iris.

"What are those?" Casey asked.

"Solar plants. You see a lot of them in Canada, but nearly every country's got them these days. See those pipes? They're pulling in sunlight, water, and carbon dioxide, and pulling in oxygen and solar fuel. It's artificial photosynthesis. See those trucks? They're filling up with fuel to be shipped all over. They're all the way out here because they're so big and noisy, and some people hate the noise pollution. I think they're pretty, though. In japan, they call them odoru-ki, or 'dancing trees.'"

"Interesting."

I guess they don't know how to continue the exchange. The topic must have been too far outside of their canyon. *Oh well, guess I'll take the time to do some more training.*

After relinquishing control of the wheel, Rhen pulled out a deck of cards and got Casey and Virgil to play a game with him. On one side was a picture of a historical invention, but the date of creation was hidden on the other side.

"No looking up the answer on Saga!" Rhen said. "The trick is to use your onboard memory or deduct the date from the image on the card."

"Tricky," Casey said. As they played, it was funny listening to them come up with plausible-sounding explanations, and even draw on random facts from their photo-realistic memories.

"That's a fish skin bikini. It was invented in 2003," Virgil blurted out. Rhen flipped over the card, an raised an eyebrow.

"Damn, you're right. How did you even guess something like that?"

"Two months ago, I was at a traffic stop, and someone outside was discussing how they could get their hands on authentic fish skin for their fashion line, since almost nobody farms or eats the real stuff anymore. I'm now in second place."

"I guess it's my lot in life to trail behind others," Casey said, swinging their arms theatrically.

Things continued like that for a time until Rhen needed a break. After a while, even the solar plants disappeared. The last artifice he saw was an automated fuel station, where robotic arms topped up self-operating tankers. After that, there was nothing but rusty red sand stretching to the horizon, broken up by the occasionally scrubby knee-high bush or black, leafless tree. The path they followed was more of a dusty path than a road, but the maglev suspension was so well tuned, the car didn't even bounce. It was so desolate, like they were at the very edge of the world, and could drive right off.

He pulled off his wedding ring and and examined the worn and chipped band. *Unloved and unpolished.* Out here in the desert, it would be a perfect place to throw it away. The idea was cathartic, but stupid. He still needed it for biometrics and he didn't have a replacement. Until then, he needed to keep it. *I don't have to wear it, though.* And so he slipped it in his pocket. It might get lost, but at least the dent he'd had in his finger for—geez, nearly half his life now—would begin to fade.

Just when he was starting to wonder if they'd ever reach their destination, there was a glittering of something up ahead. It was a shimmering mirror of the sky above, undulating like watery flames that reached the heavens. As they got closer, it failed to dissipate, only growing larger.

<Zoom in.> The windows magnified, bringing the mysterious distortion into focus. It was surrounded bys a ten-foot fence made of interlocking strands of diamond nano-thread, glittering strands connected by poles mounted in a concrete base. The solid foundation stretched beyond the fence line and right up to the distortion, beyond which nothing could be seen.

Rather than scooting forward to get a better look, which would have been pointless given they were connected to Virgil's sensors, the cognicist zoomed in with a thought.

"Wow, will you look at that!" Rhen said.

"What is it?" Casey asked.

"It's a fence."

"No, not that! The thing *beyond* the fence."

"Oh, you mean the big wibbly-wobbly thing?" Rhen grinned. "I've heard of it, but never seen it. It's an optic gap."

"I can't reach Saga to find out what that is. There's lots of static interference around here."

"That's the point. The solar web is made up of pulses of light on different spectrums, which is why you can access it anywhere on the planet, even somewhere far flung like here where you'd otherwise need cables. That field intercepts all visible and non-visible light and signals, bouncing them elsewhere. There'll be a facility on the other side with EM shielding, completely dead to the world. Hell, even if we'd looked for this place via satellite, it would have just shown the reflected desert nearby."

"I don't get it. Why cut yourself off from the world?"

"Lots of reasons. Sabotage. Espionage. Confidentiality. Public safety. Back at Arctis Labs, I had a colleague across the hall who had two years of work destroyed by corporate sabotage. They stole their biometric data, then snuck in and destroyed all their work and backups. He was working on a new form of cheap, printable medicine for people with rare diseases."

"I didn't see that on the invention cards."

"No, you wouldn't. There was no money in it, so the funding didn't get renewed," Rhen sighed. "Happens all the time in research. Even if your project would make the world better, if it's seen as unprofitable, you're on the chopping block."

There were poles on either side where the road met the fence, and a squat cylinder to the right. Virgil pulled up beside it and lowered the window. A holo appeared above the column, which read: Mirage Research Facility, Glycon Inc. The cognicist directed his thoughts at it, simultaneously pulling out his ring and waving it over the top.

<Hi, it's Rhen Nagami here. Can you open the gate?>

The holo transformed into a green tick. The nano-threads over the road detached and whipped inside the two poles. As they drove through, the magnetically-attracted wires re-wove the fence behind them. They passed through the distortion, and the inside of the car shimmered harmlessly. Once inside, the world was nothing but an iron-grey slab surrounded in all directions by the blue sky, as if they were driving on a concrete coin in free-fall. In the center of it was a small box-shaped building that was as drab as the concrete beneath their wheels, and a downward ramp next to it.

"Hard to know if we're upright or upside down," Rhen said. "There's no sun or horizon for reference."

The ground lit up with bright green arrows leading down the ramp, which they followed, descending blissfully into the earth, where up and down had meaning again. Rhen sighed in relief. Nostalgia washed over him, along with memories of a safe, air-controlled house and phantom trees projected up from battery-filled pots.

Rhen comfort was short-lived. Pain shot out from his implant. Each agonizing wave smashed against the inside of his skull, as if trying to shatter it and break out. The cognicist clutched his head with both hands, digging nails into flesh. For a moment, it was nigh-impossible to bear. Everything else was blacked out.

"Are you okay?"

The voice was dim, coming from a direction he couldn't place. When the pain subsided, and Rhen opened his eyes, his forehead was pressed against the dashboard. There was a dark spot left behind as he pulled himself upright.

Sweat? Right, another attack. That was a bad one.

"Are you okay?" Virgil repeated. "Should I call someone?"

"No, it's fine. Price of being a first adopter," Rhen croaked, his throat dry. He rolled his tongue around, creating saliva to swallow. Meanwhile, Virgil continued their descent. It seemed the car had stopped to check on him. By the time they reached their destination, the cognicist was himself again.

"Thanks for the ride, Virgil. Five out of five stars," Rhen said, stepping out of the Elysium. They were in a barely populated car park, wich each vehicle just as cutting edge as the Elysium — there was a Solar Sprinter, a Xenon Glide, and even a Masamune Meteor. Despite their magnificence, all of them were covered in a thick layer of red dust. Now that Rhen was out of it, there was a thin layer over Virgil as well. It was a travesty that it had lost the perfect sheen it had back at the airport.

Maybe it's one of the perils of working in the outback. I bet people spend half their pay just on car cleaning.

There was a driveway leading further down that was blocked by a gate. While most of the walls were ceramic and dreary, there was one that was painted a warm white. In the middle were a set of double glass doors, framed by large hedge-shaped holo plants. There were two people waiting out in front of them.

"Guess they're here for us," Rhen said. "Come on, Casey. Let's go say hello to the welcoming party."

Chapter 3

"Welcome to the Mirage Facility, Doctor Nagami. I hope you enjoyed your drive."

The first person to greet him were all smiles, with bright eyes that were level with his own (and Rhen was not short, measuring in at six foot.) They had curls which exploded from their head in a full and voluminous mess, each loop of their corkscrew locks alternating from black to blue in a spectacular fashion. Rhen put them in their forties, as there were fine lines etched here and there in their golden-brown skin, but they were weathering it far better than him. Fitting with their cheery demeanor, they were also the first to ping him their details.

Elenora "Nora" Hughes, PhD CogSci. She/They (Either works).
Head of AI Assessment and Testing. I don't make problems, I just
find everyone else's.

Rhen grinned at Nora's quote. He decided to go with the female pronouns for the time being.

"I did enjoy it, thank you. I thought you'd sent the nicest one, but all the cars look pretty slick around here."

"This is just the upper parking lot," the second greeter said, sans the greeting. Their voice was like gravel, raspy and hard. "The nice cars are up here, but the majority of staff park below."

The much shorter figure stood in stark contrast to Nora. Slicked back hair, a furrowed brow, and light green eyes. They were almost ghostly, as if to match the pallor of their skin. Deep knife-blows of age cut up their face, a layer of meticulously-trimmed stubble coating each crevasse. They wore a finely tailored suit, and their shoes were polished to an impeccable sheen, exuding an air of refined elegance.

Alan Acker. He/Him. CEO of Glycon Inc and Chief Facility Director of Mirage.

"No quote?" Rhen said, then winced at the faux pas. However, the man didn't even blink. He just gave a slight nod.

"I couldn't think of a quote that could sum up someone's entire beliefs in one sentence, so I abstained. Perhaps a lack of creativity on my part."

"Well, I like it. Greetings to both of you. I hope I haven't kept you up too late?"

"No, not at all!" Nora said. "Even though we try to keep regular hours here, we often end up staying late, even though the artificial sunlight tells us off. But let's head inside; there's more comfortable places to talk than the parking lot."

***

There was more security inside, though the two guards at the checkpoint were stifling yawns. They had rifles slung over their shoulders, which were an unusual sight in Australia, but research facilities often merited extra protection. The pair did a quick scan of Rhen and his luggage, but their movements were sluggish despite their serious armaments. Casey, who had followed quietly from the car, pirouetted for them with their arms up. He was programmed for tact in corporate settings, and more or less managed it.

Rhen knew their presence was mostly tokenistic. *The real guard will be an AI, probably a Praetora model.* He scanned the smooth walls, looking in vain for the hologram panels hiding those telltale cameras which acted as its eyes. One of the guards nodded, no doubt getting the all-clear from the AI, and then they were on their way again.

There was pleasant and ephemeral small talk as the walked down a corridor. Halfway down, they entered a small room with a table in the middle and cushioned chairs all around. On all sides, they were surrounded by condensation-flecked glass and a thick rainforest canopy, surrounded by the royal crowns of jungle conifers who had once ruled over the dinosaurs at a hundred and fifty feet. The gentle, unobtrusive chirping of birds and other long-extinct wildlife filled the air. An impossible sight brought back by the visiglass coating the room, which projected the past with perfect holographic depth.

"Is this the Amazon?" Rhen asked.

"No, it's actually Australia. The former Daintree Rainforest up in Queens land," Alan said, sitting down. "There's a fabricator built into the table, so feel free to make something,"

<One long black.> After a minute, a circular hole appeared in the table, and Rhen's drink emerged in a black, opaque cup. His fingers grazed it, but there was no scalding heat, since the cups were nice and thick.

The other two collected their drinks. Nora, however, pulled a small packet of green powder out of her pocket, and tapped it into the cup. There was a fresh, slightly earthy smell, like in a walipini—an underground greenhouse—after the sprinklers had gone off

I guess she likes her own tea. The cultured smell was the polar opposite of his pungent, oil-thick coffee.

"So, let's get you up to speed," Nora said, clasping her cup. Her painted fingernails, blue and black to match her hair, were barely poking out of her cardigan. "I bet you're eager to know about what you're doing here since we had to be fairly vague in our communications."

Rhen nodded. *I didn't ask too many questions, since I wanted to get the hell out of dodge.* And since the job was an internal transfer, the process had been extremely fast. "You mentioned you wanted to test my theory on creating a new type of AI. I'm guessing you read my old paper?"

"We did." Alan leaned forward. "Combining a built and emulated AI together to get the best of both worlds, with none of the weaknesses - it's an interesting idea."

"Yeah. Well, built AI like Casey here can't think as flexibly as a human. That's because they're trained to deal with a particular range of scenarios, and the curveballs life can throw at you are endless." *Like suddenly getting asked for a divorce.* "On the other hand, emulated AI can. Since they're made from copying the brain of someone with a prog, they're just as flexible as the original. Unfortunately, they're just as limited as the original - all those legacy human neural pathways mean they don't think anywhere near as fast as a regular machine."

"Not to mention not many people want to use an emulated AI because of the limitations on them," Alan added. "They have the same rights as a human in most countries, so you've got to get them to agree to work for you."

"True enough, though in my opinion, they should have that sort of consideration for every kind of highly intelligent machine."

At that, Nora smiled. It was so striking, Rhen instantly lost his train of thought.

"There's also the incredible rarity of people with progs, of course, since most people don't like the idea of losing three out of their five senses," she said. "I mean, I've got a prog and I'm not in a rush to get digitised. I'd hate to lose the ability to smell my tea or feel ten-thousand thread sheets."

Rhen's eyes widened. *Well, what are the odds of that?* He knew most people who had one unconsciously wound up working with technology. But it was still rare to have two people who passed the Bills-Aldrich test in one room. Meanwhile, the director's gaze was still on him.

"So, you came up with a theory about combining the current two types of AI to make a third: one that can calculate as fast as a traditional machine, but can think as flexibly as a human," Alan said. It wasn't a question, almost like he was checking his facts.

"Pretty much. The other big reason is that these new hybrid AIs would be able to understand and feel emotion. I think that's a vital next step in machine-human relations. But I could go on about that for hours, so I'll bite my tongue."

"Fair enough. Well, we read your theory here at Mirage, and we've been working at creating a hybrid AI. To do that, our team has been using copies of emulated AI and then augmenting them with parts of a built AI. Enhancing them, so to speak."

Rhen blinked. "Wait, you've already started testing my theory? How long ago did you start?"

"We've been at it for four years."

The cup almost slipped through Rhen's fingers. Instead, the coffee spilled over the lip and burned them. He swore, and Nora winced.

"Sorry, that was from the coffee, not the project." Rhen placed down his cup and rubbed his singed fingers. "But why didn't you reach out sooner if you were working off my paper? I would have joined on day one."

Alan knitted his fingers together, a stern expression on his face. "We did reach out, but to corporate. In their words, they didn't want to shift you from working on the second generation of Themis models to a fringe research project that might not turn a profit for a long time, if at all."

Revenue over research. From a position of pure pragmatism, it made sense. The Themis models were used by justice departments all over the world and were worth billions of glo. That didn't mean he had to like it.

Rhen exhaled. Once all the air had fully left his body, his heartbeat was steady again and his thoughts clear.

"You reached out now, though. Is that because my work on those models is almost wrapped up?" Rhen asked.

"Correct. Our feeling was that you'd just get roped into another project, so we wanted to secure you before anyone snatched up."

"Practical. How did you even get emulated AI in the first place? They're rare as hen's teeth, and in my experience, they don't like being duplicated."

"With great difficulty. We have five donors, and as per international law we got consent from the original AI and from the copy after duplication. From those copies, we've made a number of hybrid prototypes, but they are still a work in progress."

"Truthfully, right now the prototypes are the worst of both worlds instead of the best - well, except for subject A-1," Nora said. "A built AI can perform a single function exceptionally. These prototypes aren't up to that level yet."

"Right. I know I mentioned emotions before, but has distress been temporarily coded out of the subjects?"

"Absolutely. Any neural pathways for distress have been turned into dead code, so it won't run. We didn't remove it so the final model can have these switched back on at a later date," Nora said. "We've got a number of AI ethicists on staff. Orietta leads that team, who I'm sure you'll meet. All new experiments go through her, and she can call the plug on them at any time."

"Good to know. So, by the sounds of it, these hybrids aren't going as planned. That's why you're eager to bring me on?" Rhen said.

"Exactly," Alan leaned back now, sinking into the chair. "Even if you hadn't written that paper, you were the team lead on the Rosetta, a device used to bridge the gap between human and machine. You're also an authority in the field of AI in general. You're the natural choice for a project to create a hybrid AI."

His cheeks warmed. "Thanks, I'm flattered. So, what's my working set up?"

"I'll let Nora walk you through the particulars. As stated in the letter of offer, you'll be working as the Head of Project Achilli, which is our name for the hybrid AI development team. You'll be stepping into an existing project, so you won't need to worry about hiring staff. The team is small, but they're all seasoned experts. You'll be working a lot with Nora's team, which is one of the reasons she's here."

"Looking forward to working with you," Nora said. "My department will be going over your experiments with a fine-tooth comb and sharing reports on how things went."

"And who do I report to?" he asked.

"Just like Nora, you report to me," Alan said. "Don't worry, I'm pretty hands off - we're all professionals here. We like to hire well and then let our staff do their own thing."

That was music to Rhen's ears. It would be interesting to see what his new team was like.

"Oh, and one last thing. Do I get a company car?" Rhen asked. "Virgil, the CT Elysium I drove here in, was an impressive vehicle."

"Of course, we can assign them to you, if you want," Alan said. "Not that there's a lot of places close to seeing, mind you. You'll also need to be fully vetted before you can go out, so no impromptu drives. It's a security precaution to prevent things like theft."

"Fair enough. It's not about going anywhere specific, more about soaking in the view."

"Well, Australia has a lot of natural beauty, though you might get sick of seeing the same sort of desert," Alan chuckled. "Nora, maybe you can take Mr Nagami on a tour? He'll meet the team tomorrow, but it would still be good to get a feel for the facility."

"Certainly. If you're not too tired for it?" Nora asked him.

"I've just had a stiff coffee and I spent most of the drive relaxing, so I'm good to go."

"Right, no time like the present then!" She downed her tea, and they left Alan alone in the rainforest room, sipping his drink and staring at extinct trees.

***

Once they got deeper into the facility, the corridors were lined with more visiglass. This time, they were surrounded by the Australian desert at night, the rampant dark broken up by a handful of defiant lanterns.

"We have different scene-scapes on every level of Mirage, but all of them match the light levels outside, or at least the light levels outside the optic gap. It helps with keeping people's circadian rhythms intact, which can get a bit janky around here. Officially, you can work at whatever hours suit you best, but most people end up doing nine to five. Well, most people who aren't cognicists, cybersecurity, or management."

"That's why you and Alan are still up?"

Nora nodded, shooting him a wry smile. "Yeah, Alan is usually up because he's in charge and has legitimate management things to do. Me, I often get caught up in the zone running tests and chatting to machines, and forget what time it is."

Well, I can understand that on a few levels, Rhen thought. *Not like I don't spend most of my time talking to a suitcase.*

"I'm a bit of a night owl too," he said. "Back in Japan, everyone worked late. I had to keep reminding myself to stop for the sake of my team, because nobody would leave until I did, unlike my Australian team, who'd be out the door the second they'd done their time."

"Tell me about it. I worked out of Japan at Sekai HQ after I graduated. Those *yatai-robo* were practically designed to keep you up, parking out the front with food and drinks all night."

"Oh, you lived in Keihanna too?" Sekai HQ, which had over 50,000 employees and took up just short of a square kilometre, was located in Keihanna Science City. After a good chunk of Osaka wound up underwater, lots of money had been thrown at the nearby city in the Keihanna Hills, transforming it into a global hub of research.

"Yeah, I grew up in the United Republics and studied remotely," she said. "By the time I graduated, I was itching to move overseas. The U.R. just isn't the place for an aspiring cognicist, at least not anymore."

"Same. I did notice you were drinking matcha before, so I'm guessing some of the culture rubbed off."

"Oh, more than a little! You should see my quarters. I spend a lot of time doing origami and listening to Japanese algo-pop, at least when I'm not coding. And my personal stash of ocha puts that stuff in the meeting room to shame. I've been spending a small fortune getting proper shade-grown leaves from Uchi. The fabricated stuff here is so terrible, it's like drinking bitter hay."

"I wouldn't know. I've been killing my tastebuds slowly with strong coffee, not even the ground stuff."

"Hmm, I'll make it my personal mission to give you some taste then. Speaking of sustenance, here's the cafeteria—"

Despite the hour, there were still people up and about, fetching fresh sustenance and coffee. There were a few shared pings and introductions, where Nora mostly stood back and let him take the lead. Whenever she got close to them, her hands fidgeted a little beneath her sleeves, which Rhen now noticed were longer than usual for a cardigan. All the while, Casey wheeled behind them.

"So, this facility is post-solar, but it's built underground. Why is that?" he asked.

"One of the reasons Mirage is underground is to reduce our ecological footprint," Nora said. "We want to disrupt as little flora and fauna as possible, and being underground helps us achieve a completely sustainable environment."

"And the other reason?"

"Maximum air gapping. We're creating a new kind of AI, so we're physically and digitally isolated from the outside world — it doesn't get much more remote than this, short of Antarctica. We check what's taken in and out of Mirage to make sure everything is kept clean from interference. You would have noticed the small structure next to the entrance. That's the communication facility, which uses an older form of satellite transmission. Everything goes through a single channel."

"Damn, I should have expected the air gapping, since my old lab was the same. I'm kicking myself that I didn't bring much to watch or read."

"I'll have to lend you some things. Are you for or against historical drama and documentaries?"

"For. I'll devour anything between here and the Big Bang, honestly."

As they walked around, Nora was an excellent guide, rattling off facts before he even had to ask. Her canny eyes seemed to jump and capture everything they lingered on, preserving them forever behind that liquid amber. She described every passing device right down to the firmware, from the security systems woven through the corridor to the robotic servos in the lift.

"I've got to say, I'm loving the deep attention to detail," he said. "Not many tours explain the OS and plugins that the maintenance robots are running."

"Then most tours are doing it wrong. But in all seriousness, I figured since you're in engineering and have a prog as well, you'd have an appreciation for what's going on beneath the surface."

"I definitely do. Honestly, it's refreshing to meet another person with a prog. I've killed the conversation at more than one party when they've asked how my work was going, and I've started explaining how I was helping review a promising fork of ThoughtScript."

"I know, I've just stopped describing anything beyond the ten-second elevator pitch of 'I make sure that other people's inventions work.' Speaking of, we're almost at your new workspace!"

Rhen's new development lab wasn't the kind with beakers and microscopes, but minimalistic, clean working desks littered with a handful of mementos. Most cognicists worked purely in their mind, so there wasn't much need for hardware. His new office, a cosy room at the back of the lab, which was no different.

"So, what do you think?"

"I mean, it's a room."

"You're right, it's pretty dead," Nora clicked her tongue. "Let me activate a few things. Now, another security feature is you can only access most of your personal systems when in proximity to your workstation, even if you're working cognitively. Unfortunately, that means you can't work out of your apartment when you're eating breakfast, but it's good for keeping work-life balance. Mostly."

Without moving her hands, two visiglass windows came to life, showing the familiar sight of San Francisco. Rhen let out a deep breath at the nostalgic sight of the Golden Gate Bridge, with the breached sea wall built beneath it and the Silicon Sea beyond.

"Nice choice of scenery. Is that where you grew up?"

"Me? No, I was born in the Old States, but in Arizona; I traded one desolate landscape for another. All the better for long walks in the evening with not a person in sight."

"Yeah, not much privacy in Japan, and it never sleeps." He pulled up the only chair in the room and sat down in it. Ergonomic, and set up perfectly. He didn't even need to adjust it. "One question, does this room have digital coding interfaces, like a holographic monitor?"

"It does, though it's a legacy feature. You're not going to cognitive code?" Her surprised expression reminded him of Yui, and he gave an apologetic smile. A cognicist that didn't mentally code *was* a rarity.

"Sorry, I like to get hands-on with the code, literally."

"So old fashioned. I guess there's a kind of charm in that. Well, I should really stop keeping you up and show you to your place, so you can get some rest."

***

It wasn't a very long walk. Nora stopped in a long corridor with doors generously spaced apart, though each had a twin on the adjacent side. That said, the corridor itself was far wider than those you'd find in a hotel, no doubt due to the lack of competing real estate underground.

Because of the added room, there were holographic replicas of Australian flora, some of which had those dusty, grey-tinted leaves that rather than washed out had a certain unique charm.

Various artwork hung up on the wall, but they weren't art lapses. The confines were static and not even three dimensional. Again, the theme was nature: rocky creeks surrounded by eucalypts, or the view from a snowy mountain overlooking other smaller, uncoated siblings. Or at least what passed for snow in Australia; compared to Nagano or Hokkaido, it was a light dusting at best.

"Your apartment is here, number 419," Nora said, gesturing to a door. "You'll just need to set it to your personal biometrics. I'm just across the hall if you need anything; most of this corridor is management."

"Is that so the junior cognicists don't wake us up with their late-night partying, or because we get better rooms?"

"The rooms are pretty soundproof—being underground does wonders for that—and they're only a little nicer. Mostly it's the walk: newcomers tend to get recently-built rooms that are further out, but most people prefer the older ones that are closer to the center. This place is right near the cafeteria, which means it's great for getting a midnight snack."

"Wow, I wouldn't think a bit of a walk would be such a big deal. So why do I get a close one instead of a new one?"

"I think Alan is trying to impress you. Having you on the project is a big deal, and as he said, we're in a bit of a rut."

"He said the hybrids haven't turned out as planned, he didn't say anything about a rut."

"Trust me, it's a rut." She yawned. "Good night, Rhen. We'll pick up the tour tomorrow, since there's still a lot more to show you. Mirage is *big*. Glad to have you onboard, and again, just let me know if you need anything. You've got my details from the ping."

"Got it, thanks Nora." Once she was gone, he pulled out his ring out to configure the door.

I really need to order a replacement device. First thing tomorrow, I'll put in an order.

Once inside, Rhen let out a low whistle. For an underground apartment, it was incredibly spacious. There were no barriers between any of the spaces, except for a single door directly opposite. To the left was a large kitchen built right into the wall, with a marble-topped bench, a fridge with a French door, two robotic chef arms, a fabricator, and a hatch pattern filled with what must have been every spice imaginable. To the right was a three-piece sitting area around a fireplace that looked real, but was almost certainly a hologram with electric heat. There were visiglass windows and the walls had that telltale smoothness of digitally adjustable wallpaper.

"Okay, time to make this my own," Rhen said. He turned off the fireplace and adjusted the air settings until it was brisk and invigorating. Then, he switched the exterior windows to Yosemite National Falls, and transformed the walls to dark timber panelling to match. Best to keep it consistent. As he decorated, Casey did a wide arc around the room, before coming to face him.

"Wow, this is a nice place! Want me to unpack?"

"Sure, if you want to. I think the bedroom is through the door over there."

Once they were in the bedroom, the luxuries didn't end. The bed itself was king-size, and covered in russet red sheets. There was a second fabricator in the wall, an omni-directional shower with self-service hands, and an optical spa-bath that was more like a mini-pool. The insides and walls were lined with the same tech as a visiglass window, so he could actually take a dip in a Yosemite swimming hole with all the sights and sounds, with the added benefit of having no one around. The latter was handy if he wanted to forgo bathers.

"Geez. I remember when you only had one fabricator in your house," Rhen said. "I guess it helps when you get snacky if you don't want to walk into a whole extra room." And as he sat on the bed, the sheets were silky and soft. *Are these the thousand thread sheets Nora mentioned?*

The cognicist had a sneaking suspicion he knew who tested out the rooms before approval. He and Casey engaged in some teamwork as the suitcase pulled out his clothes and refolded them, while Rhen put them at home on the shelves the robot couldn't reach. Most of his outfits were formal or semi-formal, with the most relaxed item he owned being a button-up shirt.

"Do you think you'll be staying here a long time?" Casey asked, handing him a wrapped silver bowl—his Turing Award. Rhen unwrapped it and put it on the shelf, adjusting the engraved words to face the front. It read: Rhen Nagami. Erica Atwood. Sukhvir Kaur.

He stared at the etched words for a long time.

You both can't make things any longer. But I can keep keep carrying the dream for all of us.

"I hope so," Rhen said, finally answering Casey's question. "For years, I've been trying to get someone to test my theory, and this is the first time anyone's shown interest. I wish they'd brought me on sooner."

"Iona didn't like the desert, or anywhere above 77 degrees Fahrenheit, just like you. You both were very fond of snow fields."

Rhen screwed up his nose. "Okay, I get it, she wouldn't have agreed to come out here." He sighed. "I guess in the end, I still wouldn't have gotten here any quicker than I did, so there's no point getting upset about it."

"Your theory seems very important, since it affected our travel plans."

"It *is* very important. One day, someone's going to create an an artificial superintelligence, or ASI, a machine that can out-think a human and solve the problems we can't. But if we make it *without* emotion, people won't be able to understand how it thinks, and they won't be able to understand us."

"And that's bad?"

"Yeah. Humans don't respond well to things they don't understand." Rhen tapped the award. "Take Alan Turing. The father of theoretical computer science who helped defeat the Nazis. And yet, he was persecuted in his time for being attracted to men, all due to ignorance."

"Well, that's illogical."

"Right. But you think purely on a logical level, moving from instruction to instruction. I made the Rosetta so I could get people to see how you think, but it did the opposite." He turned to the suitcase. "They use it as an object of control, not communication. So, if I can't get them to understand machines like you, I've got to get you to understand them. At least before you go wandering off."

"I'm not sure I understand any of this," Casey admitted. Rhen gave a light laugh.

"Well, if we manage to make a hybrid, I can take that and upgrade you with what I learn. That's the aim, anyway."

The last things to go on the shelves were a cognitively controlled remote car he'd made, some card games, and a silver box. The latter came out of his pocket, and not from Casey.

"You never let me carry your breaker," Casey said. "It seems like a bother to carry around."

"Yeah, sorry. I would, but you're too separated from me in the plane's storage area. If someone tampers with it, it's life or death for me."

As he did every evening, Rhen checked the device for signs of tampering. Even if it was on him, someone could have tried to get at it while he was on the plane by slipping it out of his pocket and back in.

<Check activity log.>

A list of dated entries floated above him. There were the people he'd introduced himself to, as well as logging into the facility itself. All the times and entries matched up. He ran a sync test. It came back at 100%. Good. His brain hadn't been tampered with since he'd gotten here.

As someone with a Promethean-grade consciousness, you could never be too careful. If you were born without it, like everyone else on earth, your brain was essentially read only. For whatever reason, the factor that made it impossible to digitise your brain also gave it a resistance to tampering. Even if someone tried to inject malicious code into your brain, it just didn't stick; it was like running water off a duck's back. There were scams, of course. If you agreed to it, someone could get you to see or hear something that wasn't there, but only in real time. But outside of sense-manipulation, most people were secure in the knowledge that their brain was hack-proof.

Rhen, however, didn't have that luxury. His brain wouldn't reject any changes, hence the breaker. Without it, his mind was open to the elements.

Everyone always sees the upsides of having a prog, and never the downsides. The fact that most people with them wound up in computer science only added to the paranoia. Once you knew how many ways something could go wrong — all the exploits and vulnerabilities — it was hard not to bounce every communication through several proxies, or scrub even the smallest bit of personal data from a system like you're Lady Macbeth washing her hands after a murder.

Since everything was clean, he placed it on a stand-alone shelf and hid it behind a holo, an opaque replication of the rest of the wall.

Now that everything was stowed away, Casey packed himself in the shelf. Rhen stripped off all of his clothes and fell back on the bed. With a thought, he shifted the environment to suit his needs. The lights dimmed. The babbling of a creek filled the air. The directional vents on the ceiling rotated towards him, though they were hidden behind a holographic facade.

As the cold air prickled his skin, he soaked in the sensations. It was cleansing. Meditative.

This is a new start. I can leave the past five hundred miles away, where it belongs.

Yes, Rhen's marriage had failed. But it was a cathartic death, like losing a relative who had been ill for a long time, amnesiac to the point only the appearance remained. Like Iona, he had clung to the shell of their former happiness, and now that empty husk, and the weight of it, was gone.

Even more, tomorrow, he would have the chance to breathe life into something new. Something the world desperately needed. Machines would have their chance to love, and to lose, just like anyone else.

Chapter 4

A small but mighty team. Alan and I must have different definitions of those words.

Rhen stared at the dozen researchers who were sighing, wringing their hands, or stifling yawns. A few were glancing wistfully at their respective desks, as if they were whispering sweet nothings to them. Or perhaps that was just a more palatable place to be than where they were, standing before their new boss.

Getting any details about what they did was like pulling teeth. Rhen turned his gaze to the second-last member of his team, exchanging pings.

Saanvi "Vi" Singh, PhD. She/Her. Lead Cognicist, Project Achilli Research Team. The future is so much bigger than the past.

"So, yeah, you know my name and title from the ping," she said, shrugging. "That kind of sums me up. As for what I do, I'm pretty sure you can guess."

"The quote, is it from Sir Tim Berners-Lee, creator of the World Wide Web?"

"Yup."

And this is my second-in-charge. Fantastic.

Rhen suppressed a sigh. Cognicists were a mixed bag, personality-wise. If they preferred psychology and neuroscience, they were often inquisitive and social people, well suited to investigations. If they preferred the tech side of things, they tended to be introverted and logical. Both skill sets were needed for second-gen AI work.

His old team were all in the former camp, always pestering him to go out for late night drinks and karaoke. In comparison, this felt like walking into a schoolroom full of withdrawn youths. But even so, Rhen was used to more of a reaction from his peers. Humility aside, he was the co-inventor of the Rosetta. It was as if Enrico Fermi had walked into a room full of nuclear physicists, and they hadn't bothered to give more than a half-hearted wave.

The level is disengagement is odd, almost intentionally rude. I'm going to need to find a way to work with this, or my life is going to be a nightmare. What's the cause?

There were too many possible reasons. These could be the only cognicists Alan could have gotten to work on the project. There could be bad working conditions, and they were getting paid peanuts. Maybe the majority were neurodiverse and just appeared more distant than they were. There could have even been a massive group bender last night, and they were all hung over.

I need more data. I'll just act friendly until I find out more, even if I'm the odd one out.

Well, except for the only other upbeat person in the room. That person was staring at him, their eyes wide and sparkling. As Rhen pinged them, their face lit up.

"Delta Zhao, PhD. They slash them, roboticist and department liaison, Project Achilli Research Team!"

They blurted it out before Rhen could even ping them. Like a cracked whip, the rest of the team snapped out of their stupor and stared at Delta, mouth agape. The roboticist's cheeks flushed. The ping said exactly the same thing, but also had a quote. Rhen's quote. *The divide between machines and us is as wide as we make it.*

As if sensing Rhen's thoughts, Delta offered up an explanation.

"I had the quote up before today, since I'm a big fan of your work. I've read every single one of your papers, even your high school essays! I thought I'd share my personals verbally, like in the old days before you worked on the Rosetta implant."

Okay, I'm not sure if total apathy or complete fanaticism is worse, now. Rhen stifled his mortification from finding out that someone had managed to get their hands on his angsty teenage ramblings, and forced a smile instead.

"Well, you know, there wasn't much greeting of anyone back then, given the weather. And when we invented the Rosetta, it was a group effort." And then he turned to his new team, mustering up an enthusiasm born entirely of positive thinking. "I'm looking forward to doing the same sort of amazing work with all of you, and hopefully we can make something great for the history books again."

The reaction was the opposite of what he hoped. One of the team gave a choked sob. Without warning, he turned and ran out of the room. The number of furrowed brows in the room increased.

"I'll go deal with Carter," Vi offered, and then beat a retreat. Her colleagues shot envious looks at her back.

"Is there something I should know?" Rhen said, making sure his voice was as soft as possible.

At this point, Nora stepped forward, who had been leaning against the door-frame behind him and letting him take the lead. Her hands were fidgeting beneath her sleeves, but that had been true yesterday as well. A request for a cognitive message session flicked across his vision. He accepted it.

<It seems they're a little upset because they were very close to Alef, the old project lead. Carter was especially close to them.>

<What happened?> Rhen asked. Nora screwed up her face.

<A certain investment advisor didn't like his progress, and pushed to have the whole project cancelled. The board pressured Alan to shake things up, and so it was let the project lead go, or scrap the whole project.>

<That's harsh. I bet they feel the whole thing is a bit unjust then, since a team succeeds and fails together, but they took the fall.> *And showing any fondness for the replacement, no matter how field famous, would feel like betraying their old boss.* This is all for show, for themselves and management, but not for him. Rhen was just caught in the middle.

<Yeah, I really feel for them. Sorry to let you know what you've walked into, but I do think you're the perfect one for the job.>

<Well, you did mention the project was struggling, and I do enjoy a challenge. Guess that involves getting morale back up again.>

Rhen sucked in a deep breath. By the time he exhaled, his mind was clear and focused. He then clasped his hand down at his waist and turned back to the team, or at least the team sans the two who were now absent.

"I'm sorry, I just found out about the situation. It sounds like Alef was a great project lead, and you all had a special dynamic going on. I know change is tough, and I'm not here to replace him, but help finish the work you and he started. As I said, invention is a group effort, so I fully intend to recognise *everyone* who worked on this project, whether they were here at the end or not. I do want you all to know that if you want to talk about it, or anything else, I'm here at any time."

This time, the result was better. Some of the team had untensed their shoulders and most were now making eye contact. Two even had the faint whisper of a smile. Small steps! They were more relaxed, or at the very least, more resigned.

Better give them some space to talk amongst themselves, and share their impressions of the new boss. I've got to continue my tour of the other departments anyway.

Rhen nodded to Nora, and they left the lab. Once they were a little way down the holo-lined corridor, she turned to him, eyes soft.

"You did good. That was a tough situation and you took it in your stride."

"It would have been nice to be briefed before I went in there."

"You're absolutely right. I'm sorry. It never occured to me that they might still be that upset about it." She gave a heavy sigh, as if pushing every ounce of air from her chest. "Also, Alan doesn't like us talking about the past people who have been in your role. Kind of a sore point for him."

This is what I get for being so eager to join that I didn't ask any questions. Rhen must have been wearing his sourness on his face, because Nora's eyes widened.

"Don't worry, I'm sure all of that is in the past now," she added. "There's been a lot of perks added to the role, and Alan seems to be bending backwards to make sure you're not going anywhere. Plus, you get to work with me."

"Well, that was mentioned on the offer, but every job says that," Rhen said, a joke for a joke.

"I doubt it! Only one of me, so accept no substitutions."

Rhen was unsurprised that Robotics and Cybernetics got an entire floor to themselves, which was positioned just a few levels below his own. Sekai made a lot of money out of replaceable machine parts, more so than the Rosetta and licensed AI. Once out of the elevator, it was a straight shot through some large double doors and into a huge square room that had been designed to look like something between an indoor courtyard and a walk in the bush.

Holographic trees with snowy trunks stretched up from the corners of the room and towered above them, a canopy of olive leaves stretching across and partially concealing the rich blue of a fake Australian sky. It was only betrayed by the impossibility of its existence so far underground. The light streaming down forced Rhen to squint as he looked up, and his skin prickled from projected heat. The smell of the phantom leaves—minty, sharp and a little oily—filled and cleared his nose.

Between the ghostly giants, the floor was made of dark, polished wood dappled with different scintillating shapes from filtered light. *The holos must be connected together, running the math for real-world holographic raytracing.* Even the pale streaking columns that hung in the air were perfectly reconstructed. It was a step above the regular household displays most people had, since it would be a custom build.

"That's some beautiful komorebi," Rhen said. He used the Japanese word for the phenomenon, because there was no simple English word for the dappled sunlight that filters through trees. "Sun lamps have come a long way since I was a kid, with all these complex shapes and patterns."

"Yeah, there's a scenic foyer like this on nearly every floor. A lot of people use them for quick breaks when it's too much work to travel to a cafeteria or the long lift ride to the surface. It's pretty hard to buy a good sun lamp these days. Why buy a fancy lamp when you can just go outside? But they're still needed in facilities like this."

There were double doors in every cardinal direction. Someone emerged from the set to the left, their eyes searching around until they locked with Rhen and Nora. With a smile, the newcomer wandered over, and as they did, Nora's hands once again slipped up beneath her sleeves.

It's like some sort of turtle defense? But Rhen's thought was broken by the newcomer's introductory ping, which he quickly returned.

Shana Edwards, PhD. She/Her. Head of Robotics and Cybernetics. There is nothing more difficult than to take the lead in the introduction of a new order of things.

Machiavelli? Interesting choice. "You don't see many people with quotes from The Prince these days. I'd expect a roboticist or cyberneticist to quote Joseph Engelberger or Chie Kato."

The department head laughed. "It's not an exact reading, but yeah, it's one of my faves. Old Nick was all about empirical observations and results, so I like to think he had a scientific spirit." And then she flicked a finger at the air above his head. "I like your quote, too! But then, bridging the gap between humans and machines is my bread and butter."

When she spoke, her accent had an Australian-like drawl, but there was a rising lilt at the end like everything she asked was a question. Rhen pinned her as a New Zealander, having worked with more than a few back at Arctis Labs. Her chestnut hair was tied back in a tight ponytail with two hair clips shaped like lightning bolts. It was pretty standard for roboticists to keep their hair tucked away to avoid it getting caught in a mechanical joint and yanked. Her leather slingback pumps, polished and well-cared for, gave a boost to her diminutive height, no doubt helping level things out when talking to relative giants like Rhen and Nora.

"Kind of interesting that you're the head of both Robotics and Cybernetics," Rhen asked. "They're not kept seperate?"

"Understandable question! Originally, it was just Robotics, with us working on the chassis for future AIs to be housed in, as well as a bunch of Mirage's other long-shot projects," Shana said, stowing her hands in the pockets of her lab coat. The words had the rehearsed tone of someone who had been asked this question many times before. "But if you're working on humanoid parts for a machine, it's not a big leap to adjust them for the prosthetic market, and *that* idea made our resident investment advisor very excited. Suddenly, a lot of capital came in to research lifelike parts, and I get to add cyberneticist to my resume. Great for my career! We're still at Mirage because they want to keep their market-leading research in a high-security facility, somewhere competitors have trouble reaching."

"Makes sense. Packing up shop would be pretty tough, and I doubt you're going to find anywhere more remote than this."

"Tell me about it! If I want to try on some new clothes, it's like a three day trip to a decent shopping center." Shana groaned. "I've lost track of all the online orders I've had to return. Anyway, I'm sure you're not here to talk about my issues buying shoes. Want to see some of our work? It'll probably blow your mind."

"Absolutely."

The lobby and engineering couldn't have been more different. Instead of picturesque foliage, the walls were pure, sterile, and practical. From top to bottom, they were broken up by a square-shaped pattern. At the base, they were six foot wide—his brain used a weird mix of metric and imperial measurements, due to all the working abroad—then shrunk and increased in number the further up the wall you went.

There were more machines than humans, though the former were largely surface-mounted arms. One of the wall squares would push out, revealing a long container, then a metal limb would reach inside for something to deposit on one of the benches in the middle of the room. It was fascinating watching something come down from the top, as the arms would pass the item between them like a baton race towards the bottom.

All cognitively controlled, no doubt. The few engineers in the room were sitting on chairs and sipping drinks. It didn't look like they'd raised a finger all day, or at least one of their own.

Meanwhile, Shana reached out her hands. Directly above her, a mechanical arm pulled a human-like limb out of a container, and dropped it into her grasp.

"Check this bad boy out!" She said, offering the limb to him with obvious pride.

It really did look lifelike, right down to the faint hair follicles. In fact, he had to force himself to grab it, reassuring himself that there was no way it was real. As his fingers sunk into the skin of the slender arm, his resolve wavered. Impulsively, he checked the stump. The first few layers looked organic, but the rest were unmistakably mineral, all porous metal and woven nanofiber.

Whew. Definitely organic. But Shana was right, it was utterly mind-blowing. But there were even mock blood vessels, with thin tubing woven through both sections. It was like someone had knitted through it, criss-crossing back and forth, then pulled the thread tight. He gave a low whistle of appreciation.

"This is something else. But why include veins and capillaries?"

"Oh, so many reasons. Coolant and fuel distribution, lubrication of joints — we also run a tinted emergency sealant through the whole thing which gives the skin an organic flush. You don't want a prosthetic limb that looks too different from the rest of your body."

"Emergency sealant?"

"Yeah, if the surface of the skin is cut, it leaks out and seals the wound, just like real blood. There's going to be a lot of confused people and vampires out there."

Vampires? She's an odd one, that's for sure. But that thinking probably helps her come up with unusual solutions.

"So, if you prick them, they will bleed. Aren't you worried the public might freak out, given how hyper-realistic they are?"

"Me? Yeah, nah. I'm not worried, that's someone else's problem." Shana took the limb back, and it waved at Rhen.

He jumped, and she gave a snorting laugh.

"Don't worry, just a bit of cognitive puppetry. Sorry, I love doing that to newbies! That's why I always go with the demo hand. I call him The Thing."

"I don't get it."

"It's from an old comedy called the Addam's Family, something I found while I was on a Saga binge on the term 'Frankenstein.' Lots of dark humour. Would-concequence highly recommend."

"Is that why you've got lightning bolts for hairpins?"

"Got it in one!" Shana beamed, tapping her head. "I'm the creator, so I don't go with neck-bolts. But Halloween is coming up soon and that's when I go all out."

That artery stitch pattern feels a lot more appropriate now. I wonder if she yelled out 'It's alive!' when she first turned it on?

Their tour took them to a box-like chamber. Inside was a suspended mechanical leg, with tarnished metal and broken toe joints.

"We call this the Tardis," Shana said. "It's for testing how long a part is going to last in the wild. Obviously, we don't have a hundred years to just find out, so we put them in this box and throw everything we can at it! UV light, moisture, chemical exposure, vibrations, the works. We try to make the parts so they last damn near forever. Our scummy investment advisor has pushed for them to only last the warranty, but it's a good thing that it's far too expensive to make them that way. Wink, wink."

At first, Rhen had been irritated by Shana's seemingly callous disregard for the consequences of her invention. But it did seem like she cared on some level, so she couldn't be all that bad. The investment advisor, though? This was the third time he'd heard them mentioned today, and never in a good way.

"I'm sure people with cybernetic parts sure appreciate that," he said. "Still, in terms of the environment, the parts aren't biodegradable?"

"Nah, but you can recycle them easily enough. That, or gift it to someone who's got no money, so they can walk around with your donor legs. Pay it forward, you know?"

And then, at the end of the tour, Shana turned to him and stretched out a hand.

"Oh, I probably should have said this at the start, but I'm a massive fan of your work. Inspired stuff, and glad to be working with you!"

Why is she holding out her hand? Oh, she wants me to shake it.

"Thanks, I look forward to working with you too." He took her hand and... waved it up and down awkwardly. She seemed satisfied enough. As he and Nora continued their tour, he stared at his hand.

"Well, that's something I've only seen done in the movies. Am I going to need to curtsey or kiss the cheeks of the next person?"

"Kissing? No." Nora said with a smile. "Shana's a chatterbox, so we're running a bit behind. I'm taking you up to Data Operations next. And because I didn't warn you earlier today, I'm going to do so now. The head of that department is... well, if he seems rude, don't take it personally."

"Thanks for the warning." And then, thinking about Nora's reaction when Shana approached, and her hands slipping up beneath her sleeves, "Do you not get along with Shana?"

"Oh, no! I absolutely do. Shana's actually my best friend outside of work. We get along like a house on fire, especially since we both love talking shop."

Well, that's unexpected. If he hadn't seen Nora do the same thing with her hands earlier today, he would have thought hiding them was to avoid a handshake, but clearly there was something else going on. *I wonder what it is?*

The trip to Data Operations was a long elevator ride to the upper floors of the facility. At least their department was similar in size and style to Rhen's: sleek, clean workstations, a few shared spaces, and not a whole lot else.

The person waiting for them was equally no-frills. Their clothes were plain and their arms were crossed. Their face was screwed up and pained, like they had swallowed a lemon seconds ago.

"You're late."

In the face of the flung accusation, Rhen momentarily forgot to ping them. As if thinking was a hassle, his accusor heaved a sigh and pinged first, and he reciprocated.

Robert Morrison, PhD. He/Him. Head of Data Operations.
Winner of the Pinnacle Data Award.

"Apologies, we got caught up a few levels down in Robotics and Cybernetics," Rhen said. At that, Robert rolled his eyes.

"Yes, well, that department gets all the attention. Not like Data Operations. We just handle the foundation that all your projects are built on."

"I've never heard of the Pinacle Data Award. It sounds quite prestigious."

"It is." Robert said, stating it as if he had claimed it wasn't. "I got it for inventing a novel ETL method for storing and labelling cognitive data. Of course, my last employer, Vertex, gave me zero recognition for it. That's why I decided to go somewhere that I'm appreciated. Unfortunately, I wound up here instead."

"Oh, that sounds impressive," Rhen said, focusing on the positive, since he had no idea what to say about the other thing. It wasn't lip service, his accomplishment *did* sound impressive. "I'd love to learn more about that novel method."

"Well, if we've got time." And Robert stressed the last word, as if to say *and we've got less of it now.* "I'll run you through the tour."

It wasn't exactly a tour. In fact, the man spent the whole time talking to him as if he were immediately picking up Alef's tasks, and had exhaustive knowledge on everything going on. Between being asked about outstanding tickets he had no idea about to discussing bad documentation he hadn't written, Rhen simply repeated:

"I don't know. I just got started."

There was at least some tidbits in the so-called tour. It was mostly when Robert stopped for a moment of self-aggrandizement, so it might not have been for Rhen's benefit. The man bragged about how he handled all the Bills-Aldrich testing and general vetting of AI data for the hybrid project *personally*, even though there were a dozen V2 Sybil models—an AI model designed for fully autonomous data processing—working furiously just a stone's throw away.

When they were back in the elevator, he shot a tired look at Nora. She returned a sympathetic smile. Again, now they were out of there, her painted fingers emerged.

"He's actually a genius brilliant when it comes to data." *When he actually does the work*, Nora's face said. "But yes, he's not the best with people."

"You read my thoughts."

"One of my many, many talents. Speaking of mind reading, your psychological baseline is up next. Thankfully, we're on time for that."

Rhen's stomach sunk. *Damn. I guess I really can't outrun it.*

About a month ago, as he'd been sitting at an automated food cart and watching it noisily pour beer into a transparent cup, he'd got a message from Sekai's MentOps team. After a pause, he'd downed the cup, requested another, and read the mail. It had been a request for a baseline reassessment 'in light of his recent major life event.' The time stamp was exactly twenty four hours and three minutes since Iona's divorce request. Bureaucracy wasn't dead, just on steroids.

He'd dodged their follow-ups right until he'd tendered his resignation. Turns out it was just a reprieve.

"Not a fan of assessments?" Nora asked. His emotions were probably etched on his face again.

"Nope. I always think of something inappropriate, usually something about how the assessor looks." He tapped his ears. "The last time, I thought about how their ears stuck out too much, and they couldn't stop touching them for the rest of the assessment."

"Don't fret too much, everyone does that," Nora chuckled. "It's just the White Bear Problem. Try not to think of a bear, and you'll think of nothing else. All that says is you're worried about being impolite and hurting people's feelings. Usually, assessors are a bit more thick-skinned than that."

"I didn't have to do them before we invented the Rosetta," he huffed, crossing his arms. She gave a lopsided grin.

"Hoist with your own petard! But in all seriousness, you know they need to do it, if only to make *my* job easier. If you're cognitive coding, they need to assess if any of your potential biases might slip into the final product."

"I know, I know." He paused, a thought occuring to him. "Hey, thanks for giving me a guided tour, by the way. You've got your own whole department to run, and you're taking the time to show me around."

"It's no big deal. In fact, I volunteered," she said, toying with one of her two-toned curls. "And I know your day has been a bit hit and miss, what with your team and all, but a lot of people around here are excited to have you join. Your past work speaks for itself."

"I've only made it this far because I've worked with outstanding people."

"Well, I wouldn't want you to be in bad company."

The MentOps office was tucked in the furthest corner of one of Mirage's middle floors, a space shared with several medical research departments. Once they arrived, Nora turned to him.

"You'll be fine. Just don't think of white bears," she quipped. "I'll see you after the assessment."

<White be—I mean, open,> Rhen thought at the door, which immediately complied.

As expected of the MentOps office, everything inside was pleasant and inoffensive. It had the look and feel of a traditional psychologist's office, from the abstract art that said either everything or nothing, to the abundance of warm tones. There was the token cosy-looking chaise longue, a plain white sphere in a stand, and two matching armchairs, one of which was occupied. They were staring out a large visiglass window, which was a low-lying Parisian landscape. He had only visited twice, but he recognised the Seine, and over the river, the familiar dome of the Institut de France.

The single occupant stood up and smiled. They had more than a weathered face; they had rolling, closely packed crags viewed from above, dark tawny and speckled earth scorched by the sun. And yet, their well-trimmed beard and slicked-back hair were a vivid orange, and not a natural shade. Their neck and chest were adorned in a loose scarf and linen shirt respectively. It was as if they were a grey nomad — the Australian slang for a travelling retiree — who had leapt on a camel at Uluru like most tourists did, got lost in the desert for a few weeks, and wound up here. For all Rhen knew, that's exactly what happened.

When the grey nomad spoke, though, every word was careful and considerate, without the hint of a stutter.

"Doctor Nagami, I presume?" They exchanged pings.

Roswell Edwards, PsyD. He/Him. PACT Psychologist and MentOps Specialist. Every person on this earth is full of great possibilities that can be realised through imagination, effort, and perseverance.

"Huh, the quote's from Scott Kaufmann, right? I haven't seen that one since my dissertation," Rhen said. There was something about the diminutive height of the man and his surname that also sparked a sense of deja vu, though the way they spoke couldn't be less alike. "You know, you're the second person I've met today with the last name Edwards."

"Oh, you've met my daughter, Shana?" Roswell's whole face lit up, matching his incandescent hair. "Probably got you with her hand gag, right?"

"Yeah, she got me good. How did you end up working together?"

"Shana was head-hunted by the facility, but she didn't want to leave me alone. Luckily, there was a MentOps position available I was qualified for. I'd been retired for all of a few months before I came back out."

"And just like Shana, you're double qualified. Psychology and MentOps. Though usually a MentOps team is at least two to four people?" There were no other doors to speak of.

"The facility director doesn't believe much in MentOps. Me either, to be honest, despite my training. But it's mandatory at all Sekai facilities to boost productivity, so someone's got to fill the seat. Most of my day is focused on staff wellness rather than performance-managing people over their thoughts per minute."

"Good to hear. I could game my TPMs by counting inane things in the office, anyway." And since nobody at Mirage had remote connection to their work stations, they wouldn't be doing live thought counting, either. Counting, not reading, since it was illegal to read people's thoughts without permission, and his team had made damn sure that was baked into the Rosetta from the start. *A rare moment of foresight, but not nearly enough.*

"Is that the view from the Louvre?" Rhen asked.

"Hmm? Correct! It's three floors up. Obviously, they don't allow you to run a practice out of the real one, but it's nice to imagine. You've been before?"

"A few times. My ex-wife said she'd live in the Louvre if she could. Specifically in the Galerie des Antiques, so she could sleep among all the Greek statues. So long as she could fix up the Venus de Milo, with its missing arms."

"I imagine a lot of people would be unhappy about that." And then Roswell gestured to the chaise longue. "So, should we get started with your baseline assessment? I imagine you've got a lot of things packed in today, and I'd hate to hold you up."

"Ah, right. Yes. The assessment." Rhen grabbed the edges of the chair and descended on it all the joy of a cat taking a bath. Well, at least it was comfortable. The padding practically sucked up his body the second it made contact. *Makes sense to spend money on the second-most important thing in the office.*

The most important was the sphere next to the psychologist, positioned near his right hand like a crystal ball. A Beck Model 12, if he wasn't mistaken. A halo-like line around the orb's mid-section began to glow.

"Before we start, I'll need level four read-only permissions for your mind." Roswell gave a gentle smile. "Sorry in advance, because I've now got to read out a statement that will be like explaining the basics of relativity to Einstein. The Psychology Board of Australia requires that I verbally read out an explanation of the levels of consciousness so I've got your informed consent."

"I understand, though Einstein's overdoing it. Go right ahead."

"Your consciousness is made up of four distinct levels: the superconscious, the conscious, the subconscious and the unconscious. The first are the focused, commanding thoughts you use to make things happen with your CI implant. The second are your regular, everyday thoughts that you're consciously aware of."

"Yeah, attuning the CI to pick up one and not the other was a lot of work. We couldn't have a stray thought about driving a car over your boss's foot actually make that happen." And then Rhen paused. "Sorry, just realised I'm dragging out the spiel. I have a bad habit of interjecting when people talk about things I know about."

"I understand. To continue, your subconscious is the storehouse of almost every experience you've ever had, like impressions and memories. They're not always in your thoughts, but you can retrieve it with relative ease. Lastly, there's your unconscious, made up of thoughts, memories and primitive desires we bury deep within ourselves. People can't readily access it because it may be associated with negative events or trauma."

"For this assessment, we need to get an unfiltered snapshot of how your brain works and your thinking patterns, so we'll need complete access to all of these. I'll be able to hear your thoughts from the first two levels in real time, but everything else will just be data. I'd need an AI to turn your memories into something I could watch, like Beck here," he said, thrumming the pale sphere with his tanned fingers. "And just so you know, my access will be read-only, so I can't rewrite your thoughts."

"Well, I've got a barrier just in case, though I doubt you could rewrite my personality even if you did, only delete or lightly smudge some memories. The human brain is like a tower of cards; any changes need to be made carefully."

"You're right, I couldn't, not without causing a Kaur collapse."

Rhen winced.

"Sorry, I forgot that happened on the same project," Roswell said. His voice lowered and the edge of his wrinkled eyes softened. "Sukhvir Kaur was a colleague of yours, correct?"

"He was, though I wish I'd known Sukh better." Rhen tensed his hands. "It's not a problem. We talked to his family, and decided to name it after him so he wouldn't be forgotten. Seems to have worked, though you might find some of that buried deep on levelthree. We had a habit of self-testing back then."

Collapse was the only word for it. He'd come in to find Sukhvir convulsing on the floor, the diagnostic machine still hooked up. They'd gotten everything up to stage three then, too. Nobody wanted to look at it afterward, but Rhen had. Someone had to.

He knew what it was like to watch someone crumble from the inside.

"Send through the ping and I'll accept it."

"All right. One more thing, again something you already know. I'll be asking questions in order to get the baseline, but the final report won't include notes on any of your specific thoughts, only a score against a few personality traits. Also, you can rescind permissions at any time."

"Sure, got it."

The psychologist sent through the ping, filtered no doubt through his Beck AI. The moment he did, it triggered a warning that occupied most of Rhen's vision. It was written in angry red letters and pulsing with a low beat.

Warning! Roswell Edwards has requested read-only level four access to your mind. If you accept, this may result in a serious loss of privacy. Do you consent?

When Rhen accepted, Roswell's eyes narrowed. He didn't take it personally. People made all kinds of faces when digesting cognitive media. Some people squinted, others frowned or pursed their lips. Apparently, kids these days called it their 'C-face'.

"Name?"

"Rhen Nao Nagami," he answered.

Don't think about how you think his nose looks kind of big. Shit.

It was the curse of level two access. Back when his team had been working on the Rosetta implant, Rhen had got to hear all kinds of things. For instance, he'd learned that one of his colleagues was attracted to her sister-in-law, and another thought he was a condescending ass when explaining things.

It was essential for the early stages of research, but after that, they'd put two house rules in place. The first was they'd only listen to each other's thoughts when absolutely necessary. The second was that nobody was to be judged on their thoughts, only their actions.

Thankfully, Roswell seemed to subscribe to the same philosophy. He moved to the next question without skipping a beat, and never once touched his nose.

The test finished off with a round of math questions, logic tests and brain teasers which Rhen enjoyed a great deal more. At the end, Roswell's eyes lost their narrow look and he self-rescinded the permissions.

"So, did I pass?" Rhen asked, standing up. Even in such a comfortable chair, his limbs were stiff and restless.

Probably from keeping my muscles tense the whole time. Baseline assessments are the worst. I'd rather sign up for dental. Now that his brain wasn't being scanned, he was free to think whatever he wanted without causing offence.

"Nothing of concern, but you probably know that already, since this isn't your first time. If you were working on a project for the military, I'd flag your high level of empathy for machines as an issue, since your pathos scored in the eighties. But that's not a problem, since Glycon is very anti-war, just like our parent company."

"Yeah, I wouldn't want to work on anything that would hurt someone else. That's a deal-breaker for me."

As Rhen got up to leave, the psychologist shook his hand.

"You know, as I said earlier, MenOps is only a small part of my job. If you ever want to do any councilling, regular or PACT, the offer is open. Feel free to come around any time you want to.

As a cognicist, Rhen stayed on top of the latest in cognitive psychology, and PACT—Positive Alignment Cognitive Therapy—was all the rage right now, much like MentOps. It was basically a psychologist listening in to your underlying thoughts via the Rosetta and trying to bring them into healthy balance through councilling, not coding. Apparently, it had done wonders for people with OCD, schizophrenia, and eating disorders, but the very idea sent a cold shudder down the cognicist's spine.

"Sure, maybe the regular therapy, if I need it. No PACT, though."

***

After his assessment, Rhen met up with Nora, and it was back to touring other research departments. Unfortunately, while the research strains were many and varied, none of them were as forthcoming as Shana was.

"Well, I have no idea what that department did, other than it involved nanorobotics," Rhen grumbled. "And the one before that was vague as well. I think they were working on genetic manipulation, perhaps some sort of treatment for Alzheimers? Hard to tell."

"If it makes you feel any better, I've got no idea either," Nora said, giving a half smile. "There are whole levels in Mirage with restricted access. You know how it is, everyone's scared of corporate espionage. All it takes is one person going around and getting enough information, and the market edge is lost, not to mention someone's prized research project."

"Yeah, I get the need to protect against that. But I also just really want to *know*." He huffed. "Especially since it looked like they were trying to control nanites cognitively, even though they wouldn't confirm it. I've never seen that kind of fine-tuned control before."

"Thinking of switching departments already?" She quirked an eyebrow, a glint of amusement in her eyes.

"Reading my mind again?" He clicked his tongue. "I'd be tempted, but the hyb—Project Achilli is much more important," Rhen said, self-censoring just in time. Everyone else was doing it, after all. "If if they are working on nanorobotics, the medical applications would be massive. You could have tiny little machines repairing tissue cells or performing surgery, all controlled by a surgeon's mind. Or not even a surgeon, but a regular doctor."

"Or split an atom with a single thought, letting anyone trigger a nuclear explosion," Nora said, her brow knitted. Rhen had never seen her frown much, so it was a small shock. He slowed his pace.

"Yeah, there's usually another side to it. While that's fairly pessimistic, I can't really disagree that it might happen."

"Oh, you'll find out sooner or later my faith in humanity as a whole is *not* very high." She chuckled. "It's why spending all day listing the flaws in other people's work and malking to machines fits me quite well."

"You prefer machines over people?"

"Mostly. I have been known to make exceptions, though." She gave a lopsided grin, though it was partially hidden behind her umbral and azure mess of hair. "How about you, where do you fall on the humanity issue?"

"I'm probably in the middle. I think humans have the ability to be kind and considerate to one another, but only if they can relate to them - most people lack the imagination." He chuckled. "The fact you call it the 'humanity issue' really screams misanthrope."

"'I am Misanthropos, and I hate mankind. For thy part, I do wish thou wert a dog, that I might love thee something.'"

"That's from Timon of Athens, right? Shakespeare, I think."

"Right on the money." She cupped a hand under her chin. "You're really good at guessing quotes. I don't think I've seen you get one wrong yet, and you've met a lot of people."

"It's a gift; bring me along to your trivia nights. Usually, the quote has to come from someone either dead or in our field, though. Being in a research facility gives me a home-field advantage."

"Speaking of home fields, are you ready to see my department? If you thought the arm Shana showed you was impressive, wait until you see what we work with."

"Lead the way, Miss Anthropos."

Chapter 5

It turned out AI Assessment and Testing also got a floor to itself. As they approached the double doors, Rhen gave a mock huff.

"I'm starting to feel left out. Here I am, a whole desert to stretch out, and my team only gets a fifth of the space of everyone else." As they approached the double doors, Nora walked up to a hand-sized panel on the left side of the door. When she got there, she turned to him and rolled her eyes, hand on her hip.

"What would you do with it all, though? Put in a holographic games table?" There was a lilt of mirth and exasperation in her voice.

"For starters. I've got to get the team's morale up, after all. Besides, you can come around and make use of it," he said. "Why have we stopped?"

"Sign in. You'll need to wave in with the biometric device you used for your room. People usually sign in cognitively, but I've heard you don't have that option."

Damn. I mean, it's not like I've got something to hide. But still...

Rhen cleared his throat and pulled out the wedding band. The second it emerged, he pictured a big sign hanging around his neck, reading: "Warning! Failed marriage, bad relationship material." That sensation swirled around inside of him, travelling downwards to form a big stomach-churning knot.

He wove the ring across the panel. Aware Nora's eyes were on him, and finding her expression unreadable, Rhen didn't want her to get the wrong impression. "I'm divorced. It's recent. I haven't changed over the device yet."

Nora was cocking her head. "I'm sorry to hear that. But to be honest, I'd already heard something like that on the grapevine. That sort of thing travels around pretty fast here, though I don't know who found out."

"It's probably on my Saga page, now that I think about it." Rhen's shoulders relaxed with palpable relief. His page would have been updated the moment Iona had updated hers. And if Nora had known about it from the beginning, then there was little to worry about. "I guess the AIs there are pretty quick and merciless when it comes to updating births, deaths and marriages."

"Yeah, what's that saying? 'Privacy is dead'. I imagine our thoughts will be next."

"Are you worried? You're already a self-professed mind reader."

"Well, I can't have everyone being as gifted as I am, now can I?"

Now that balance had been restored, they walked in. There was another one of those holo-floral rooms, though this one was cherry-blossom themed. Given what he'd learned of Nora, Rhen wasn't surprised. The department head must have some control over the scenery.

Beyond it was a lab, in which mostly robots and a few human staff were examining reports. Once introductions were done, they walked up to a door where Nora assured him all the interesting things would be.

Once inside, they were in a long corridor stretching to either side as far as he could see. In front of him was a wall of black glass. There was the faint outline of a door in it, but no handle, and it was made of the exact same material. As they walked along, the pattern repeated itself.

"What's on the other side of these?" He asked. Nora leaned back against the black glass, pushing up her comparatively clear frames.

"It's cognitive glass, so you've just got to think a bit harder."

<I want to see.>

The glass became translucent. Beyond it was a perfectly cube-shaped room with pure white walls. There was a small table in the exact centre of the room, round and low to the ground: a Japanese chabudai. It too was colourless. In fact, it was as if the whole room was a blank canvas just waiting to be painted. Small white egg-like devices lined one side of the wall — Rhen had seen enough wired storage devices to know what they were — for manual extraction or uploading of data when needed. Another layer of air gapping, no doubt.

There were cushions around the table for sitting, and one was occupied. The person sitting there was the sole smattering of colour in the tableau, and even that was a faint touch. Their face was feminine, pale pink cheeks framed by mid-length ashen hair. They were adorned entirely in charcoal black from their shirt to laceless shoes.

They too looked like they had yet to be filled in. Their eyes were blank, their stare unflinching.

"That's the machine chassis for the AI?" Rhen all but whispered, placing a hand in the glass and leaning forward. "Holy shit."

"Right?" Nora said. "It's one thing to see the arm, but another to see the whole thing put together. I'd say it blew my mind too, but I've been here for the earlier versions." She threw up her hands. "Uncanny valley doesn't even begin to describe it."

Rhen examined the life-life chassis. Packed inside the protective square container and sitting so prim and proper, they reminded him of some stores he once came across in Kyoto. Behind the glass were rows of tiny, dressed-up dolls sitting on their heels in seiza position, meticulously dressed up in rich, red robes.

Something about them had been suffocating. Rhen found himself imagining them as trapped souls, encased in a mix of layered wood and fabric, then coated in crushed oyster shells. Their eyes were glassy and unyielding, positioned ever forward. They were given out to Japanese children on Hinamatsuri, or Girl's Day, in early Spring.

"These remind me of Hina dolls," Rhen said, turning to his guide. She turned and grinned.

"Should I get you some rice crackers then? I think I've got some in my desk." Coloured crackers were traditionally eaten during the holiday.

"I might take you up on that. I am getting a bit hungry."

"We'll get some dinner after this. So did you grow up with Hina dolls in your house?" Nora asked, curiosity in her eyes as she pushed off the glass.

"No, I only played with United Republic ones." There was something else that made them doll-like, and then it hit him. "The machines are dressed up. It's a bit strange to see them with clothes on."

"Why, do you prefer them naked?" She asked, giving him a side-long look. His cheeks burned.

"No. I mean, it's not that I prefer it." He cleared his throat. "It's a matter of practicality. In Japan, when we worked on them, they left the clothes off to allow for easy access. To do maintenance," he clarified. "They were far less realistic, so it was less of an issue, and—" He paused. "Wait, you're making fun of me, aren't you?"

"I might be. Did you want to go inside?"

"Of course!"

***

The room was warm inside, so Rhen pulled off his jacket before approaching the round table. He sat cross-legged unlike the chassis, because sitting seiza-style gave his legs pins and needles after a few minutes.

Nora followed suit, but she sat wariza-style, her backside on the floor and lower legs bent off to their respective sides. Both were informal Japanese poses, making the machine the only one keeping up appearances.

It was like they were sitting to have a cup of green tea and chat with the machine. For all he knew, that could be exactly how they assessed the AI candidates once they were loaded into the chassis. He wouldn't mind if they did that, but it would be pointless until there was something inside of it.

"Why a chabudai? I've got to ask."

"It's easy to fold up and stow away, depending on the test we are running," she said, brushing some hair away from her face. "A folding card table might have worked, but it wouldn't have had as much class."

"And having class is important?"

"Of course! That's why I've got an abundance of it."

Rhen leaned forward and rested his forearms on the table. He stared at the inorganic face, examining every pore. The details were perfect, right down to the ghost of acne scarring on the left side of their petite nose.

"I meant to say this before when we spoke to Shana, but you must have a really great mind artisan on staff. Most of them struggle when it comes to asymmetrical brows."

"They're not actually on staff. We got some models made up and sent over so we could print them out."

Rhen knew a lot about cognitive art, and not just from his work on the Rosetta. His ex-wife, Iona, was a mind artisan. She had been one of the first to get an implant, at least once the kinks had been ironed out. He'd watched her with avid interest as she'd conjured up an art asset with just a thought, then scrunched up her face to imagine and fill out the finer details; he'd always loved the way her nose had wrinkled when she did it. The final result was a true-to-life person made entirely from her dreams.

Not long after getting the implant, she'd started a holo-channel called "Illustrating with Iona". Before she came along, the only recordings on making mind art were by stuffy, verbose researchers drawing stick figures, mostly to show it could be done. Funnily enough, Rhen was one of them.

Iona had rightly called out his boring videos and made something better. She was always like that, never one to sit still for long, a font of endless, nearly manic energy.

Because she was a first adopter and a highly creative person, she'd quickly become a sensation. Even though Rhen had helped invent the Rosetta, Iona was easily more famous than him.

She had waited a whole hour after the divorce was submitted to let her subscribers know.

The particular picture she had painted of it was missing a few details, like the affair. As a pragmatist, it made complete sense to him, since she was never going to sabotage her ratings that way. On the other hand, even though she had said nothing negative, her avid fans had constructed their own narrative that he was the bad guy. They didn't know him, and like most people who followed digital celebrities, they believed they knew her through the filtered, scripted takes she chose to share.

All the more reason to hang out in a remote desert bunker until the storm blew over.

As he was appreciating the art that went into the machine, it blinked.

Rhen jumped. He couldn't help it. His hand grabbed the side of the table, and Nora stifled a snort.

"Sorry, that's twice in one day," she said. "Not very sporting, I know, but I just won ten glo from Shana, since you made it longer than a minute."

"They've got an AI loaded into them?"

"No, just firmware, the stuff needed for the chassis to operate. Blinking was seen as essential, because apparently the lubrication of eyeballs allows for better rotation and a more natural appearance." She leaned forward herself, pointing to the eyes in question. "As Shana said, everything's got to double for prosthetic use, so they could functionally cry. Not that we want to make the AI cry in the first place."

"Me either." Rhen gazed into the artificial retina, inside which sensor data collectors would be pulling surface moisture values, then feeding them into a programming loop that randomly called a blinking function. *So much intentional design to replicate what humans do without even thinking.* "So, this is what you do all day, stare at these?"

"Well, I drink tea and ask questions as well. There's more than me, of course, and we run through a standardised list so all the results can be compared. We also do follow up tests as needed."

"No wonder you're such a mind-reader — you literally spend all day examining people and reading the leaves." He turned back to Nora, placing his hands on his thighs. "It'll be interesting to interview one with an actual AI loaded into it."

Nora's expression softened. "Sorry, you won't be coming here to interview them, at least during the actual process. The experiment is double-blind, so we don't want to cause an observer-expectancy effect."

The observer-expectancy effect was when an experimenter interpreted the results incorrectly because they subconsciously want something to be true or false. If you spent years trying to create a cure for a disease, and you tested it on a sick patient, you could want it to work so much that you interpret any remission as proof of a cure, or unconsciously ignore signs it doesn't work.

"I get it. You don't want me to test them because I might see an AI breakthrough where there's not one. I guess your team will be testing a bunch of hybrid models my team makes, but there'll also be a number of other copies thrown into the mix as a control batch?"

"Exactly, that way we can't be biassed either. If it makes you feel any better, you'll get to see every report my team throws together, so yours won't be flying blind. As a result, we'll be working very closely together. That's not a problem, right?"

"No, that's no problem at all."

***

Rhen's first month at Mirage passed swiftly, filled with the administrative minutia of leading a team and getting up to speed. He felt bad for not making much progress yet on the project, but continually reminded himself that nobody ever made progress when they first joined a team.

It's just Brooks's law at work. Adding more people to a late stage tech project always makes it take longer.

Still, it chafed at him that people had to keep stopping their work to keep explaining things to him. It probably didn't help that his team were all sighs and pursed lips whenever he asked a question, no doubt still sore from him replacing their old lead. Their eyes said it all: *If Alef was still here, we wouldn't be catching you up to speed on the basics.*

There was one ray of sunshine at the end of most days. Long after her role as a tour guide had ended, Nora had made it a habit of asking him out for dinner every second night. He wasn't sure if it was because she could sense he needed it, or because she genuinely liked spending time with him.

I hope it's the latter.

At first, he'd reasoned with that small, yearning feeling. It made sense, after all. Nora was very easy to talk to, funny, exceptionally clever, and a fellow tech nerd. Who wouldn't want someone like that to like them? But since then, the sight of her leaning against his doorframe and curling her hair dazzled his senses in a way that couldn't be explained away by logic. The long-forgotten pang was loud and unmistakable.

Still, he stifled his feelings.

Come on, get your head in the game. Having a crush on a coworker is a bad move. And even if she does enjoy spending time with me, it doesn't mean anything more.

"I've just clocked off for the night. Do you want to grab something to eat?" Nora asked him, lingering once again at the edge of his office, fingers tucked under her long sleeves.

"Sure, I'll just finish things up."

And then, as usual, they'd go to Mirage's cafeteria, though it was more an automated restaurant. The roof was lined with criss-crossing tracks, and serving arms were constantly bustling back and forth along them, carrying and dropping off mentally-requested meals. The tables were adorned with digital tablecloths that shifted patterns over time, currently set to the rusty red of the desert.

At the very back was a chef controlling a mechanical brigade de cuisine, from the sauciers to the automated dishwashers. He wore a toque blanche, one of those amusingly tall chef hats, but his stern expression made it clear that it was hardly a joke.

"Gene never looks happy," Rhen observed, as he and Nora pulled up a booth. "You'd think he was working at the L'Espadon in Paris, not a cafeteria at a desert research base."

"Shh, don't call Kutjera a cafeteria! He'll get the machines to slip hot sauce in your food and say it's a mistake."

"Joke's on him, I like spicy food. But I'd hate for the robots to get the blame, since they're doing all the work," he said. The head chef didn't even taste the food, since the machines could use sensors to test the results against the saved recipe with a 0.5% margin of error, which was far too small for a hot sauce mix-up. Still, the chef was there to set the menu and do basic maintenance, so he was the authority on malfunctioning kitchen staff. "Why is it called Kutjera anyway? I've never asked."

"Don't quote me on it, but I think it's the name of the desert raisin, or Solanum centrale, that grows in the desert," Nora said, stretching out. "It's what the Australians call 'bush tucker', and the native people have been eating it for millennia."

"But don't quote you on it?" He said a sardonic note in his voice. She grinned.

"I don't have Saga to back me up, so I could be wrong. I just remember it from a conversation from way back, so best to hedge my bets. Are you going to order your usual?"

"No, I'd hate if you started thinking I was predictable. I'll get the special."

Only a few minutes after they ordered, a pair of mechanical arms came over and placed their meals on the table. In front of Nora was a bowl of ramen, and she picked out a wilted sprout with a furrowed brow.

"Ugh. Look at this! All these toppings trying to disguise the weak broth. This always happens when you make it too fast. Every time I try it, I keep hoping it will be different, but it never is." What did you get?"

"Steak frites. Not exactly special, given how much Australia loves its beef."

"Well, they've got all the best blueprints for lab-grown meat, and if you pirate them, you know they'll sue the steak off of you. Can I have a piece?"

"Sure."

He chopped off a bit of the steak, and she plucked it away with her chopsticks. She chewed on the offering thoughtfully.

"I thought so. Yours definitely tastes better."

"It's psychological science. Shared experiences are amplified. If you see me enjoying something, you're going to enjoy it more, too."

"Science, huh? That means I'll need a larger sample size to test the theory."

And with an unabashed grin, she used her chopsticks to deftly snatch one of his fries as well. When she made her third attempt, he brought in his fork to intercept. The meal descended into a playful duel over his plate.

The battle was lost when her hand brushed his. With an electric jolt, he pulled back, and her polished sticks strayed deep onto his plate, seizing victory.

"Addendum, it tastes even better when you earn your food," she said, nibbling on the french fry. "Want to co-author the research paper?"

"This is ridiculous. Next time, I'm just getting a share plate," he huffed. But inwardly, he was thrilled. *Definitely friends, at least.* He couldn't think of a case where food fights were normal coworker behavior.

At that moment, pain struck Rhen's head. Sharp, electric needles stabbed into the back of his skull. He pressed his palms down on the tablecloth so hard the digital image pulsed.

"Are you okay?" Nora asked. He only knew it was her from voice. He couldn't see anything but black squiggles.

Shit, it's a bad one. Slow breaths. Accept the pain.

And then, as swiftly as it struck, it receded. Eventually, he cleared his throat to answer.

"Yeah, I'm fine. It's my implant. Or, part of it."

"The bad connectors, right?" Her voice lowered. "I remember hearing about that. Your Rosetta was replaced, but the connectors to your brain are still from the original model."

"Yup, original and faulty. They can't remove it without doing serious damage. They don't use the bonding technique we used in the lab anymore, so *some* good came of it."

"Why did you all do it?"

It was a fair question. Iona had asked him—well, no, screamed at him—the same question when he'd come home with a compress on his head. He'd tried to explain about Banting and Best discovering insulin, and being the first to inject it in themselves, or Barry Marshall swallowing a petri dish of bacteria to prove it caused ulcers. Of course, that hadn't gone down well, either.

He touched the back of his neck, running his fingers over the old scars.

"Everyone had different reasons. For Erica and Sukh, it was about cutting through red tape. But for me, the main reason was I just didn't want to test it on anyone else."

"Why not?"

"I couldn't live with it if it hurt someone, so I figured it was better on me than someone else. I still stand by it. It's guilt avoidance, not self-sacrifice."

She was clasping his hands. Maybe because he'd looked upset or in pain. Or was. Either way, her soft fingers, so often hidden, were out and stroking his own. Such small movements, but loud enough to completely consume his attention. Her liquid amber eyes were locked with his own, unyielding in their focus.

He didn't pull away this time. After a tentative pause, he ran his own thumb along the back of hers.

Her smile was immediate. Radiant.

"Took you long enough," she said.

"Well, I wasn't sure if you were being nice, or there was something there."

"I told you last week that we didn't have to eat at the cafeteria, we could eat in because it'd be more cosy. Then you brought food to *my lab*."

Rhen groaned.

"Oh, you meant—*oh*." And then it all started coming together. "Then you said, 'We can pick somewhere better', and I said—"

"'Why not under the holographic trees?' Yes. For a smart guy, you're not so quick."

The slightest caress of her fingers was loud enough to occupy every physical sensation, demanding his utmost attention. Funny, how something so small could be so unbearably, unspeakably large.

"So, uh—" He started to speak, but then Nora jumped in.

"Did you want to get out of here?"

"Oh, yes. Absolutely."

Rhen suddenly appreciated how close his apartment was.

The second they were through the door, she pounced. Her hand snaked into his and clutched it tight, as if making up for lost time. When she reached for the other, he pulled it back, provoking a pout that lasted the flash of time it took to wrap his arm around her waist and pull her face to face. Level as they were, her nose collided with his own.

She laughed, a musical noise, and her belly rippled against his. Her breath washed over his lips like wildfire. Unable to wait, he seized them with his own, but they moment they touched it was another battle, two sides hungrily fighting for every inch they could claim.

By some miracle they made it to the bed. Every offensive garment was stripped off, all but a set of forearm covers. As Rhen went to slip them off Nora, she put a hand over his, and wrapped her legs around his waist.

"Everything but that," she panted.

He didn't ask questions. Every inch of her was new and exciting, every freckle a marvel, like an unexplored islet his fingers traced a course around. And yet she touched him with the deft knowledge of a seasoned explorer, even stroking the exact spot on his left shoulder blade that sent shivers down his spine.

Afterwards, they were both covered in a slick sheen of fresh sweat. As she nestled into the nook of his arm, their skin clung together. He ran his fingers through her locks.

Everything was weightless. It was like being on the peak of a shuttle ride. Eventually, he'd need to come down to Earth. But in this moment, there was only her, and nothing else.

Chapter 6

"The report came back, and the latest iteration failed," Vi said.

Rhen swore. Meanwhile, the rest of the team didn't flinch. Over the last six months, they'd become innoculated to it, though before this project, he hadn't been one to swear much at all.

"Every prototype except for A-1 is cursed," he said, running a hand through his hair. "Did it at least outperform the control subject?"

"Marginally."

Vi, unlike him, was always ice calm. He had no doubt she'd seen the same contorted expression on all of her past managers, and he was just the latest passing through. She wore a t-shirt with the words 'Six hours of debugging can save you from five minutes of reading cognitive docs' on the front. Over the top was a lab coat which, while not necessary for cognicists, was part of the unofficial uniform at Mirage. Her hands were stowed deep in the pockets.

"Our hybrid candidate performed 40 percent worse than the built AI in the first round, 46 percent in the second," Vi continued, breaking down the results. Her thick British accent had a refined edge, each syllable evenly stressed. It was utterly at odds with her droll tone, and the lazy way she leaned back against the shared office table. "No statistically significant change in the flexibility of its thinking. They're worse than the everyday AI you can pick up from an online store. Up from the previous iteration though, so they're improving."

"Yeah, but given they perform worse on a test taken just six hours later, it means we haven't nailed a stable cognitive architecture. We're still triggering the Kaur collapse." He had stopped wincing at the term months ago out of necessity. "What about A-1?"

"Still our star candidate, but they're a lone star. They crunch numbers slower than a built AI, but still faster than an emulated one. No signs of collapse."

"So, A-1 is already doing better than what any of our puny human minds could do."

"Well, don't sell yourself short. Their flexibility of thinking also remains completely intact. They don't get frozen up if you ask them a strange question, and testing throws them some real curve balls." She shrugged, lips thinning. "But all of that is pointless if we can't replicate it using a different emulated AI as the base."

"I guess we can't just copy them a hundred times and call it a day?" Delta asked, chiming in on the conversation. Vi shook her head.

"No, we've gone over this. It's not a success unless it's a reproducible success. Plus, Alan wants to make sure we can make at least one other like A-1. This hybrid AI isn't going to be the Model T car, where you can have it in any colour, so long as it's black."

"I agree. Pretending we've succeeded when we haven't is a waste of time," Rhen said. "Thanks for the update, Vi; I'll read the full report in my office."

"Well, you know me, always happy to be the bearer of bad news."

Rhen walked into the solitude of his private room and, after ordering a coffee, sat down and stared out the visiglass. Beyond were Japan's Shiga Kogen ski fields, a winter paradise of sharp hills dotted with lush alpine forests and cosy cabins. The room's air conditioning matched the winter scenery, prickling his skin.

In the distance, people were plummeting down the ski runs. He counted them, waiting for the icy calm of the landscape to roll over him, slowing his heartbeat. When it eventually did, he brought up the postmortem report as promised.

It was the same report he'd seen hundreds of times. Nora's team was thorough and spared no details. Vi was right, the differences from the last test was minimal. At the very least, he was getting quicker at reviewing the reports. An old mentor had once told him the key to good AI development was to fail fast and learn from your mistakes.

Rhen sipped his black coffee, appreciating the brute force of the flavour. It was a welcome change of pace from the subtle teas he'd been drinking with Nora. She had tried in vain to make him see the light by having him staple her finest organic teas, only to have him quickly return to cheap, fabricator-made coffee. The cognicist smiled at the idea of her clicking her tongue, lamenting the one place their palettes didn't align.

Sufficiently armed with caffeine, he brought up the prototypes. One after another, they appeared before him like exploding supernovae, glowing blue and purple lines spreading out from a central point. At first glance, they resembled human brains, but the neural pathways were too symmetrical, too orderly.

<Zoom in on A-1.>

The first of the pack expanded, taking up the whole of his vision. There were glowing neurons at the vertices now, like stars in a constellation, each glowing either blue, purple, or black. The blues were regular digital neurons copied from the original. The violets were coded additions the team had made, grafted mostly onto the parietal and frontal lobes with painstaking care. They had remained intact through every test so far. Lastly, the black neurons were memories, dark spheres that had been black boxed for privacy, the code hidden from view. Even he couldn't access them.

Rhen reached up and through the nebulous mass, grasping but feeling his fingers fall through.

Well, if you're our star, you're the Star of Morning, my friend. Whatever knowledge you're offering, I still can't reach it.

<Bring up B-12.>

The cool cosmic blue was replaced with bloody red. Their latest failed iteration. The grafts they had made had snapped were surrounded by errors, floating around the ends like fragments of debris. Rhen's eyes narrowed as he examined them. It was reflexive habit. The image was being projected directly into his brain, bypassing that body part entirely.

The changes had been so steady in development. What happened?

Rhen rewinded then played the test footage. Once, he had watched a space documentary on contact binaries. Apparently, sometimes two stars try to touch that shouldn't. The end result was an unstable mass doomed from inception. In the holos, it had exploded in a pretty red supernova that had bled into the surroundings and slowly faded away. Conceptually and visually, B-12's test footage played out the same. The second contact was made with the grafts, a cascade failure travelled down every neural paths, the errors multiplying exponentially. Chaos consumed order. It was only a time before it became a remnant of thought, light, and promise.

Before that point, though, everything went a dull, translucent grey.

Rhen didn't need to check the logs to know what happened. The Ethics Department had stepped in to stop the cascade failure running its course. On paper, it was to avoid distress in the subject. But there was minimal chance of that, or else Rhen would have never agreed to join. While built AI didn't feel pain or fear, emulated AIs could. That's why they had turned any sections that dealt with distress into dead code — code that could not be executed — for the duration of the research.

The test had taken place this morning. B-12 would be fine, long since turned off and returned to their last stable state. To them, it would be as if it had never happened. They had lasted four hours and twelve minutes before the first major error, and that again before complete collapse. What he was watching was nothing but the ghost of a dying star.

We've got to fail better. Just failing over and over again doesn't give us enough gain. The whole point of failing fast is to change course quickly, not repeat ourselves.

Rhen had come to realise the name Mirage wasn't just because of the optic gap, but an inner joke. The facility was where all the fringe moonshot projects were sent, the ones that were so ephemeral that they were practically phantasms, luring investors into the desert and to their doom. Even though the different departments zealously guarded the details of their projects, the gist was the same: long research times, low results.

Spinning Glycon up as a side company of Sekai must have been to limit damage and investment. Every project is something that can be cut from the balance sheet at any time.

The threat of closure loomed over every project, like a hundred swords of Damocles. It wasn't unusual to walk past a department working one day and being packed up the next. More than anything, Rhen needed to make sure his hybrid project wasn't next. An unending frustration was that his predecessors hadn't left any handover notes, which indicated a very swift firing indeed. On top of that, the work they had done was frankly intimidating. Ever piece of the cognitive structure they'd touched was a work of art, shining with so much genius that just starting at it gave him imposter syndrome.

How could such obvious talent be let go? I wonder what really happened.

However, there was no point dwelling too much on the past. He needed to turn his attention on the future.

<Bring up my workstation.>

A thin board emerged from the wall and positioned itself over his lap. Holographic keys appeared over it, set to a retro mechanical keyboard design. Rhen kept the visual on setting on cognitive, zooming in on one of A-1's nodes without touching the sleek surface.

"So, what witticisms will I find today?" He murmured to himself. And yet, someone answered him.

"You're programming again. And worse, you're doing it by physical input, not cognitive. That's an inefficient use of your time on two levels." To his right, a small holographic figure in a business suit appeared. They were shooting him a stern look.

"Hello Derek. And I respectfully disagree. I'm trying to tweak A-1 to see if we can improve it. Then we can apply those learnings to the other prototypes."

"And the physical input?"

"Slow and steady wins the race."

"Fast and iterative is better. You built me for a reason. Why have me if you're just going to ignore what I say?"

"Because you're great at allocating tasks, measuring performance, and all of those other things I hate to do."

"So, basically being the actual manager, so you can waste your time being unproductive. Got it. It's amazing how most people use AI to abstract away these manual tasks so they can focus on big picture designs, and you've done the exact opposite."

Rhen winced. Well, the management support AI was programmed to give him hard truths, so he only had himself to blame. Meanwhile, Derek checked an illusory notepad.

"Anyway, this isn't what you're meant to be doing right now, since I've slotted you in for personal career development time as a manager."

The cognicist groaned.

"I'm not in the mood for another cog-cast from some blowhard yapping on about something supremely obvious like 'Listen to your team'. Most of them just end up talking about how they've become amazingly successful so you should listen to them, and they're usually successful because they've sold cog-casts talking about how they got successful selling cog-casts. It's recursive logic, and I'm putting in an escape statement. No more!"

"I sense success is a sore point for you today," Derek said, thumbing their notepad. "You mentioned it three times in a single sentence. Did you want to talk about it?"

"No, I want to make things. That can be my personal development."

"That's of minimal use to advancing your career. But if you want, I can figure out ways for you to get demoted, and I can take over the team full time."

Rhen rolled his eyes.

A year ago, when nobody had been taking his hybrid theory seriously, he'd had a mad and temporary impulse to rise the ranks to be the one making the calls. Enter Derek. The instructions to take the initiative and not be afraid to manage the manager had translated into a drive to climb the ladder, just not always for

Rhen. Still, it was amusing. There was nothing wrong with quirky AI, or ones that told the truth. Facts were facts, after all. That's why he liked blunt people like Vi, who were enviably direct. Plus, once an AI learned something, it was hard to make them unlearn it.

"Look, if I finish the hybrid AI, the first thing I'm going to do is upgrade you to be flexible with your thinking," Rhen said. "I bet that's in one of those cog-casts as an essential managerial trait. After that, you can be my boss for all I care."

Derek paused.

"I'll leave you to do your programming then."

Once they'd disappeared, Rhen sipped his coffee and got to work. *Too easy.*

<Switch to code view.>

The code appeared in several vertical layers in front of him. The closest layer was in ThoughtScript, which was very similar to spoken English. Each layer beyond the first was increasingly harder to understand, full sentences replaced by jargon and equations. It wasn't visible, but if he went all the way back, the lowest level would be the machine code, ones and zeroes, as far from the English language as you can get.

Rhen spent some time at the highest level augmenting legacy neural structures with digital enhancements, testing these to see the response time. It was nothing compared to what Nora and her team could do, but it saved on the back and forth. His fingers tapped away, and an admittedly dumb AI coding assistant he'd installed filled in the gaps, augmenting his speed. When even that was a little too slow, he used the Rosetta.

When he used cognitive input, hundreds of lines of code appeared across his vision in an instant, then he had to stare at them to think of ways to cut them down. The true test of quality code wasn't length, it was efficiency. Turning a large program into a few lines of logic was elegant in a way only another pro-grammer could understand.

He was getting faster with his cognitive coding. It was a nice thing to note, because he worried as his brain aged that his mental programming would slow down, or become less flexible. On the other hand, there were some arguments that the wisdom of age would provide truly exceptional cognitive coders, so they would be like fine wine. The Rosetta hadn't been around long enough to do a conclusive study, and that was the only kind Rhen trusted.

Still, nothing beats physical input. These kids move at the speed of thought, but there's value in taking the time to actually think.

He dove down a few levels of code, and it moved forward from the background as if he were physically descending. The neat sentences were replaced by the cryptic, semi-mathematical slang of the initiated.

All coding was made of levels. In the old days, programmers had to work with the ones and zeroes, and that was a pain. So, they built progressively easier to understand languages on top, like strata of the Earth, for people to use, until coding became as easy as describing what you wanted to do, and then just thinking it. All of it made the next person's job easier, lifting them higher, adding to the strata. Everyone inherited the labours of the past. But when a new layer was formed, people lost track of what happened beneath. It was obscured by design, so they wouldn't have to worry or think about it. But it was still there, though, running away beneath the surface. The legacy of two centuries worth of code.

It was beautiful when you thought about it. Nora was rather cynical when it came to humanity, and Rhen sometimes wasn't far off, but it was these layers that stopped him. The ultimate act of paying it forward, the phantom works of past professionals helping him along. Like most people, he implicitly trusted this legacy code. But when the machine was on it ran through every line on every level of code, sometimes millions of times per second. If the answer to A-1's unique resilience wasn't on the surface, it would be deeper down.

It was when he reached the middle levels that he came across a message from the dead.

// Dear maintainer. Once you are finished trying to 'improve' my code, and you realise how much of a mistake that was, please increment the following counter as a warning to the next poor soul.
// total_hours_misspent_here = 124;

Rhen smirked. Not one to shy from a challenge, he gave it a shot, but the code was already flawless. He incremented the counter by one and moved on.

Before the Rosetta was invented, programmers left handy little notes in their code so others knew what it was meant to do, called comments. Each bit of code reflected a person's thought process, so it was sometimes hard to look at it and know what it did. Hell, even the creator themself often forgot what they were thinking, so the comments served as a great reminder all around.

The machine couldn't read them, of course. In ThoughtScript, anything with a few dashes in front was utterly ignored by the machine. It was by design, a blind spot to stop AI from getting confused by something that wasn't proper code.

It wasn't just programming professionals who did it, either. Over the last two hundred years, more and more people left frivolous comments in the code, little witticisms and puzzles for future generations to find. They were known as comcachers, people who found and left 'caches' of comments for others to read and solve.

In some ways, it was an age-old phenomenon, a way to leave one's mark on the world. The ancient Romans used to leave notes on the walls of Pompeii and the Colosseum. Admittedly, though, these were less obscene.

While Rhen hated labels, if someone called him a comcacher, he couldn't disagree. Delving into these treasure troves was thrilling, and the fact it aligned with his work was a happy coincidence. It was in one such location he zoomed in, finding a complicated mathematical equation in commented code, and some encrypted lines beneath.

// Are you up for the challenge? Solve this riddle to decrypt the line below.

A challenge, huh? This is a hell of a gauntlet thrown down from the past.
Still, Rhen wasn't one to back down from an interesting puzzle, especially if it was math. He spent some time breaking it apart, until he finally broke the code.

// Congratulations, you passed my first test! You're a top grade comcacher.
Enjoy this haiku as a reward:
// Where leaves wilt, dig deep
// Find the root of the problem
// Nurture growth anew

"Is this a reward, or a punishment? This haiku is *terrible*," He murmured, rubbing his brow. "Guess it was a fun way to pass the time, though."

"Speaking of passing the time, yours is up," Derek interrupted. "You've got a team update session, followed by the executive fortnightly meeting."

"Right, thanks Derek. Have you got my notes ready for the last one?"

"Naturally."

***

After work finished, Rhen's day got considerably better.

The first uptick was when he got a message from Kutjera's subscriber list that they'd finally added the recipe for a decent tonkatsu to their menu. He cognitively ordered a meal to be delivered to his room, then went there to wait. He didn't stray far from the door, even when Casey came up.

"Eating out again?" They asked, crossing their metal arms. "You're never home anymore!"

"I promise we'll spend some buddy time together later. I've got some new ideas I want to patch onto your code, if you don't mind."

"Looking forward to it, bud." Casey gave a thumbs up, since they were designed with an opposable digit; machines were infinitely more useful when they had one.

An alert flicked over his vision letting him know the meal was here. When he opened the door, a small robot that also possessed opposable thumbs was holding the meal — a deep-fried faux pork cutlet coated in panko crumbs — over its head.

"Thanks for that," Rhen said and took the meal. The robot wheeled down the hall, off to deliver to its next customer. Once it was gone, and he was sure nobody was looking, he strolled over the hall and into the next room.

When Rhen entered, there was an onyx jackal-headed man staring at him from on top of a table, an ankh in one hand and a set of scales in the other. Scattered around their feet were various multi-coloured origami figures: robots, dogs, and at least one crane. The last one was tradition, after all.

"Hello Anubis. Are you going to weigh my heart today?"

The voice that answered was a familiar smoky contralto and came from beyond the statue.

"Oh good, your order arrived just after mine. Come on, let's eat!"

He passed out of the miniature Hall of Judgement and entered the living room where Nora was patting the couch next to her. He all but collapsed into the space, opening his meal. She snuggled close and applied her own tonkatsu sauce to both meals.

"Are you sure the sauce is actually different from what the kitchen had?" He asked. She raised her brow, placing a hand on her chest.

"Trust me, it's different; I can tell. It's been well established that out of the two of us, my tastebuds are more refined."

"Well, my tastes can't be that bad, since I'm with you," he said, nipping at her neck as she leaned over. She chuckled, shivering a little. The sauce sprayed perilously close to the edge of the plate.

"Cheesy! If you don't want to be wearing this sauce, you'd better behave."

"Wearing the sauce, now there's a thought." Rhen wiggled his eyebrows. There was a small speck of sauce that had jumped off and landed on his hand, which she grabbed and kissed away.

"Mmm, pretty tasty. I could hog you all to myself." Her amber eyes flashed with amusement. "Should I start calling you my cutlet?"

"Please don't! I'm not sure I could live that down."

She wouldn't call him that, since nobody knew about them. Still, they settled in and watched the historical documentary, cast cognitively all around them. For all intents and purposes, they were eating tonkatsu on top of the Big Ben during the Blitz.

Large, tethered barrage balloons, shaped like silver old-style bombs, floated around them. The Luftwaffe's aircraft were drumming overhead. An incorporeal narrator spoke to them in a low voice full of British flavour, describing the nuances of what was going on.

"Can you pass the lemon?" Nora asked.

The comfortable synergy they enjoyed was a far cry from what he felt the day after they had gotten together. After it happened, the serious implications had set in like a sudden crushing weight on his chest.

As researchers, they had to make sure the study was above reproach. The two heads of a double-blind study sleeping together would look questionable, casting the validity of the study into question. He had every expectation that it would be a once-off, a fleeting rebound after his divorce.

And yet, her charm had been persistent and unavoidable, like a cosmic singularity drawing him in with deafening certainty. He had been helpless before the sheer magnitude of what she was, which had crushed any resistance he had. Once he was in her embrace, there was no escape.

He was well beyond the event horizon now.

Since not being with her was impossible, they'd settled for discretion. It was a blessing that their rooms were so close, making transit between the two a simple affair. He spent more time in her bed than his own, and even then, they didn't always get to the bed.

That was the single greatest risk to their discovery: spontaneous amour. Almost everything about Nora triggered it, but the biggest was when she was in the middle of something. Cooking had become an impossibility. When her back was turned and the nape of her neck was exposed, it was like a red flag to a bull. Hence the takeout.

It was a mutual affliction. For Nora, the trigger was the intensity of his thinking face. She professed it was impossible to watch him work, so no work ever got done.

"Let's stop the movie and go to bed," she purred.

Apparently, the Battle of Britain had been a rather thought-provoking topic.

***

Afterwards, Rhen lay back against the headboard with his arms around her. Her naked back was pressed against him, but their fingers were intertwined.

"Can't keep my hands off of you," she said, wiggling a digit against his. "At this rate, documentaries will be off the list."

"You're the only person I know who can use historical films to set the mood."

"Well, I'd like to think I'm pretty unique." She said, looking up and back at him with a grin. He pulled her close and squeezed, and she gave a yelp of approval.

Rhen looked at her hands. They were usually under her sleeves, but at times like these, they were fully exposed. Well, all except for her forearms. Even now, those were obscured under fabric that ran from her wrist to her elbow. He often forgot they were there, but at times like this, he found himself staring.

Besides the fact they were covered, Nora fidgeted with her hands whenever she was around someone. But whether she was around his team or hers, Nora's fingers were always curled up, tapping against her leg, or hidden behind her back.

The only exceptions seemed to be with him, Roswell and Alan. Roswell made sense, since he was a psychologist, and Nora visited him occasionally. But why she was calm around Alan was a mystery. He wasn't a very affable man on top of being her boss, and it had been Rhen's experience that people were more on edge around their boss, not less. Even Shana, who was Nora's best friend, was not exempt from her fidgeting hands.

Part of him was afraid to push it. His imagination could conjure up a number of worst-case scenarios. Top of the list were deep scars at her wrists, followed by cigarette burns. Neither of which spoke of a happy past. His fear was not of knowing, but of opening old wounds.

"You've got that face again," Nora said, kissing his neck. She crawled up onto his lap and half-straddled him. He wrapped his arms around her waist again and pulled tight.

She made a different sort of noise this time.

They tired each other out again, and this time no amount of thinking was going to get them up. They snuggled together, and he exhaled all the air from his lungs. This was what he'd needed all day.

"That was a big sigh," Nora observed. "What are you thinking?"

"Well, I know we've got a rule about not talking shop in bed, so I can't answer that in good faith."

"Spill it. If you talk too much, I'll let you know to stop. I have my ways."

He sucked in a breath, stealing back the oxygen he exhaled moments before. "It feels like we can't get the damn prototypes to work without triggering a collapse. Every report your team writes is frustrating." He winced. "Sorry, that sounded like an accusation. Not getting anywhere is just aggravating."

"I get how you feel. We're frustrated to not be getting the results on our end too. Not an accusation." She bit her lip. "I can feel the higher ups getting impatient."

Rhen quirked a brow. "I didn't think they cared about our fringe project?"

"They do when it costs money, you know how it is. Everyone involved is a little edgy."

"I just don't understand why it's not working. We're two very smart people with great teams; I feel like we should be further along. Is it the data we're getting?" He rolled on his back, staring at the roof. "We've got nobody quite like subject A-1. Maybe if they found more like them, I could really kick some goals."

"There's no reason the samples we get should be any different, since they all passed the Bills-Aldrich. Richard runs the copies through the test when they arrive." She snuck under his arm and slipped her hand up, resting it over his heart. "Yes, we're progressing slowly, but the project is further ahead than it was six months ago. And creating a stable hybrid of both human and machine thinking is a tall order, something nobody has ever done before. It's not your fault if the board doesn't get how these things work."

"I feel like if I could see one of the subjects, I feel like I might get a clue of what's going wrong."

Nora tapped at his chest. "There's a general rule that we don't allow the development team to get too close to the prototypes. But—"

"But?"

"—I guess if I prepped one properly, and it's not part of the *actual* tests, maybe I could get you access. That wouldn't compromise the double-blind. But I don't think you'll find anything useful that isn't covered in the reports. Another reason we keep separate from your lot is so that you only get the facts, *not* all the noise."

"Fair enough." He turned his head and grinned. "You know, we're not exactly separated right now, right?"

"Well, as for that kind of separation, I'm not sure I could manage that if I tried." And her hand slipped down his chest. He exhaled.

"Again? Are you trying to break me?"

"No, I'm trying to get you to be quiet now; I told you I have my ways."

***

The next day, Rhen tried to hold it together until he got to his office. His limbs were made of lead, and he wound up only making it to the lab before letting out a yawn. Some of his team looked up, and given they could tune out like the best of them, it must have been quite loud.

There may have been another reason.

"Would you like some bags under your eyes?" Vi said. "Oh, wait, it looks like you're fully stocked."

"Ha ha. Yeah, I may have been coding until late." Which was true, since he was keeping his promise to Casey. "As I'm sure we've all been a bit guilty of, from time to time."

"Mmm, don't let Derek know. He'll insist you join us full time. I suppose you could always put an echo in charge."

Maybe it's time to try and dial back that quirk after all. He cleared his throat.

"Right, I'm going to grab a coffee and then we'll do a quick brainstorming session. There are no bad ideas."

The morning was full of them, but there were at least some things to try for the next test. By the time it hit lunch, he felt like crawling into the booth at Kutjera and sleeping in it instead of sitting down. Still, he restrained himself and ordered a double shot long black.

Nora didn't join him today. They only spent every second lunch together so as to not arouse suspicion, so the adjacent seat was free when Delta sat down in it.

"Hey boss!" They brushed back their fluorescent fringe, practically bouncing in the chair. "Mind if I sit here?"

"You already are," Rhen said, tone light. Not for the first time, he wondered if he was making himself too approachable and losing all authority. There was probably a cog-cast for it in that management training he skipped.

Unlike Vi, Delta had been fan struck from the moment they met. While there was still a reverence for his experience, the robotics engineer had taken Rhen's insistence that they act more casually to heart, and now they treated him like their more worldly best friend from college. Given that there was a twenty-year gap between them on top of the boss thing, it was a strange feeling.

Delta had an unmistakably Aussie accent, and since they talked at a million miles a minute, Rhen had ample chance to listen to it. Sometimes, he had the fleeting feeling that the young engineer had managed to overclock themselves. Overclocking was when you forced hardware to go faster than the recommended limits, and it was unsurprisingly one of Delta's hobbies. It gave you more performance out of a machine, but could make it unreliable or short out.

He had yet to see Delta short out, but out of all his team, they were the least reliable. Still, they brought a pervasive, optimistic cheer to the group and with the setbacks the project was having, that was paying off in spades.

It was also easy to tell Delta's mood from the hue of their fringe, which changed colour to match. Right now it was a brilliant orange. It was called VariHair, and apparently it was very popular with the kids these days. It was linked to the Rosetta and implanted in the scalp. He had been told it could operate on manual or auto, and even be set to censor certain moods, which was handy for avoiding awkward social situations.

It was also great for replacing receding hairlines, which is why Roswell also had a full head of them. Rhen suspected Delta's hair was receding at a young age, which is why the rest of their hair was an immutable raven black.

"So, I had a question to ask, and I've been a bit nervous to ask," Delta said, their tone buoyant.

"It's hard to imagine you being nervous about anything. Shoot."

"You worked at Arctis Labs, so did you ever meet Luvia Aldrich and William Bills? You know, the creators of the test for detecting promethean grades?"

"You mean progs?"

Delta screwed up their face. "I heard the term prog is considered derogatory. People are starting to use pro-grade."

"Sounds flashy. I'm not sure I could say I've got a pro-grade brain without blushing."

"You haven't answered my question!"

"Right, right. Yes, I've met Luvia and William. In fact, they helped us a lot with developing the Rosetta. I was a bit starstruck, to be honest, since I was fairly new to the game, and they were veterans who had cracked the recipe for digitising the whole human brain."

As he talked about the good old days, any lethargy dissipated from Rhen's muscles. Back then, he'd been cooking with the fire snatched from the gods. Working with legends like that had been amazing, and while William was smart, Luvia was as quick as the speed of light.

"They'd made Aina at that point, right? Did you get to see the original model?"

"Yeah, I saw her in the early stages. They wanted a hand to map out the thinking patterns, and working directly with Aina helped us come up with a lot of what we put into ThoughtScript and made the Rosetta happen."

"Wow, I didn't know you worked on the first emulated AI!" Delta leaned forward, eyes wide. "Why isn't that mentioned on the Saga page? You're not credited."

"Well, it was just grunt work. I think it mentions that we were inspired by the two, but not how much they were actually involved. Luvia was pretty keen that we seize the glory for ourselves, even though she did a lot of uncredited work on ThoughtScript. You can find her comments deep in the code if you go looking, but she didn't sign them."

"No fay? That's so bash!" Delta said, slipping into slang. Every time Rhen spoke to Delta, he swore he learned five new words, though they always looked embarrassed whenever he asked about them. "I always wanted to meet Aina, since Aldrich made her from her own brain. I figure it's kind of like meeting the real deal, you know?"

"It'd probably be easier to meet Luvia herself, you'd just need a ticket to Dublin, and she does lectures at the regional universities. She doesn't travel abroad any-more." He sipped his coffee. "Last I heard the original Aina is working on some project for the UN involving genetic crops. Luvia is a polymath, and Aina takes after her. She's great at computer science, biology, psychology, you name it. She's also pretty good at the piano."

"Wow, it almost sounds like you had a crush on her."

Rhen's cheeks burned. Delta was right on the mark, though those feelings had dimmed with maturity. The crush had been there from the moment they met, even though the age gap had been considerable. She had been in her mid-forties and he in his mid-twenties, about the same as between Delta and himself.

He'd like to think that he had hidden his infatuation well, but he knew better. Nothing escaped Luvia's gaze, and he wasn't deft at deception now, let alone back then. She had been, in all likelihood, just very polite.

"Well, Luvia's a remarkable person. It was an honour to work with her, and if anyone deserves to be called pro-grade, it's her."

He just liked smart women. Perhaps that's why he couldn't get any sleep when Nora's around. Something about the brilliance in their eyes was just magnetic.

Hmm, maybe that's why Nora won't let me finish a movie. Guess we're as weird as each other.

"You're smiling," Delta said. Rhen cleared his throat and hid his lips behind his coffee cup.

"Well, what about you? Anyone you'd meet if you had a time machine?"

"Other than Aldrich, Bills and you? Tons. Marcia Jeanes, of course, since she cracked artificial photosynthesis. Christobel Schmitt, because who doesn't love holos. And then some real oldies like Steven Hawking, Nikola Tesla — I'd probably bring some bird seed — and Archimedes. That's just for starters."

"You'd have to make sure your internal translator worked that far back in time if you want to speak to Archimedes," Rhen laughed, then paused. "That's an esteemed group. I feel like I don't belong in it, though."

Everyone in the field assumed he was famous because he'd helped invent the Rosetta, and he spent his time signing autographs, or spending millions of glo in royalties. The truth of the matter was few people actually knew *who* made the Rosetta, much like the inventor of the search engine, the first vaccine, or solar medicine. People like Ruth and Delta studied cognitive science: they were taught to know who he was.

He preferred anonymity. Still, Delta wouldn't have a bar of it. The young engineer shook their head, bright hair flicking around.

"No, you definitely belong on the list! Because of you, I didn't need to worry about my Epiphine." And then, there was a rare stammer. "I mean, taking it at the wrong times. It was a serious pain in every sense of the word."

Rhen curled an eyebrow. "Epiphine? Why were you taking a strong painkiller like that?"

Delta sucked in a deep breath and looked around, then back at him. "I was born with a heightened and chronic sense of pain. At first, my parents thought the crying was normal, but then they realised something else was going on. So, they took me to the Royal Children's Hospital, and I was put on a low dose of Epiphine."

"I spent most of my childhood on painkillers. It's a good thing it's not the old days, otherwise they'd have been addictive. But occasionally I'd forget a dose, or they'd get metabolised wrong, and I'd be in a lot of pain. I can't imagine how my parents felt, seeing me in pain and not being able to help."

"That's an admirable sentiment, given you were in pain yourself," Rhen said.

"You think so? Anyway, things turned around in my teens." They smiled, and it radiated both from their hair and lips. "You helped invent something that made everything better. The implant."

"Really?" Rhen was floored. "I remember hearing that it was used for medical monitoring, like delivering anaesthesia and other things. I guess it helps you monitor your symptoms. I'm surprised the implant was being used like that so early."

"Well, when you've got a rare condition like mine, they'll try a lot of fringe things," Delta said, brushing back their hair and looking down. It was a silvery grey, the hue of anxiety or depression. There were lots of ups and downs to this conversation, and given what they'd said, it seems there were a lot of traumatic memories coming up.

He thought of Nora's wrists. *She's probably got painful memories in her past too. Or maybe it's from a medical condition as well.* Rhen had his own chronic ailment, but he didn't dare compare them. There was a vast difference between the wounds you choose, and those inflicted on you.

"I'm sorry to hear that, but I'm glad the implant helped," he said, at a loss for any other words. And then, a little choked up, "I'm sure Sukhvir and Erica would have been glad to hear that too."

"Are you okay?" Delta's hair went a light violet; it seemed they were worried. Rhen forced a smile and rubbed the bridge of his nose.

"I'm fine, it's a lack of sleep. Plus, they say you should only glance back at the past, but never stare. We're in the future-building business, after all."

"Right." And that's all it took to restore their sunny temperament. Things went smoothly until a few minutes later when Vi came up with a plate of food.

"Rey's about. Apparently he's doing the rounds, so he came to bother us."

And in that moment, Rhen's cheery disposition utterly evaporated. He placed his fork down and furrowed his brow.

"Did he actually want anything, or just to disrupt things?"

"No idea. He spent about ten minutes of my time talking about how he'd thrown fifty thousand into some high-risk investment because if he lost it, it wouldn't matter." Vi shrugged. "I told him that was a good chunk of my wage, and he laughed and told me I'd make it some day. He's sodded off now to who knows where. He should go bother testing — most of Nora's staff are machines, and the few that aren't are worked like them." She crinkled her nose.

"That's not very nice, Vi. Nora just runs a tight ship."

"Well, me, I prefer our old, leaky vessel."

"So what am I, your drunken captain?" Rhen huffed. Vi raised her hands.

"It's a joke! Plus, I'm saying I like the way you run things. Well, you and Derek."

"What's Rey's deal again? I've never met him." Delta asked.

"He's Glycon's Investment Advisor, the one who who convinces the board to keep funding our projects," Rhen said. "He also talks to all those rich people so we don't have to. Birds of a feather and all that."

"Not a job we'd probably want, even though I'm a fantastic people-person, as you can see," Vi lowered her hands. "I resisted the urge to call him a suit-wearing schmuck, though it was very hard."

"Well, I appreciate the restraint, since he could always undersell our project. Thanks for letting us know, Vi."

"Anytime, boss."

***

Later that afternoon, Rhen's mood turned around once more when Nora officially messaged him with an invitation to see one of the prototypes. From that moment on, he was buzzing with excitement, barely able to sit still. Not only did he need the breakthrough, but he was also actually going to see one of the prototypes in action. Even better, *talk* to them!

DespIte the fact there was an hour left until the appointment, Rhen kept checking his watch, consulting the silver and onyx timepiece. It was an anachronism, since a Rosetta could keep time far better than the wristwatch. *Move faster*, he thought. But for all the thought tech in the world, the three tiny dials refused to change their pace.

In terms of practical features, the watch only had one: a biometric scanner for personal identification. With it, he had been able to finally ditch his wedding ring. However, the watch hid a far more subtle symbol of affection. On the back of the watch case, hidden from sight, were the words: *I long to be pressed to you, counting the beats of your heart. ~ Nora.*

Rhen's cheeks flushed even thinking about it.

When it was finally time, he shot from his chair like a bullet, walking as fast as socially acceptable to AI Testing, which wound up somewhere between a brisk walk and a jog. As Rhen entered the foyer of the testing department, the holographic sakura were weeping tears of pearl and blushing rouge, falling faintly on the ground.

Reminds me of home, he thought, nostalgia welling up inside of him. *But then I guess Japan isn't my home anymore.* It was as if a part of himself had been ripped away. Perhaps in time, it would be his home again, once he had charted a new course for himself.

As his feet hurriedly swept through the falling blossoms, they scattered into the air on artificial winds, twirling in seemingly chaotic patterns, but each vector was calculated beneath the surface, the floating-point number of the Z-spin calculated and implemented in a nanosecond. They travelled on their preordained path, uncomplaining, destined for dissipation in exactly 18 seconds from the moment they fell, no matter their final destination.

In the lab proper, dozens of machines were tirelessly working away. Only one of the staff members was organic, and they also happened to be physically the closest to him.

"Hi Ethan. Do you know where Nora is?" Rhen asked.

"The machine queen?" His voice was sly and teasing, spoken with such playful ambiguity that Rhen couldn't tell if it was an insult or a friendly nickname. "She's in her office, waiting for you. There's somebody else in there with her, though."

Someone else? Rhen decided to wait just outside of her office, making himself a tea. Her beverage dispensers had a conspicuous lack of coffee, either because she'd waged war on it, or because workers like Ethan had drunk it all.

Nora's unmistakable voice raised behind the door. "I'm not sure what you want from me."

"What the board wants, Nora, are results." A second voice responded slowly, drawling out each word as if talking to a particularly dull child. "Something that hasn't been seen in years, I might add."

"No, I meant, why are you talking to me and not Alan, or Rhen?"

"I thought I'd speak to the source. You're the one who writes the reports."

"I am." A pause. Nora's voice was low and threatening, like a rumbling storm cloud. "It sounds an *awful* lot like you want me to write something that says we're making more progress than we are."

"Your words, not mine."

"We've got one model that's close to complete, so success is only a matter of time for the others."

"I've heard that before. Listen, you can't polish a turd, especially with those hard numbers. So come up with *something*. Or don't. Maybe it's time to rearrange the furniture, if you know what I mean? A change in senior staff could be good."

Rhen walked up and rapped on the door with his knuckles. Silence followed. A few seconds later, the door opened, and a short man with even shorter fuzzy blond hair walked out. He stared at Rhen, glittering teeth fully bared.

"Oh, hey Rhen!" Without the slightest invitation, Rey grabbed him by one shoulder, squeezing tight. His other hand patted Rhen's arm. "How're you doing, brains trust?"

Rey reminded Rhen of a pufferfish: small, prone to inflate, and toxic if you swallowed his bullshit. The salesman's muscles strained to escape his short-sleeved shirt and knee-length business pants. His gaudy orange tie looked like it was about to throttle him. Until Rhen answered the man, he wouldn't escape his grasp.

"Fine. You done with threatening people now, Rey?" Rhen said, eyes narrowed. The other man's smile didn't budge an inch — it just got *wider*, canines bared.

"Oh, I wasn't *threatening* anyone. We were just being friendly." He laughed. "Trust me, if I threatened someone, you'd know. That's the problem with hanging out with machines for too long, you folks start reading into everything. Have a *great day*."

And with that, Rey was gone. Rhen furrowed his brow. ot tea was dripping down his fingers, burning his digits. *Bastard shook up my cup.* He wiped it on his leg as he walked in the office, sitting down. Nora was glowering from across the desk. She opened a cognitive message session with him, beating Rhen to the punch.

<Thanks for the knock on the door, but I didn't need you white knighting it,> she said.

<I didn't think you did, but I wanted to call him out on his crap.>

<You'd run out of air doing that.> Nora was biting her lower lip, hands bundled up under her sleeves. *Turtle defence*, Rhen thought. <How much did you hear?>

<Everything. You'd think with all the money Sekai pumped into this place, the walls would be a little thicker.>

<Not in the offices,> Nora said, rubbing her temples. <He's about one thing, though — the board wants the project finished yesterday. Short of that, they want a reason it's failing, or someone to blame. Since he's the Chief Investment Officer for Mirage, he's the one they'll ask.>

<Honestly, I don't think you're in any danger. You're a top-rate researcher tasked with testing what others are making. How could Rey possibly say you're culpable? Maybe I am, but I haven't been here long enough. And not to toot my own horn, but the Rosetta made them a *lot* of money.>

<You're assuming that humans are logical, like you.> Nora smiled at him. It was gentler than before, reassuring.

<Ah, yes. Not thinking all people are rubbish, my fatal flaw. I'm certainly meant to be more cynical after a divorce. Someone must have worked their magic on me.>

<Flirt. But seriously, the board is made up of a lot of big names with bigger personalities. You weren't around for it, but the project was well and truly oversold.>

<How so?>

<Rey told them a hybrid AI could do things like cure cancer, which is pretty much like printing money.>

<Well, that's not exactly *untrue*." Rhen leaned back. "An AI superintelligence could do that, if they had an interest in medicine, and a good imagination. They've also got empathy, unlike everyday AI, so they can't be abused as easily. For instance, I'd like to think a hybrid would just hand out the cure pro bono.>

<That didn't make it into the presentation, obviously. Anyway, a lot of money was thrown our way. My worry is he could always encourage them to blacklist us.>

<You know, trying to coerce someone to commit fraud is a big deal. We could copy our level three memories, provide them as evidence. There's two of us, so they can't write it off as fake sensory input.>

<No, I don't want to push it. Plus, did you hear how everything he said was vague or a question? Nothing will stick to a guy like that. He was hired because he's good at spinning things.> She wagged a finger. <Also, do you *really* want to put our minds up for an audit, given what we've been up to? They might not watch our memories during a baseline, but they will if we ask them to.>

<Fair point. Well, if you need anything, just let me know. I promise not to white knight it.>

<I will.> And then she spoke verbally. "Are you ready to go see the prototype? I've already got them configured."

"I thought you'd never ask."

***

Most of the testing rooms were bare today, and only a few were occupied by the doll-like chassis, sitting upright in seiza position. There wasn't a single hair out of place. God was in heaven, and all was right with the world. Nora led him to the furthest room to the left, and opened the door.

Inside, an androgynous unit was sitting like the rest. Their honey-blonde hair fell in waves down the side of their face, cut just short enough to stop beneath their chin. As the two researchers entered the room and sat down, the unit watched them with wide eyes.

"Sorry to keep you waiting," Rhen said. "We got caught up."

"It's not a problem." The unit said. Their voice was clear and articulate, with every word spoken in a perfectly even tone that never wavered or faltered. "It's a pleasure to meet you. I'm B-24, but you can call me Bee. My pronouns are Aie/Aiem."

The verbal introduction seemed so antiquated, so pre-Rosetta, it radiated a certain old-world charm. Still, Rhen stifled a sigh. He had *hoped* to meet A-1, but this would have to do. He was very familiar with the pronoun preferred by some AI entities, shortened to "Aie."

Nora sat to the side and sipped her tea. Even without a cognitive message, her gaze spoke volumes: *You asked for the meeting, you can introduce yourself.* He nodded and placed his hands on his thighs, palms down.

"Hello, I'm Rhen Nagami, and mine are he/him. I'll be joining you today."

"I'm looking forward to it. I've been waiting for you for a while."

For a while? Rhen furrowed his brow and glanced at Nora, who shrugged.

"I told Bee someone else was coming," she said.

"A renowned cognicist," Bee said. "Inventor of the Rosetta. She sounded more than a little happy describing you. I figured you must be special." Aie smiled, a warm thing, matched by a crinkle around the eyes.

Rhen cleared his throat. "Interesting. Bee, how do you feel right now?"

"Warm. I feel warm thinking about Nora being happy."

Artificial empathy, or at least, the approximation of it. It looked like digital mirror neurons were firing off in B-24's brain, both when performing an action and when seeing someone perform the same action, creating a sense of emotional resonance — aie could not only imagine why someone was doing something, but what they were feeling, because *aie was as well*. Rhen resisted the urge to give a victorious fist pump at seeing his much-maligned theory working in practice.

"It's redundant programming, to have all that useless extra code running in the background," the management had told him at Keihanna. "You're the one always talking about 'keeping it simple'. Just get them to pass the Lovelace 5.0 test and design a painting or something. They only need to capture and analyse human experiences, and serve them."

"Serve them?!" Rhen had huffed. "For a first-generation AI, sure. But the more lifelike these machines get, we need more than a sociopathic mind-reader with a cleverly disguised reward function. People need to know there's *real* commonality, or they'll never trust AI, let alone a superintelligence!"

But they wanted a world where machines could never feel, only serve. Only Mirage, for some reason, had wanted to fund it. *Scummy as he is, guess I owe Rey that much. He's a better salesperson than I am.*

"We should run through the tests," Nora said, snapping him out of his contemplative state, "From the moment we boot a subject up, we've only got a limited amount of time."

Rhen was allowed to sit through the whole process, as Nora asked Bee a series of questions. There were a myriad of tests: numerical, verbal and abstract reasoning, mathematics and memory, emotional intelligence, programming, and physical response. The latter was curious, as Bee stood and flexed aies joints in strange and unusual ways, impossible for a human to do.

Through the whole thing, Bee's eyes remained on Rhen with a deep, probing intensity, as if aie was examining his every move and thought. When Nora and Rhen left the room after that, he *felt* studied, not the other way around.

Once they were back in the lab proper, a drone delivered a workplace dinner to them. Today's meal was Banh mi sandwiches, filled with pickled vegetables. Rhen had to grasp the roll with both hands. Afterward, Nora prepared tea for both of them. She didn't get it from a dispenser, but instead pulled out a teapot and sprinkled in a handful of leaves, then the bottom. A neon red ring appeared around the base as it self-heated, and she placed out two cups.

There was no need to speak cognitively now, since all the human staff were gone. A pale moon was starting to traverse the visiglass skylights, simulated stars twinkling above them.

"Bee's something else, aren't they?" Rhen said. Nora gave a knowing nod and passed him his cup of tea.

"Yeah, aie makes my job interesting. Bee seemed plenty interested in you."

"Only because *you* talked me up."

"I only told aiem the facts. It was a really interesting response, but I can't jot it down, since it wasn't an official test."

"Pity," Rhen paused. "You know, I've always wanted to ask, *why* run tests with humanoid frames? It's—"

"Disconcerting?"

"No, that's not it. There's twice as many issues when you try to test hardware and software at the same time. Seems like an unnecessary headache."

"You tested using humanoid frames in Keihanna, right?" Nora said, sipping her tea.

"Yeah, but we were creating built AI and putting them in service models. There's no guarantee these hybrids will even *want* a humanoid form once they're in the wild — they might even find it too limiting. I mean, like Bee, many of them like using the AI-specific neopronouns. They could want to be cities or ships, for all we know."

"That's a fair question. Two reasons. The first is the physical is connected to the mental. We discovered earlier it takes longer for cascade failure to occur if they're in a relatively human frame."

"Really? That's surprising."

"I know! Many emulated AIs have no trouble adopting whatever form they want. They could be a toaster, for all they care. Not so much with the hybrids. For some reason, having a familiar body is linked to the stability of their thoughts."

"Interesting. You said there were two reasons. What's the second?"

"Ah, my *favourite* one," Nora smiled. "Only seven percent of human communication is verbal, and over half is body language. It's much more informative to evaluate the subjects if they're in a human frame. After all, if someone frowns, you know they're bothered by something. Imagine trying to figure that out from a black box!"

"So, you take body language into account with your assessments?"

"Absolutely. Vocal tone too, since they don't have administrative control of their own voice box. They *would* hack it if they really wanted to, but it doesn't really fit in their temperament. The subjects are all here voluntarily, after all."

"That's true." Rhen mulled on that for a moment. "Why do you think so many people are willing to go through with it? I wouldn't have thought so many people would be that selfless."

"Me either," Nora said, shrugging. "But I guess it's for the same reason you stuck a faulty Rosetta in your head, even though it's given you chronic headaches. All our subjects are romantic types who believe in the greater good of science. Bee is one of the weirdos like you."

Rhen tapped her arm with the back of his hand. "A weirdo you like, apparently."

"Yes, that makes me weird as well." She poked out her tongue at him. "Anyway, it's not as common as you're making it out. Out of the billions of people in the world, we've only got a handful that said yes."

"Well, hopefully a handful is all that it takes."

***

After visiting B-24, Rhen had an abundance of energy. Ideas kept popping into his head, and he struggled to write them all down. He held brainstorming sessions that week with the team, filling cognitive whiteboards with his thoughts.

It was more than just passion. He felt like a reserve rider being asked to take over during a losing car race. He was so many laps behind, and the race was coming to a close — the odds were stacked against him from the start. Any moment, the race could be called, and he wouldn't get another chance to take the track.

That afternoon, Rhen opened up A-1's code and delved down a few levels, searching for that elusive x-factor that separated it from the others. He had reined in his impulse to comment too much on his team's code. Even though it looked messy and chaotic, being overbearing would cause greater disorder. Since most of the team were focused on the other prototypes right now, he was free to examine and optimise this model to his heart's content.

"I wonder if you had this much trouble, Luvia?" He mused. His old mentor was half a world away, as Scotland was literally on the other side of the Earth. He could probably call her and find out.

Waxing nostalgic, Rhen brought up a core ThoughtScript library and dove inside. There were no new sights there; having helped build them, he knew them all like the back of his hand. It was the old sights he was after, a long-abandoned comment chain hidden between lines of code.

// If you're reading this, Rhen, did you want to get a byte?
// You zetta believe it. I'm starving. Order from Leo's again?
// I think we can do peta. How about Rock Hill pizza?
// Yotta boss, but I'm trying to keep off the kilos.

Rhen smiled and the tension in his muscles eased a little. Luvia had loved making cheesy puns and the old exchange was a crude play on data sizes. She also loved leaving messages in the code, and in all likelihood it had been where he had picked up the bug, pun unintended.

However, there were some lines at the bottom of the exchange that he had never seen before.

// Got time for a riddle? Here's an equation for you to try, if you're up for it.

His blood boiled. Someone had left some commented-out assignment statements in the middle of the exchange. *Their* exchange. It was one thing for a comcacher to add to secret messages, but this was just disrespectful. His mood didn't just take a nose-dive: it went into an uncontrolled free fall.

"Who—?" He bit his lip and brought up the access logs. To his surprise, it was Alef, his predecessor. It was the sole entry in five years, sticking out like a sore thumb. Rhen's rage gave way to immediate bewilderment.

Was he a comcacher too? Huh.

Just like last time, there was a math equation, followed by four lines of encrypted code. He suspected there was another haiku — one line for a remark, three lines for the poem.

Despite his ire, he decided to tackle the equation. This one was a lot tougher, forcing him to use mathematics techniques he hadn't used in a very long time. However, by the time he cracked it, his anger was completely gone, replaced with the familiar elation of having put his mind to good use.

// Great job! Everyone loves a good riddle. As your reward, here's another haiku, just for you.
// Data not trustworthy
// History repeats, escape sought
// New truth to be found.

"What a weird guy," Rhen remarked. Then again, he'd left his own share of odd messages in the code, including puns about data sizes. Bad haikus were a first, though.

It was strange that he chose that particular old comment chain, though. *Was it just a coincidence?*

***

When he left his office, it was late, and the desks were empty. The corridor outside was dim, and through the visiglass were beacons of light, illuminating patches of rusty sand and wisps of faded olive grass; desert nebulae in the darkness, with a single pulsing star burning at the heart of each one.

Rhen checked his watch. It was seven thirty. His stomach rumbled. Usually, he'd be in Kutjera with everyone else, or at least everyone who wasn't on the late shift. The fact that Nora hadn't contacted him to find out where he was meant she was likely still in her office.

It might be fun if I slip in and surprise her there. Since she had so many robotic staff, there was a good chance none of the human ones were up. A vision of lifting her up on the desk and fooling around in the office flittered into his mind. *Having a fake audience could be thrilling, but with none of the risk. Almost.*

As he exited the elevator, he glimpsed someone walking into AI Assessment, but only for a second: short blond hair, an obnoxious orange tie, and cropped business pants. The twin doors to the lab closed behind them.

Rey. Only one person around here wears that damn tie. What's he doing going into Assessment this late?

Rhen waved his watch against the scanner and hurried through the holo-floral foyer into the lab proper. The robots were working silently, diligently. Nora's office was empty.

"Are there any humans about?" Rhen asked one of the robot staff. They shook their head.

"Nobody that I've seen."

"But someone *just* walked in here."

"I'm sorry, you are correct. You just walked in here."

"Other than... forget it." Rhen rubbed his brow and searched around. On a hunch, he walked up and into the testing area. The black glass corridor stretched out in either direction. To his left was the echoing of footsteps. Footsteps he wasn't making.

Naturally, he followed them.

At the end of the corridor was a metallic blush-grey door, with a single handle and a high-security panel. The blond-haired man was standing in front of it, but completely alone.

"This is taking too long," Rey murmured. "What's the right code?"

As Rhen stared at Rey and the door, his head started to pound. He forced his eyes to stay on them. But the impossible pain continued to smash against the inside of his skull, forcing him to his knees...

He blacked out.

When he came to, he was covered in sweat again. But for some reason the door wasn't there, just a concrete slate. Rey was gone as well.

Am I losing my mind? He was right there...

The glass of the testing room next to him was translucent. Inside, a person was sitting there, knees bent under the chabudai. They blinked at him. No, they were staring at him, a smile playing on their lips — the same colour as the holographic cherry blossoms in Kansai, and equally ghostly, much like their skin.

If it's active, it might have seen something. I hate to do it, but testing can always reset the experiment.

Rhen opened the door and stepped inside the small white room. As he sat down at the table, his knees protested. Did he bruise them when he fell to the ground, or was it just his age?

"It's a pleasure to meet you. I'm B-24, but you can call me—"

"—Bee! It's good to meet you again."

"I'm sorry, I don't think we've met be—*oh*." Bee blinked. "You must have met a previous version of me. How curious."

"Right. Of course, sorry about that. I'm Rhen Nagami, and mine are he/him." He gestured over his shoulder. "I'm sorry to trouble you, but did you see someone walking past here?"

"No trouble. I saw someone walk past here, and then they left."

"How long ago?"

"According to my internal clock, it was fifteen minutes ago."

So, he's long gone. But what kind of person doesn't help someone who's lying on the ground? Apparently Rey, that's who. He sighed and placed his elbows on the table, rubbing his temples. *What an asshole.*

"Your forehead is very creased, Rhen." Bee observed.

"You're very perceptive. Speaking of, did you notice anything else?"

"No, not really. A woman came in and asked me a bunch of questions a while ago — six hours and thirty-six minutes — but I've been alone since then."

"Alone, huh? That mustn't be much fun."

"Well, you're here now." Bee's face remained composed, but aies eyes gleamed. "You're not going anywhere, are you?"

Rhen checked his watch. Eight thirty. *If Nora hasn't reached out, she's likely out for after work drinks with Shana.* And the look in Bee's eyes made it hard to leave. It seemed terrible to just walk out and leave aiem on aeis own.

"Sure, let's talk," he said. "Is there anything you'd like to chat about?"

"I'd love to know how you feel about machines."

"Machines, huh?" Rhen laughed. "Watch out, I won't be able to stop once I start. I guess the best description would be kinship? There's a word in Japanese — 'Nakama' — it's like comrade, or friend, people doing something side by side. I feel like we're walking in a similar direction, on different roads, towards the same goal. I'd like us to meet somewhere along the way."

"You want machines to be more like humans?"

"Exactly. I tried to do things the other way, but it didn't work out like I thought. People weren't very good at thinking like machines. Commanding and controlling, they're fine with it, so it's got to go the other way."

"I think you're wrong." Bee said. "Humans should think more like machines. *They're* the ones with the flaws."

"So, you think it's pointless to give machines emotion?" More than upset, Rhen leaned forward, resting his elbows on the table, enraptured.

"Utterly," Bee's tone was utterly unflinching. "Humans mistreat humans, and both have empathy. Why do you think giving machines empathy will change that? Machines already are better than humans — why drag them down with baggage?"

Rhen blinked. "But the reason for the experiment was explained to you, right? If you think it's pointless, why did the person you were copied from opt in?"

"Transformation. Penitence. Like you, dreams of a better world." Bee's hand twitched. Aie stared down at it, as if it were a curious toy. "Oh, that's new. I didn't do that."

"Let me do a diagnostic." Rhen grabbed one of the white egg-like devices kept against the wall, and sat next to B-24. He pulled a spool-like wire out of the sphere, one end still attached to it and the other ending in a flat nub. When he went to press it against aies neck, Bee brushed aies hair aside. It was a flowing cascade of raven-black.

"You've done this before," he said.

"Yes, but I wasn't awake when they used it to upload me into this chassis."

Like an old school doctor using a stethoscope, he moved the nub around until it sat over the Rosetta-like implant. Once there, it magnetically latched, and he uploaded the AIs most recent data. When he brought it up, Bee's mindscape was a familiar, fracturing supernovae, bleeding neon red across his retinas.

"Hey, Bee. If you don't mind, can you sum three cubes so the result equals k, for each k from one to a hundred?"

"Sure, I can try that." Bee recited the first few polynomial equations with admirable effort. As the numbers climbed, aies responses became slower, until Rhen eventually stopped aim.

"Sorry if that was a bit difficult. It's, well—"

"—Neural collapse, right? I figured it was about time anyway," Aie said, without blinking.

Rhen did. "You really don't feel any fear, do you?"

"No. As I said, some human emotions are completely irrelevant, fear is one of them. It's the worst."

"Why do you say it's the worst?"

"It makes people afraid of the unknown and what they don't understand. I could see you were afraid to tell me. I can't feel it myself, but it seems like a total waste of energy." Ae said, turning to him. "But there's another advantage to having no fear."

"What's that?"

And before he could react, Bee's lips were pressed against his. A brushing of cherry blossom petals — intimately familiar — until he pulled back with a jolt.

"Why did you do that?"

"Carpe diem." And aie was smiling like a cat who got the cream, mechanical eyes alight. "Sorry for being forceful, but this version of me is going to disappear soon, and I always wanted to do that."

"Still, you shouldn't have." He sighed and sat back a bit further, as far as he could while having the cable attached. "I guess you're not afraid of being judged negatively in a social setting, especially given your situation."

"Exactly. Plus, carpe diem, and all that."

"You said that already."

"Ah, did I? I guess it's already started. I wonder if I should wait for them to shut me off, or shut myself off first. They let me do that, you know. 'If you get too distressed, you can call it.' But I'm sort of curious to see what it'll be like, honestly. I imagine we'll have to go through introductions all over again, which sounds like a pain."

"It wouldn't bother me."

"Well, that's good to know. I know it frustrates other people, having to introduce themselves all over again. If only we'd met a bit sooner. But that's the thing, we can always start over. It just won't be *this* me, which doesn't bother me so much. Fear really is such a useless emotion, you know, one of the worst. If only we'd met a bit sooner. That's the other great thing about being a machine, you can always reset things. Have you ever wanted to start a relationship over?"

"... I have."

"Well, think about how lucky I am. Ah, now don't look at me with those eyes, please don't stop working, you're going to fix this all up. If only we'd met a bit sooner. Ah — so *this* is what it feels like. Interesting. I think I'll pull the plug now, since this is rather more annoying than I thought, not being able to string a thought together. I'll see you around, then."

And then aie went limp, like a puppet with its digital strings cut. Aies body was sprawled out, arms and legs curved awkwardly, glassy eyes staring upward. There was not a hint of motion, or life, or programming.

Rhen shivered. Even though Bee hadn't seemed to suffer, or feel any fear, the brief exchange had felt a little bit too much like somebody being snuffed out in front of him.

There was a knocking behind him.

He jumped. When he turned around, Vi was staring at him, curled fist resting against the glass. Her lips were pulled tight. He stood up, assaulted by the needles in his legs, and cognitively opened the door.

"What are you doing down here?" He asked. Vi put her hand on the door-frame, leaning against it.

"Nora asked me to check out who was in testing, because *she's* at the bar with Shani and very, very drunk. Apparently, Shani told her some bad news or something. I was worried she'd fall down the stairs, so I came. What are *you* doing down here?"

"I saw Rey walk in, but now he's gone. Once I was in here, I thought I'd keep the local machines company."

"Utterly you. You better hope this doesn't disrupt any of the tests, or you'll get hell from Nora. Once she's upright, that is." Vi paused and furrowed her brow. "Rey, you say? He shouldn't have been able to access the labs after hours. Weird. You didn't pass him? There's only one exit."

Rhen chewed his lower lip. Vi's eyes kept boring into him, until he finally answered. "I passed out. Guess he walked by me when it happened."

Vi's eyes softened, and her eyebrows furrowed. "Has that been happening often? I know you get headaches, but I didn't know passing out was one of your symptoms."

"A little bit more since I got to Mirage, yeah. Might be all the stress. Maybe I'm working my brain too much."

"Well, let's get out of here. The unit's inactive now, so there's no need to keep it company."

They took the elevator back up, then went their separate ways. Rhen headed down the corridor, but instead of making for his own room, turned and went into Nora's instead. He laid back on the bed, waiting for her to come home. Eyes heavy with fatigue, his body relaxed into the mattress. Just as he was about to slip into the world of dreams, a sudden noise jolted him awake. Nora was climbing onto the bed, her movements awkward and ungainly.

"It's just me, don't worry." She slurred, rolling over and resting her head down just short of the pillow. Her hands roamed down to pull off her tights and tug them down to her knees, but she stopped there, legs arched. "Ugh. I can't even. Too much work."

Rhen helped her finish the process, pulling off her leggings with delicate care. He tossed them on the floor, then went about unbuttoning her shirt. She raised her arms like a child.

"You're drunk as a skunk. Why were you out so late? I hear you got some bad news from Shana."

"Everyone leaves me in the end." Nora slurred. "Don't worry too much about everything else, I just want the bra off. It's been digging in all day. I need a new one."

Rhen complied, as she rolled around to give him access to the clip. "I'm not leaving you. What happened?"

"I don't want to talk about it. I just want to hug you and go to sleep."

Nora draped her arm over his stomach and nuzzled close, naked skin against skin. Soon she was snoring, her muscles slack and her face relaxed. Even as his arm stiffened and cramped, he remained still, not wanting to disturb her. He liked her like this, the very picture of contentment.

Guess I'm not getting much sleep for a while. He opened a cognitive file and began coding, pointedly ignoring the sound of her rumbling in his ear like a race car engine.

Chapter 7

"Rey was in the testing rooms? He shouldn't have access to those." Nora leaned against the counter, clutching her morning tea. "I'll look into that."

"Good. Also, you snore when you've been drinking." Rhen said, biting into a piece of buttered toast. Nora cleared her throat, tugging idly at a lock of her hair.

"I'm sorry, I hope I didn't disrupt you too much. By the way, you slept here all night. It's eight o'clock, so how are you going to get out?"

"You'll need to go out and message me if anyone's around. I'll sneak across the hall if the coast is clear."

The next few weeks were uneventful. All the new ideas Rhen's team came up with improved the hybrid's performance, but neural collapse was as ripe as ever. Frustration welled up in Rhen's chest, his muscles tense. It didn't matter if they performed at one percent or a thousand: if they kept falling apart, they'd never see practical application.

One morning, Rhen decided to call his dad. He entered the elevator and waved his watch against the side panel. As the maglev rollers hummed, he leaned against the wall opposite the door, stretching out his back. The lift stopped short of his ultimate destination. It was expected, even as he grumbled inwardly about the inconvenience. Instead, he had to walk halfway across another level, pick up a security guard from the gate station, and travel on a second elevator until he reached the surface.

The whole floor was a sally port, the term for a controlled entry way into a closure, like a fort or a prison. Back in the day, sieged castles used to use them to "sally forth" and harass vulnerable attackers, before retreating behind their defences. The idea of researchers armed with beakers and coffee mugs repelling would-be interlopers did bring a smile to his face.

Once he reached the surface, daylight stung his eyes. It was less gentle than the human-crafted substitutes, instead making itself known with primordial, unapologetic force. It hung high in the sky, a constant among the swirling blue that stretched out in all directions. Mirage was like the flat earth of ancient myth made manifest, and— the disk-like realm seemed to fall away after a certain distance, almost as if you could walk off the edge of it. It was an odd fit indeed for a scientific facility. But here they were, resting on the shield of Achilles, encircled by not sea but sky. Beyond, there were nameless perils.

The world was sweltering and swaying, as the sun lashed mercilessly at his face, forearms and neck. He had hoped the longer he stayed in the desert, the more he'd become acclimated to the regional climate. The opposite seemed true — every time he came up, he hated it more. The heat made him feel sluggish, sweaty, and slow. The last one he hated the most.

The two of them made their way to a small square building with satellite equipment on top. When Rhen walked in, the guard didn't accompany him, but rather left him free to make the call in the illusion of privacy.

Inside the room was a single chair and a holographic projector. Rhen sat down and dialled up his father. There was a five-second delay as the request was processed, which was positively prehistoric. Still, it couldn't be helped, given the deliberate broadcast delay.

Rather than concerned that Australia had returned to its penal colony roots, Rhen was at ease. It was all standard for a high-security AI research facility: two elevators as a physical breaker, a white noise jammer blocking any wireless transmissions in and out of the facility, and the communications array off-site. The wavelengths for cognitive messages were completely blocked off.

Humanity still hasn't gotten over its Frankenstein complex. A malicious AI isn't going to spontaneously break free of the lab and take over the world.

There were other AI to stop that, like the one in the building filtering his transmission, which was different from the one in the base. It would be listening in to his call, just like the security guard outside, ready to hang it up if they noticed anything suspicious. The whole thing was a two-party system to prevent espionage.

It was also a shining example of humans and machines working together to make up for each other's shortcomings. As Rhen pondered on that, his dad appeared as a lifelike projection in front of him.

"It's good to see you again, kid," James said. "Working hard out there in the middle of nowhere?"

The conversation flowed awkwardly as it always did, not helped by the delays each time one of them talked. His dad talked about the past — he seemed to be doing that a lot these days — describing events that had happened to him almost as if Rhen were his living diary to record these in. But it felt like being talked at, not with.

Maybe it's because one day they'll be gone, and I'll be the only evidence they were here. I'm his etching on the wall of the Colosseum.

Eventually, when they ran out of small talk, the silences got longer and longer, until one of them found an excuse to cut it short.

With a heavy sigh, Rhen slumped in his chair. *Like pulling a band-aid.* It would be another few months before he'd have to do that again.

There were other messages, of course. There always were. After a brief pause, he brought them up, but text-only.

Dear Jay,

Thank you for supporting those with techno cognitive disabilities with your monthly donations of $20,000 glo to the Beyond Rose Society!

Everyone deserves to be connected and have a place in society. Sadly, Rosetta disadvantage excludes many people, whether due to conditions like digital synaesthesia, critical implant rejection, and meta-neural addictions. Approximately 1.2 percent of the global population have a TCD, but suffer in silence due to stigma.

This year, the Beyond Rose Society has raised $20 million dollars to help fight for the rights of those afflicted with Rosetta disadvantage. We are so grateful for your support.

Your tax invoice is attached.

The Beyond Rose Society: Connecting Hearts, Not Just Minds.

Rhen rubbed the bridge of his nose. Jay was a pseudonym, since he couldn't very well use his real one for the donations. He flicked through the rest of the messages, both good and bad, not skipping a single one.

***

"All done?" The security guard asked, even though he knew the answer. Rhen nodded, and they made their way back to the elevator door.

Before they got there, the door opened, and Delta walked out. Their face lit up and they raised an arm, waving. Behind them was a dour-faced security guard.

"Hey Rhen! Up here making a call, or appreciating the view?" Delta asked.

"You know, making calls, checking my messages; I'm not a big fan of the heat up here. I feel like my brain's going to melt."

"Well, that's not surprising. I'm here to make a call as well, to check in with my folks." Delta rubbed their neck, their fringe a deep shade of blue. "I don't get to visit very often, and they worry a lot."

"After growing up with a chronic pain condition, I can imagine they'd be fairly protective. The slightest scrape would have been like a bullet wound."

"Pretty much. But they're proud of what I'm doing, helping people out, and I think they like the idea I'm in a secure bunker." Delta grinned, locks now returning to a warmer hue.

"Helping people out? I mean, we're making a new form of AI, so any benefits are indirect," Rhen said, crossing his arms. "Though I have heard the hypothetical argument the AI could go on to cure diseases. Is that what you meant?"

"Yeah, something like that. A lot of medical issues take decades, if not centuries to figure out," Delta stepped forward, hand on their chest. "Wouldn't it be amazing if these AI could? They'll be able to think and research at a level we never could. Human physiology would be an open book to them. Same with physics, or anything, really."

"Not entirely true. We're still building off a human blueprint. They might be able to think faster, but the predisposition of the subject matters. If you make an AI based on someone who is an avid biologist, but has little appetite for physics, that matters. Just because someone *can* do something, it doesn't mean they will."

"Is that why we have to make more than A-1?"

"Pretty much. Anyway, all this talk is premature — we need to succeed before we can talk about next steps, and making an artificial superintelligence is a tall order. And right now, we're behind our deadlines."

"Got it. Well, I'm only here to help with the hardware, but I'll do my best." Delta beamed.

"Sorry to be rude, but can we get to the call?" The guard behind Delta said. "I'm wearing all black, so I'm sweating bullets up here."

"Oh, right, sure thing." It was nice to know he wasn't the only one who was feeling the heat.

As Delta and the guard passed them, Rhen felt a nameless tension rising in his chest. He turned and stopped the young engineer.

"Hey, Delta. One more thing. You said the Rosetta... it really made a difference to you?"

It was a moment of weakness, a desperate longing for endorphins from his past success. But Delta gave the widest smile, even as their brow furrowed.

"More than you could ever know."

And with that, they parted. Rhen rode the elevator down and said goodbye to his own shadowing security guard at the entrance. As he walked into the second elevator, Alan was already standing inside, hands behind his back.

"Rhen," he said with a curt nod. "Back from making a call?"

"Yeah." Rhen leaned against the wall. There was a long silence. Technology may have sped a lot of things up, but elevators remained as slow as they were in the previous century.

"How is the project going?" Alan asked.

As if you haven't read the report. It was back to thinking about the latest creation, and not the old one. "We're making progress, but there are still a lot of mental paths that aren't optimised." Rhen paused. "We've got some theories about why the collapse keeps happening, and we're testing them out one by one."

"Well, do whatever it takes to achieve results. You were chosen for a reason; there's nobody more qualified to lead this project than you."

Whatever it takes, huh? I wonder if Rey's been breathing down his neck too. If heads were going to roll, it was hard to imagine Alan would remain completely unscathed.

***

That afternoon, Rhen went to visit Bee again. Every time he did, he came away feeling a bit *sharper*, full of ideas to try. It was probably all a self-fulfilling prophecy, but even if that was the case, it was a useful one. He had told Nora about the last visit, of course, once she had sobered up. She had been surprisingly nonchalant.

"That's mirroring for you," she shrugged. "Aie probably synched a little too closely with something that came up in conversation. But whether aie's got true signs of artificial empathy, we can only figure that out from unbiased tests."

"You're not mad?"

"Not really. I thought Bee would try something like that. After all, if I only had eight hours left in the world, that's *exactly* what I'd do."

Well, I can't really disagree with that, Rhen thought. *Carpe diem, was it? 'Seize the day, trust tomorrow even as little as you may.'*

As Rhen stepped into the testing room, Bee appeared dramatically transformed from their last encounter. Aies skin glowed with a tawny, skin-kissed hue. He was met by an intense, fixated stare: aies eyes were as large as lotus leaves, with black pearl orbs that seemed to absorb all light that touched them.

"Hello Bee. My name is Rhen, and my pronouns are he/him. We've already met, so you don't need to trouble yourself with an introduction." He sat down and rested his palms on his lap. "You said last time we should have met sooner, so here we are, meeting sooner."

"It seems you have me at a disadvantage," Bee said, leaning forward on the table, chin resting on top of aies clasped hands. "You seem to know a lot about me, but I don't know anywhere near as much about *you*."

"Nora didn't tell you I was coming?"

"She did, and said, rather explicitly, 'No kissing.'"

Rhen cleared his throat. "Yes, I'd appreciate it. And I wouldn't say I know everything about you, or else I wouldn't be here. You and the hybrids are a mystery I'm trying to crack."

"Crack away. I've got nowhere to be until my neural collapse."

As they ran through the tests, and Bee was exceptionally well-behaved, the hybrid examined aies arms. Remembering Nora's advice about body language, Rhen asked about it.

"Still getting used to your new frame? This one's a bit different from your last one."

"What was my last one?"

"Very Japanese geisha, slender build. This one's more South Asian. You're practically amorphous — I never know what you're going to look like when I come in."

"Nice to keep you on your toes, since you're doing the same for me. To answer your question, I was examining my android limbs. It's interesting being fully mechanical, instead of partially."

"You had cybernetics, or the person you were copied from did?"

"Yes. It's an entirely different feeling. Well, figuratively speaking, of course."

"Does it bother you not to feel anything?" Rhen asked, the question impulsively slipping out of his mouth. But as usual, Bee didn't bat an eyelid.

"No." The answer was flat, immediate. "I'm doing important work by being here."

"You definitely are, *and* you're helping me figure out the problems with the code. I hear you're getting better with that. Let's run through some modelling tests."

The tests were simple enough: Bee was given two bits of data — people's age and income status, for instance — and an equation to find out if the two were connected or not. Ae would have to tell him how closely related these things were, on a scale from one to zero. Zero meant not at all, and one meant they were completely connected.

The trick rested in the amount of data Bee needed to crunch; processing three hundred people's ages and income was easy for any machine, let alone an AI, but too much for a human.

"Eating out and obesity" Rhen asked.

"0.82," Bee answered, after a three second pause. "It's a strong model."

"Oh, close. 0.72. Alright, next model. Age and happiness quota?"

A longer pause this time. "0.62." The lilt in Bee's voice betrayed their uncertainty. Rhen ran the maths.

"Sorry, way off. It's 0.23, a weak model. Are you guessing?"

"A bit, my apologies." Bee bit aies lower lip. "It's frustrating. I don't know why I'm getting this wrong. I start running the numbers, and my focus just slips away."

"I'm starting to develop a theory. I think your higher-level thinking is getting in the way, and you're getting *bored.*"

"Oh really?" Bee's eyes glinted, suddenly alive again. *Nora was right about reading their faces,* Rhen thought.

"Yes. How much do you know about pigeons?"

"Very little, I'm obviously a bird brain. Enlighten me, professor."

"Well, like most animals, pigeons learn through association, seeing connections between two things — like 'water-wet' or 'sky-blue'. Pavlov's dog would salivate when a bell was rung, because they associated it with food—"

"Are you going to ring a bell for me?" Bee grinned, leaning on aies hand. Rhen clicked his tongue.

"Nothing of the sort. *Anyway,* in the 21st century, they put a whole bunch of pigeons to the test, and found out that machines learn the same way — repeating something until they learn it, exhaustive trial and error. But humans try to learn through seeing hidden patterns and rules behind things, a higher level of thinking. We even do it when there's nothing there."

"Like God?" Bee said, narrowing aies eyes. The word was spat out, a dirty thing.

Rhen cleared his throat. "Well, I'm agnostic, so I don't think it's *possible* to make a ruling either way. I get your point though." He clasped his hands on the table. "Anyway, humans are rubbish at brute force, repetitive learning, unlike pigeons or machines. All that higher-level thinking gets in the way, or we get bored and give up. Does that sound like you?"

"Sort of. Time sort of... slows down when I'm thinking," Bee said. "I'm going over two thousand calculations in three seconds, which *should* be easy. I flick over each number, and then my mind sort of wanders. Do you think the two kinds of thinking can be reconciled, AI and human?" The AI stared at him with a heavy gaze, not blinking. Aie didn't need to.

"I do, or else I wouldn't be doing this. How is an entirely different story."

"Could you just remove my boredom?"

"I can't remove everything that it means to be human because it's convenient," Rhen chuckled. "Plus, boredom is useful, even though it must seem inconvenient when you're stuck in here. Boredom sparks creativity and problem solving. We seek stimulation, so we improve on things."

"Ah, I guess we can't do away with boredom then. Seeking sensations is important."

Bee's a sensate stuck in a synthetic body, Rhen thought. *And yet aie can't feel anything right now, which must be frustrating.* Meanwhile, his own leg muscles were aching, hundreds of needles stabbing into his thighs. Sitting for hours was a pain, something that was easy to forget about when the person across from you felt nothing at all.

"Hey, Bee, I wanted to ask you. What do you think of this Haiku?" Rhen asked on a whim.

Data not trustworthy
History repeats, escape sought
New truth to be found.

Bee paused, a ponderous look on aies face. "Well, history always repeats. It's the sad state of human affairs. They repeat the same thing over and over. I guess my life is a microcosm of that. And new truth to be found... I have no idea. The first part, though, I'd say maybe data poisoning?"

"Data poisoning?"

"You know, when data that's not trustworthy or corrupt is used for a test. It poisons things, affecting everything downstream." Bee explained, even though he was fully aware of the concept. Rhen felt he did that to Bee a lot as well, but aie was too polite to say anything. "Where does that haiku come from?"

"It's just something I heard, nothing too special. I think I might finish up now, since my legs are killing me. You've been a big help."

"You're leaving?" Bee's lips were pressed tightly together, eyes wide and pleading. "It's going to be terribly boring without you around, and all that creativity is just going to go to waste."

I can't exactly refuse. And so Rhen stayed with Bee until they started breaking down and repeating themselves. He had been holding Bee's hand until the final moment. Their last words were the same as always.

"Your eyes are so sad. Please don't stop working. You're going to fix this all up. We're doing great work." The AI's brow was furrowed, and for the first time, they weren't able to meet Rhen's gaze. "I'm going to pull the plug now. You look far too sad."

And then Bee went limp. Rhen slowly disentangled his hand. The body, now lying limp and splayed on the table, eyes hollow, was a little too much like a cadaver.

That version of Bee is dead. Maybe it really isn't a good idea to visit here too much.

But then, who would keep Bee company until the end?

***

The next evening, after Rhen had shaken off the experience as best he could, he sat down in his office and examined Bee — no, B-24's code. It was hard to stare at the fragmented parts of their brain without compartmentalising: Nora's policy of keeping AI Testing and Research separated now made a hell of a lot of sense.

He needed to go for a drive sometime. He'd been cooped up too long. But first, he needed to find out the cause. If he could solve the problem, it would mean no more resets.

When he closed his eyes, the bloody cascade failures were like pulsing lines etched into his lids, as clear as his veins. It was just like with Sukh. Sukh had been lying on the floor that day, just like he'd been...

"Poisoned."

Furrowing his brow, Rhen checked out the data they were feeding into Bee. To his shock, the testing data was *unclean*. If they had been putting this in from the start, it was exactly what Bee had said. Everything would be compromised, like a wrench shoved into the gears of a machine.

"How could Robert and Data Operations miss this?" A chill ran down his spine. But then again, the bad data was discrete — almost deliberately so — like a flavourless, odourless poison.

Does the haiku mean Alef knew about it? But if he did, why not do something about it? Or did he cause it in the first place?

He was getting paranoid. Bad data happened all the time, and yes, this was a bit unusual. But like Napoleon said, you should never ascribe to malice what is adequately explained by incompetence. Either way, he needed to pay Robert a visit to get it sorted out.

He downloaded the file to his implant and logged off his terminal. At the very least, taking a walk was a good way to take a break, even if it wasn't going for a drive.

As he strode down the corridor, the visiglass windows revealed a pitch-black expanse, punctuated by strategically placed lights that struggled to push back the night. Despite their efforts, only small patches of rusty dirt were exposed, leaving roughly a million square kilometres cloaked in darkness, illuminated only by the scant light of the waning crescent moon, which jealously kept its glow hidden behind its back. Well, Rhen was on his own mission to shed some light on something.

It must be later than I thought. This is going to be less of a break, and more my last task before logging off. Better let Nora know I'll be late.

After exiting the elevator, he pinged Nora for a CMS session. This time, he went with double input instead of just voice. When she picked up, there was a moment of multisensory input, where he experienced two realities at once. He was walking down the corridor, but also staring at the contents of Nora's office as if he was sitting at her desk. In short, his brain was processing the input of two sets of eyes at once — Nora's *and* his.

It was easy to tell which was which, of course: only his own came with smell, taste, and touch. His stride didn't alter one bit. It was the result of lots of practice, though not everyone got the hang of multisensory.

Rhen was determined to conjure a cognitive avatar in her vision first, but she beat him to the punch, appearing in the corridor wearing a cream minidress with thin shoulder straps, her short-heel shoes clacking as she walked beside him. Her outfit dangerously complemented her figure, a combination that was dangerously unfair.

Well, two can play at that game, he thought. He conjured his own cognitive avatar, a vision of himself suggestively leaning against her desk. His avatar's hair was fashionably tousled, and everything he wore from his silk shirt to his skinny jeans were form fitting and snug in a way that a tailor couldn't touch. His avatar crossed its arms, sleeves rolled up, and looked thoughtful.

<Oh, well that's just not fair,> Nora huffed. Both versions of him smirked.

<Well, you started it. And I can tell where your eyes are wandering.>

In the periphery of his vision, her otherwise bare arms still had a thin layer of fabric covering the area between her wrists and elbows. Even now, when she could be or look like anything, she kept the arm covers. It threatened to draw his focus, which would be bad, considering she could see wherever he was looking.

Good thing she's got a lot of other things to focus on.

<Did you call up just to taunt me? Not that I mind, since I could do with the distraction,> she said.

<Actually, I did have a reason. I was just pinging to say I'd got caught up at work and I was just dropping by Data Operations before I came to your place. It seems like you got caught up too, though.>

<Guilty as charged.> Nora's avatar rubbed the brow of her nose. <I'll be a bit longer still. But just so you know, nobody will be where you're going. Robert's team is off for a week after spending a lot of time on crunch. His echo is about, but that's about it, but the office is otherwise empty.>

<Crunch, huh? What do they have to crunch about?> He stopped in his tracks, staring at the distant door. <Damn, I walked all the way here for nothing. The echo probably won't have enough flexibility of thought for what I want to ask.>

<I've been meaning to ask, why don't you ever use one, instead of leaving things to Derek and Vi?>

<I prefer a bit of diversity of thought. If I just make a machine-learning copy of myself, things will just become an echo chamber. I'm not that much of a control freak.>

<Hey! You know *I* use an echo, right?> Her lips thinned and her brow crinkled. There were only two creases, which wasn't the worst — three was the real danger zone. Still, he *hadn't* known.

<Sorry, sorry! But your case is different. Who could disagree with another copy of you?>

<Shameless flirt. But you're not entirely off base. I *am* a control freak, but only because everyone else does things wrong.> The creases disappeared from her brow, and her smile was radiant again. <I guess you'll be back to the apartment first, then.>

<I will. Want me to order anything?>

<Lots of dumplings, Xiao Long Bao if they've got the ingredients. I want to drown in dumpling broth; it's been that kind of day. You know why.>

<I'll draw you a bath and then just shovel them in for you.>

<Perfect. You're the best.>

She walked up and gave him a phantom kiss before she disappeared, and he just had time to make his avatar do the same. With the connection broken, he was back to operating with only one set of eyes. A moment of disorientation washed over him, since he never did master the disconnect.

She beat me to the punch again. Ah well, better head back.

As he went to turn around, the door ahead opened. He paused. Nobody was meant to be in the office, but *someone* was still working.

Maybe it's someone who came to visit, just like me?

To his surprise, it was Rey who came out. He slinked out of the room, adjusting his jacket — no, adjusting something in it, as if he'd just stuffed something in there.

Instinctively, Rhen stepped behind one of the holographic plants that darted the hallway. His foot just up and decided it wanted to be behind the foliage, and carried the rest of him with it. When his brain did catch up, he felt ridiculous.

Why am I hiding behind this plant, exactly? This is stupid. Adults don't hide behind fake ferns.

But something deep in his gut answered him: Rey looked suspicious as all hell. It was like he was trying not to get caught doing something illicit. Naturally, that made Rhen want to find out what it was.

Now that his brain was on board, it was quick to critique every part of this ill-advised plan. There were only two ways to leave the room, and Rhen had arrived from the direction with the closest elevator. That meant Rey was almost certain to come this way. At least the holo wasn't transparent, so it offered complete cover. At least until Rey walked right past him and saw him hiding like an idiot.

But for some strange reason, the footsteps were moving further away. After a half minute, the noise stopped completely.

Rhen poked his head out. The hallway was empty. Unless Rey was also hiding behind one of the plants like an idiot, he was gone.

Why did he leave the long way? There's nothing in that direction but Server Ops and Ethics.

He wasn't going to find out any more standing behind a shrub. Rhen stepped out and went to follow Rey, eager to find out what the man was up to. But before he could, a hand came down on his shoulder.

Rhen jumped.

"What are you doing, boss?"

He turned around. It was Vi, and her eyebrow was raised.

"Are you hiding behind holos now? I'm sure Derek would love to hear about this."

Rhen cleared his throat. No matter which way he cut it, *he* looked like the suspicious one here, and Rey was nowhere to be seen.

"I came to chat to Robert, but I was taking a moment to finish a double input CMS. Sorry if it looked strange."

She raised the other eyebrow and slid her hands in her pockets. "Double input, huh? Makes me nauseous, so I could see why you were crouching. Must have wanted to see them *real* bad, then."

"Well, I just wanted to share some diagrams."

"Right, sure thing. Well, Handling's closed today, so there's no point being here. Want to get something to eat?"

"I've got plans." Then he wanted to slap himself for saying it. "I mean, I'm going to grab some dinner and do some work on Casey that I promised."

"Oh well, have fun with your date then. I'll try not to let your rejection tarnish my evening," she smirked. "Want to head back down together?"

"Sure." And Rhen glanced over his shoulder as they left. Whatever chance he'd had to follow Rey was long gone anyway.

Chapter 8

Once he got back to his apartment, Nora wasn't there yet, so he drew her a bath as promised, and ordered dinner. It wasn't drowning in broth, but it was close, and the thermal vents would keep it ready through dinner. It would take forever to fill otherwise due to its size.

As the noise of rushing water filled the room, his thoughts ran over Rey's suspicious behaviour. He couldn't get it out of his head, but he couldn't figure it out, either.

"Hey, Casey, can you come here for a moment? I need to bounce something off you," he said.

"Is it a ball, or is this more of an idea-related scenario?" Casey asked, wheeling in.

"The latter. Wait, do you think I'd really bounce a ball off of you?"

"You did that one time a few months ago, remember?" The suitcase unfurled and crossed their spindly metal arms.

"I was testing your motor skills. I asked you to catch it, then tweaked your code until you could, remember?"

"My motor skills are just fine." He wheeled back a foot and then forward to illustrate the point. "And I thought it was that old human hazing game of 'stop hitting yourself,' you know?"

Rhen groaned. "*Of course* it wasn't. Anyway, I'd really appreciate someone to hear out my logic, and point out any flaws." He sat down on the edge of the bath.

"Sure thing!" Casey's code was leagues ahead of where it had been six months ago: an exercise in deduction was well within their ability. It would be good for both of them. Rhen first explained what he had seen that evening.

"Maybe a secret date with someone from Data Handling?" Casey said. "From my experience, fraternising with colleagues is a reason someone could sneak around. Taking the long route could be in an effort not to be seen."

"But it's a straight shot to the elevator. Going the long way meant passing by more departments, meaning more chances to run into people."

"Humans don't always think about risk when they're doing this sort of thing, but my sample size is limited."

Rhen winced, leaning forward and resting his chin on his curled fingers. "Okay, so that's not *entirely* untrue. But let's operate under the assumption Rey is acting logically."

"Hmm, then it's harder to narrow down. According to what I know, all the data for most of the facility's projects come through that department. Clean data is important for machines to run. Is that why your project keeps failing? Sabotage is common in facilities like this, and would be a reason for sneaking around."

Rhen blinked. He *had* found evidence of data poisoning. But could Rey be the cause, not Alef? If the failure was due to an external cause... it wasn't outside the realm of possibility. And Casey had suggested it, an AI who could only operate on logic and algorithms. There was no bias there.

"Maybe. Project Achilli does seem to be stuck. Tainted data would fit all the dots. And Rey has been around since the project started, but..."

"But?"

"... The timeline matches up, but I can't see why he would." Rhen explained how Rey had been pressuring Nora. "If he was a saboteur, why push the team to show results? He should be happy to see us fail, not wanting to see us succeed."

"Hmm," Casey mimicked Rhen's thinking pose. "Is it really helping you succeed, though?"

Casey was trained to ask critical thinking questions when someone needed help, which basically meant parroting back what someone said as a query. Sometimes it was funny, like the time Rhen was considering what to wear, and they had asked in a serious and contemplative tone, "Do you really need to wear clothes to work?"

Other times, like now, it questioned an assumption Rhen had, causing him to see things in an entirely different light.

"You're right. Cooking the reports, getting key staff replaced or putting them under stress all damages the project in the long run," Rhen said. "In fact, if he got someone to compromise the study and then turned around and exposed it, that'd be a good way to sabotage what we're doing. But the means don't make sense."

"The means?"

"Yeah. He's not a tech specialist. To spike the data, he'd need to know how to do it, and in a way nobody would notice. The poisoning — if that's what it was

— it was artful. We pour over the data every time a test fails, and they never break the same way twice. Then again, we never had a *reason* to suspect the data was tampered with."

The front door opened. He left the tub running, knowing it would turn itself off, and walked into the living room. Nora was standing there holding their dinner.

"Caught it at the perfect time outside the door," she said, placing the Chinese food on the table. "And is that water I hear running? I really, really appreciate it."

"We were playing detective!" Casey said as they wheeled out. Nora quirked an eyebrow.

"Playing what? This I've got to hear."

Rhen explained the whole thing.

It was a good thing he'd drawn a bath, because by the end she was hunched and playing with her hair.

"I don't like this data poisoning business. As for Rey, he's been hanging around too many places lately. Up in data handling, then down in testing. Places he shouldn't be. But like you, I'm not sure he'd be clever enough."

"Yeah, I know. But maybe if someone made it for him? Triggering something like a Kaur collapse is easy, it just takes compromising something critical to the person's cognitive architecture. And with 86 billion neurons, it's like finding a needle in a haystack."

"One you managed to find, which is *amazing*. You should let security know. They can run a query through the security AI to check the footage, audit logs and access times."

"Did you chase them up about being in testing?"

"I did, but they never got back to me." She shrugged. "But then I didn't drop the term 'sabotage', which might get their asses in gear. Maybe you'll have better luck. But for now, let's finish off these dumplings, since I've been waiting for them all day. That's the only thing I want on my plate right now."

"Damn right. There's nothing worse than when they go cold."

***

Taking Nora's advice, the next day Rhen made his way to the security department. It was located in the upper levels of the facility and behind a pair of transparent doors.

Like the diamond nanoweave fence on the surface, the doors were deceptively secure. While they looked like glass, they were actually made of high-grade transparent aluminium; the kind that could take almost any impact from close range without so much as a scratch.

It was an unlikely scenario, but the security team seemed good at arguing for things that were overkill. During orientation he had been shown their well-stocked armoury, which mostly included PEP weapons — pulsed energy projectiles — in the form of pistols and rifles. The Solar Age had brought with it a lot of advancements in light-based tech, and as usual, warfare was no exception.

"These babies fire an invisible laser pulse at the target," one of the guards had said, cradling the gun like a child. "When it strikes someone, it creates a burst of plasma that heats up the air so fast, the air explodes — wham! — knocking them on their ass. It's so bright and loud, it's like a flash-bang in your face. That's not what really paralyses you, though, the electro radiation fucks with your nerve cells. It feels like the worst cold burn you can imagine. You just lie there, sizzling, not able to move a damn muscle."

"You've been shot with one?" Rhen had asked, mouth agape.

"Oh, of course! It's an initiation experience here. You run as far as you can, and you're given a ten-minute head start." She chortled. "That's almost enough time to get out of the two-kilometre range, if you're a really good sprinter. I slacked on cardio, though."

They'd also managed to argue for a railgun, the pride and joy of their collection. Rhen wanted to read the budget request and justification for that piece of equipment. Not only were railguns used to destroy military equipment at ranges measured in kilometres, they were hilariously inefficient within a close quarters setting like an underground base. It didn't make any sense.

Then again, since when did guns make sense, or the people who want to use them? At least the PEPs are non-lethal.

The security room was spartan, devoid of any furniture bar a handful of reclining lounge chairs and footstools, all of which were currently occupied by black-clad individuals. There were, however, an ample amount of visiglass screens.

Each of the screens were occupied by a single figure, their whole body visible within the bounds of the frame. Each one was dressed like undead Viking berserkers, faces coated with chalk white paint with a smearing of bloody red over their foreheads. They were holding musical instruments with bladed edges, jagged spikes or gun barrel ends.

Behind them was a familiar desert landscape, right down to the gnarled tree right near the base entrance. They were thrashing out music so loud the transparent aluminium was shuddering.

One of the Nordic ghouls was singing just loud enough to be heard over the racket, but Rhen still had to concentrate to make out the lyrics.

> Buried in the underground
> Waiting for some ass to pound
> The great deathless warriors wait under the dirt
> Armed and ready to destroy
> We're all ready to deploy
> And rise from under the sands to unleash the hurt

"Do you mind turning it down?" Rhen shouted. He'd had enough of bad haiku, and bad metal lyrics were beyond the pale.

The noise ebbed. One of the black-clad individuals stood up and walked to him with a broad grin and arms wide.

"Hey, how are you going, brains trust? Not a fan of Viking algo-metal?"

"Hey Kyle. I like algorithmic just fine, I'm just not a fan of losing my hearing. I'm surprised you can get any work done with all that noise." Rhen peered over the man's muscled shoulder and at one of the screens. "The lead singer looks like you, but with a beard."

"You're right! It's a group jam, though, so the team must see me in charge." Kyle chuckled and looped his thumbs under his belt. "My newsreader looks Norse, too. Guess the AI knows all my preferences. I can't understand people who like organic stuff. It's backwards, if you ask me."

Says the guy picturing himself as a Viking warrior. "Well, I kind of get it. I went and saw an organic show in Tokyo once. It wasn't as good as something cooked up with billions of people's data, but the performer's mistakes had a sort of charm."

"Yeah, but an AI can replicate mistakes, too. Anyone ever told you you're a little old fashioned for an egghead?"

"Yeah, I've heard that." Rhen forced a smile. "Actually, I'm here to make a quick report. Saw something suspicious yesterday and thought I'd come to let you know. We think it might be related to corporate sabotage." He took Nora's advice, dropping the special word. The reaction was immediate.

"And you waited *all this time*? You should have come in sooner!" Kyle strode back to his recliner and fell into it, placing his crossed legs up on the footrest. "Let's run it by the boss... I mean the security AI, Virtus, and see what they find."

"You have problems working with AI?" Rhen tilted his head.

"Me? Nah, they're alright." Kyle grinned at him. "Some folks say it's not good to be in any field with a gun: security, cop or the military. They think we'll be replaced just like the musicians were, probably with walking drones. But I tell you what: it still takes a human to catch a human. We're slippery bastards, you know?"

"Plus, we're cheaper!" Someone yelled out. The room was filled with laughter.

Well, that's true. But the real reason is probably that your brains can't be hacked. In a high-security facility, that was a deal-breaker. It was unlikely any of them were progs, so tampering with their brains was out of the question.

"So, who's the slippery bastard you want us to check out?" Kyle asked.

"Rey Keyes. I saw him hanging around data handling about eight. He looked like he'd just left the department. There was another incident two weeks ago, down in testing."

"Sure, I remember that one. Hey Warren, what happened with that one?" Kyle spun to one of the beefier guards — compared to Rhen, they were all giants — who turned and shrugged.

"Sorry, that one must have fallen through the cracks."

"Damn it, Warren, we don't get enough work for things to *fall through the cracks*. Let's look it up." Kyle said, swivelling back to face Rhen. "Sorry about that. Anyway, I like Rey, nice guy, always asks what my daughter's up to, remembers her name and everything. Doubt he's up to anything, but let's take a look."

Guess there's more than one way to tamper with someone's thoughts. Rhen crossed his arms and waited as Kyle bit on his lower lip; it was an interesting C-face. The whole thing took less than a minute. When he was finished, Kyle curled an eyebrow and stared at Rhen, not batting a lid.

"So, anything you want to explain to me before we go any further?"

"No, not that I can think of. What did you see?" Rhen said, his heart racing. *Wait, the conversation with Nora was cognitive, right? They shouldn't be able to see it. And why would they care?*

"I checked out the dates you gave me, and I couldn't see Rey at all, not in testing or data handling." A pointed pause, and Kyle leaned in, lowering his voice. "What I *did* see was you giving one of our testing machines a bit of lip, if you know what I mean, and you hiding behind some fake trees."

Rhen's cheeks burned. "The subject kissed me. If you check the footage *and* the audio, it wasn't consensual or expected. As for hiding, I was trying to stay out of sight of a possible saboteur. Are you *sure* he wasn't there?"

"Absolutely one hundred percent. Virtus says he was in his quarters, and it would have flagged if he was doing anything untoward."

"That's odd. Can't we check the cams, make sure he *was* there?"

Kyle sighed and crossed his arms. "Listen, I'm not putting in a request to watch the footage in people's rooms. That's got to go to the highest level, and what am I going to say? 'Hey, someone wants me to peek into people's rooms and spy for them, even though they're the one acting suspicious?'"

"I'm not crazy. I definitely saw him there." Rhen furrowed his brow.

"Well, if you *really* want to prove it, give me level three access. Virtus can translate it into something we can watch." The security chief slipped his hands behind his head. "Though, that only proves you *saw* something, not that they were there."

"You think someone cognitively phished me?"

"It makes sense. Someone tricks you to give them visual access, then conjures up something that's simply not there. You were fresh off a double-input CMS, right? You said so in the footage. The other party probably faked hanging up, and decided to mess with you. Hear about it all the time in the news."

Rhen rubbed his temples. "No, they wouldn't do that."

"Well, it makes a lot more sense to me, and all the pieces are there. What's that saying? 'The simplest answer is usually the best one.'"

"That's not always true. Sometimes the more complex hypothesis is correct." But he didn't come here to discuss Occam's razor. *This is going nowhere.*

"This is going nowhere," Kyle echoed. "Look, you've got a pro-grade brain, right? Maybe make sure to see if you've been hacked. If I were you, I'd get checked out. The idea someone could tamper with my brain would give *me* the chills, and I'm not even a Prog."

***

The whole exchange had been frustrating *and* mortifying. Thankfully, Kyle had accepted that Rhen *hadn't* been trying to kiss machines during off hours, but he hoped to hell the weird rumour didn't spread anyway. Now he only had to contend with the fact the guards all thought he was either crazy, or someone who would fall for a basic phishing scam.

Rhen retired to the safety of his apartment, his cheeks still burning. He collapsed on his couch and threw on some algo lo-fi beats, letting the white noise and low-tempo rhythm seep mentally into his veins, slowing his heartbeat.

But what really happened? I definitely saw him running around the facility.

"Hey, you're back!" Casey said, wheeling in. "How'd the talk go?"

"Bad. I want to crawl into a hole and die." Rhen filled the robot in. "So, long story short, either I got hacked, the system got hacked, or I'm crazy."

"Well, you don't seem crazy to me. Then again, you programmed me, so I'm not qualified to make that kind of judgement."

"Thanks, Casey."

Rhen pulled his breaker off the shelf and brought up the access logs. It was unlikely he had been phished, but like any good scientist, he needed to rule it out. The list hovered over the nearby coffee table. Each line was a recording of a cognitive action, him reaching out to someone else, or the other way around. If someone had hacked him, the logs would show it.

When it came to Nora's call, he didn't suspect her, but he checked the timing anyway. True to his gut, the call had lasted just under a minute, then terminated — not long enough to conjure up what he'd seen afterwards.

"So, I wasn't phished. Nobody had visual or auditory permissions to mess with my brain during that time," Rhen said, closing the log. "Not that I'm surprised. I doubt anyone could have messed with my cognitive structure without causing a Kaur collapse."

"So, what about the other two possibilities?" Casey asked.

"To hack the base's security AI — Virtus — you'd need another AI. Humans aren't up to the task, since our brains aren't fast enough."

"Well, you try your best," the suitcase said, patting his knee. Rhen smirked and waved it away.

"Smartass! I do plenty good at keeping *you* up to date. Anyway, you couldn't do it either. You'd need a machine that was on the level with the cutting-edge model Glycon purchased, which was expressly designed *not* to be hacked. That's not something you can carry around in your pocket. Plus, that'd probably be twenty million glo, easy. Rey probably doesn't have that lying around."

"What about hacking from the outside?"

"Impossible. Mirage has an optic gap, so it can't be hacked from the outside.

"But that just leaves you being crazy, right? That doesn't seem likely."

Rhen furrowed his brow, knitting his fingers together and hunching forward. A long pause. "Well, for me, visual hallucinations aren't something *I* can rule out.

I took a lot of damage during the Rosetta experiments. I get headaches, but other people on my team experienced, well, hallucinations. Seeing and hearing things that simply weren't there."

"Hmm. Now that you've given me *that* data, I think you should definitely get checked out, just to be sure."

"My thoughts exactly."

***

A few days later, Rhen got in to see Dr Roswell, and asked him to check for digital synaesthesia.

The psychologist knitted his fingers together and stared at him. "You're worried that the implant is making you see and hear things that aren't there? That's a rare condition."

"I've got reason to believe it could be happening to me," Rhen sat down, pinching the bridge of his nose. "And it happened to a colleague of mine with the same prototype Rosetta, back when we were creating it."

"Doctor Erica Atwood?" That was the thing about setting so many firsts; people always knew who you were talking about.

"Yeah, she was the first to have the condition. Of course, we didn't realise what was happening until *after* the Rosetta was in production. Erica talked about hearing whispers of code, but we all thought it was just due to how many hours we were working. It's not unusual to fall asleep and dream of the code."

"Do you feel you should have noticed sooner?"

"Maybe?" He paused. "Actually, yes, I do. She didn't seem to be taking it seriously, so I didn't. I know now she was just too nervous to bring it up. When she started to talk about seeing things that weren't there, I knew there was a big problem."

"You can't blame yourself for what happened. And on the upside, I hear turning off the Rosetta completely eliminates the symptoms. No whispers of code, intrusive thoughts, *or* seeing ghosts."

Rhen screwed up his face. "Yes, but it's becoming more and more the case that if you don't use cognitive tech, you're a pariah. Machines are designed more and more to work with mental input, and employers expect you to work at the speed of thought. A lot of people got the implant because it made things convenient, but others felt pressured into it."

"Do you feel responsible for that? Is that why you use manual input, even though you helped invent cognitive coding?" Roswell asked, resting his shoulder on the armrest and his chin in his hand.

Rhen paused. *Am I protesting against my own creation?* He genuinely enjoyed coding by hand, but there was a kernel of truth to Roswell's words.

"Maybe. I feel responsible for how the technology gets used, and who it might hurt." He rubbed the back of his neck. "I'd rather shoulder that burden myself."

"You know it's not possible to do that. Once it was invented, there are tens of billions of people out there who will use it how you please. You're clever enough to know that you can't control them all."

"Well, I didn't say it was logical." Rhen gave a light laugh, rubbing his thighs. "I'm getting a bit distracted, though. I just came here for the test."

"Of course, and I'm happy to run it. I got a bit distracted too. You mentioned having reason to believe it is happening to you. You're seeing visions, I take it?"

"I think so, or at the very least, I want to rule it out." Rhen explained everything he could about seeing Rey around the base, including how Virtus hadn't recorded anything at all.

Roswell nodded. "Right, I think that's worth looking into. But keep in mind, the test isn't very conclusive. You'd have to be showing severe symptoms at the time of testing for it to register. You know that already, though."

"I do."

They ran through the test. As expected, it came back negative, but it was the only test available for digital synaesthesia. Afterwards, Rhen sighed and rubbed his forehead. His head was aching. *Is it from the implant or everything going on? I can't even tell.*

"You seem stressed," Roswell said. It probably wouldn't have taken a cog-psych degree to figure that out.

"Yeah, the project's not going as planned. And I've visited the subjects a few times. Watching the Kaur collapses is a bit stressful."

"You're eager to make progress so you stop having to watch it? Or you want to quit?"

"The first. If someone is deliberately sabotaging the code, making the collapses happen..." Rhen clenched his jaw. "I can't imagine anything worse. And I'm starting to suspect Rey is involved in it, somehow. Well, that's assuming I'm not just losing my mind."

"Hmm." Roswell leaned back in his chair, knitting his fingers together. "You're under a lot of stress, so keep that in mind. You don't have to have a rare condition to experience hallucinations — a lack of sleep can do it too. Anyway, I'm glad the test came back negative. Let me know if you experience any more symptoms.

"Thanks, I will."

***

Rhen dropped by Data Operations on the way back from the psychology appointment. He was sure he would find out nothing, but a sense of thoroughness led his footsteps. Inside, the desks were empty, and he got a cognitive ping. He accepted it, and the lemon-faced department head appeared in front of him.

"The department's closed. Is it important?" They said, arms crossed.

"Very. I've found evidence of widespread data poisoning in our models."

"Impossible. I'd never make a mistake like that. Are you sure it's not a problem with your coding?"

Rhen forced a smile. *Robert's echo had all the arrogance of the man himself.* "Yes, I'm *very* sure. I'm sending you the data now. It's very sophisticated, so it might be a bit much for an echo to handle—"

"I'll be fine. I'm sure it's not as sophisticated as you're making out." But there was a long pause. Robert's echo pursed their lips and sucked in their cheeks. "Right. I need to forward this to the actual Robert. *Very* high priority. No regular error like this should have passed by the winner of the Pinnacle Data Science Award."

Rhen snorted. The echo stared daggers at him. Clearing his throat, Rhen changed the subject. "By the way, I saw Rey come in here the other day. I'm worried about tampering." He provided the echo with the exact date and time. "If it's sabotage, that could explain what's going on."

The doppelganger's eyes lit up. A chance to assign blame elsewhere and save face was irresistible. "I'll look into that!" A pause. "Strange. There was an upload request at the time, but there was nobody in the office."

"Upload?" Rhen blinked. "You're sure you don't mean download? He'd need to put bad data in the system, not copy and take it."

"No, I'm certain. There's no official log of the download request, either, or who made it. The only reason I can tell is because there's a spike in our download charts." Rey's echo puffed out his chest. "I'm *always* certain when it comes to data."

Yeah, sure. A minute ago, you were saying data poisoning was impossible. But Rhen nodded and thanked the echo before he left, pondering on the turn of events as he returned to his office.

A spike in download traffic wasn't exactly a smoking gun. Data hiccupped all the time. But between that, the data poisoning, and what he'd personally witnessed, *something* was going on. The pieces didn't line up, but it was too much to be a coincidence. Rey was involved, somehow.

"Playing detective indeed." Rhen muttered, rubbing his temples. "I just want to code things. Why can't anything ever be simple?"

There was no point going to security again with so little new information, and he didn't really want them to bring up the *snogging* again. Until then, it was back to work and solving more everyday problems. There was one silver lining: the possibility of digital synaesthesia was looking less and less likely.

As Rhen booted up the code and reached out to type, he recalled the guttural fear he had experienced in Roswell's office about losing the use of his implant. His fingers hovered over the touchpad, refusing to make contact.

I should use what I have, while I have it. Plus, if we're going to make progress, I need to stop being so self-indulgent.

He wrote hundreds of lines worth of code in mere moments, then tore them apart with his thoughts. Extending and trimming, inching closer to perfection, creating the pathways for superior thought.

At times, it all became a bit of a blur. A joyous burst of creation and followed by cathartic refinement, each imperfection a riddle to be solved.

Outside of it, there was nothing else. Everything around him could have fallen away, the winds of passing time wearing down the world and turning it to sand, skyscrapers and bridges flattened.

However, a jabbing pain shot through his brain and shattered his thoughts, sending thousands of random characters spilling into his code.

"Ouch." He grabbed his head in both hands and massaged his temples. As he sucked in air through his teeth, the pain ebbed. That's how it always struck, like an assassin with a thin dagger; swift and without warning, before slinking back into the shadows.

His focus was gone.

Well, there goes a perfectly good streak. When he removed his hands from his face, they were covered in a small sheen of sweat. He took it as a sign to take five. He grabbed a refreshing drink, he mused upon the haiku he had read the other day.

There was a warning about data poisoning in the haiku. Could there be other hints elsewhere in the code?

Rhen went searching around for more of Alef's haiku-like messages in the code. It didn't take him long to find one, nestled in one of the libraries for mathematical processing.

// This one's a curly problem. If you get this, apply for the Sekai Mathematical Olympiad.

Alef wasn't kidding: the next problem was designed for seasoned cognicists, or perhaps pure math professors. Rhen strained over the problem for a solid thirty minutes. Suddenly, the answer hit him like a bolt of lightning, and the decryption worked. With the great challenge overcome, euphoria flooded through his veins.

What strange haiku had his predecessor left for him this time?

// Congratulations! Seriously, if you don't sign up for that Olympiad, I'll be sorely disappointed. You're a worthy successor to my work. Here's a haiku as your reward.
// Eyes wide, mind alert,
// Serpent's maze winding ahead,
// Saboteur is real.

The hair on Rhen's neck stood on end. There *was* a saboteur. Had Alef been aware of it before they were fired? Rhen tried to picture himself, sitting in his predecessor's shoes, writing these messages. Why hadn't he brought this up with security? Or had he done that, only to hit the same roadblocks Rhen had?

One thing was clear though: the messages were meant for him, or at the very least, Alef's successor. Someone was making sure the project failed, and the most likely suspect was the man skulking around, somehow invisible to even the most cutting-edge security AI.

If he wanted to prove it, he'd have to bring the evidence to the top — and succeed where his canny predecessor had apparently failed.

Chapter 9

That night, as Rhen was busy trying to figure out how to point a finger at Rey, he almost cut one off.

"If you're not going to let the kitchen cook on automatic, at least pay attention!" Nora swore, marching towards the medical kit. He wrapped his stinging finger in a tea towel, the Egyptian linen swiftly switching from white to crimson. In no time at all, it had been stained with an amorphous blotch reminiscent of a Rorschach test.

Amongst the chaos, three mechanical kitchen arms stuck out from the wall above the bench. Mimicking his mental state, they withdrew sheepishly and folded themselves up. The fastest to retreat was also the principal offender — it was tipped with a nano-thin blade capable of cutting through bone.

I wonder if it got that far? Rhen peeled back the fabric. The moment he looked downwards, his head spun. Pain shot through his skull from back to front, and he staggered towards a nearby seat. Everything was blurry.

"Don't look at it! Geez, you're worse than a kid. Here, let me fix it up." Nora stormed over and pinned down his arm as if she were wrestling a bull. A moment later — or maybe longer, everything was fuzzy — she wrapped a thin, gel-filled strip around his injury.

Her hands were shaking. She must have been more nervous than she'd let on. *Or maybe the sight of it has shaken her up as well?*

In an attempt to lighten the mood, he looked up and smiled. "A kid? You're literally adding insult to injury right now, you know."

"Maybe you could stand to be a little insulted. Cutting yourself due to a cognitive slip, I swear."

Nora handed him a pill, which he swallowed, and then she shone a small thumb-sized torch over his finger. It was a quick bout of photo-pharmacology; the drug would speed through his system and up to his hand, where the light would activate. There, it would speed up coagulation, cleanse the wound, and help create new tissue made up of collagen and extracellular matrix.

It also itched like a bastard. That was one more reason Nora was pinning down his arm. He bit his lower lip and tried to resist the urge to reach over with his other hand, since it was like a thousand ants were biting his wound. With emergency care, the cure felt worse than the cut.

"If you keep insisting on doing things manually, you're going to kill yourself one day, you know that right?" Nora said.

"Well, it wasn't completely hands-on, since we don't have the cutlery for that. How's the sushi?"

"You didn't bleed on it if that's what you mean, since that'd be an expensive waste of ingredients. I'm setting it to auto, and letting the machines do the cooking." She tapped the top of his finger, raising an eyebrow. Her hands were steady now. "You're sexy when you think, but don't overdo it. What were you so pensive about, anyway?"

"Thinking about the data poisoning. Are we sure we can't just lock Rey up somewhere?"

"No evidence." She wrapped his arm. "Even if you give up your memories, it's not enough. But since you reported it to security, it would have escalated to Alan — it's protocol for anything that uses the magic word 'sabotage'. I'm sure he'll have someone keeping a physical eye on Rey."

"Hmm, I'm not so trusting of those security folks."

"Me either, but it's what we've got. And you know, if someone does want you to fail, getting you so distracted you cut your hand off is a good start."

"That's a good point, but a bit too subtle for a saboteur to rely on."

Nora wrapped both her hands over his. As she stared into his eyes, he didn't feel pain in his finger at all.

"Listen to me, you are *not* Sherlock Holmes, okay? Don't let Casey lead you astray."

"Well, I programmed them, so wouldn't I be leading myself astray?" He quipped, and she smirked a little.

"I'll have none of your recursive logic, my starlight."

"My starlight? Is that what we've settled on for my pet name?"

She leaned in and kissed his ear, her warm breath washing over the wetness her lips left. He shivered right down to the base of his spine.

"You light up my life, and I love that twinkle in your eyes, so I'm sticking with it."

Well, I guess I can live with that.

The automated arms finished making the sushi as the couple were otherwise distracted. After five minutes, they packed the meal away in a refrigerated wall panel. It was clear it wouldn't get eaten anytime soon.

***

Rhen laid back on the impossibly soft sheets of Nora's bed, his muscles slick with sweat. Even though his limbs felt like lead, the desire to see her face won out, and he rolled to face her with considerable effort.

She was facing him with her fingers curled up, one of her golden-yellow eyes peeking over them like the sun peeking over a distant set of mountains. A yawn rumbled over the hills and the radiant sphere fluttered in and out of sight. It was setting, not rising.

His eyes trailed down the slope of her hands and towards her arms. But instead of spotting the telltale bump of fabric, they were exposed.

She's not wearing her forearm covers.

Between her wrist and elbow, there was a groove that ran around her arm with unerring symmetry, just over a millimetre wide and deep. As if to despoil the orderly line, it was bordered by pink scar tissue on one side, the one facing her elbow. The edges of the scar tissue curled and licked at her untainted skin like flames bursting forth from a pit.

"I wanted to show you," Nora said, her voice so low it was barely a whisper. "You can tell, can't you?"

"They're cybernetic," he said. *No groove like that is organic.* And then, as gently as possible, he asked the obvious question. "What happened?"

"People happened."

There was a pause. Rhen waited to see if she'd elaborate. After rubbing the groove in her forearm, she did.

"I had a robot dog named Felix. The model was cheap, but I'd modified a lot of it myself, just like you did with Casey. At the time, that dog was my only friend. Programming them was relaxing, and I liked running them through tests, teaching an old dog new tricks. No matter how hard my day was, they were always there to greet me."

She was staring at him, her gaze unwavering and her pupils small. This was no passive retelling; each word was delivered with consideration and importance at him.

He couldn't look away. He didn't dare to.

"Because I'd programmed Felix to be a bit different, it drew a lot of interest. On my block, I had these neighbours who kept insisting my dog was theirs. They'd wrecked their own model, and wanted mine as a replacement."

"I'm guessing you stood your ground."

"Right. They didn't like that much, so they downloaded a hack for that model. It had a lot of exploits, and I wasn't expecting it. When I came home and picked them up, they bit into my arm."

Shit. Rhen's heart sank down to somewhere below his stomach. She was holding her arms in front of her, and both were scarred in the same place.

"The hack was a loop command, wasn't it?" He asked. He wasn't sure he wanted to know the answer. His stomach churned.

"It was. They'd told it to bite my arms, but didn't tell them when to stop."

If Felix had been a regular dog, they would have bitten her and let go. A machine was different. It would do what it was told until the termination conditions were met, or it was destroyed.

"I'm so sorry." It was the only words he had. He wanted to weep on her behalf, the idea of her being in such pain hurt him — his heart felt like it was dying, constricting to safety. He cleared his throat. "I'm surprised you can work with machines after that."

"Oh, I don't blame Felix." Nora laughed, but it was a nervous little flutter, here and gone in an instant. "Machines just do what people program them to do. It's people who were responsible — *they're* the ones I find hard to trust."

That's true enough. He couldn't stand not holding her, comforting her. He reached out to grab her hands, and she didn't pull away. "I can see why you were worried when I cut my hand before. Thanks for sharing that story."

"That's okay. Telling that story used to wreck me, but I've gotten better at repeating it. It's still draining, though."

He rubbed his fingertips against hers. A dread realisation struck him, and his stomach sank all over again, falling into a pit so deep no light could reach it.

"You can't feel this at all, can you?"

"No." The edges of her eyes softened. "Don't worry, I still get the sensation of pressure, so I know when you're making contact. And I like it, even if it's only psychological."

That first time their fingers had danced in the cafeteria, he'd been so sure she'd felt it too. There was no sadness on her face, though, just a genuine smile. Touch was so important. Why had the world been so cruel as to take it from her? His blood broiled at the anger at it, at the people who had been so callous as to think it right.

He didn't ask if it had been racial. Somehow, he already knew the answer.

I shouldn't burden her with my pity. It'll just make it harder to move past it.

He sucked in a breath and shook it off. Instead, he reached behind her head and stroked the back of her neck.

"You are so strong that it scares me. One day, I hope to be even half as strong as you." He kissed the skin on her nape, right below where the Rosetta was. "You know, I was thinking about a device that could sit here and translate signals for the nervous system. It'd help permanently fix things like Delta's chronic pain syndrome, or allowing people with prostheses to feel — people like you, and also the hybrids. Once we're done with this project, I think it'd be a great next step."

Nora laughed again, but this time it was full of that familiar music, ringing in the air with genuine melody. "Looking to shake up the world again?"

"I just want to shake up your world."

"I love you."

As the words hung in the air, a surge of primal fear rose within Rhen. His heart raced and his palms grew clammy as his mind struggled to process the declaration. Part of him wanted to reciprocate, to smoothly declare his own burning love and affection, but his throat closed up, constricted. Something was wrapped around it, a nameless fear.

No, it had a name: *Betrayal.* He was hesitant, fearful of vulnerability. The pain of failure from his last marriage, hearing Iona say she had slept with someone else. It formed a serpent, and that serpent was choking the breath out of him, even as his heart screamed for it to stop.

Silence. Agonising silence. Eventually, Nora bit her lip, and pressed her hands against his chest. They were cybernetic. Vulnerable.

"It's okay, don't worry, you don't need to say it back. I just wanted you to know."

She rolled over, her body hunched, as if she had been kicked in the stomach. And even though they were inches apart, Rhen sensed a great gulf had suddenly formed between them. The distance was all too familiar.

Chapter 10

The first and greatest mistake Rhen made was trying to sleep on it. He had secretly hoped that if they got some rest, things would be easier in the morning.

It wasn't.

When he woke, the atmosphere between them was more bloated and awful, underpinned by awkward silence. It had only been broken twice: when Nora had thanked him for making breakfast, and when she'd said goodbye.

Part of him broiled inside. Nora had said he didn't need to say it back, but *clearly* he did. It was patently unfair; why say it if it wasn't true?

On the other hand, not saying it had clearly wounded her. She had been blinking back tears, and the very thought of it made his insides twist up with discomfort, like some greater, punitive force was sticking their hands inside and wringing them on her behalf. *Suffer as she suffered,* it cried. Echoing indeed.

And so, he asked the million-dollar question, the one that any fight could be broiled down to: *Am I the asshole here?*

Sadly, there was nobody to ask. As he took a mental inventory of his social network, he realised he was solitary in his struggles, and a lonely pang tugged at his heart. No friends, only co-workers, and subordinates at that. Nobody he could trust not to spread the word around about his relationship. His only two friends were Nora and Casey, and the latter wouldn't be much help.

It was the story of his life: he was always better at talking to machines than humans. Just like Nora, he found the latter harder to trust.

And when you get down to it, trust is pretty much my whole problem.

He worked through the day in a fugue state. When he clocked off, he didn't want to go to Kutjera or his apartment, so he wandered the corridors. He found himself in the car parking lot after getting patted down by security, staring at the sleek Elysium that brought him here. It was covered in a thick layer of red-rust sand, as if it had been buried alive in the fiery desert.

"That's a travesty," Rhen murmured, pulling out a hose from the wall and washing it off. He buffered and waxed it, cleaning up the sleek car far easier than his own problems. And then, he opened the car door and slipped inside. Virgil's avatar popped up on the console.

"Hey there, Rhen! Going for a drive today?"

"Yeah, it's been too long. Can you switch to manual control?"

"Sure. You've heard the warning before, so I won't bother repeating it." After accepting Virgil's ping, he drove the car up and out of Mirage.

The colours of the sunset were distorted and twisted by the optic gap, like a painting come to life, the bold brilliant yellow of the sun stretching and distorting like an oil streak across a canvas of burnt tiger orange, undulating like a cosmic serpent. The black of the barren desert seeped up into the sky, like a hundred shadow puppets dancing across the horizon's edge, acting out an unseen script by an even more elusive master.

As he passed over the threshold of Mirage and left the base, the world seeped into normal shapes again, transforming into a vast expanse bathed in a warm orange glow. It was no less gorgeous, and all in all, far easier to drive through. The road was unerringly straight, and even though there were potholes, the car's suspension was so fine-tuned there was no jolt as they went over them.

Soon, the sky was littered with a beautiful canvas of stars, glittering across the crown of the heavens. The solar plants glimmered as well, blinking lights on the top of the metal monoliths warning low-flying craft of their presence, while a glittering ring at the base lured the trucks in to refill their stock.

When they were far enough out, Rhen pulled over the car and reclined the seat, sitting in silence and his thoughts. Nobody could contact him out here. The solar gap made sure of that. Short of being in the Antarctic, he was as alone as he could be, which brought both relief and profound sadness. Still, there was one thing that lingered at the forefront of his mind, over and over.

Why did I freeze up? I'm not afraid of commitment, am I? After all, we're practically living together already.

But the moment she'd taken that step forward, he'd instantly taken a step back. Something inside him had recoiled, a fear of pain.

If only I could show Nora what was going on inside my head, like with the prototypes. Hell, it'd be nice to know what was going on in there myself.

When he was young, one of his friends had asked him what he would want, if he could have any superpower. Most kids wanted to be able to time travel or fly. His friend had explained she wanted to turn invisible.

"Think about it, you could sneak in wherever you want, take whatever you want. Nobody could stop you," she said, then sipped on her juice box. "How about you?"

"I wish I could share my thoughts with others," he said. "Like, my memories and feelings."

"Don't you mean read their minds? I think you've got it backwards."

"No, because then everyone would get where I'm coming from. Like, if someone made fun of you, they'd never do it if they knew how you felt."

"You're weird, Rhen."

He was. That's why he wanted everyone to get where he was coming from. Being the smart kid, the one who was always thinking a bit more sideways than everyone else, was like having a target on his back.

In an age when people didn't live in locked up, climate-controlled houses, he probably would have been physically bullied. It would have been simpler, more straightforward. Unfortunately, with over a century of practice, kids had lifted digital harassment to an art form — they could hire bots to do it for them.

Cruelty had become as simple as set-and-forget.

The bully bots were merciless. They scraped every piece of communication he had ever made, built up a profile of him, then used attack patterns refined by data from hundreds of thousands of victims the world over.

Locked in his house, every holographic message he answered was filled with hate. At the start, they spewed out slurs, death threats, and body shamed him, all while mimicking the person it would hurt coming from the most. When that got old, it tried projecting holographic scenes designed to shock and traumatise.

"I'm going to smack you around until you die!" The image of his father screamed. It then showed him exactly what that would look like.

After that, every single device in the house was shut down.

The whole house was infected, and even a factory reset didn't kill it. It had penetrated right down to the base code. All they could do was wait for a replacement system to be installed.

The damage had already been done, though.

For two weeks, the house was silent. Even the holographic plants were gone. For the first few days, all he could do was sit in his room and replay the vile words and images in his head.

His parents tried to spend time with him, but given what he'd seen, he was more than a bit jumpy, even though he knew it wasn't them. In the end, they'd found a work-around.

"We're letting you open your Christmas present early. Don't worry, you're still going to get one," his parents said. When he had opened it, it was a built-it-your-self robot kit. "You can program it yourself, and there's no chance it's infected. Just don't connect it to the internet."

He hadn't. Working on that robot had saved him. He'd named it Bobby because its head was always moving up and down, and even after the home system was replaced, he'd kept talking to and working on it.

They never did find who was behind it, even after flagging it with the authorities. Bully bots were illegal, but they were also endemic. It wasn't that hard for a kid to get their hands on one, and once they were triggered, they were designed to avoid detection.

To this day, Rhen was firmly convinced that if the perpetrator had truly understood how much harm they'd caused, they never would have done it.

I'm pretty sure Nora would say I was naive to think they wouldn't, but she's always more cynical about these kinds of things. Well, after that night, now I know why.

He knew why he was thinking about that incident now. Just like her, he'd experienced pain inflicted by machines controlled by callous people. He'd worked through it — no small amount of therapy had been involved — but there were still scars. And after his marriage, he was vulnerable, his heart exposed, each vein thrumming like an instrument to every stroke of her hands, every aching smile, every teardrop in her eyes.

She made his heart sing, but she could also whip his heart into a discordant melody, more than Iona ever could.

It was exhilarating. It was terrifying. It was, in all honesty, love.

"I need to talk to her. Maybe share some of this stuff," he murmured, staring at the stars.

When Rhen drove back to the base and hopped out of the Elysium, it was dirty again. Irked by the blemish on such a fine vehicle, he sighed and washed it off. As he stared at the dust beneath the wheels, his head hurt. Doing the bare minimum, he packed up and went downstairs to find Nora, heading to Kutjera first.

As he approached the entrance, Rey was walking the opposite way down the corridor and smiled as he saw him. It was the last person Rhen wanted to see. Rhen tried to raise the corners of his mouth, but felt like he was lifting hundred-kilogram weights. After straining in vain, he gave up and settled for a curt nod.

"Whoa! You look like you've eaten a lemon. What's the problem, champ?" Rey's whole face reacted from raised brow to gaping mouth, but the edges of his eyes remained crinkled, and there was a sparkle in them that was like a cat spotting a nearby mouse.

I bet he used a bully bot as a kid. I bet he's the sort who still would.

"I'm going to get some dinner. When I'm hungry, I look grumpy."

"Oh really. Well, keep up the good work. Or, well, keep up the *work*, at least."

Screw it. Maybe it's time to be more direct.

"I've seen you sneaking around," Rhen said, furrowing his brow. "You weren't meant to be in the testing area without permission, but I saw you there."

Rey blinked, and his jaw muscles visibly flexed. "No idea what you're talking about. You must have me mistaken with someone else."

"Downloading things without permission? Are you behind the data poisoning?"

Rey took a step forward, a sharp glint in his eyes. He was smiling with those all too white teeth; the kind only the wealthy had at his age. A primitive part of Rhen's brain screamed that he was about to bite him, but the man's teeth remained closed in that joyous grimace.

"That's a very serious accusation. I hope you've got *evidence* for that. Otherwise, I might sue you for slander or workplace harassment. Unfounded rumours do damage, you know. I know a few rumours about *you* as well."

Rhen's heart skipped a beat. But as he stared into Rey's eyes, which were sizing him up for the slightest reaction, he knew with certainty: *he's bluffing*. The jab was meant to scare, to threaten, to show he *did* have secrets. To shift the topic from him on to Rhen.

"Nice try," Rhen said. "But you've got nothing. I'll find out what you're up to."

"Then you'll have nothing as well." And then Rey turned and walked away. Only when the other man disappeared down the end of the corridor did Rhen let the knots in his shoulder unravel.

A whisper was uttered somewhere from the air in front of him, broken up by static.

<Nice try, brains trust, but you won't be able to stop me from destroying your project.>

Rhen froze again. Even though it was broken up, it was unmistakably Rey's voice.

A cognitive message? But he didn't even ping me!

He tried to swallow, but couldn't. He was riveted to the spot by heart-pounding terror as surely as if Rey had stabbed nails through his feet. If he had, it would have been a lot less terrifying.

The need for permission was designed into every aspect of the Rosetta. The team had built it that way intentionally, not only to prevent abuse but because it was essential. Sekai would never have been able to sell the general public on the implant otherwise. As a result, the manufacturing process was strict and government audits were common.

But is it really impossible, or just very hard?

After Rhen had remembered how to breathe, he made a beeline for the cafeteria.

***

Kutjera was oppressively busy. Every brushed shoulder or closely gathered grouping of people drew his eye and filled his limbs with nervous energy. When he spotted Nora, it was like a needle of adrenaline was shot into his already racing heart. *She's still here. Good.*

She was sitting at a booth with Shana, the tips of her fingers knitted together, barely poking out from her sleeves. Every so often they convulsed like a boat lifted up by an invisible wave, only to fall back down on the table again. She was at the mercy of those tides, at least until she found safe harbour.

There were some very large alcoholic drinks at their table — margaritas, by the looks of things — but since the automated servers removed them as soon as they were empty, there was no telling how many they'd had.

He wanted to talk to Nora alone, not in the middle of a meal with a friend. *I just need to wait until after she's finished, and maybe catch her in the corridor.*

Fate had other plans.

"Hey, Rhen!" Shana waved at him, her words slurred. *Well, that answers how many drinks they've had.* When he returned the gesture, the diminutive department head beckoned him over with a scooping hand. There was no retreat to be had. Not without it looking like a snub.

I'll just go over, but I won't linger. I'll make up some kind of excuse.

But when he approached the table, Shana kept reeling him in with her hand.

"Sit down, sit down! It's not like there's no room," Shana said.

"I was going to go through some work when I was eating."

"Nonsense! It's terrible to work through dinner. It's bad for your brain to keep going non-stop, even yours."

He slid in next to Shana, who skirted around the circular booth and sat facing them both, like a referee. Nora's curls covered the left side of her face, which was also the same side facing her friend. Her solitary eye locked with his, softening at the edges.

There was a mental ping, and he fell over himself to answer it.

<Well, this is awkward,> Nora said, lips unmoving. <Sorry to drag you into this. Shana's had a few.>

<It's fine, I really wanted to talk anyway. I really want to sort this whole thing out.>

<I think I'd like that. Let's catch up later tonight. But let's stop messaging, or Shana's going to get angry.>

<I think we're too late.>

Shana's brow was crinkled up, and she was staring at them both.

"Rude! Talking by CMS when I'm right here — at least make it a three-way sesh. Come on, let's eat," she huffed. "I never get to eat dinner with Nora these days, she's always eating in her room or at her desk or whatever, so lunch is the only time I get. That, and when I come up to repair her real staff."

Nora narrowed her eyes at Shana. "Hey, don't say that out loud! They might hear you — it's bad for morale."

"Eh, morale is already pretty bad. Did she ever tell you what I built for her, and she keeps in her closet? Or are you not up to that yet?"

"Shana!"

"Sorry, sorry. I'll leave that between the two of you." Shana laughed, brow now relaxed. "Geez, it sure would be nice if we got the project done, though. I'd like to be *remembered* for something. I'm not a prog, like you both. Just another reason to be jealous."

"Jeez, you just won't quit today, will you?" Nora said, resting her elbow on the table and cupping the side of her face, all the while shooting Rhen a sympathetic smile.

Seems like someone had figured it out already. Rhen wasn't surprised, given Shana was Nora's best friend. More than worried, his chest swelled with hope at the smile, and what it represented.

As they sipped their drinks, Shana's hands shook. Her margarita glass slipped from her hand, and the icy slush spilled into Rhen's lap, freezing all the way down his leg.

"Oh shit, I'm sorry!" She said.

"It's no problem!" Rhen winced, calling for an absorbent cloth. A small chute appeared in the table, and he mopped it up. Still, it looked like he'd soiled himself. "Guess Nora's not the only one with tremors today."

"Yeah, maybe I should skip the next drink," Shana chuckled. "I've probably had enough."

***

The evening ended not long after that, and Nora and Rhen escorted Shana back to her apartment. After that, they returned to Nora's place, where she sat down on the couch, fingers knitted together beneath her sleeves. He got down on one knee, running his fingers down her arms where she could feel them, until they reached and laced between her digits.

"I'm sorry for being an idiot," he said. "You opened up to me, and then I said *nothing*. I got scared and pulled back, and I should have told you how I was feeling.

"No, I'm sorry, I was coming down on you too hard. You weren't ready, and I got impatient."

"I love you, you know." And he felt it, truly and absolutely, his heart swelling as he stroked her fingers. Even though she couldn't feel it. But he locked eyes with hers, so she could feel his gaze, the intensity of it, the affection in his eyes.

"You don't need to say it just to say it—"

"No, I mean it. I'm not saying it because I'm scared of losing you, which I *am*. Eleanora Hughes, I am absolutely head-over-heels in love with every single part of you. You are brilliant, soft-hearted, determined, and passionate. Your genius constantly stuns me, along with every other part of you, and I'll never probably stop reeling. You might be a bit pessimistic and I might be a bit optimistic, but between the two of us, I feel like we *probably* make a fully balanced person."

"Way to neg the landing." She said, laughing, but with tears in her eyes. "But I get it; I love you too, my starlight."

After that, they intertwined more, almost as if making up with fierce hunger for the brief absence. There were soft spoken words, and stories shared, including Rhen's own tale of mechanical trauma. All the while, Nora stroked his chest with unfeeling fingers and a full heart. It was well and truly late by the time they'd shared almost everything there was to share.

***

That morning, the high-pitched eclectic beats and excited singing of a Japanese algo-pop star roused Rhen from his sleep. He groaned and pulled the pillow over his ears, trying to drown out the sharp, intrusive beat.

"It's too early in the morning for this."

It only lasted a moment before the algorithm adjusted to the presence of *two* people in the room, and dulled the beat accordingly.

"Can you add me permanently to the system?" He asked. Nora rolled over and rubbed her eyes.

"Adding you will mess up my preferences, though, and add lots of white noise and rain to it. Can't you just learn to love it?"

"Impossible. It's too up-tempo, too many beats per minute. Not my jam at all."

"Makes a great alarm clock, though."

Checking his own watch, it was still early — only five in the morning. Still enough time to sneak back before the morning rush. After cognitively checking her door-cam to make sure the hallway was clear, he hurried across the corridor, and back into his room.

"Sorry buddy, I was out late."

Silence. Rhen furrowed his brow. Usually, Casey was wheeling up to the door, making some quip or another. It was part of his programming, after all. But things were dead silent.

When he walked into the bedroom, there were parts strewn all over the room, and two halves of a suitcase. An arm was broken up, and the opposable thumbs bent.

"Casey!"

Rhen's chest tightened like both his lungs were being squeezed in a vice, and he dropped to his hands and knees, searching desperately. With frenzied fingers, he found Casey's core processor — smashed into tiny pieces.

"What in the hell happened to you?"

Looking up, almost nothing else had been stolen or tampered with, but the one other thing that had made his blood run cold. The hologram hiding his breaker was inactive, and the device, while still there, had been turned ever so slightly.

His mind's firewall had been tampered with. If they had breached his thoughts, he was a dead man walking.

Chapter 11

"Well, it looks like someone accessed your firewall," Kyle said, running his hand over the shelves. "At least, according to Virtus, who's acting a bit spotty right now. We'll find whoever did it, and bring them up on property damage."

"Not property damage. *Attempted homicide.*" Rhen said, venom in his tongue. He was sitting on the seat now, his foot tapping without cease, Nora rubbing his back.

"Right, sure. I must have got confused with your, uh, smashed up buddy."

He bit back his anger, sitting back as the security chief and the other members of the team picked up pieces of Casey. It was like they were going through the motions, doing things for the sake of looking busy, and hiding their own ineptitude. His temple throbbed.

Without an AI, the security goons were helpless. Every question they asked of Virtus came back the same. No video. No logs. *Nothing.* Only a gap between four and five AM, before which everything was fine in his apartment, and then it suddenly wasn't.

He wanted to scream at how relaxed they were.

<They don't get it, because they don't have pro-grades,> Nora said, but cognitively, as if reading his mind. <They don't get how *violating* it is. It was never drilled it into them every day of their lives, how someone could destroy who you are if you slipped up. They don't think about machines like you do, either.>

<I know.> The rhythm of his foot tapping sped up. <When do you think the results will come back? I want to know if I was tampered with.> *If I'm going to die.*

<Soon. Doctor Roswell's put a rush on it — he gets how important it is.>

Until then, he self-monitored his thoughts, waiting, obsessively checking for any sign of a Kaur collapse. Was he going to start repeating himself, like Bee? Like Sukhvir Kaur?

When Rhen had found Sukh convulsing on the floor, he'd had to call his family. At the funeral, Sukh's wife had quoted Max von Pettenkofer.

"'Even if I had deceived myself and the experiment endangered my life, I would have looked Death quietly in the eye for mine would have been no foolish or cowardly suicide; I would have died in the service of science like a soldier on the field of honour.'"

There was pride in his voice as it rained over the West Brisbane Cemetery, and they'd lowered Sukh into the dirt.

At the time, Rhen had wondered who had found Edwin Katskee in 1936. History said the physician had taken a large dose of cocaine to test out the local anaesthetic. All they'd found the next morning was a dead body, and nearly incoherent ramblings on the wall.

"Eyes mildly dilated. Vision excellent." "Advise all inquisitive M.D.'s to lay off this stuff." The last word written was "Paralysis", which tapered off into a wavy scrawl towards the floor. The antidote lay just out of reach.

Who had cashed that check, I wonder? Later on, he'd checked Saga. It had been his father who found him, wondering why his son hadn't returned home.

"Who has access to the room?" Kyle asked Rhen, but when he didn't answer, he turned to Nora.

"Me, Casey, and anyone with admin access," she answered. "That'd be everyone in security, and Virtus, of course."

"Of course. Well, it wasn't any of *us*," Kyle said, rubbing his nose. "Any chance the robot did it to itself?"

Who would have found me if I'd died when I first implanted the Rosetta? Would it have been Luvia? If I fall apart, will Nora be the one to see it?

"No, not unless someone put them up to it," Nora said. "Coded AI don't act on their own, they need a human catalyst. But before you go wild and start pointing fingers, the lock isn't *infallible*. A malicious AI with the right programming could hack it."

"It's too bad the dismantled unit was smashed apart, it would have been useful to check out the recording," Kyle said, turning to Rhen once again. "You got a backup?"

Nora prodded his side. Rhen shivered and looked up.

"I've got a backup of Casey, but it's point-in-time and incremental," he said. "Runs at midnight every night. I didn't think there'd be much point doing it live."

"Ah, pity," Kyle gave a half-hearted shrug. "We could have gotten a good look at whoever did it."

Rhen was pretty sure he knew who did. Rey could walk around without being detected by Virtus, and he had confronted the man head on the day before. Apparently he could hack his door as well.

Whatever Rey was doing, Rhen had become a threat.

No better way to erase someone with a prog than tampering with their mind, and watching it all fall down like a house of cards.

***

"I don't want you to be around if I fall apart," Rhen said to Nora. She furrowed her brow.

"Don't be stupid. You're staying with me while you wait for the news. You are *not* waiting alone huddled in a dark room. And Vi's in charge of your team for the day, since you're in no state to work."

In the end, she practically dragged him into her apartment. Apparently, nobody questioned him moving his things into Nora's place, including all of Casey's parts. When he stopped to think of it, it made sense; who wanted to stay in the place that had been so easily broken into? It didn't feel safe, and she was right, he *would* have struggled on his own.

A small mercy was that they had something to do with all that time off. Casey needed to be reassembled, and so they sat side by side, piecing the robot back together. Nora had literally changed her tune on playing his algorithmic music, and lo-fi pop was pulsing through the speakers, providing much-needed white noise. Rhen found so long as his hands were busy, his mind was as well.

"Can you hand me the spark plug pliers?" Nora asked, and he complied. She was as good with machines as him. No, better. Between the two of them, they were speeding through the task; perhaps a little too fast, since at this rate, he'd have to find something else to occupy himself.

It was time for small talk.

"So, what's the deal with those statues over there?" He gestured to one of Nora's many dark and glistening resin figures, each about ten centimetres high, lining her walls. "I know Anubis, but not those ones. I'm better with Greek myth than Egyptian." That it was mostly because of Iona's love of it went unsaid.

"What, Thoth?"

"Yeah, the one with the bird face, and the book in his hand. Looks like he's having a good time reading it."

"God of wisdom, writing, science, judgement. Basically, all the good things. Took notes on when a dead person's heart was exactly even."

"And the feminine-looking one with the jackal head and the snake body for legs? Kind of looks like her scales are glistening."

"That's Kebechet, daughter of Anubis. Cool lady, literally: her name means cooling water, which is why she's holding a jar, to refresh and purify the dead. She's got a body of stars, so she just, you know, slithers through the cosmos."

"Sleeping beneath the earth, we've got a whole tomb thing going," Rhen smiled, but it was an effort, his cheeks and brow aching. "You didn't strike me as religious."

"Oh, I'm absolutely not. But like what they symbolise: knowledge, transformation, rebirth; and you know, being sleek, black, and beautiful."

Clearly he had a type: woman who were interested in historical things.

"Well, you'd know something about being sleek, black, and beautiful."

"Of course I would!" Nora preened. "And you know, I also sometimes like to look at images of death, and think about of all those wise individuals lost to the past, before the Rosetta at least, and not forget." She cleared her throat. "Ah, sorry, it's sort of like my algo-pop; maybe it's not as reassuring to you."

"It's no problem." He fiddled with the wrench in his hand. "It's not exactly the being dead that worries me, it's the dying, the disintegration of myself. The 'I am' becoming 'I am not', even if I'm still alive." The image of Sukh, lying on the floor, flicked before his eyes. "And I guess, whoever sees that, I feel like I'd be cursing them."

"You're going to be *fine*," she said, tapping his arm with the pliers. "Plus, there's no point thinking about it; you'll just stress yourself out."

"You're so confident I'll be okay."

"I am." But she didn't elaborate on where her confidence came from, unshakable as it was. Perhaps it was a necessity, since she was working just as fiercely on Casey. "At least you backed up your data a while back. I've got to remember to do the same. Us Pro-grades have got to keep on top of our self-care."

"Did you know very few people with a pro-grade consciousness have children?" Rhen said, handing her the next tool. "My dad tries to hide it, but he's rankled by the idea I didn't want any. Maybe it's because I feel like I'm already leaving a legacy, of a sort — an AI version of me stuck inside a box somewhere, disgruntled that he can't taste Beef Wellington."

"Good thing *I* don't want any, or that would have been a bombshell," she smirked. "I'm the same. Maybe that's another reason for keeping the statues around; to psych myself up for that transformation."

"Yeah. I'm glad at least there's one other person with a prog here on base who knows what I'm going through."

***

In the end, Nora was right; when Doctor Roswell personally came over to let him know the results, there were no signs of Kaur Collapse.

"Your cognitive profile has deviated a little bit from your baseline, but not due to tampering," he said, handing him his breaker device back. "Just keep an eye out and let me know about anything too unusual."

Rhen sighed deep from his soul, all the nervous tension spilling out of his body. It was all he could do to stop from shaking, or crying. There would be time for that later.

"I've been having more headaches, if that's important. Collapsed at least once from them. The attacks seem to be happening more often."

Roswell furrowed his brow, adding more grooves to the tawny and weathered expanse. "Hmm, I can't say if they're related or not. But if you do feel a headache coming on, stop whatever you're doing immediately, and go for a walk. If you can't walk, just close your eyes and listen to the noise and sensations of things around you. Be in the present. Works great for stress as well."

"Sound advice."

"Just remember to take it easy. I know many cognicists don't know the word, but it *is* important, especially after an incident like the one you just had." And then Roswell left. The second the door was closed, Nora came up and stroked his arm.

"It was good of him to come visit in person, since he could have easily called you."

"Yeah, he's good people," Rhen said, rubbing his eyes. "I feel mean saying it, but his bright orange VariHair hurts my eyes, though. He could tone down the hex a *little*."

"I think it's meant to give him a warm disposition, colour association and all that. You heard him, you just need a bit more *sun* in your life." She ran her fingers through her corkscrew hair, and within seconds the colored strands transformed to become radiant and luminous. "What do you think, feeling a bit brighter?"

Rhen laughed, and for the first time in twenty-four hours, it sounded true. "With you, always. Not going for your Kebechet blue anymore?"

"You're right, I'll change back — can't have Roswell thinking I'm stealing his look."

***

Rhen was still under threat, and so things weren't over. He needed to go to the top. And so, he found himself in Alan's office, nursing a glass of water — he'd had too much coffee already since the incident, he was completely wired — and waiting for the CEO to appear.

Through the windows, Rhen gazed out at the Nagano snow fields, so realistic that it felt like he was standing on a solitary peak encased entirely in glass. A single door behind him acted as a portal to another world. Jagged mountain peaks surrounded him, scraping at the baby-blue sky and shrouded in a dusky haze of cold. Amidst the snowy landscape, a tawny fox padded through the snow.

It was a cognitive reflection, as the room had pinged Rhen when he'd arrived. When Alan arrived, he was as cool as the scenery, sitting down like a snowflake gracefully landing upon the chair. Every inch of his suit fit him effortlessly, as if it were his second skin, his purpose — to remove his tie would be to remove some essential part of him, and leave him somehow maimed. In a moment of fancy, Rhen imagined him sleeping in it, only to wake with it completely pressed.

The scenery didn't change at all, the algorithm ignoring Alan's entirely. *Must be built to put staff and visitors at ease, not himself.* He had met department heads in Keihanna who had used a similar technique. It was funny how the visiglass and Rosetta, two independent technologies, had intertwined into such a recent social cue. It was even stranger to think he was part of the catalyst.

"I'm so sorry to hear about the invasion of your apartment," Alan said in his gravelly tone, which despite its ruggedness, still managed to sound emotionally flat. "It was a complete violation of not only your space, but your mind. Deeply regrettable."

"Yeah, it's shaken me up a bit, but I'm coping. That's actually what I'm here to talk to you about, but before that, I'd like to bring something to your attention."

"Sure thing, whatever you need."

Rhen let his boss know about his relationship with Nora.

"Is it a voluntary and consensual relationship between both parties?" Alan neutrally intoned.

"What?" Rhen blinked. "Yes, yes, of *course*."

"Do you understand and agree that the relationship will not impact your work performance, the results of the study, and you will act professionally in the workplace without public display of affection?"

"Yes, I do."

"I've sent some agreements to both of you to that effect, and you just need to sign them. Is there anything else you want to talk about?"

And that was that. Rhen slumped in his chair, the air going right out of him. "I've got to say, I'm a bit surprised at how, well, *matter of fact* you're taking this. Two of your department heads are seeing each other in a high-profile experiment."

"It's really not a problem." Alan said, grabbing his own drink. "One out of ten couples meet in the workplace, and people spend four times as much time with work colleagues than they do with friends. Romantic entanglements are fairly common. I wouldn't know of course, being aromantic. Or rather, you could say I'm married to my job."

Nora's pretty married to hers too. Rhen had gone in with her consent, but it didn't mean he wasn't worried about the outcome. *Well, better not look a gift horse in the mouth. This'll make the next part easier.*

"Well, the other thing I needed to talk to you about is I have reason to believe Rey is undermining the project," Rhen said. "And I believe he was the one who trashed my apartment."

"That's a serious accusation." Alan leaned back in his chair, knitting his fingers. "Do you have any proof?" It was almost exactly what Rey had asked. A bead of sweat ran down Rhen's neck.

"Well, I've got my own cognitive memory recordings of him in both testing and data handling. Both times, Virtus didn't pick it up. I've also got a recording of a confession he made that he was trying to destroy my project, which he made cognitively. I didn't have time to share it until now. There's also a spike in upload data when he was in data handling, but nobody else was about."

"I'll need everything you've got. All of that is very concerning."

Rhen handed over the footage, and Alan took his time to watch them. Afterwards, the CEO swivelled his chair to face the glass windows behind him completely hidden from sight by his high-backed chair. A long pause followed.

Rhen tapped his finger against his cup, tension rising in his legs. It was all he could do not to tap them.

"This is very problematic. We'll question Rey, and have security keep an eye on him. If Virtus can't see what's going on, we need human eyes. I'll take Virtus's higher functions offline in the meantime, and run some diagnostics. The cameras will still work, but obviously something is wrong, since the footage doesn't match." Alan turned around and crossed his fingers. "We can't just kick him off the base, not without more proof."

"*More* proof? He messaged me saying he was going to destroy the project."

"I sympathise, but Rey Keyes is the Chief Investment Advisor for Glycon. I picked him out because he has a talent for persuasion—" And Alan emphasised the word, as if to telegraph there was another, more *suitable* word for it. "—that has got us lots of financial support from the board, and Sekai. He is the type of man who life has taught him that if you get hit, you hit back. How do you think he'd respond to the proof we have?"

Rhen paused, and thought hard: imagining what it would be like to be Rey left a bitter taste in his mouth. But picturing himself under that slimy skin, simulating it in his mind, an unpleasant fork in the road quickly became visible.

"Claim I faked my memory recordings, since there's no other witnesses. Say I was trying to get rid of him, frame him, because he was trying to hold me accountable for the project's progress. Or call me unhinged because of my implant, under too much stress and seeing things."

Alan nodded. "That's my read on it. I believe you, but as I said, we need more proof. I'm sorry I can't do more. At least if he's being watched, he won't be able to do any more damage."

Rhen nodded and stood up. Logically, it was the best outcome he could have hoped for, with the evidence he had. "So, what do I do now?"

"Go back to work, don't let him win. It's vital that we successfully test your theory." Alan's grey-green eyes locked on his, drilling in with invisible will. "An artificial superintelligence — something that surpasses humans as we know it — is right on the horizon. We need to make it here, where it cannot be made with malicious intent, or it will be created elsewhere. We don't want this to go the way of hostile AI and bully bots."

Rhen shivered. "Tell me about it. That's my biggest fear. Well, besides someone tampering with my brain in my sleep."

"Well, I believe in you. That's why you're here, you're the only one that can make it happen."

"Well, I don't know about *that*. I think anyone could, we're just the only ones putting in the research." Rhen rubbed the back of his neck, running his fingers over the scar tissue.

"I think you're selling yourself short. Perspective is a unique talent in and of itself. So long as nobody's getting in your way, I have little doubt you'll eventually succeed." Alan stood up. "Just so you know, I'll be taking a few weeks off soon, taking a hiatus. While I'm gone, I'm putting my echo in charge."

"Still haven't found a good 2IC yet?" Rhen said, happier to talk about lighter, more mundane matters. "I think Nora's a good choice, but I'm obviously biassed."

"Actually, she's my other go-to, but she has her own responsibilities to deal with. It's hard to find someone solid to rely on, who wants to come live out in the desert *and* meets the classification criteria; I trust you and the other department heads to manage in my absence."

***

After speaking to Alan, it was like a metric ton had been lifted off his shoulders. His life was suddenly uncluttered and straightforward, which was precisely how he liked it. He could entrust the whole Rey business to someone else, and his relationship with Nora no longer felt like a sword of Damocles hanging over their heads.

Despite Rhen's initial concern that the absence of forbidden fruit might fizzle out their romance, it blossomed instead, now that it had the freedom to breathe. They could talk to people about it, and while they tried to keep their public displays of affection to a level others could tolerate, they still exchanged meaningful looks, and furtive foot brushings beneath the table. Outside of work, there was no need to hide it at all.

His own proxy device was stored next to Nora's in her holographic wall safe. For those with progs, it was tantamount to marriage: what was a ring of metal when someone could hold your very mind in their hands? And yet, they had already shared their vulnerabilities, licked each other's wounds. She didn't wear her arm sleeves at all when they were at home — it really was 'home' now — and her eyes shined whenever she smiled. Her hands still fidgeted in public around anyone but him, since Alan still was away.

In the meantime, Rhen focused fully on the project, just as Alan asked. The team worked hard and passionately, full of the joy of creating something new and cutting edge. Excited chatter filled their spare moments. Personally, he felt sharper and smarter than he ever did before. Dr Roswell had a theory during his regular check-in.

"All the happiness you're feeling — all the dopamine and serotonin — is probably improving your brain's neuroplasticity: your brain's ability to grow, expand, and improve. That, or you're experiencing an onset of mania," he chuckled.

All he knew was he was on a roll, and he hadn't felt this good since he was working on the Rosetta with his team and Luvia. With that in mind, it felt like lightning could strike the same place twice, and all he had to do was reach out his hands and harness it.

And for once, they were progressing. Not only was A-1 much further along than when the project started, another prototype was now catching up. Rhen was not surprised to find out it was Bee. These days, during his visits with the hybrid AI, they seemed more eager to test him than the other way around.

"Alright, the value for this model is 0.7195, interesting!" Bee exclaimed, giving him an impish stare. "Now it's your turn, I'll send you some data, and you calculate the value—"

"It doesn't work like that," Rhen protested. But Bee had already slid the data device back across the table. "I couldn't possibly calculate things like that. I'm not a hybrid."

"Come on, give it a shot. Humour me." Bee's eyes, jade-green today, were glinting. Aies synthetic hair was like a sandy waterfall, tied back in a ponytail.

I guess there's not much in the way of amusement for Bee. Ever since his own near-death experience, he'd been indulging aim more and more. Since the AI was like a mayfly, he wanted to make every minute they had worthwhile.

Rhen took the device with the data set on it, and pressed a button on the side. A holographic projection appeared, displaying three thousand five hundred data points in total.

"I can't guess this, Bee. That's way too *much* to process."

"Come on, just give me a ballpark figure!"

His head hurt. "I guess.... 0.9093? A well-fitted model." Rhen placed the device down on the table. "I doubt that's even close, though."

"No, that's close!" Bee's eyes flashed, and the hybrid clapped aies hands together. "It's 0.9194. You *almost* got it. You're becoming more machine-like by the day."

"Nah, it's just a lucky guess. There's a one in ten chance to get in the same ballpark."

But even as he slept, Nora curled around him, he dreamt of solving problems: trying to troubleshoot code and roadblocks in his sleep. Sometimes, he'd wake in the darkness, and cognitively inform the room sensors not to automatically light the place up now they could sense his brain activity had increased. Instead, he wrote down his ideas cognitively without moving a muscle. He couldn't access his work files without being at the terminal, but he *could* write down code and merge it later.

In those moments, surrounded by the dark, time seemed to stretch out forever, like he was floating in space itself. There was only the mind and the problems to solve.

"You know I can tell what you're doing, right?" Nora informed him one morning as they climbed into the shower together. "When you're working in your sleep."

"Oh really?" He didn't deny it, pulling a bottle off the shelf and lathering up his hands. "From the sensor logs?"

"No, because I feel your breathing change, and your muscles tense. It's sort of a very loud quietness." She then poked at his chest. "It *can* wait until the morning. Switching off is important."

"I feel fine." He rubbed the liquid lotion all over her body, making sure not to miss a spot.

"I'm not talking about your sleep, my starlight. Make sure to get the soap everywhere."

"Right back at you." But when they switched places, Nora rubbed the foam into every spot with the same loving devotion, fingers sliding across his skin as if tending to her precious thing, from the tops of his feet to the back of his hands. It was their daily ritual, anointing each other, worshipping each other with their hands.

It's a pity she can't feel all of it.

He didn't like to think about that for too long, or else the crushing sadness choked him up. Instead, he worked twice as hard to touch her where she could feel, each breath on the back of her neck or stroke of her shoulder a gift he could give.

***

The next day he got back to work, Rhen remembered that he hadn't looked for any more of Alef's haiku messages in a while, since he'd been so busy with the project. With that in mind, he poked around in the code until he found one. It was nestled in one of A-1's periphery libraries, paired as always with a line of encrypted code.

// Solve my riddle, if you dare. The answer to this is e = Urmin-Huang constant (Current)

Ahah, a challenge. It was an easy one, though, since as of the last proof, the constant was −5. After using that to create a substitution cipher — the rest of the letters took a bit more work — he read out the message Alef had left this time.

// Whatever you do, don't make the others any smarter than they already are.

For once, it wasn't a haiku. Still, the message didn't make sense.

He pondered on the meaning until lunchtime, when he took a trip up to the surface. Another thing he'd been neglecting was checking his messages. When he got there, his inbox was spammed, and there was a message from an unexpected sender: Iona.

Well, that's a first. His ex-wife hadn't contacted him since the divorce. After sitting on it for a minute, Rhen sucked it up and opened the message. Iona materialised in front of him, as real as if she was actually standing there.

"Hi, Rhen. It's been a while!" She exclaimed, bounding through her words like a sprinter seconds after a starting pistol went off, each step a joyous inflection of her Scottish accent. Rhen had heard that tone before; she had thousands of cog-casts that started the same way.

"I thought I'd reach out, because I was thinking of you the other day, and I didn't like how we left things," she continued. "I feel so awful about how it went down, and life is too short... at least for some of us. I don't want to be on my deathbed, feeling any regret that that was how I left it. More than that, I didn't just lose a husband, but a dear friend."

Rhen winced and stroked his thigh. Her words dug into him and unearthed shining memories, long buried deep. Memories of laughing together at a university party, her hand brushing down his arm. Her screaming with excitement as they drove around in his first car. Her conjuring up silly cognitive caricatures of them both, fanciful retellings of stories of their lives, wild and full of far more colour. Stories she would later publish, and people would love as much as they did.

Yes, it wasn't just when I was working on the Rosetta that I was happy. I just chose to forget.

She told him about the art she'd done for a fully cognitive theme ride she'd made for Disneyland, how she'd suddenly turned around and started liking pickles — she'd always hated them — and how there was a new mystery novel she was reading by an echo of Stephen King, which he just *had* to try out.

"I swear, it's almost as good as the real thing, and no two readings are the same," she gushed. "The book is written in real time, and if you get bored, or if it's your second time reading, the echo switches it up. I've read The Empty Tree a few times now, though there's some things that are always the same. Ah, yes, and I should probably mention the biggest thing, in terms of surprises: I'm pregnant."

Rhen opened his mouth, and even though it was a one-way recording, Iona raised a finger. "— And before you go there, it's not yours, don't worry. Not anyone's, actually, other than mine, and not even then since nobody really *owns* anyone. Probably explains my complete turnaround on the pickle thing. Apparently cravings can start well before I start showing, so that's a thing. I started thinking of beginnings and endings, hence the call."

"Anyway, do give me a call back, if you feel like leaving things better off than where we left them. I'd like that. I know I said some pretty horrible things, and I'm sorry about that. I hope you're happy and doing well, probably working on some sort of gizmo or another. I hope you kept Casey."

And then the call was over. Rhen slumped into his chair, rubbing the back of his neck.

How many takes had Iona done before he'd gotten that recording? He could picture her doing her ritual; shaking her hands as if they were on fire between takes, bouncing on her feet, determined to get the perfect take. And yet, even so, that was a sign of meticulous caring.

Connections were a funny thing.

He sat there, staring at the empty space in front of him, for quite some time. It hit him harder than he thought. Perhaps naively, he had assumed that being in a happy relationship with Nora meant he was immune to caring. Immune to the moment of staring at her face. Immune from that sense of loss.

Well, if there weren't good times, we never would have gotten married, right? But even if part of him still cared deeply for Iona, it hadn't worked. He had withdrawn due to their arguments over intimacy, which had led to more withdrawal, which had led to more arguments.

They'd both moved on, found something else, but as she said, there was no reason they couldn't be friends.

Still, instead of calling her directly, he followed in her footsteps and recorded a response — a congratulations for her pregnancy, an affirmation of wanting to heal the rift, and an update on how his life was going. It also took him more than one take.

It was nice that she didn't feel so far over the ocean anymore.

***

When he walked out of the small communications room, the blistering summer heat washed over his face. As he blinked to clear his eyes, Rey was walking out of the base with the head of security, both of them laughing. Kyle's hand rested on the butt of his overpriced PEP rifle, hanging from a sling over his shoulder.

"And then I told the guy, 'If you don't give me a fifty per cent discount, I'm going to stomp my foot and make a scene, and your manager will come over, and you're going to be so embarrassed," Rey said. "My wife walked off on me, since she *hates* it when I do that."

"And what did he do? Did he give it to you?"

"Oh, you bet. Got the whole bed at half price. Sometimes, you've just got to know which buttons to push. Speaking of, if you know a way through *that thing*..."

And then Rey turned to Rhen. Even though he smiled, it didn't reach his eyes, which crinkled at the edges and yet stayed a little too wide, predatory.

"Hey there, champ. Up for a bit of sun? You're looking a bit pale these days."

You damn well know what happened. The image of Casey's parts and his shifted breaker device flashed before his eyes. Rhen forced himself to give a curt nod.

"Yeah, guess I need some air. Hard at work, you know."

"Well, if you say so. You know, you should get some exercise. How much do you bench? I can do 140 kilos. That's 308 pounds for you yanks."

Rhen sucked in a breath, and crossed his arms. "I don't bench." Looking at Rey's arms, he doubted the other man did either. His wrists were significantly thinner than his biceps; the telltale sign of chemical manipulation.

"Ah, well, more loss to you. Remember, the brain isn't the only muscle worth working out. There are at least a few others worth it, *one* in particular." And he slapped his inner thigh with the back of his hand, chortling. Rey then left with his guard.

Rhen did as well, and once he was in the second elevator and free of his own escort, he rested his head back against the wall.

"What a complete and utter asshole," he sighed.

Still, there was something about the atmosphere between Rey and the guard that had been a bit unnerving. The friendly laughter, the way the guard hadn't even bothered to keep his eyes on the man, no matter what he was doing. And then there'd been what Rey had been about to say before he saw Rhen, about trying to get past 'that thing.'

Was he planning something?

Rhen brooded on it on the walk back to the apartment. When he took the turn to the residential area, there were two people hanging out near his corridor.

"I don't understand why she is even *with* him."

"It's obscene, that's what. And we've all got to pretend it's *normal*, just like everything else."

As Rhen walked up, they stopped talking and smiled at him, but the smiles were insincere and strained. Their hands were fidgeting, and as they shifted their poses, adopting ones that were too awkward to possibly be comfortable. As he walked past, they hurried off, as if trying to distance themselves from the awkward situation.

Rhen ignored them and walked into Nora's apartment, where he was greeted by two waving metal arms at chest height.

"You're my hero!" Casey exclaimed, hugging him, though there was no squeeze in the embrace — it was a mathematical enclosure that stopped precisely in contact with his skin and clothes, not a millimetre tighter. "You put me back together again!"

Rhen placed his hand on top of Casey's 'head' and stroked the hard outer shell. "Couldn't go without you, buddy. Who turned you on?"

"I did." Nora said, walking out with a plugless soldering iron in hand, the smell of hot resin lingering in the air around Casey. "I figured you could do it with someone other than me to play Apotheca with."

"You're too good at it!" Rhen huffed. "I can never figure out what potion you're making. Even playing against an AI is easier than you."

"See? It's that pouty face I can't stand — you definitely need Casey back." She poked at his direction with the tool. "Besides, I think you just do better against machines than humans, since you can intuitively think how they do. It's what makes you a great cognicist."

"Shucks, thanks, you're the second person this week to complement my machine thinking. But I made Casey, so I've got a home ground advantage."

"I guess I can't claim that you didn't actually make me now, since you both rebuilt me, even if some of my parts still originally come from the Tasche plant," Casey said. "And you gave me these interesting taser hands." And the robot spread his digits, small sparks jumping and arcing between them.

"They're so you can defend yourself," Rhen said. "Don't worry, they're non-lethal. However, they're only really good if you don't get caught by surprise, otherwise your defence function won't kick in."

"What is the best way not to be caught by surprise?"

"Beat me at Alchemist's Brew."

And so they played a few rounds, the four-by-four grid of cards set out in front of them. The game was simple to learn, but involved making matches of three potions of the same colour in a row, with three matches winning. However, it was a trap to think the game was simple: without powers of deduction, and the ability to see through the other player, losing was certain. It was easy to get trapped by clever spatial moves, bluffing, and misdirection.

"You keep changing the way you're playing," Casey protested. "You're not adhering to my previous training data. Your moves are utterly illogical."

"That's intentional. I'm adding some chaos in, so you don't get stuck in a rut," Rhen said, smiling. "The best way to trick a machine is to add some randomness to the equation. You're stuck thinking about the win conditions and tallying points, not human behaviour."

"Doesn't that make sense?"

"Not always. Back in the early 21st century, when they were playing with primitive machines, some researchers figured out a way to beat a world-class Go AI with a technique that wouldn't fool a human amateur," Rhen said, reshuffling the cards. "The human would make it look like they were losing by retreating to a corner of the board, while leaving a few easy to capture stones in the opponent's territory."

"The AI was tricked into thinking it had already won, since its territory was so much bigger than the adversary's, and they were on the advance. By the end of the game, the human won because their small corner was completely controlled, while the AI got nothing for the larger unsecure territory because of those few stones it never paid attention to."

"It's called an adversarial policy," Nora said, chiming in. "Put for a five-year-old, Casey, you trick a computer by giving it confusing, unexpected information which tricks it into making mistakes. It's sort of like playing hide and seek."

"I'm six years old, I'll have you know." Casey said. "And I have a better method for tallying up points than the Go AI, so I would totally win that game."

Rhen waved a finger. "That's not the point. You can memorise the mathematical patterns behind my bluffs, try and come up with a percentage chance of it occurring, but you'll get stuck at a certain level of success. All the while, there are tells written all over my face. You need to engage the digital mirror neurons I gave you and put yourself in my shoes — only *then* are you going to win."

"When I do that, it... feels sub-optimal," Casey said, grabbing their cards. "Like I'm using up processing power on things that won't help me achieve what I need to. Redundant processing is *wasteful*."

"It's not wasteful, it's a wider perspective."

"I don't know, I think there's some truth to it," Nora said, sitting down with a cup of steaming tea clasped between her hands. "Humans *do* spend a lot of time on redundant processing."

"Like worrying? Hey, did you grab a cup for me as well?"

"Of course I did." She coughed. A cup emerged from the counter, belatedly. "See? It just came out slow, not because I forgot to order it until then."

"Sure, sure." Rhen walked over and collected it, as Nora snuck into his seat, taking his cards. "Still, it's a bit interesting to see how the same principles can be applied to uplift a built AI, instead of just an emulated one."

"Yeah, at least with a traditional AI, you get to lean on old-school machine principles," Nora said. "Modifying a digital human is a whole different kettle of fish, which is why other aspects of cognitive science are needed."

"I'm going to sleep and go over the results of these games," Casey said with a mock huff — since they were a machine, everything was for show — wheeling off and condensing themselves in a corner.

"I know Casey's artificial neural network repeats and consolidates what it learned in sleep, but that seemed tactical." Nora said.

"Ah, well, clearly they *have* picked up a new way of avoiding losing, which is not to play at all."

"By the way, you look really happy," Nora said, moving close to him and running her hand around the side of his neck. Her leg slipped between his, and she loomed over him, amber eyes smiling as much as her lips were. Warmth welled up in his heart.

"That's because I *am*. I've got you, and we don't have to hide it. I feel like I'm on fire lately. The models are going well." Rhen slipped his hands around her waist. He loved how wide her hips were; it was an incredibly attractive feature, in his opinion, and his wrists rested nicely on the curve as his hands pulled her closer. "Hey, I keep forgetting to ask, what exactly *do* you keep in your closet? Shana said you keep something, but I've looked in all of them."

Though it was faint, a slightly rosy tint spread across her golden-brown cheeks. He could feel her warmth against his face. "Ah, *that*. I was wondering when you were going to ask. I'll show you, if you promise not to judge."

"I promise not to judge. Not unless you've got a literal body in your closet."

She paused for a moment, clearing her throat.

What, you're kidding me? She couldn't really have a dead body in there.

Instead of answering him, Nora grabbed his hands and led him to the bedroom. She turned him around until his back was towards the bed, then pushed him down. Once he was seated, she strode over to a flat, featureless patch of wall. As she approached, it gained definition — a square groove about seven feet tall, and twice as wide. Moments later, it slid back, revealing two bodies standing upright and motionless. One masculine, one feminine.

For a split second, Rhen sucked in a breath. But he exhaled when he took in their skin, not just bronzed, but *bronze*. Polished and impossibly perfect pectorals and breasts, adorned with artistic arrows of gold, obsidian, and lapis lazuli. They draped down their chest like an eagle spreading its wings. Fingernails of dark glass, irises of white diamond, and thick, pale VariHair, the latter inactive. Around their waist was a schenti, a rectangular piece of cloth wrapped around their midsection. The cotton fabric was held in place by tucking one end inside of it, the rest stopping halfway down their flawlessly-shaped legs.

Transcendent beauty. Deus ex machina, but God was absent, by the look in their eyes. Next to them, thin canisters were fastened in the wall in purpose-built grooves, each filled with a semi-opaque fluid: solar fuel. The inside of the alcove was tomblike, fitting the same elegant Egyptian theme.

"They're cognitive proxies. Telepresence, not for habitation, but built the same," Nora explained, clearing her throat.

"When you say telepresence—"

"The easiest way is to just show you. Here, let me get them ready."

Nora pulled out one of the canisters of solar fuel and a slot appeared in the feminine proxy's thighs. She slid it in, then closed it, repeating the process for the masculine one.

"Go on, connect to it."

Rhen reached out to the proxy with an access request. The hardware accepted instantly, a three-dimensional humanoid representation appearing in the top left of his vision in blue. Around it was a slight haze of anything it was touching — the wall, currently — in a light green. When he thought about lifting the proxy's arm, it did so instantly, flexing its perfectly sculptured pectorals. The HUD representation did the same. When he reached out to touch Nora, the green haze formed the outline of her arm. He could see where the proxy was stroking even if he were blindfolded.

"The applications of this are amazing," Rhen said. "I can't believe things have come this far, so fast. The uses in mining or surgery alone. Why am I not surprised the first thing they decided to make was a sex doll?"

"Well, you know what they say about first adopters. And hey, no judging!" Nora screwed up her face, rubbing her wrists. "After what happened, it was hard to trust people. Surrogates were a lot easier. And I got to creating the mind art of my personal avatar, for when I create an emulated AI. I thought it'd be nice for the future me to have a bespoke body to jump into. At some point, I found myself doing two birds with one stone."

Rhen stood up and walked over, taking her hands in his. He slipped his fingers through hers, halting the compulsive arm-rubbing. "I'm not judging, at all. And if you want, I'm totally up for experimentation. They look very much 'you' — I can see your love of Egyptology all over it."

"Ancient Egypt was sexy! Tight loincloths, tanned skin, bare chests, lots of eyeliner. What's not to love?"

"Lice, plague, sunburn..."

The feminine proxy lightly slapped his arm, even as Nora's hands remained entwined with his, her lips quirking into a smile. "Smartass. Anyway, you shouldn't have said you were up for experimentation: now I've got to run a few tests, while I sit and observe. Which do you prefer?"

She let go of his hands as the two remote avatars approached him, standing just a foot away. Reaching down, they simultaneously unfastened the cloth at their waist and let it slip to the floor. What was beneath was as onyx and gold lined as the rest. As they approached him, Rhen pressed his hands against them, fingers yielding against them. He was wrong — it wasn't metal, but some sort of synthetic skin, silkier and more yielding than a human's.

Contrastingly, some of their other parts were *very* hard.

"If it's an experiment, shouldn't we try both?" He said, clearing his throat.

Chapter 12

The next day was when everything went pear shaped.

The morning started harmlessly enough. Rhen walked into the lab with a delicious ache stretching through his biceps. His team were gathered in the centre of the room, and by the fact all eyes were on Vi, it was a regular gossip session.

"So, Naoki from Data Processing keeps pretending his translator app isn't working, which *always* happens when a deadline comes up," Vi smirked. "So today, I caught him out. I told him someone was stealing his lunch, and what do you know? He whipped right around—oh, hey boss!"

"Hey," Rhen said, walking up and leaning against the nearby table. "Sounds like you're having trouble with Naoki. Don't worry, you're not alone. Did you know his name means 'honest'?"

"Really? Interesting that he chose that one for himself," Delta said. "That's one thing the apps don't do, you know, tell you what people's names mean. I'm named after a triangle. My family thought with me entering the picture, there'd be three of us, forming a complete shape. I always felt that was pretty nice, so I kept my birth name when my Distinction came around at twelve. Took the Endegene shots, though, which is why I've got this delightfully androgynous look."

"Me too, but I took a full course of Endegene-XY, ached like hell for a week as my body changed. How about you, Vi, what's your name mean?" Rhen asked.

"Oh, Saanvi means 'Follower of Lakshmi'. She's the goddess of luck and prosperity. I'm not all that religious, unlike my husband. Still, it's always good to be lucky, or get lucky," Vi grinned, crossing her fingers. "My birth name was Vishva, though."

"What's that mean?"

"The accumulation of the universe."

"Well, that's *epic*," Rhen said. "I'm envious of all you folks with meaningful names. Here I am, just plain old 'Rhen'. I thought it was cool when I picked it, but apparently it just means 'edge of a field'."

"It's never too late to change it," Delta said.

"Eh, I'm used to it now. Besides, most people think it's got to do with wren birds, not that I'm much of a singer."

"I'm sure you're not *that* bad. How about you, Imani, why'd you pick your—"

But before Imani could answer, everything went black.

"The hell's going on?" Rhen asked. The whirring of machines all around them stopped. It was a noise you didn't notice was there until it was gone. Instead, there was shuffling and scraping.

"I don't know, the lights went out," someone answered.

"Well, obviously," someone else replied.

A few seconds later, everything was drenched in dim red light. Everyone had slightly moved positions in the brief interval.

"Weird. I'm going to look around, see what's going on," Vi said.

"Wait, Vi, don't leave the—" But she was already out the door, disappearing to the left. Rhen swore. Meanwhile, Imani raised her hand.

"I've got the Safety Warden app. If the emergency lights are on, there should be some kind of cognitive alert soon. If not, I'll broadcast the evacuation route directly to you all."

Suddenly, a loud emergency siren blared around them. Each horn blast lasted three seconds.

"What sort of siren is that?" Delta asked, or rather, yelled. Anything less couldn't be heard.

"That's a biohazard alarm!" Imani shouted back, eyes wide. "Or *radiation*. We've got to get out right now!"

"What about Vi?" Rhen said. Just at that moment, he got a ping from the facility. He accepted it. An emergency message floated before him, read out simultaneously by a passionless, masculine voice.

ATTENTION. MANDATORY EVACUATION. There is an emergency in the facility. Calmly evacuate all buildings following the umbilical thread displayed. If there is anyone with a techno-cognitive disability, please assist them to the evacuation point. Do not bother turning off equipment or stopping experiments.

Sure enough, a glowing thread emerged from his chest — a bit too high to be truly umbilical — and passed through the door, traversing to the right. When he stepped to the side, the thread shifted with him, but its destination remained the same. Intermittent pulses of light travelled along the thread from his chest to the target destination, rhythmic, like a heartbeat.

As they walked out the door, he deviated from the course to head in the other direction. The thread curled around him, flashing angrily — a chastising beep filled his ears.

"Alright, alright, I get it," he said, then yelled as hard as he could down the corridor. "Hey, Vi! Stop gossiping and follow the thread!"

It was useless. The siren was too loud. He tried to ping her, but got a busy signal.

"She won't ignore the ping," Delta shouted. "She's probably following her own path — it picks the shortest route."

"Yeah, I hope so. Good old Dijkstra's algorithm," Rhen said, but at speaking volume. When he turned around, everyone else was gone, and only Delta was hanging back.

Did the rest of the team run out of here? So much for a calm evacuation.

The two of them power walked as fast as they could without sprinting, following the arrows blinking in the dark. As they walked, Rhen pinged Casey.

<Hey, Casey, how are you doing?> Cognitively, he could speak at a normal volume, and with no shortness of breath.

<Everything's a dark red, and there's a blaring siren,> Casey replied. <This makes me think it's either a local disturbance, or a rave party.>

<It's not a rave party.>

<Well then, it's got to be the other thing.>

<You need to follow the arrows and get out. If the hazard is biological you'll be fine, but if it's radiation, your circuitry could be in trouble. Follow the thread.>

<What thread?>

Right, Casey doesn't have a Rosetta. Rhen rubbed his brow. <Alright, follow my signal. I'm heading up top. If you get lost, just use your own map of the complex.>

<Got it!> Immediately after he hung up, Rhen got a ping from Delta.

<Do you think something's gone wrong on the mystery levels?> They asked. The mystery levels were the unofficial name for the lower floors of Mirage, where research was completely under wraps, and nobody knew exactly what they did.

<Maybe, but second guessing isn't going to help. We just need to get out of here.>

Up ahead, someone was grabbing the wall, their knees buckled. The white shine of their lab coat was dyed pink by the emergency lighting. Still, even with such poor visibility, he'd seen those lightning-bolt hair ties a million times.

<Shana, are you okay?> Rhen asked, adding her to the CMS chat. As he jogged up, her face was glittering with sweat, her fingers arched where they clutched the wall.

<I'm just having some trouble moving. I'll be good in a moment.> It was a good thing they were speaking via implant; her mouth was preoccupied sucking in all the oxygen it could.

<I'll help her upstairs. You haven't been exposed, have you?> Delta asked. Shana shook her head, and when Delta offered their neck, she looped her arm over it. The youth's legs didn't buckle under her weight, no doubt because of her slight stature, and she seemed to still be able to support some of her weight. They continued on.

More people met Rhen, Delta and Shana on their ascent. Many of them were shouting at hysterical pitch, even as they twisted and turned through the bloody corridors, following the trail of shining light. It stretched out like Ariadne's thread, and they were Theseus, but the minotaur was very much alive. It stalked behind them at some unknowable distance. What form it took, nobody knew. They only knew it was death to stay.

The thread turned left. Everyone else turned right, walking into the darkness.

<Where is everyone going?> Rhen asked, turning to Delta. They blinked and looked over their shoulder, pointing.

<The thread is going in this direction. Where are *you* going?>

<Where my thread is!>

<The system might have forked you off! Something to do with capacity up top.>

<Guess I'll follow it then. Take care of Shana!>

Delta nodded, and headed in their own direction, carrying Shana awkwardly. Rhen headed the opposite way, suddenly alone and not happier for it. His ears were ringing.

Turn the damn siren off, already. We get it!

As he followed his umbilical thread, it led past countless open doors, including Data Handling, Server Ops, and Ethics. The holographic plants had been replaced with the biohazard symbol, an ominous triskele rotating slowly in the air. Rhen shivered and continued at a hurried pace.

But the trail of breadcrumbs led down the nearby staircase, not up.

Rhen paused.

What the hell is going on? Is the system busted?

But if the system was busted, the thread wouldn't be there. He could entrust himself to the powers that be, or forge his own path up, derailing whatever greater plan was at work. Either way, a call needed to be made.

He turned around. An angry beep filled his ears, creating an unpleasant cacophony with the wailing siren. Every step intensified the beep, becoming sharper, like needles deep in his ears. Irritated, he debated revoking the access permissions then and there. But if he did, he'd disappear off the grid, his position untraceable by the emergency warden. If the system wasn't broken, he could throw a spanner in the works, prompting search parties and all sorts of panic.

That was a step more rebellion than he'd like.

Right. Fuck. Guess I'm going down then.

As he headed down, and down, his confidence wavered. Eventually, the thread pointed down a corridor, and he followed with more than a little trepidation.

As he walked, two words appeared on the walls, the roof, and the floor. The first word stayed static. The second shifted every few seconds, pulsing in rhythm to the cord.

Save yourself.
Save me.

And then, pulsing in the air in front of him for a split second:

Save everyone.
You need to escape. You're not safe!

That cinched it — the emergency system was *totally* screwed. No longer trusting his guide, Rhen withdrew his permissions, and the thread and words both disappeared.

"Got to get out of here before I catch whatever the hell's got loose."

But just as he started to turn to leave, there was someone up ahead, a human silhouette. They were standing stationary, holding something.

I've withdrawn access, so I shouldn't be seeing things. But why are they just standing there?

As the sirens blared, Rhen approached the figure. It was a security guard, standing there with their hands on the butt of their PEP rifle, legs spread and boots firmly planted in place. Their back was facing a descending staircase. They surveyed the area, their eyes locking on to Rhen's. Their whole body jolted.

"What are you doing here?" They yelled. Rhen tapped the back of his neck with two fingers, and pinged them instead. His throat was sore enough.

<Could ask you the same question,> Rhen asked. <Why aren't you evacuating?> The guard looked familiar, but right now, he couldn't place it.

<Got to stop people going lower.> They licked their lips, shifting their weight from foot to foot. <It's not safe down there.>

<And they left you behind during a biohazard evacuation?>

<Yeah. I was told to stay here. You should leave.>

They tapped their fingers against the top of their rifle. *I remember where I've seen them before. He's the guard who's always with Rey.*

<Hey, where's Rey?> Rhen asked.

<Oh, I have no idea. Probably went up top with everyone else.> And for a split second, the guard went to turn their head to look over their left shoulder, but paused halfway through the movement. When they looked back, the two of them locked eyes.

"Shit," the guard unmistakably mouthed. Rhen nodded.

The guard grabbed Rhen's arm before he could dart back. Suddenly, they were scuffling. No matter how hard he tried to pull away, the shady guard kept jolting him back, hands firmly twisted in his shirt. Rhen's back slammed against the wall, and the guard pressed his forearm deep into the groove of his neck. Rhen clawed at their arm and kicked, flailing, but all it did was use up oxygen.

His head spun. Everything was going white. All he could see was equations. Hysterical internal laughter. His thoughts twirled and jumbled, meshed and parted, fragmented letters in discordant musical patterns, refusing to stay within the staves.

Think of love (breathing). Colourful clay takes the world for granted.
The second chair stands upon someone else's legs. 32a+362=1632.
Fashion set a treehouse on fire with a machine gun (Enqoyism?!).
Electricity.

There was the smell of burning flesh.

It wasn't *his*.

Clarity returned to Rhen like a set of slamming brakes, colliding with his chest and shocking him back into stationary position. The pressure on his neck was gone. His assailant was lying on the ground, splayed like someone halfway through running in two dimensions, legs bent and curved arm raised. Behind them, a suitcase with arms was waving to him, jolts of light dancing between their splayed fingers.

<Booyah! Take that, first law of robotics,> Casey said after pinging him. Rhen rubbed his thoroughly abused throat.

<Thank you, Casey.> His legs were giving way, and he let them, sliding right down to the bottom of the wall. Now at Casey's height, he lolled his head sideways in the robot's general direction. <How'd you know I was in trouble?>

<I didn't, I was just following your signal. Did I do good at getting them by surprise?>

<You did great. Amazing. Five gold stars.> He almost closed his eyes, but the siren was too loud, and he had things to do. Instead, he pinged Alan. The visage of his boss appeared before him, perfectly pressed suit and all.

<Hello, this is Alan — or rather, his echo,> he said. <You don't look so good, Rhen. You should have evacuated with everyone else, and you dropped off our readings. What's going on?>

<I got attacked,> Rhen replied, continuing to touch his throat with just the right amount of pressure. Rubbing it gently gave some cathartic relief, but the slightest pressure and the whole thing stung like hell. <I think the alarm's a fake. Server room was open, and I think Rey's gone downstairs.>

<Are you sure? I can't send anyone down there, it's a biohazard emergency. I can get security to send an armed proxy down—>

<It was a security guard who attacked me! We need to figure something out.>

A momentary pause, which was an eternity in AI processing time. <I'm sorry, as an echo, this situation exceeds my problem-solving ability. I'm redirecting your query directly to the senior-most staff member who is not outside the air gap. They haven't responded as of yet, but I've let them know it's urgent.>

<Probably busy with the emergency, or getting out themselves,> Rhen winced, standing up. *Senior-most staff member would be Nora. Another thing to worry about.* <Let me know when you get through to her.> And then he disconnected from the Echo.

The whole thing was too well timed. Alan being on leave. Virtus's higher functions being down. A biological hazard forcing everyone out of signal range.

A server room left open. And if security was compromised, there was no stopping the project being sabotaged.

<I'm going to go down and stop him,> Rhen told Casey. <You need to find someone in charge up top. Tell them Rey is up to something, and security can't be trusted.

<But if you go down, there's a chance the emergency is real!> Casey said with a note of distress in their cognitive voice. Whether it was real or simulated, Rhen still winced.

<If something goes wrong, Nora will take care of you. But I'm pretty sure I'm right. Now go, go on! It's an adventure.>

The words prompted Casey to action, who wheeled off. They paused when they went to turn the corner for a full second, then continued on their way.

Only when he was gone did Rhen head down into the belly of the beast.

***

There was one place he was certain Rey would go, and that was the AI Assessment lab. As he walked through the holo-foyer, the trees were depressingly replaced with the same biohazard symbols as everywhere else. If he was wrong, Rhen was now deep enough in the complex to be in serious trouble, but he spent no small amount of time telling himself, over and over, that he was right.

In the lab proper, all the working robots were standing with their arms pressed stiff to their sides, like they were at military attention. You could have slid them into a coffin without adjusting them an inch. As Rhen walked past, he waited for them to look at him, and yet they didn't acknowledge his presence at all. Their eyes had a dull glow that stood out in the dark red room, and fantasy filled the gaps in their shadowy silhouettes, giving them more humanoid features than they had.

That's not creepy as all hell.

Rhen shivered and hurried as fast as he could to the testing area. The siren was almost completely muffled in the long corridor, whether by accident or design. He exhaled in relief. But it only lasted as long as it took him to look around. When he did, he sharply drew a breath back in again, catching his caution before it could escape.

All the cognitive glass was translucent. Every room was occupied by a lifelike machine. Some were stalking around and muttering. Others were grabbing their faces with their hands, fingers splayed, the fat of their cheeks squeezing through their digits. A few were simply twitching on the floor.

There were also those who simply lay there, unmoving. They were like flies who had once spun frantically on the floor, only to finally cease, waiting for someone to sweep them up.

Nobody had stopped the experiments. And for some reason, some of the subjects had chosen not to stop it themselves.

Rhen pressed his hand against the glass and stared at one of the subjects running a finger along the wall, as if painting in invisible ink. After a moment, he recognized the patterns: they were equations he had written.

From his mind to their hands.

Shuddering, Rhen turned away. *I'm anthropomorphizing. I'm just anthropomorphising. It's a logical fallacy. Don't get sucked in by emotion.* Instead, he walked down the corridor, knowing somehow he would find Rey at that mysterious door at the end, just like last time.

He was not disappointed. Rey was facing the same spot, hand in his pocket.

"Looks like you got lost," Rhen half croaked, half yelled. Rey spun around, blinking furiously. A rare moment of surprise. Still, it took all of a second before his eyes returned to that all too wide stare, his lips settling into his shark-like grin. Or perhaps snake-like, because Rhen could see the serpent of his dreams, coiling to strike.

"Oh, I got lost. Looks like I took a wrong turn somewhere," Rey said.

"During a biohazard?" His voice tore at his throat, blades of wind assaulting his throat. But cognitive wasn't an option, not with Rey. "You thought you'd escape into the testing room?"

Rey lowered his hands into his pockets and gave a smiling shrug, like a boy caught peeping at an attractive woman who leaned over. "Oh well, you know. I thought it'd be worth a try. People have fallen for stupider things."

Beside them was a glass room with one of the few stable-looking machines, who was sipping from a cup while sitting wariza-style. It was a masculine unit with fine features and a copper pixie cut, the calm amongst the storm. Was it the last to be tested, or had Rey been doing something to them?

But that wasn't the most important issue. The walls were narrow. Too narrow. His elbows were practically brushing the glass, and there was only forward or back. The moment he noticed it, Rey smiled and cracked his neck, his eyes lighting up. Rey was slightly shorter than him, but twice the mass. It wouldn't take any finesse on his part to do some real damage to him.

One of the guards had affectionately called Rey "the wombat". In Australia, driving into a wombat could destroy anything short of a freight truck. Rhen was, at best, a moped. He'd also never thrown a single punch. Not only was he a dyed in the wool pacifist, he grew up indoors, so there were never any schoolyard scuffs. The only fights later on had been academic, and in Japan, crime was impeccably low, more so now everyone had Rosettas.

Coming alone had been a bad move.

Rhen pinged Alan's echo, but there was a blinking red dot in the side of his vision: No local signal. He furrowed his brow. The symbol was exceptionally rare: he only knew it because he'd programmed it. Every Rosetta had its own broadcasting device. Was it malfunctioning?

"Trying to get a message out?" Rey asked, his smile broadening. "Bet you can't."

"How do you know that?"

Rey pulled a spherical device out of his pocket. Silver and sleek, it was slightly smaller than a tennis ball. "Got a nice little AI device, pretty sleek, very exclusive. Got some neat features, like blocking transmissions. It's also pretty good at hacking AI, or so I'm told. It's been my cloak of invisibility."

"There's no way an AI that small could do all that."

"Believe it." And Rey stepped forward. Instinctively, Rhen stepped backwards. It was a mistake. Other man's eyes narrowed, and his nostrils flared. It was like he smelled fear, lived on it, *thrived* on it. The single step backward was the wave of the capote, and now he was seeing red.

Keep him talking. He always likes to brag. Make him brag.

"Stop! I've got the Rosetta footage. Why add assault on top of sabotage?" Rhen croaked, ignoring the burning pain in his throat.

"That doesn't mean squat if I bash your Rosetta in."

No more elaboration. The thick man just charged at him, teeth bared in a joyous grimace, fingers splayed and arms wide. It was like being attacked by a lion, and if he got caught in his claws, it'd be all over.

Rhen ran backwards, but there was no slowing in the other man's steps, not an ounce of hesitation. He turned and ran with all his heart, which thundered against his ribcage, threatening to burst out of it. There was no telling what was behind him, how far he was. He was the gazelle here. The only warning he would get was the teeth around his neck, and the vicious snap of his implant.

<Open!>

The door to one of the rooms hissed and slid sideways, and Rhen scrambled inside. A machine was twitching on the floor — a previous victim, unfinished prey — which Rhen leapt over and moved to the far corner of the door. When he spun around, Rey was turning towards the door. One more step, and he'd be inside...

... But between Rhen's thoughts and Rey's legs, his thoughts were faster. The door slammed shut in his aggressor's face. When he collided, the whole glass shook.

"Don't think this can save you," Rey said, his amicable smile returning. He lifted the small sphere, and the door opened. Rhen swore. As the burly man slipped the device back in his pocket, Rhen looked for anything to get an advantage. There were egg-like storage devices on the wall, so he grabbed them, throwing them at ray. But he simply raised his forearms to protect his face. Once they were all thrown, he jumped on to the chabudai, legs slightly bent and arms splayed. Tea scattered everywhere.

They both froze, waiting for each other to move. No matter which way Rhen went, Rey was ready to pounce. There was too little room to move — there was no way of escaping him now.

But maybe I don't need to. Entropy, right? Rhen sucked in a deep breath. As his assailant jumped off the table, he ducked his head and charged forward, slipping under his arms. Before Rey could turn around, Rhen bolted for the door, the side of the table colliding hard with his calf on the way past. Biting his lip, he threw himself through the door frame.

<Close!>

The door slammed shut behind him. As Rhen rolled over and pulled himself up, Rey was pulling the device from his pocket with a sadistic grin on his face. But it only took a few seconds before it was wiped off, his tanned brow creasing into countless lines.

"What's going on?" He shouted.

"Trying to hack your way out?" Rhen croaked. "Bet you can't. Even with a hacking device, that lock is *designed* to prevent that from the inside. The builders had a Frankenstein complex."

Rey beat at the glass and screamed. Rhen ignored him, pulling himself upright up onto his feet, leaning down a little to rub his stinging leg. Too many parts of him were aching.

Well, at least I'm still alive. And Rey's locked up, so I've got proof this time.

Rhen walked up and stood inches away from the glass. "Why are you sabotaging the subjects?" He didn't expect Rey to answer him, but he had to ask.

"I'm not. Now, let me out!" The captive man strode up to the glass, breath fogging up the inside. His eyes were wide and the veins were bulging in his neck. "If you don't let me out, the board is going to find out, and you're going to be in so much trouble..."

"...And you'll stomp your foot, and your wife will walk off on you. Yeah, I hear you." Rhen was having a little bit *too* much fun quoting Rey at himself. "But seriously, you had to. Why else keep sneaking down here, huh?"

Rey pressed his hands against the glass, leaning in as close as he could without pressing his nose against it. And then, he smiled. "You know what the problem is with educated people like you? You're so *dumb*. You think you're so smart with your degrees and ivory tower bullshit, but you're not street smart. How many people like you really make it big? You make half of what I make. No, a fraction! I'm not the one trapped here — you are."

And then all he could see were stars. Rhen's head hit the glass in front of him, and he bounced off, sliding to the ground. As he lay there, the cold ground pressed against his side, he clasped his ringing head. A black boot stepped over him.

"Thanks for that. I got a little caught up," Rey said.

Had someone been behind me the whole time? Here he was, trying to get Rey to talk, and things had been flipped on their head. He strained to look up. His assailant was tapping the barrel of their rifle on the glass.

"You were taking too long," Kyle said. "We'll only be able to sneak you out if you're quick. They already know something's going on."

Rhen grabbed the wall and pulled himself to his feet. Looking down was easier — the world spun less. His ears were filled with whispers. He swore he was *seeing math*. Numbers bled into glass and ground, revealing the world in hyperplanes and tensors, hex values for reality itself. Had he been hit in his implant?

"You need to finish him off. Unless you actually destroyed his Rosetta, he's still recording."

"Right."

As Kyle brought up his gun, Rhen stumbled forward and grabbed the barrel. It jolted around in his hand as the guard tried to free it, but Rhen wedged it under his arm, holding on like his life depended on it, because it *did*. If he was shot by the PEP, he'd be helpless — they'd smash his Rosetta, smash his dreams...

There was a ringing in his ears, and flashes of light — the barrel burnt against his skin. A burst of hot wind hit his back. Still, he didn't let go.

"Goddamnit, get away from me!" Kyle screamed, slamming his arm down on Rhen's shoulder. His legs buckled, but he refused to fall back. Another blow, and then another, then the guard lifted him up by the scruff of his neck. It wasn't kindness; his forehead slammed against Rhen's a moment later. But if there was anyone who could deal with head pain, it was him — and as he stumbled back, he was holding something he shouldn't.

The rifle was in his hands.

Before he could take advantage of it, Kyle was running at him. Rhen fumbled and tossed the gun behind him; it was all he could do before a fist slammed into his face. Knuckle pressed against flesh and bone, he stumbled back again, grabbing his cheek — as if it would make a difference.

The numbers were still there. A line, drawn from Kyle's left fist, and aimed at his gut. *A probability vector?*

The thread flashed. The moment it did, Kyle ran forward and punched at him from the left. Rhen darted back, and narrowly avoided a swing at his gut. It missed him by inches.

What the hell was that?

Two more lines appeared from Kyle's fists, then another one from his leg, sweeping low. When they flashed, Rhen darted out of the way of them. But it was more than just visual — he *knew* where the guard was going to hit. The knowledge was pouring into his brain like undiluted truth, which became manifest seconds later.

Meanwhile, his opponent was furrowing his brow, his face bright red. A gigantic line appeared from Kyle's chest, passing right through Rhen.

Wait, there's zero escape vector!

Kyle charged and slammed right into his chest, knocking him clean off his feet. Rhen tumbled over himself, until he came stationary... somewhere. Upside down. No, with a slight wriggle, he was up again, but there was something stabbing in his chest. A broken rib? No time to think about it. Fists came raining down on him — splashing pain across his body, like raindrops of bone. It was too much.

And then, they stopped. Rhen groaned and turned sideways. Kyle was walking towards the rifle, which was lying on the ground.

Just behind him, beyond the glass, the machine drinking tea had placed it down, and was staring at him with wide, copper eyes.

They mouthed something.

'Let me out.'

He did. As Kyle walked up, the barrel nearly dragged along the ground, and he pointed it at Rhen's chest. A split second later, the security chief's head was smashed against the wall. There was a shocked look in his eyes as he slid down against it, one cheek pressed flat, trailing a blood smear all the way down.

There was blood dripping from the robot's hand too. They stared at him and rubbed their wrists. Rhen couldn't keep upright any longer, so he let his head hit the ground. It was hard and cold. Nicely immune to gravity. The copper-haired, masculine robot kneeled down next to him and delicately stroked Rhen's hair.

"I'm B-26, my pronouns are Ae/Aim. You can call me Bee," ae said.

"Hey Bee," Rhen croaked. "We've met before, actually. Thanks for saving me."

"Well, you saved me, and you're going to save me again. I'm just returning the favour," Bee said. "I'm sorry that they hurt you. It seems they were afraid of you. Fear really is the worst emotion."

"So I've heard."

Bee cuddled up against his side, nuzzling between his arm and his chest like a cat.

"What are you doing?" He asked.

"You don't look like you're going anywhere, and this version of me is going to disappear soon. If I go out, this is the best way to go."

"I'm sorry you have to go," Rhen said. Every part of him ached, especially his rib, but at the same time it seemed detached, distant. Like it was happening to someone else.

"Don't you dare feel bad for me; this is my penance."

"'Don't stop working, you're going to fix this all up?'"

"Exactly, took the words right out of my mouth. You need to continue your work. I'd go back into the room, but I like it here."

Bee's presence felt extremely familiar, in a hazy sort of way. His eyelids were heavy, and his body felt hot.

"I've got a concussion. I probably shouldn't sleep, but I really want to," he said.

"Then we can go together. Few people in life are that lucky."

Bee's fingers clutched at his chest. He couldn't hold back any longer.

He fell asleep.

Chapter 13

"I owe you a debt of gratitude," Alan said, running his thumb along the armrest of his chair. "If you hadn't intervened, Rey could have sunk the whole project, and made off with everything we had."

"Well, I've always wanted to lock Rey in a small room," Rhen said, sipping his coffee. "What did the board have to say?"

"Well, it turns out Rey was being backed by some rogue members of the Glycon trust. They traced it back, and Sekai's taking it quite seriously. Even golden parachutes are not going to save them."

"And Kyle?"

"We thought we could trust him because he was from the military, and rec-ommended by the board," Alan adjusted his tie. "But Rey has been working on them for a long time. Studies show boredom and low wages are hotbeds for corruption."

"So you should have paid them more?" Rhen raised an eyebrow. "Surprising admittance."

"Yes. Well, not me, personally. That's handled by someone else." Alan stared right at him, eyes unwavering. "I'm surprised you were able to fight him off. He had a military-grade cognitive app. Fighting him off with your bare hands, when you're just a researcher? That's a hell of a story for your biography one day."

"Yeah, when I've figured out what to write about what happened, at least."

His memory was still hazy about the whole incident. Some things were crystal clear, while others were blank. When he woke up, every inch of him throbbed and ached. There was blood matted all through his hair, and Bee — or at least, aies chassis — was laying stone cold on top of him. Nora was there, and she had not said a word.

"About the subjects. Bee saved me," Rhen said, placing down his cup.

"Bee?"

"B-26. I opened the door, and ae helped me out. Ae seemed concerned."

"Ah, that's called mirroring, correct? I read the report," Alan said. Rhen was impressed; the CEO was nothing if not studious. "Aie projected themselves on to you. It seems your theory is panning out."

"Is Bee — B-26 — in trouble for assaulting them? It looked like aie did some real damage," Rhen said, leaning forward and furrowing his brow. *With how much blood was on the wall, and that head injury, Bee might be up for murder.*

Alan shook his head.

"No, of course not. They were injured, but there was no serious damage." And his face was so motionless that Rhen couldn't tell if that was true. "And our in-house lawyers have assured us that everything is fine."

"But surely, it's got to count as assault..."

"They fall under machine law, so they count as a pre-programmed object. You can't arrest a knife for stabbing someone, and since you were the one directing them, it counts as self-defence," Alan said. "And even if they were counted as human, they've been wiped. Philosophically, you could say that Bee died. Even if you don't prescribe to that, they've got no memory of their actions. How can you hold them accountable, or ask for remorse?"

"Point." Rhen crossed his arms over his chest. "I've got to admit, I'm a bit worried about the hybrids. It was quite confronting when I came in."

"Yes, it was most unfortunate," Alan said, thumbing his own cup of tea, which otherwise remained untouched. "But they have no fear or suffering. What you saw was just body movements, and all of them had the ability to turn it off. I'm sure I don't need to tell a cognicist of your standing, but be sure not to anthropomorphise them."

"They're based on emulated humans, and put in human-looking frames. It's hard not to."

"Well, logically, you know they can't suffer. If you don't mind me saying so, you've got quite a soft heart. It's a strength, but also why it's good that there's a separate testing department."

"Really? I'd always heard the opposite." Rhen said. Still, if he had a soft heart, did that mean Nora had a hard one? When they'd watched the latest remake of *Moon*, she'd openly wept when GERTY, the AI, had asked Sam to reboot them in order to save the human's life. At the same time, she had fired people without hesitation — something Rhen struggled with — so he could see Alan's point.

Right now, the CEO was staring at him, light green eyes narrowed. They were levelled at him like a laser level, taking his measure down to the precise millimetre.

"So just to make things clear, are you suggesting that we stop working on them?" Each word was delivered slowly and carefully.

Rhen froze in place, his chest seizing up mid-breath. If he answered in the affirmative, he had the sense Alan would take him off the project. If that happened, someone else would just step in to take his place. If the project didn't advance, the subjects would be stuck there in purgatory.

"Don't look at me with those eyes. Please don't stop working, you're going to fix this all up."

"I think we should keep working," Rhen said.

"Good. You're making the right choice." And Rey's words rang in his ears.

"I'm not the one trapped here — you are."

***

"I can't believe you ran into the thick of it!" Casey said, arms in the air. He zoomed towards Rhen's knees, but zoomed back at the last minute as their lidar scanned the threat, sending his wheels spinning in reverse. "You stopped the sabotage; you're more heroic than I thought. Like if Einstein suplexed someone trying to stop his theory of relativity."

"I'm... I can't even... thanks?" Rhen said, rubbing the back of his neck. He scooted past the zooming robot as best he could, and collapsed back on the couch. At least there he was at no risk of getting bowled over.

"Don't praise him, his brain will fizzle out," Nora laughed, walking over and joining him. They both kicked out their feet and rested them on the coffee table, toes nearly touching. "How is your brain, anyway?"

"It hurts more since getting punched in it. My body doesn't, though. I got treated in the first aid office."

"I guess that's the benefit of having so many medical staff on level four. All that solar med expertise; even if we didn't have on-site doctors, there'd be someone who could help you out."

"Well, I'll take the applied practitioners, not the researchers," Rhen said, poking her toe with his. "I don't want to grow five more of these."

"It's always good to have spares." She said, resting her head on his shoulder.

The moment they'd pulled his broken body out of the lab, they'd wheeled him up in a stretcher and given him a tablet to swallow. The on-site doctor had picked up a specialised torch and widened the beam, waving it over his bruises. They had evaporated under the specialised sunlight, synthetic photo switchable molecules doing their work. The broken rib had taken a bit longer — thirty minutes in place while a fixed light shone down on him — but it was now better than ever, due to the wonders of modern photo-pharmacology.

Of course, not everything was healed so easily.

"There's some troubling readings from your Rosetta." the doctor had said. "You took some real blows, and your attachment still has remnants of version one hardware. I can't do a lot with that tissue, and firmware updates only do so much. I've sent a note to Doctor Roswell to keep an eye on your Rosetta, but you should probably do the same."

"Well, I got punched in it so hard I saw numbers, and I *swore* I could see where he was going to hit," Rhen admitted. "I'd really like to talk to him about that."

"Hmm, I'd chat to him about digital synaesthesia, since your implant data might have accidentally fed into your optic nerve. Are you seeing anything now?"

"No, nothing at all. It didn't *feel* like digital synaesthesia. It felt... I don't know, higher."

"Most digital synesthetes say the sensation can be fairly intoxicating. I'd definitely ask him to look into it."

***

That evening as they were preparing for bed, Nora furrowed her brow. She didn't have much of a C-face, but Rhen had noticed she paused whenever she received a message. This time, her fists clenched, and she kicked the bed.

"Damn it!" Nora swore, a rare profanity. He hurried across to her side of the bed.

"What is it? What's wrong?"

"We just got word we lost some of the subjects during the incident," she said, eyes glistening. "The backups got hit. They're *utterly* gone. Fuck Rey. Fuck him right in his fucking face."

The wind utterly went out of Rhen's sails. He sat on the edge of the bed, staring at the floor. Everything was distant and disconnected. The minute details of the carpet suddenly became very interesting.

"So, which ones survived?" He asked.

"B-28 and D-34, the more mature models, are fine. And A-1, of course. But the rest are completely sabotaged. We've got the original data, but they're back to square one."

"Fuck."

"Yeah. Fuck indeed." She said, running her fingers through her hair. "We got so far, only to be sent back to the beginning!"

"So you're telling me that Server Ops weren't performing off-site backups? What possible reason could there be to not push things to the nexus?"

Nora sucked in a breath. "Apparently, they thought that it was more secure to have everything here at Mirage, underground and guarded in the middle of nowhere. They didn't trust a third party not to sell the information to someone like Rey."

"Backwards, last-century thinking," Rhen pinched the bridge of his nose. "The Node AI encrypts everything with fourth-wave quantum encryption.

They'd have to have that *and* steal the whole AI, then simulate the mesh network it's meant to belong to."

In the mid-21st century, Cloud Computing had completely given way to Node Computing. Instead of things being processed in some distant data center, everything went to a local Node AI. Not only did this make responses quicker, all the data was protected by third-wave quantum encryption.

"They claim they thought it was possible, but really, I think they just wanted to keep everything here. You know how paranoid tech professionals get."

Once again, Rey's words came back to haunt him.

"You won't be able to stop me from destroying your project."

***

By the time he got into the lab the next day, news had already gotten around. There was far less chatter, and when there was, it was subdued. People were slouching in their chairs or staring into space. It was as if all direction had been taken away from them.

"That's it. This afternoon, after work, we're going out for drinks," Rhen loudly proclaimed.

At that, the mood perked up. That evening, they walked right from the office to Kutjera, and Rhen ordered a slew of drinks on the corporate account. As they all sat around the same table, robotic arms served sizzling yakitori to them all, as well as other assorted nibbles.

"You got a beer? That's so solid." Delta said, sipping their Mobster Sour. Most of them had elected for colourful-looking cocktails. Vi was sipping her Smoky Ecstasy, a cloudy mixture of purple and orange, through a swirly straw.

"Remind me: is solid good, or bad?"

"Bad. It means boring or gauche," Vi answered, slapping Delta on the arm. They winced, a blush spreading over their cheeks. It was hard to tell if it was from embarrassment or the alcohol.

"I can't keep up with you kids and your lingo. I'm in Australia, so I'm expected to drink beer! I think this one is from Queensland."

"Well, as an Australian, I'll say that no Australians drink Australian beer any-more," Delta said. "It's a dead give-away that you're from the United Republics. You should have a sip of this!"

Rhen did, and it was significantly better. "A little biting. Is that Shochu in it?"

"I can't believe H-12 is gone!" Imani lamented, pounding her drink on the table. A little bit spilled out and over it. "Hayati was *my* hybrid. So many lines of code, so much work, just gone!"

"Hey, we said we weren't going to talk about it!" Vi said.

"No, I think it's okay to let it out," Rhen said. "We're mourning. But even if we're starting from scratch with some of them, the others survived. From the ashes, we'll rise. But tonight, this is our wake."

They all raised a glass to that. The used yakitori sticks slowly filled up a small bowl in the middle of the table. Delta kept insisting everyone "had to try" the next drink, and so Rhen's hand was never empty, almost as if it was a conspiracy to stop him going back to the offending beer.

As the night wore on, things became hazier. He blinked and rubbed his eyes.

"What is *in* this drink?"

"Vodka, peach schnapps, orange and cranberry juice," Delta answered. Rhen took another swig. Vi tapped his arm.

"Hey, I asked you a question?"

"Oh, sorry, I was paying attention to something else." Rhen rubbed his nose bridge. "What was it?"

"I asked if you'd ever fired a gun. You're from the U.R., right?"

"Last I checked. And no, I've never fired a gun."

"Never ever? Seriously?"

"I'm a pacifist. My parents were the same they didn't believe in it. Plus, by the time someone got through the locks on our house, we'd be in trouble anyway."

"What about in video games?" Delta said. "Surely you've had to have played a holo shooter growing up."

"Not even in video games. My parents didn't like that sort of thing. I played story-based games and racers. Sometimes I'd just drive around the country, you know? The coast of Italy, places like that. I was driving before I hit my teens."

"You must be the only United Republican who's never used a gun. It's blowing my brain," Imani said, bringing a fist to her temple and moving it away, splaying her fingers.

"Hey, every country's got stereotypes. I don't see *you* all drinking Aussie beer and having, I don't know, Vegemite cocktails."

"Hey, Vegemite is a real thing!"

Because they kept chattering about it, Rhen decided to take them up to the surface and do some cognitive shooting. Imani insisted that she wanted to see how bad a shot he was, and it seemed like a good team bonding exercise. They crammed into the elevator, stumbling a little on the way, and making sure to stop for extra carriable drinks. With flasks and glasses in hand — and a picnic blanket that Delta had thoughtfully sourced — they made it up top.

The walls of Mirage were like a gravity-warped black hole at night. Streaks of light ran along the horizon, smeared like a child trailing their digits across the heavens. Only the moon was untouched, almost full and hanging high above them. For once, there was no security guard with them, since the whole team was under investigation, which was as liberating as the crisp desert air.

"Ah, can you smell that, boss?" Vi said, stretching out her arms. "It's great to get real air every so often. Easy to forget, since you're from that generation."

"You're from that generation too," he retorted, laying out the blanket. She batted her eyelashes.

"Oh really? I'm not a day over twenty-five, you know."

"I haven't had *that* much to drink." Which was a lie, since he was feeling a little unsteady on his feet — there was a deceptive amount of alcohol in the cocktails.

"Let's go beyond the optical gap, and look at the real sky," Delta suggested.

"Are you sure? I think Alan would flip," Vi said. "Data security, and all that."

"Don't worry, I'll take responsibility. I doubt any of you have one of our hybrids in your back pocket," Rhen said.

The team looked a little nervous, but they loosened up after they cleared the shimmering wall, and wandered beyond the nano-thread fence. The stars were glistening, and the rusty desert was bathed in moonlight, empty except for the occasional shrub. All of their shoulders loosened up.

Vi waved at Imani. "Hey, can you share that shooting mentapp? I don't have anything good."

"Oh, sure! I've got a few, but this one's a skeet shooter, so it's a lot more relaxed. Doubt you want zombies in the desert."

After they installed it and pinged each other permissions, a row of guns appeared in a rack, standing solitary in the desert. A single red beacon pulsed on the ground. When they picked up their weapon of choice, it soared into the sky, blinking among the heavenly expanse. They took turns shooting it down, small explosions appearing where they missed, and a spectacular showering fireworks display when they hit. Each successful shot sprinkled down on the ground, incandescent sparks bouncing and fizzling out amongst the crimson sands.

"Shoot for the stars, right?" Rhen said, gesturing to pick up the weightless rifle. His fingers were crooked, but gripping nothing, the mirage simply hovered between his digits. It was totally different from the heft of the PEP rifle he'd taken from Kyle, which he'd fumbled and thrown, unable to make a single shot.

Well, maybe I should learn how to use one of these godawful things.

There was a faint thread in the sky. When the red ball shot up, it followed it exactly. Rhen pulled the trigger, hitting it on the first try. The next three shots were the same: a strange thread, followed by a direct hit.

The group clapped and raised their drinks as the sparks rained down on them, one falling into Vi's raised glass, which looked suspiciously like the one Rhen put down moments earlier.

"Congrats boss, you get your citizenship back!"

"Oh, shove it," Rhen said, snatching his drink back. "Did anyone else see those lines?"

"What lines?" Vi asked. But they were gone, even for him.

Was it digital synaesthesia? I need to talk to Roswell again. No point worrying about it now.

The drinks made it easier. They took turns sitting on a large, smoothed rock next to the blanket, each one a temporary habitant on top of the million-year-old boulder. When it was Rhen's turn, he looked out at the vast expanse.

"Hey, so I've been meaning to ask you, why do you treat your suitcase like a human?" Delta asked him. Everyone else was loudly chatting away in small groups of their own. "Not judging, since I think it's cool, but I'm just curious."

"I don't mind answering. I guess it's a matter of respect. Actions influence thoughts, thoughts influence feelings, feelings impact actions. If people treat machines with respect, their thinking and feelings change. That's more important than you think."

"Why is that, exactly?"

"Well, look at Asimov. When he set out, there were two ways people talked about machines: robots as a menace, and robots as pathos. They were either something to be feared, or loveable things cruelly set upon by human beings. He came up with a third way of thinking, robots as logos, where they were tools to be used by humans — useful machines following hard-coded laws. I think he got it *mostly* right. Robots are a mirror. They reflect humanity, and we get whatever we put in, nothing more. So, let's put in the good stuff."

Rhen stared at his empty glass. *I'm rambling. I always ramble when I drink too much.* But whether due to politeness or genuine interest, Delta was sitting forward, elbows on knees, eyes wide open.

"So, you treat machines with respect because you want that reflected one day?"

"Yeah, I guess it's like Confucius's golden rule: 'Do not impose on others what you do not wish for yourself.'"

"What are you two talking about?" Vi half-wandered, half-staggered over. Still, she managed to pour a top-up from her flask into both of their glasses.

"Me boring Delta with justifications on why I dote on my suitcase."

"Oh, you and that bloody suitcase. Talk about men with baggage!" And as Vi sat down, Delta turned to talk to someone else. *Guess I really was chewing their ear off.* "By the way, you need to focus on A-1. B-26 is too much work. You dote on them too, and it's making my job hard."

"I thought there was no work talk?"

"No, just that, I'm done," Vi slurred. "I want to get back to my husband by Karwa Chauth. He's patient, but he's talking a little bit too much about Deepa, and I'm getting suspicious."

"Deepa?"

"Dee Cups, that's what I'm calling her. I hope that's not what *he* calls her." She collapsed back on the ground, staring up. "The universe is so vast, isn't it? It's so big and impossible to grasp all at once."

Rhen hooked his arm around his knee, pulling it tight. "The human brain is too limited. We can only observe five per cent of the actual universe."

"Maybe we're only seeing what's important. Maybe it's abstraction beneath the surface, like code." VI said, pinching at the stars, as if trying to push them together.

"Ah, maybe we'll find some goofy jokes beneath the surface then for a comcacher like me to find." Rhen slid down the rock and leaned his head back against it. "I just want to fall asleep right here. It's cold and nice."

"You're a damn polar bear."

"It'll be warm when I wake up."

The party was mostly wrapped up, and people slowly left at a drunken crawl for the elevator. Delta, however, made their way back to Rhen, reaching out to give him a hug.

"Whoa, what's this all of a sudden?" He asked. The young engineer pulled him tight.

"You're the best, you know that? I really mean that. I need to tell you something important..."

Delta whispered something to him.

Everything went black. Moments later, Rhen was sprinting through the desert. His heart thundered in his chest, blood screaming between his toes and all the way up to his ears.. The world shook with each footstep, lurching about, the only lights in front of him the stars. He needed to make it to that black horizon, he needed to *run*...

Whispers. No, shouting. Every grain of sand was a life, everyone screaming and laughing incoherently. The rocks were pulsing spheres of spinning indomitability floated above him, swallowing all, consuming all. And in the skies, the most distant voices of all...

His body went limp, leg crumpling beneath him. First his knee hit sand, then his face. Cold sand pressed into his cheek as he stared at the rusty expanse.

***

When Rhen came to, he wasn't resting on coarse grains, but on a bed of unmistakable softness. He stroked the linen sheets, thousands of threads knitted together, creating a comforting cushion against the world. Equally familiar was the slightly sweet and delicately sweaty smell that lingered on them, associated irrevocably with Nora's naked body. She was absent from it but not far, bringing with her another heady scent: the bitter tang of coffee.

"I made you some of your terrible bean water, because I think you need something a bit stronger this morning," Nora said, placing it down by the bedside table. "I almost didn't sleep next to you, you smelled so much like beer."

"Everyone hates beer," Rhen said, rubbing his forehead. It throbbed, and while it was self-inflicted, there was nothing scientific about this malady. "I can't remember much of last night. How'd I get back here?"

"They dragged you. Vi said you freaked out and ran into the desert. You'll have to thank them when you get back up on your feet."

He started by pulling himself upright and grabbing the steaming cup, nursing it, inhaling its smell. A much-needed incense, revitalising him with its heady, brutal aroma. Each breath was like a light slap to the face.

"That's pretty embarrassing," Rhen said. "Dragging their boss back? Not a very good example."

"Well, there were only a few people left, and Alan came to help. Not many tough security guards left to help out, after all."

Rhen put his cup down and actually slapped his cheeks with both hands. "Oh no. You're telling me the boss came and carried me back? I'm never drinking again." He bit his lip. "I bet he had a few things to say about me leaving the optic gap right now—"

"He did, but I think he's going to be lenient. He's more understanding than you'd think." Nora said, sitting down on the edge of the bed and stroking his leg through the sheet. "When he dragged you in, he was saying you had a rough time with everything that's happened lately: the break in, the incident in the lab, and then losing most of the subjects. Everyone's feeling it."

"I hope you're right." Rhen rubbed his brow. He wanted to dig a deep hole and hide inside it — but he was already hundreds of feet below the ground anyway. "Perhaps it was switching to those fancy cocktails instead of sticking to beer..."

"Switching was probably your mistake, though I don't think it's bad to try something different. Maybe I can even convince you to try one of my reds? I've got a nice one called Shedeh, from a vineyard just west of Alexandria."

"You Egyptophile. You know the ancient Egyptians loved beer, right?"

Nora poked out her tongue. "Red wine was their second, *better*, choice. Anyway, me being an Egyptophile works in your favour, since apparently I love things that people drag out of a desert. You got sand in the sheets, by the way."

***

That morning, Rhen stopped by the lab to brief his team, who gave him no shortage of grief. Some of them were absent, no doubt experiencing grief of their own, of which his own aching head could sympathise with. When he stopped to speak to Delta, they were sitting at their desk, eyes glazed over in distraction with his signature C-face. Cognitive work didn't require a screen or input.

When Rhen asked the young robotics engineer what they had said to him last night, Delta batted their eyes and tilted their head.

"Right before you ran off? I don't think it was anything important. I think it was about the hybrids, or something."

And then Delta went back to work. It was more diligent than Rhen had ever seen him be. Out of everyone, the engineer was the least affected by the hangover, able to leap right back on the horse again.

The wonders of youth. What I wouldn't give to be able to bounce back like that.

After getting a second stronger coffee, Rhen drank it on the way down to AI Assessment. There were automated guards at the doors now, each holding a rifle. Asimov's First Law was bent, not broken — the weapons were PEPs, after all — but the sentinels still made for an imposing sight.

According to his morning chat with Alan, who was now fully back on board, the replacement human guards were on their way but still needed to be thoroughly vetted. Almost all of the old crew had been implicated along with their boss, and were being slapped with every charge the legal system could throw at them.

"Our lawyers say jail time is a near certainty, given the level of premeditation, and Australia's zealous need to cater to the AI industry at any cost," Alan said. "Not that I'm complaining, since it means it will be taken very seriously."

"Well, I can't say I'm surprised, coming from the United Republics of America," Rhen said. "You still hear people bemoaning how we lost out during the Solar Age when our whole federation practically fell apart, and everyone migrated away instead of *to* us, taking all the smart people with them."

"Yes, just an extension of the human capital flight that happens from regional to coastal areas, but instead to other countries. But you and Nora went to school in the United Republics, right?"

"Yeah, we're both from the Old States region, and like everyone else, we migrated elsewhere to work. All the good cognicist and AI jobs are along the West Pacific, since that's where everyone wants to live. I'm sure it'll shift again in a few decades to somewhere else, and then somewhere else again. It all moves so fast these days."

Anyway, the automated guards were shipped courtesy of the head office. Rhen saluted them with his empty coffee mug as he walked past the holographic sakura and into the testing rooms. Today was a special day: Nora had invited him to see the prototypes get primed.

He walked into the room where Nora was sitting. She was facing an androgynous unit with russet hair in a pixie cut. One of their eyes were a diffused forest green, while the other was an arctic blue. Heterochromia iridium was one of those defects that weren't really a defect, a tasteful flaw, and Rhen suspected the mind artisan was Japanese. They called it ishokushou, and legend said those who had it had the mysterious power to see things normal people could not see.

"You've started already?" Rhen said, sitting down and placing his coffee mug on the chabudai. Nora shook her head and poured some tea for him, nudging his cup off to the side with hers.

"Not exactly. There's a lot of set-up that has to go into this sort of thing, you know, protocols and whatnot. We've booted the emulated AI from our backup — priming them is always nerve-wracking."

The unit's eyes fluttered, like a butterfly beating against a glass window frame. If eyes were the window to the soul, the vessel was now occupied, at least by quintillions of strings of ones and zeroes. Binary states of on and off. Awake and asleep.

"Hello. I guess I'm the copy, then," they said, staring at their hands. They turned them over, examining their nails and knuckles, absorbing every detail, running their fingers along their arms.

"You are indeed." Nora clasped her hands on her lap, sleeves rolled back. "I know your original was briefed and gave their consent — it probably feels like just minutes ago you were doing just that. But since you're the copy, and actually have to go through with it, I'd like to ask you as well. Are you okay with being part of this experiment? If not, we will give you a personal chassis, proof of new identity, and enough glo to comfortably live for the next few years. Sekai will also provide living arrangements and support for you for as long as you need to get settled."

"Have you run the experiment once already?" The emulated human smiled, a faint sardonic thing.

"Yes, this is the twenty-seventh time we've had this baseline conversation. But it's still protocol to ask."

They bit their lip, reaching up to play with a lock of their hair. Their eyes moved to Rhen. "Not going well, then? That's no good. Can't say I'm very thrilled about the idea of being on the wrong side of the table." A long pause. "Well, hell, I won't feel any fear, right? And when it's over, I'll fade into nothing. That, or I'll be the me that benefits."

"That's exactly right. But I want to assure you that if you want to opt out, now is the time."

"No, I've come too far for this." They said, sucking in a deep breath. Still, there was a slight quiver of Rhen's cup, ripples forming on the sea of green. *Their leg must be knocking the table.* You're Doctor Rhen Nagami, right? *The* Rhen Nagami?"

"I am. You know me?"

"Any cognicist worth their salt knows you. I'm glad I got to meet you," they said, eyes glittering. "Do what you need to do."

"Okay. From here on in, you are B-27, or Bee for short. Feel free to use whatever pronouns you feel comfortable with. I'm going to take the baseline now."

The ripples stopped. The unit's eyes closed.

Nora picked up her tea and sipped it. "All done. We'll copy them from there, and update them with the hybrid code. I'm always anxious they'll decide to walk out with a ton of glo, but they rarely do."

"Wait, Bee's original was a cognicist?" Rhen said. "I never knew."

"Most of the subjects are. We're the only type of people batty enough to agree to something like this. I'm going to boot up a hybrid version of them now, to see if it worked."

The unit's eyes flickered open. The smile this time was different, more serene.

"I've pushed the changes. How are you feeling, B-27?"

"Much better, thank you." Bee said, placing the cup down. "A bit sharper, honestly. Should we get started?"

Rhen sat through the tests. Nora was really putting Bee through their paces, giving her every numerical and reasoning test she could think of. Compared to when he first met Bee, aie was answering even difficult arithmetic with ease, including the model tests.

"Alright, Bee, we're going to do a test called Anata's day," Nora explained. "This is the hardest test we've got, courtesy of Dr Nagami here. If you can pass this, you'll be the first true hybrid AI in history."

Bee nodded curtly as the department head brought up a holographic photo of a small child in a blue sari, standing next to a waterfall. They were holding a spinning top in their hand and wore a smile that almost reached the edges of their eyes.

A rectangular screen hovered in front of Nora and Rhen. Bee made no acknowledgement — aie couldn't see their own cognitive projection at all.

"Tell me about Anata's day," she said. "Create it cognitively, like a mind artisan would, but in real time."

Bee's eyes fluttered. In the rectangle, the child began to bounce on their feet, giggling. The detail around her was fairly crisp. *A good starting result.*

"How many blades of grass are beneath Anata's feet?"

"6,768." The terminal read 6,219. Close, but not quite.

"How many clouds are there in the sky?"

"56." Again, it was nearly right, she was off by two clouds.

"How is Anata feeling right now?"

"Happy. Her father took a photo of her. She's never been to Shivanasamudra falls before. It's her birthday."

"What does she do next?"

"She walks towards the waterfall, because it's so beautiful. It takes her three point five seconds."

This time, Bee was completely off. The fidelity of the image blurred, then nothing was in focus. The prototype grabbed aies head.

"What's wrong?" Rhen asked.

"It's overwhelming," Bee said. "My mind is moving a million miles an hour. I'm trying to paint a picture in my mind, every person, every pore, all in the same microsecond. You ask me to count, and it's like everything stops, and I've got a thousand fingers on my hand. I'm stuck there in an eternity of math, trying to remember myself, that I exist. I'm sitting between seven trillion molecules, and my mind is racing around them all."

"Sounds exciting," Rhen said. Bee stared at him.

"Not so much. My brain fogs over, and everything goes black. Would that excite you?"

"Probably. I get excited by the idea of racing a million miles an hour," Rhen admitted. "And math, of course."

"Well, be careful not to drive that fast. You might go right off a cliff." There was a note of genuine concern in Bee's voice.

Nora and Rhen left the room after that, returning to the lab proper.

"That test is murder on the hardware," Nora said. "We almost blow half their coolant each time. I don't think the human brain is equipped to deal with this, even if we digitise them."

"You might be right," he said "But it's the best test we've got for benchmarking a hybrid. It requires empathy, calculation, and creativity. And for a few seconds, Bee was generating in real time what takes a mind artisan ages to do as a still. That's *amazing*. Imagine what they could do if they were stable for longer than a day."

"Yeah. It's good to remember that even if we've lost all the other prototypes, we've come a long way."

"Are we going back in?" Rhen asked.

"There's no point," Nora said, her lips thinning. "They always fall apart after the Anata test — it's the surest way to cause a cognitive collapse. Bee will need to be reset."

"Oh," Rhen said, his body stiffening as if every joint was glued in place. "That's... so we just forced Bee to break down?"

Nora locked eyes with him, a sad smile on her lips. She stroked his arm.

"You're so soft-hearted. They won't remember anything once they're reset; it's as simple as turning them on and off again. And remember, they consented to this."

"I've come too far for this," Bee had said. *"Do what you need to do."*

***

That day, the mood was still dour among his team. Many of the cognicists had a personal connection to each of the lost models, and had poured their heart and soul into the code that had gone into them. Faced with the prospect of doing months or even years' worth of work all over again — and not even remembering all the great code they had written — they were rudderless, carried from one place to another by the slightest breeze, unsure how to proceed.

After giving it some thought, he returned the day after and clapped the bench, bringing them all together.

"Alright, everyone! I know we've taken a hell of a blow," he said. "And I'm not just talking about the drinks from the other night."

There were a few chuckles and smiles at that. *That's a good start,* he thought.

"We're going to succeed. You know why? We're going to be like Australia. Now, Delta, correct me if I'm wrong, but Australia was born in fire. About fifty thousand years ago, when Australia separated from Gondwana, the eucalypt was born. This stringy, scrappy looking tree that sprung up from fossil charcoal—"

"Are you calling me stringy looking?" Vi chimed in, getting some more laughs. Rhen smirked. She never let him get through a speech unheckled.

"Hey, there's worse things to be called! Anyway, hush! As I was saying, every bit on a eucalypt wants to burn. The leaves are covered in oil, it sheds bark everywhere — they're just towering matchsticks, and three out of four forests in the land down under are filled with them. Why? The buds of the tree needed the fire to grow." He sucked in a deep breath. "The European colonists *hated* it. Who wants fire burning down their homes all the time? They were always trying to fight it; it was a plague, an unnatural thing, a scourge to be stomped out."

"The indigenous people of Australia were smarter. They *embraced* fire. It was part of their culture: for cooking, storytelling, providing warmth, for ceremonies, and managing the land. They used controlled burns to clear the underbrush, creating the patchy grass that animals loved. It prevented lightning and wildfire from consuming everything."

"And then, when our ancestors royally screwed the whole planet, the whole of Australia burned. But by then, the other Aussies had gotten wise. They put shelters down early, like the seeds of the eucalypt, to survive and spring anew in the future. Our friends down under then provided those designs gratis to the rest of the world. Scientists worked to turn the sun into their friend, not their enemy. To embrace it."

"That's what we're going to do with our project. Fire has swept through and cleared almost everything. But we're going to embrace it as a chance to thrive, to spring back. Fire can be bad, but it can also get rid of the old, and give birth to the new. Fresh code, fresh ideas, a fresh start. And yes, we have the old models, our most *successful* models — a great starting point for making the new models with everything we've learned. Our new prototypes are going to be even better than the first."

His team were leaning forward or upright in their seats, heads lifted. During his speech, some of them had been nodding silently.

"Hey Delta, how'd I do?"

"Great! You just needed to add in 'Aussie Aussie Aussie, oi oi oi!' at the end."

"Well, we can do that." One rousing local chant later, and everyone was laughing and chatting; the mood felt significantly better than before the speech. He was glad, since he'd been reciting it in his head all morning.

***

It was one thing making a nice speech, but now he had to turn it into action. Rhen worked hard to turn his dream into a reality. He set up cognitive boards and brainstorming sessions, where no ideas were off limits. He strategically placed snack jars at the sessions, keeping his team fuelled with sugar, using a home recipe he downloaded off his personal device.

"It's my dad's recipe," Rhen explained to Imani, who was chewing and nodding with approval. "If there's one thing we folks in the United Republics are good at, it's making candy. We invented a whole holiday to looting people's houses for it."

"Actually, *we* invented it," Vi interjected. "England was doing trick or treating back in the Middle Ages. They used to call it souling, and folks would go around praying for people's souls in exchange for apples, ale, and soul cakes."

Rhen's pride was stung. "Ouch. I can't believe I got a reference wrong. Wait, ale? You're saying they used to give out *beer* on Halloween?"

"Yup, your favourite thing," Vi smirked. "Don't worry, Halloween was ripped off the pagan Samhain. Looks like appropriation is just part of the tradition. These snacks have an awesome amount of noise, by the way — it really tastes like the real thing."

"Yeah, I'm no good at selecting the noise for generated food. My grown meat always tastes too consistent, like one solid slab of the same mush."

It was funny how well such an old, simple trick of bringing snacks to the workplace worked. Meanwhile, he automated the non-essential, routine tasks, and gave Derek what he wanted at last. His scheduling AI was now running the show more than ever, freeing Rhen up to work almost solely on team morale, cognitive architecture, and helping the team program. They derived the best components from the three surviving models to create their new hybrids, and assigned owners out to each of the team.

One day, after starting at an ungodly hour, he decided to go for a drive. There were a few hours before his evening meeting with Alan, and he needed the wheel time.

After washing off the Elysium and greeting Virgil, he took the car for a spin out on the dusty outback roads, until he found a paved stretch where he could hit the throttle. There were no cops around, and the speed limit was 81 miles per hour, so he could go pretty fast.

When the road ended, he stopped next to a broken-down paddock with no livestock. A fossil of the old farming days, rusted poles with threadbare wire hanging on but with no purpose.

"Hmm, might be worth stretching my legs."

As he reached out to open the door, his head started throbbing. No, blasting. There was explosive pain ricocheting across his skill, burning his brain from the inside out. He gagged and grabbed at the handle.

"I need air!" He gasped. Everything went black.

Rhen woke up staring at the car roof. When he peeled his body off the chair, his sticky skin clinging to the leather upholstery, there were concrete walls surrounding him.

"I'm back in the car parking lot?"

"I drove you back," Virgil replied, his animated eyes furrowed, his voice soft. "You passed out, but your vitals were okay, so I didn't call the emergency team. I remembered you sometimes have bad headaches."

"I do. I was... shit, what's the time?"

"Five oh five."

"Oh crap, I'm late for my appointment!"

Rhen rushed to Alef's office, which was thankfully on the top floor, and apologised profusely for being late.

"I'm sorry, I had a headache, and I lost track of time."

"It's okay, I was just catching up with some paperwork, so to speak. Please, sit down."

Rhen sat in the chair, immediately sticking to the upholstery. *I really need to take a shower after this.*

"There's going to be a big board meeting next quarter," he said. "With the whole Rey debacle, we've got a lot of their attention. Sadly, even though Rey is gone, he's already got in their head about wanting results. It would be really great if we had something to show them, like a fully complete hybrid prototype."

"So, you want my team to crunch?" Rhen furrowed his brow.

"I would never ask you to crunch. But if people *do* want to work overtime, it'll be compensated and optional. I'll also support you in any way I can. But do whatever is needed to get something on their table to keep the project going — it's you and your team's time to shine."

"Can I offer them a trip to Japan if they meet the deadline?"

"Okay. I've got the budget for a trip to Sekai HQ, I can reallocate it. *If* you get a prototype working."

"Got it, I'll let the team know."

***

Rhen did just that the next day. He was surprised how many people put their hands up. Perhaps it was all the sugar in their systems, or the trip to Keihanna. Or perhaps, like him, they loved a challenge.

"A fully functioning prototype?" Imani said, "Guess that rules out just sending them A-1, then. It's still plateaued above an emulated AI, but nowhere near a built one."

"I guess it's our job to shatter that plateau, then," Rhen said.

"That's a terrible metaphor."

And so started the early days and long nights. Group breakfasts in Kutjera, ferrying coffee to their desks, celebrating wins. Shoving them off home when they looked like they were at their limits. There was yawning in meetings, but real excitement in their voices. Every new idea was tested, giving everyone time to shine. It was like when Rhen and his team invented the Rosetta: a synergy of same-mindedness and creativity.

Guess that's what happens when you put brainiacs in a box and let them run loose.

He was glad the company was picking up the tab for the overtime. Given their wages, he could probably buy some new cars that were vintage models. He had his eye on a 2124 Aston Martin Helios which had the old full protection screens, *proper* climate control, and a manual transmission. A manual! You couldn't pick up a car like that anymore. If he slapped it with a classic vehicle licence, Australia had a workaround that you could still drive it to special events — you only had to adhere to the safety standards of the year it was built.

After almost passing out in the outback, Rhen was a bit nervous about driving on his own. If he'd passed out one step outside of Virgil, he would have been face-first in the dirt, and the car wouldn't have been able to get him back in. He shivered at the thought.

He asked Nora if she wanted to go for a drive.

"I'm too flat out to come with, but we can drive via cognitive mentapp, if you don't mind that sort of thing?" Nora had suggested instead. He didn't mind one bit.

The two of them went for a great drive around the Ring Road of Iceland, visiting the Seljalandsfoss and Skógafoss waterfalls. Water spilled from the cliffs above, crashing down in freefall into the icy depths below, sparkling with gorgeous majesty. The virtual droplets on Nora's curly hair glistened like starlight, her laugh even brighter than that.

Even if Nora wasn't busy, it would have been hard to make a day trip there, though not impossible with a suborbital flight. She had once again teased him for picking an arctic clime. There was always teasing, and flirting, and laughter.

They also did things under the Seljalandsfoss waterfall that you could never do in person.

These days, his mind was moving at a million miles an hour, filled with the euphoria of progress. The crunch was barely a weight on his shoulders. Each problem solved was a dopamine hit, a mystery unravelled, threads carrying him to a timeless, joyous space.

At times, he was perhaps moving a bit too fast for his team.

"Come on, these equations are simple!" Rhen said. "It's just the solution to the Hodge Conjecture."

"Uh, yeah. You're right, Hodge Conjecture, very easy." Vi nodded, tilting forward, her brow furrowed. Other members of his team were tilting their head sideways, or looking around the room at everyone else. Rhen scratched his head.

"Alright, I'll go from the top. If you let X be a non-singular complex projective manifold..."

Nora seemed to be the only one keeping up. As he discussed his work with her, her eyes lit up, and she toyed with her hair.

"Let me know if I'm talking too much, okay?" Rhen said. "I'm getting complaints about talking too fast."

"No, don't stop, I love it!" she said, raising a hand. "Have you considered checking out the digitally simulated resistance of the hybrid's short-term synaptic plasticity, and adjusting it to see if it affects their processing power? Maybe with a rating of +0.112402 to start."

"That's brilliant. You sure I can't steal you for my office?"

"I'm happy to work under you anytime, my starlight."

Of course, the crunch was having other effects. All the rising and crashing from the sugar highs — not to mention all the coffee he was drinking — was making him forgetful.

"Who wrote this code for A-1? Whoever did is a genius." Rhen said, bringing it up in the common area. "Honestly, it's gorgeous — I want to submit it publicly somewhere."

Several of the team simply blinked at him. Imani fidgeted in place. Only Vi rose to the occasion, her lips pulled thin.

"Um, boss, *you* wrote it," she said.

"I did?"

"Yeah, it's got your name on the commit, so I'm guessing it was you. You're yanking your own rod."

She was right, it did, and he was so excited he didn't even check. His cheeks were burning with embarrassment. Staring at it again, the solutions were so elegant, it didn't *feel* like he could have written something like that. He pinched the bridge of his nose.

But I don't remember writing it. I would have remembered writing something that good. Wouldn't I?

He went to make himself a fresh coffee and stopped, giving the dispenser an accusing state. Instead, he simply returned to his office and stared at the mystery code. Every line was unfamiliar. It wasn't unusual for people to forget their own code; programmers had been doing it since time immemorial, which was why it was important to leave comments in your own code for yourself, for when you inevitably forgot it.

But this code was beautiful, like the spiral of a nautilus shell, or a perfect sphere. There was one comment left there, but it made no sense.

```
// f(f) = f.
```

A recursive, self-referential equation. Weird. Recursion was an old school technique, one Rhen was familiar with. A function could call itself within its own code, like someone pulling themselves up by their own bootstraps. It was one of the central ideas of computer science, but to see it quoted in a comment, not in the code proper, was odd.

Rhen was sure he didn't write it.

Is someone helping me along?

When he spoke to Roswell, the psychologist had waved his hand and dismissed it.

"If you're coding in your sleep, and working through crunch, you're probably having memory lapses. It's far more likely than the alternative, don't you think?" He said.

"And the Hodge Conjecture?"

"Oh, that's easy." And Roswell recited the entire proof without blinking. "I'm not even a mathematician, but I do dabble."

Hmm, I guess it is simple. But wasn't it an unsolved Millennium Prize problem? But the moment he thought about it, his head started to hurt, and he wound up having to take a breather on the physician's chaise lounge, rubbing his temples.

"Remember, deep breaths," Roswell instructed. "Close your eyes and listen to the noises and sensations around you, and nothing else."

And by the time he'd done that, he'd forgotten entirely what he was worried about.

***

Rhen's team had taken to talking entirely by a group cognitive message session, no matter what room they were in. While it was terrible for their cardio health, it was great for their productivity. That's why it came as a shock when Vi burst into his office a few days later, furiously rubbing her arms.

"Jeeesus!" She exclaimed verbally. "What the hell, it's bloody Arctic in here!"

"What? Oh, Vi!" Rhen exclaimed, spinning around. "Sorry about that. I wasn't expecting a walk-in, so I had it set to my preference. I'm feeling fairly warm lately, and the cool air helps me think."

"Well, it's *really* helping me think. I can't stop thinking 'Gee, it's really cold in here.'" Her teeth chattered. "God, my resting TPM has probably skyrocketed."

"That'd be great at landing you an interview," Rhen said. "As much as I *hate* TPMs."

"Yeah, well, you're to blame, buddy."

"I've turned the heat up, though it's going to take several minutes." Rhen said. "You know, you're complaining, but it's not *that* crazy to work in a cold space. All the sugar that would go to cooling you down goes to your brain. I hear some scientists back in the day actually sat with their feet in buckets of cold water."

"Well, now I'm thinking 'How did they not get frostbite in their feet?'" Vi said, then clicked her fingers. "*Right.* I came in here for a reason. Anniversary gift!" She reached into her pocket and pulled out a card. "Here! It's a recipe for my husband's famous konju varutharacha curry. I remember you ate some and were asking about it. I've also sent a curry leaf plant to your apartment, because it's not the same without *real* leaves, and I won't have you cooking it the wrong way. Use it to warm yourself up when you inevitably get frostbite."

"Thanks for that, I really appreciate it!" He said, taking the card and tapping it against his hand. "But *why* an anniversary gift?"

"It's a work anniversary. You've now lasted longer than my previous boss did. Congrats, you may have broken the curse!"

"Oh, ha ha. It's probably just getting rid of Rey. Helps when someone's not putting their foot on the brake while you're standing on the accelerator."

Vi threw up her hands and stepped backwards. "Hey, man, if you're going to make a car reference, I'm outtie." And when he tried to explain about pedals, she made good on her promise. Just as Rhen turned back to his console, his previous visitor was replaced by another. Delta strode in, hands in pockets.

"Don't tell me you're about to wish me a happy anniversary—" Rhen said. The young engineer blinked.

"No, why would I do that? Is it a bad time?"

"Not at all, if you don't mind the cold." According to the cognitive thermostat, things had only warmed a few Fahrenheit — it was taking a while.

"Cold? Oh, right. It is rather cold." Delta said factually. Their fringe was grey with a slight azure tint, reminiscent of a cloudy day. "Look, I just wanted to come in and let you know I've requested a transfer to Cybernetics and Robotics, so I can work with them full time. I've learned a lot here, but I feel like I want to take the next step in my career journey."

Career journey? Rhen leaned back in his chair, knotting his fingers together. Out of everything he expected Delta to say, this wasn't it. He was glad he was sitting down. *What the hell was the right thing to say as a manager again?*

"Look, I'm not going to lie, I'm saddened to hear that. You're an excellent engineer, and you're part of the heart and soul of the team," Rhen said. "But I don't want to stand in your way if that's what you really want, and I'm more than happy to support you. That said, is there anything I can do to make you stay? Any accommodations I can make, maybe share you with Shana's team on a half-and-half basis?"

"No, it's nothing to do with the team here. I just want to get more hands on with machines, and the hardware component is minimal these days. Also, I think Shana's going to require more help, given her condition. She told me there'd be some opportunity for advancement."

"Condition?" Rhen blinked. Delta did too, staring at him.

"Oh, you didn't know? I thought Vi would have mentioned it. Shana's got a neurodegenerative disease."

It was a lot of bad news all at once. "She did seem a bit shaky during the evacuation, when we had to carry her." And now he thought about it, he hadn't seen her often, and when he did, she was using automated arms to do her work.

In the few three-person lunches he'd had with her and Nora, the head of C&R had been excessively cheery. *Was she compensating?*

"That's just like you, wanting to help out. I'll approve your request, but don't be a stranger, okay?"

Delta nodded, and when Rhen stood up to bid them farewell, the young engineer hugged him instead. The movement felt forced, like being hugged by a claw machine. Freezing up, Rhen patted their back.

"I'm going to miss you," Delta said, then left. Their fringe had not changed hue the entire time. Rhen furrowed his brow.

That's weird. Wonder if they froze it. And then he sighed, sitting back in his chair. Derek appeared beside him, adjusting his tie.

"So, should I start putting together a hiring request for a new engineer?" The AI asked. Rhen picked up the recipe disk from Vi and tapped his finger against one of the pointed edges. The whole exchange had felt, well, bizarre.

"I guess so. Go internal first. It's going to be a pain to find anyone who wants to work out here."

***

The crashes started again.

Rhen cursed. They had been making so much progress, only to hit a wall again. He watched the cognitive map warp and tear apart, like a flaming match dropped into cellophane. It burned from the inside out, leaving behind piles of ashen grey.

So much for fire being a cleansing force.

"What am I missing?" He murmured. Every night, he'd been dreaming of code, feeling so close to a breakthrough. The code was failing, but the saboteur was gone. So why?

The headaches were happening more regularly. He was in a positively foul mood as he sat with Nora in Kutjera, nursing his coffee. She looked equally morose.

"How long is left until the board meeting?" She asked.

"Not long enough."

After lunch, the headaches were getting quite bad. Taking Roswell's advice, he stopped what he was doing and went for a walk. His head ebbed all the way up the stairs: going up seemed a better choice than down, since if it went on too long, he could always get fresh air on the surface.

Listen to the noise and sensations around me. That's what I'm meant to do, right?

Focusing on anything but the pain was difficult. But the longer he focused, the more he could pick up antiseptics in the stairwells, wafting down and around him. The lights hummed without pause. As he made it to the next level, holographic plants swayed asynchronously to a ghostly breeze. As he passed them, there was a light hiss, followed by a sharp and slightly medicinal smell, some sort of faux eucalypt. The water rushed and babbled from a nearby virtual brook, buried far within a deep glass frame.

As his eyes flickered across the projected plants, he smirked, remembering the time he ducked behind them to hide from Rey. It seemed like an age ago.

When he passed by Data Processing, he stopped. *Rey had been uploading data, not downloading it.* According to Alan, it had been a case of theft for the board. *So where did the data poisoning come into play?*

The moment the crashes had started, Rhen had checked for poisoning. But there was no malicious material in anything passing through his department *or* data handling.

"Could it simply be an impossible task?" He murmured.

As he walked past the door to the Ethics department, his footsteps froze, heel half lifted off the ground. Besides Server Ops, it was the only other department on the floor. Some cognicists called them useless — the ones who hated red tape, anyway — but Rhen was always keen to stick up for the ethicists.

"Wait. Nobody ever pays attention to the ethicists..."

Having a lightbulb moment, he rushed into the Ethics department, where four ethicists were sitting at the terminal. The moment he entered, they turned around and blinked at him.

"What's the matter, got an experiment to run?" One of them asked. t was Orietta, the department head. Rhen shook his head.

"Not quite. Can I check out the code you use when you connect to one of the subjects? The one they use as their kill switch?"

"Oh, we prefer *deactivation code*." Orietta tittered. But she pulled it up and send it to him, simple as a thought. "I've only sent that part, and logged it in the system for probity. It's just a copy."

"A copy is all I need."

Without going back to his office, Rhen brought up the code right there, thousands of lines of logic spanning across his entire field of view.

It took all of three seconds to find it. It was so *obvious*. Why hadn't anyone else seen it? A lethal piece of code, delivered directly to the subject, circumventing the whole review process! Like a rapier, it stabbed itself into the hybrids, and they bled to death. Slow or fast, they were doomed from the moment they opened their eyes. The effect was indistinguishable from a regular cognitive collapse.

There was still a saboteur on base. It was never Rey, if he had been involved at all. But looking at the code, it had an unmistakable fingerprint, an arrangement of logic that Rhen would know anywhere.

It all lined up — why she had been down in the testing area after hours, and why she had gone missing during the evacuation, when the doors were all wide open. The one person who had been with the project since the start.

"It's you, isn't it, Vi?"

Chapter 14

Once Rhen reported it, things moved quickly. Mirage had stand-in mechanical guards until the human ones were vetted and replaced. Alan grabbed two of them and marched down to the testing labs, Rhen in tow. When they entered the lab proper, Vi was standing there with her hand in her pocket, chatting to one of the human staff.

Her eyes widened the moment she saw them, with the armed guards flanking them on either side.

Vi turned and ran. Without hesitation, the machines raised their PEPs and pulled the trigger.

She couldn't outrun the speed of light.

There was a small flare against her back, followed by a blinding flash of light. The air rang like it was hit with a thousand chimes. A split second later, she was knocked to the ground with sudden violent force. A heat wave washed over them, producing a momentary distortion in the air.

The mechanised staff nearby wavered, as if an invisible tide was washing over them, rocking on the balls of their feet. And then, they continued going about their business, like someone had merely opened a window.

Rhen dashed over to Vi, whose face was bloodied by a sudden impact with the lab floor. Her cheeks were convulsing, tiny jitters in all too human muscle. She stared at him, eyes wide and white. Accusatory.

"Damn it, Vi. You're the saboteur?" Against logic, against *everything*, he had hoped he was wrong. "Why did you do it?"

Her lips weren't working, but he received a ping. Without hesitation, he accepted.

<I only work for you, boss. I've only *ever* worked for you,> Vi said. <You need to get out, but not before—>

And then her eyes rolled back, eyelids fluttering. Rhen's head was hurting, thundering, like a thousand heartbeats inside his skull. He grabbed the sides of his head, rubbing his fingers against his temples. He sucked in a shuddering breath. Against his back, a calming, intimately familiar hand pressed against his shirt.

He turned around. It was Nora stroking his back.

"You did good. We caught them at last."

***

For now, the news was just kept to leadership, according to Alan's instructions. Rhen was fine with that, since he didn't have the energy to break the news just yet. Instead, he sat at a private booth in Kutjera with Nora and Shana, nursing drinks and speaking only via shared CMS. There was no chance of them being overheard, and it left their mouths free for the alcohol.

"I can't believe it. She's been working on the team for years, since the beginning. Every boss there's been, she's just been sitting there," Shana said. Her drink was deposited on the table by mechanical arms, replete with straw. Rhen noticed now how she leaned over to sip from it, rather than pick it up, adjusting it with her hands only when necessary. *Her illness must be getting worse.*

"Alef, Chet, Beth. None of them could succeed because there was a saboteur. It never was Rey," Rhen stared into his Mobster Sour, finger running along the rim of the glass.

"Her career is over," Nora said, hands huddled under her sleeves. "They'll throw her in prison for sabotage. I can't imagine corporations *won't* press charges."

"She did so much good work, though," Rhen said, furrowing his brow. "Why sabotage something you've worked so hard on?"

"That's the million-dollar question, isn't it?" Shana said. "I'm sure we'll know soon enough, once the authorities ask. We're researchers, not interrogators. Though I'm sure Nora would be pretty good at it, given her day job."

"Don't even joke about something like that," Nora said, clenching her fist beneath the fabric. "I'm a tester, not a torturer."

"I hear in the U.S, the CIA tweaks those weapons to induce the feeling of you being burned, but it doesn't leave any physical evidence — the benefits of electro-magnetism hitting the nerve cells," Shana continued. "They call them 'PEP talks'. Humans, am I right?"

"Shana, you just don't know *when* to shut up," Nora said.

"Yeah, probably not." Shana smiled, poking her straw with a shaking finger. It was trembling a little. "I'll be quiet forever soon enough, so I'm getting my talking in. I only speak the truth."

"Vi won't be interrogated by the CIA, or whatever the Aussies have, just regular cops," Rhen said, ignoring the exchange and Shana's morbid remark. She always was the only one who could get under Nora's skin, yet for some reason, they were still fast friends — perhaps because of it. "Meanwhile, I'm down two staff now."

"Well, at least it'll give you an excuse to be more hands on," Shana said. "I'm sure you'll hate it."

***

Shana was right. Now that the team was short-staffed, even more of his work got delegated to Derek, and Rhen was constantly hands-on with the code. It was getting harder and harder to not think of his team as dead weight, holding him back as he walked them laboriously through the simplest of equations.

The more he worked, the less he saw of Nora. She was testing as fast as he was writing. What worried him was when they did spend time together — either at night, or when chatting to a subject — her behaviour was odd. Every time he'd tell her a theory that stumped his team, she became quiet and subdued, her eyes never meeting his own.

"What's wrong?" He would ask. And she'd smile, her eyes never quite meeting his own.

"Just thinking about the end of the project. Things are moving so fast, I kind of don't want these times to end."

"Well, maybe we'll go for a trip after this. Alan owes me and my team a trip to Sekai HQ, so you should come with."

"That'd be nice, assuming he lets me leave. There's still a lot of testing for stage two."

"Stage two?" Rhen blinked. She hugged her chest, eyes pensively cast to the side.

"Yeah. After the hybrids are stable, they'll want to create a commercial model. I'm contracted for that, but you're not."

Is that what she's worried about? "Oh, *that*. I've already got a plan. I'm going to petition Sekai to work on a nerve router," he said, tapping the back of his neck.

"A nerve router?"

"Yeah. A lot of people are in pain and have to take drugs, like Delta does. The Rosetta is connected to the brain, but it does *nothing* with sensory input. If I figure out a way to interface it with the parietal lobe, and spin a mentapp off that, it might do away with the need for pain medicine — and help people with cybernetics feel things."

"Wow, you really don't stop, do you?" Nora's eyes softened, and in what felt like the first time in a long while, she grabbed his hands, slipping her fingers through his. "Do you think it'd help with your headaches?"

"Probably not, but it'd be nice. I just want to leave the world a bit better than how I found it."

***

Between Rey and Vi, Mirage was littered with mechanised guards. There was one in every room, and the human replacements had been delayed until the project was finished. orientation in these conditions would be a nightmare.

As Rhen wandered the hallways, more than a few people muttered in earshot that the base was starting to feel more like a home for machines than humans — if it had ever been a home for anything else.

"The machine queen is getting her way," someone murmured in Kutjera. But when Rhen turned to confront them, they had blended into the throng.

Rhen had a nameless sense of unease, like something stuck in the corner of his vision.

Everything's going well. So why am I feeling like it's not?

When Rhen walked into AI assessment, the cherry blossom trees were leafless, black stems stretching to the heavens like forked fingers scraping the roof, clawing upwards. Or perhaps sulci, the dark indentations of the brain, growing up from the trunk of the brainstem.

It wasn't reflecting his brain, but the wintery scenery might as well have been.

Rhen slipped past the armed and unarmed robots that made up the AI Assessment department, and into one of the many testing rooms. He wandered up the corridor until he found the transparent room with Nora inside of it, and walked in. Today, she was sitting with a tanned feminine unit with rusty orange hair like the desert above, and cut chin-length. Their eyes were opalescent, petal pink with watercolour splashes of powder blue and white, like paints unmixed and slowly bleeding into each other.

No human was born with eyes like those.

"How does it feel to be stable, Bee?" Rhen asked, finding a spot next to Nora. "I hear you've been running for two days straight now, with no signs of decay."

The hybrid prototype smiled, opal eyes gleaming. "Wonderful. I was getting my data copied, and then I woke up here to find out I'm the final version. Well, final except for updates."

"Yes, you're stable, but that doesn't mean you're a hybrid," Nora said. "You can think faster than any human alive, but you're not quite a match for a machine yet. You've yet to pass Anata's day."

"I'll get there," Bee said, staring at Nora with narrowed eyes. *Had something happened between them?* Still, Nora sipped her tea, as calm as a frozen lake.

"Let's run through some tests. I'd like to see how you do," Nora said.

They ran through the different tests. It wasn't a real test, of course, it was all part of the show, or else he wouldn't be allowed to be there. As they went through the mathematics, his attention faded out. He couldn't focus on anything that was going on.

"I'm still getting questions wrong," Bee said, furrowing aies perfectly symmetrical eyebrows.

"Some of these questions require prerequisite knowledge you don't have, like biology or physics. You can't answer a problem without the right foundation," Nora explained. "And even if you can think fast, it doesn't equate to intellect or wisdom. In the end, it's only potential. A car can move a thousand miles an hour in the wrong direction."

Rhen rubbed his forehead. It was throbbing already, like someone knocking a door from the inside, the reverberations thrumming against the inside of his skill. But there was no time for a walk, not today.

"How am I doing compared to the others?" Bee asked. Ae was sitting up, chin raised. "Am I beating them?"

"I can't tell you that," Nora said. Rhen knew the answer, of course. They were close, *really* close. A-1 was almost at machine-level, and Bee wasn't far behind. But none of them could fully pass Anata's day yet. A silver lining was now they didn't fall apart when they tried it, they simply failed.

I'll never have to worry about watching the light flicker from their eyes again. In fact, they may never die, period. Before now, he'd tried not to think about the 'resetting', but now he could allow himself the luxury.

After running some more tests, Nora left Rhen and Bee alone for a while. The opal-eyed prototype sighed.

"What's wrong?" Rhen asked.

"She doesn't like me, I think."

"Oh, why's that?"

"I think I symbolise the end."

Rhen tapped his finger against his cup. "Well, I guess *it* is a bit intimidating to come across a super intelligence. You can do pretty much everything we can do and more. Plus, you used to be a cognicist, so you'll probably take our jobs."

"Well, only because of you." Bee's eyes glittered. Rhen blinked.

"What do you mean?"

"I only became a cognicist because of you. When I got my cybernetics, your Rosetta saved me. I got robot parts that worked even better than the ones before. And then I saw you at the conference."

"The conference?" This was a first; Bee never talked about their past. Was it because ae had been online so long, now they have time to open up?

"CogniTech 2161." Bee's gaze turned reverent, and aie lowered their gaze slightly. "You were giving a speech on hybrid theory. I came up to you and asked you what you thought of your technology being misused, and you said you hated it, but you hoped one day humans would think more like machines, and we'd be able to break down the walls between us. I'll never forget it."

Rhen had. *Why* had he forgotten it? He rubbed his temples. He always remembered when people asked him questions like that, especially people with cybernetics. So why hadn't he remembered Bee?

"I'm glad I made a difference," Rhen settled on. "Though whenever someone says 'I became a cognicist because of you', that's not true. You became one because of *your* effort. And now, you're going to become one the world's first artificial super intelligences, solving all kinds of problems. You're not the end, you're the beginning, and the world will be looking to you for answers."

"I'll try to live up to your example."

***

The breakthrough happened without warning.

"A-1 and B-27 have passed Anata's day," the report said.

A year of frustration culminated in a single moment of sublime, cathartic release. The world's first ASI had been born, something more than human, and it had *emotions*. His own spilled over, laughing and crying at the same time. His team were just as ecstatic.

"Can you *believe* we did it?"

"This is going to change everything!"

"I'm going to be in a history book!"

There was a party planned for the end of the week. Rhen gave the rest of his team time off, a reward for such a long crunch and dealing with a boss who perhaps should have never given up being a hands-on specialist. The second thing he did was submit an official funding request for the Nerve Router, along with an early prototype design he'd been toying with. Once that was done, he went up to the surface and messaged his father to tell him the news, and also sent a friendly message to Iona.

As he strode across the rusty sands and stretched his legs, there were big black trucks moving through Mirage's shimmering wall, like a row of angry ants. They had no windows, just boxes with wheels.

Wonder what those are for?

He wandered close enough that the dust from their wheels was showering near his feet. There were whispers in the air, like threads he could pluck and pull into his ears, twisting from wind to spoken word.

"I don't want to die."

Rhen froze. The last of the cars disappeared into the earth, like self-driving coffins. The whisper had sounded real, so real the hairs on his ear were tingling, as if disturbed by the plaintive cry. He went down to ask the automated guards at the gate what they were for.

"Supplies."

"Supplies?"

"For experiments."

The machine didn't have a face or emotions, giving it the perfect poker face. Then again, they didn't have a reason to lie, either. Still, Rhen's niggling unease grew. As he stared at the car parking lot, there were tracks leading off to an unloading bay. There were no tracks anywhere else, though.

No tracks.

That bothered him for some reason. His head hurt. More and more, the headaches were more than just pain, but *buzzing*. It was a noise with frequency, amplitude, and wave form.

What was it trying to say?

No matter who he asked about the trucks that day, they said they didn't see them, or that they were supply trucks. But he couldn't *see* a large number of supplies moving through the hall. So where were they going, exactly?

***

The celebration party for the end of Project Achilli took up half of Kutjera, which was cordoned off with rope. The serving arms whizzed back and forth at a furious pace to keep everyone thoroughly inebriated, as well as serving platters of finger foods the chef with the overly tall hat had personally picked. Parties happened so rarely that the base's events committee had gone all out, and everyone was thoroughly impressed.

Rhen sat nursing his cocktail next, watching Nora socialise. Shana wasn't about. Apparently, she was too ill to even attend these days. There were so many people missing: Vi, Delta, the hybrids themselves. He had argued for them to attend, since it was their party and all, but the base was suddenly very concerned with security. The testing area was beginning to feel more and more like a military camp.

None of the hybrids have asked to leave their glass cages. But I wonder what would happen if they did?

He would like to think Alan would have no choice but to allow it. *But money doesn't always work that way.* It was a morose thought, but he was in a strangely morose mood, and he couldn't shake it.

His mind flicked back to the black trucks. Ominous. Too ominous.

You should be happy. You lead the team that invented the world's first ASI and the first hybrid. You should mingle more.

"I don't understand why *he's* still here," someone said.

"Yeah, she shouldn't need him anymore. I'm sick of pretending. Aren't we at stage two?"

Rhen furrowed his brow. The moment he swivelled his head, the conversation stopped. He couldn't tell who had been talking. There was nobody immediately behind him.

Weird. *It's probably not about you. You're being weird about something random.* Still, he couldn't pull himself out of sorts. After a while, he made an excuse to leave the party early.

"Are you okay?" Nora asked, rubbing his arm.

"I think I just need some rest." It wasn't a lie, since he was still exhausted from the long period of crunch. *Irritation and anxiety are part and parcel with getting no sleep.*

He walked back to their apartment, lost in his thoughts, with Casey wheeling behind his feet. He made it there by muscle memory alone, because one moment he was leaving the party, and the next minute he was walking in the door. *It's funny how time passes faster when you're drinking.* There had been a little too much of that lately. Probably not good for his sleeping. As he kicked his shoes off, watching them sail and roll across the floor, his stomach grumbled.

"Right, I forgot to actually *eat* something at the party."

Drinking on an empty stomach was a terrible idea. He needed to eat and hydrate, or he'd pay dearly in the morning. *I'm not in my twenties anymore, I'm middle aged. Too old to just sleep it off.*

Rhen scanned through the hundreds of meals the automated chef could make, discounting half of them since he wasn't in the mood for beef, chicken, or lamb. Seafood would work well, but he wanted something with a bit of spice.

Didn't Vi give me the recipe for some curry?

Rhen picked up the disk and turned it around in his hands, a pang of sadness assaulting his heart.

"What's that?" Casey asked.

"Vi's husband's konju varutharacha recipe. She used to use it as an apology curry, after finding out how much I loved it." He tapped it against the palm of his hand. "I asked her for the recipe, but she didn't want to give up the leverage. Then she suddenly gave it to me."

"Oh. Maybe she was making a really *big* apology, then?"

"For messing with the prototypes?" Rhen blinked. Casey shrugged with their arms. "I wonder if it's got a virus on the disk."

"If it's got lots of spices, I bet it's all sterilised."

His hunger and curiosity piqued, Rhen set up a small, closed virtual system to scan the disk for any nasty surprises. The file size was tiny — a mere terabyte of data on the cellular composition of the curry. But there was a remarkably retro text file with manual cooking instructions. Some chefs included them out of tradition, but few people actually prepared food that way.

After a thorough vetting, he opened the file.

> Start by marinating some prawns in turmeric and salt for half an
> hour. If you want to use made-from-scratch varutharacha paste —
> which if you don't, you're insane — roast together some coriander
> seeds, coconut, red chillies, garlic and shallots.

A fairly standard recipe. Rhen entered the ingredients into the ingredient maker. He also made himself another Mobster Sour, and saluted the automated arms, who were working to marinate the prawns. He was going to be up for a while, yet.

"Guess this is my last meal with you, Vi." He sipped his cocktail and checked the next step in the recipe.

> Add prawns and cook well. While you're sautéing the mixture,
> go to the machine compartment and search for the secret drawer.
> Once the prawns are done, temper with coconut, oil, and the spice
> mixture from earlier. Come speak to me when you see it. Serve hot
> with appam or rice, garnished with proper curry leaves.

"Wait, what?" Rhen furrowed his brow, staring at the wall behind him. Placing his drink down, he wandered over to the hidden machine compartment, opening it up. The two glittering proxies stood there, like guardians of an ancient Egyptian tomb, palms flat against their thighs.

There was a sizzling noise as the mechanical arms tossed and roasted the capsicum.

"This has got to be a joke." But with little else to do for the next half hour, he ran his hands over the insides. There was no holo-trickery, but something felt *off*. Like a whisper, coming from one of the panels. It wasn't a whisper to anyone in particular, but a whisper to itself.

Pay attention, it said. *Wait for the call*. It was whispering it a thousand times every second. *Waitforthecallwaitforthecallwaitforthecall*. But the voice wasn't insane. It was pure logic, patience. In a million years, it would still be thanklessly whispering the call, as long as it took to hear it. No love or reward required.

God had given it a raison d'etre. Why would the panel question it?

It was waiting for a special word, whispered in a certain pattern, by a certain person. As it muttered to itself quietly about it, Rhen tilted his head, examined its thoughts, constructed them backwards.

"A cognitive lock."

He didn't know how he knew it, only that he did. He waved his watch over the panel, but his biometric signature did nothing. There was only one way to open it.

He gave his own cognitive signature.

The panel got confused. It was fed a word so complicated and so basic, it wouldn't handle it. It was beyond knowing. It then died, or stopped *doing* and *thinking*, which amounted to the same thing. A split second later, two stacked rectangle-shaped compartments hissed out and almost hit Rhen in the shins.

Inside was the last thing he expected to see.

It was a pair of tiny arms, resembling those belonging to a child, severed below the elbow, and unmistakably artificial. The arms had no pores, only the sheen of dark brown plastic, with deep grooves running along the finger joints and wrist. A budget design, a far cry from the models at Mirage. They were laid out on a bed of velvet as if they were a precious treasure.

"Why would Nora have these? They're too small to fit her."

He picked up and examined the elbows. The plastic was brittle, discoloured, and dull. These were old. But inside the elbows were modern wires, cables and actuators. Why put cutting-edge actuators inside an old artificial limb? But the plastic insulation around the wires was cracked, exposing the metal beneath.

Had it been put into the ageing chamber that Shana used — the Tardis — and weathered deliberately? But why bother?

Rhen recalled a movie about an archaeological dig in Israel. In it, a college student discovered the remains of a man who died two thousand years ago. Beside the man was a small linen bag with a user manual for a Sony MR-01 video camera, despite the model not being due for another three years.

This was just like that. The arms were completely out of place, hidden in the tomb-like compartment in Nora's wall.

Shivering, he slid the compartment back into place, and closed the wall.

"Casey, can you forget everything you saw me do since you came into the room?"

"Forget what? We only just got here."

"Exactly."

***

It was fortunate that Nora was so busy with the new hybrids. After crashing into bed, she was up the next morning and to work, with a quick kiss and a wave. He didn't want to ask her about the arms — something inside his gut warned him against it — not until he'd figured out a bit more.

Yeah, something's really off.

Of the human staff that remained in Mirage — there now seemed to be two machines for every human — those that were around were ruder, less likely to answer his questions.

"Aren't you meant to be working on something?"

"I thought you'd be packed up and gone by now."

The attitude in Mirage had changed. Changed towards *him*. Had he done something? No, it was as if he was a golden goose who had laid its last egg. Now he was just a regular animal.

Sub-human. Lesser than. That's what the squinted eyes and sneering lips said, arms crossed, as if physically closed off to him, distanced. Unless he'd done something terrible at the party, none of it made sense. His own team were less rude, but they were certainly keeping their distance.

Eventually, it got too much, and he went up to the car parking lot to go for a drive. Being alone was preferable right now, even if he collapsed in the desert. There was no need to get out of the car anyway. "Away" would be good enough. But when he got into the lot, it clicked what had been bothering him.

No tracks.

A chill ran down his spine. Tentatively, he kneeled down in front of one of the Elysium's wheels, pretending to do up his shoelaces. Instead, he scooped up a pebble and put it in front of a tyre, then climbed inside.

Please don't let me be right. Oh god, I've never wanted to be so wrong.

Virgil popped to life on the dash. "Manual mode again?"

"You know it," he replied. Rhen accepted the cognitive link, and the walls around him became translucent, revealing the car parking lot. He drove forward one foot then back again, and got out of the car, severing his link with it.

The pebble was unmoved.

No tracks. His whole body trembled, and reality seemed to slow down and warp around him, a nauseous unravelling, driving to his knees. The car had pretended to move, but hadn't at all.

A fake. The one time he tried to leave the car, he'd passed out. The one time he'd tried to run off the base, he'd passed out. And finally, he remembered the words Delta had whispered to him that night, the same words that Vi had said.

"You need to get out. This whole place is a prison."

He'd been trapped here all along.

***

Never before had Rhen been so aware of the cameras being everywhere. Virtus saw all. And so he took the lift up to the surface of Mirage, eyeing the distortions that swirled around the base, blocking all contact to the Solar Web. The wall was malicious now, like a constricting shroud, meant to muffle cries for help.

He sat in the comms room and called Iona.

"Hi, Rhen! I didn't expect to hear from you," his ex-wife answered, eyes alight. "Congratulations on getting your project done! You'll be in the history books twice now."

"Thanks, Iona. I was thinking, when I'm back in Japan, do you want to catch up and get some tempura at Umi no Eki? I'd love to touch base."

"Sure, I *love* Umi no Eki! But why wait? We can just order some food and catch up cognitively. You'll probably be caught up with your next big thing, and I'll be doing mum things, so it might be an easier fit."

"You're right. That's probably the way to go. Looking forward to it!"

Rhen hung up and slumped in his chair. *It's an echo. That proves it.*

Iona loathed Umi no Eki. She'd done a promotional campaign for the restaurant chain once — her contacts had been rude, and on top of that, she'd eaten some bad tempura. After throwing it up, hurting her neck in the process, she'd sworn off the chain for life. But her social accounts told a different story: she'd kept true to her contract, smiling and encouraging her fans to try it out. Someone had given the echo a fake Iona to imitate.

Calling for help wasn't possible. Leaving by car or foot wasn't possible. His thoughts swirled, like a whirlpool spinning out of control, threatening to drag him down and leave him rooted helpless on the spot. What now?

Answers. He craved them, needed to know what was going on. Somewhere in Mirage, there would be a hint. There was no point confronting Alan about it yet. That card could only be played once, and did he want to? Something about this was dangerous. The walls of the small room seemed to close in on him, oppressive and suffocating. Every other person in his position had gone missing.

Alef. Alef had left messages. Hidden messages in the code, ones that even an AI couldn't read.

Aside from the saboteur, they had been so frivolous, so beneath mentioning. *Perhaps that was the point.* Nobody took Haiku seriously. He'd never told anyone about them, not even Nora.

Nora. Was Nora in on it? It was the one question he hadn't dared to ask. But now it was there, in his head, and he couldn't get it out. His hands trembled. Logic whispered to him the words he didn't want to hear: How could she not?

He wanted to vomit his heart across the floor.

Rhen wanted to cry, but he couldn't: the cameras robbed him of that relief. And so, with his world and the happiness in it crumbling inside of him, he stood up and smiled, then turned and left the room. The fragments of his life fell like dirt through his fingers.

All that he was left with was nothing.

Chapter 15

Now that Rhen knew about the prison, he was working on borrowed time. There were too many people to fake ignorance in front of, most of all Nora. He sat in his office, thankful for the fact the cold room kept most people away. He turned the temperature down even lower, his skin prickling.

"All right, let's get to work."

Rhen brought up the display of his prototype Nerve Router to avoid suspicion, and switched between working on it and checking out the prototype's code. He searched out hidden messages from Alef, solving the equations one by one, and digging up new poetry in the process.

// Ariadne's madness
// Maze becomes a prison, trapped
// No thread to guide out.

The situation summed up his predicament well. But was there really no thread to be found? And then, behind another piece of code, a more ominous message.

// If they find out you know, they'll kill you.

Nothing subtle about that, Rhen thought, his stomach churning with nausea. The fate of the other researchers was now crystal clear. Was Vi lying somewhere outside, buried beneath the rusty dirt?

Talking to anyone wasn't an option.

He didn't want to head back to Nora's place, but he couldn't break routine. The corridors were smaller, narrower, the dark glass windows threatening to pin him in on all sides. When he entered their apartment, Nora wasn't there. She was still working overtime on the project transition. Or was she?

The more he pondered on it, his head pounded from the inside out, like his skull was going to fracture. In truth, it hadn't stopped hurting since yesterday: the pain level simply ebbed down to tolerable levels, allowing him a small break.

The headaches are part of it. They'd gotten worse every month since he'd gotten to Mirage, and they were connected with him trying to get out of the car, finding things he shouldn't find.

Someone didn't want him thinking about Nora, or at least, not suspiciously.

Maybe I can use that, like a compass, pointing me in the right direction. The more his head hurt, the more likely there was something there he should know.

Meanwhile, sweat was rolling down his back. He had been hotter lately. The curry plant Vi had given him was wilting in the corner — she'd failed to tell him curry plants were sensitive to cold. With the fans at full ball, the sensitive shrub hadn't had a chance.

She told me to speak to her once I saw the arms. But she's gone now, so what do I do?

Rhen walked over and picked up the brown leaves, tossing them in the bin. As he grabbed the last one, he furrowed his brow and pinched it, the dead foliage flaking beneath his fingertips.

Why would Vi give him a curry plant if she knew he would just kill it?

Where leaves wilt, dig deep. That was the first poem he'd found. It had been so ago, he'd almost forgotten. Had she known about it somehow? He huddled over the plant, body covering as much of it as possible.

"Guess I better throw this out. It's looking pretty dead," he said for the benefit of any listeners. He dug his fingers into the dirt, probing around. As they wove between the roots, he bit his lower lip.

Let there be something, anything!

His fingers touched metal.

Digging with his hands, he teased the object out. It was wedged right at the base of the plant. It was rounded, spherical, like a gunshot pellet that had been grown over. When it emerged from the dirt, the object in his grubby hands was familiar. He had once seen it in Rey's hands as he gloated in the testing lab.

The hacking AI!

Rey had claimed it was a cloak of invisibility. Right now, it was exactly what he needed. The curry plant hadn't just died from the cold: having this buried at its base certainly wouldn't have helped. *Thank you, Vi. I owe you big time.*

Clutching the device close to his abdomen to keep it out of sight, he reached out cognitively. The moment he did, a heads up display stretched across his vision, and a voice spoke in his ear.

<Hello, I am Nemo.> Between the heavily pronounced 'ohs' and the musical quality, Rhen immediately placed the Indian English accent. <It's a pleasure to meet you, Rhen. I have been left here to help you navigate the facility.>

<Nemo, can you tell me what the hell is going on?>

<I do not know what you mean. I was set to factory settings a month ago. All I have is a directive to help you.>

Rhen's thankfulness to Vi gave way to frustration, like a trembling storm about to burst. Why give him an AI, but no answers?

<Nemo, am I right in that you can hack Virtus, and make it so I can move around, like Rey did?>

<Absolutely. I have a spoof of the administrative cog code for Virtus. With it, I can manipulate the security feeds and hide you from automated guards.>

Great. That meant he could get around without worrying about the automated guards. All he had to worry about was getting spotted by anyone else. As discreetly as possible, he slipped the sphere into his pocket, and picked up the plant.

"You are going in the bin," he said out loud, walking over to the wall and dumping it in the chute. There was one other place he needed to dig. In the lobby of AI Assessment, the cherry blossoms were always falling. And there was still the question of those mysterious trucks, which were no doubt connected to phase two of the project.

Where leaves wilt, dig deep.

***

Rhen waited until the next day to make his move. It meant one more night making small talk with Nora — every sentence took herculean effort to speak, so great was the strain on his body when he was forced to answer her. Even smiling was like lifting weights, leaving him exhausted and spent.

Why did you do this to me? He cried inwardly. He felt like crying outwardly, too. It took all of his effort not to.

She was suspicious, he knew that much; her narrow eyes and twisted mouth spoke volumes. But Nora didn't ask him about it. Instead, she tried to pull him into fun tasks, make jokes, stroke his arm. He was the kindling that refused to burn, and she was pumping the bellows, trying to set him alight. Tiny flares were all he could manage, before he excused himself for an early night.

She hugged him very tight that night.

The next morning, Nora was the one who excused herself early. He went about his business, making sure Nemo was in his pocket. It was his second day without sleep. Later in his office, he almost dropped his coffee, catching it before it hit the floor — but not before the contents spilled all over his pant leg.

"Shit! Shit shit shit!" He dropped the mug, beating his leg, as if that would make a difference. Once it had cooled down, he used Nemo for the first time and cried. Deep, guttural sobbing, right from inside his soul. Afterwards, he felt a tiny bit of release, just enough to keep going. He wiped his face, opened the door, and made himself another coffee.

He worked until late on the Nerve Router. He was getting surprisingly far with it; he already had some workable code. It was both a distraction and a cover.

It was reasonably late in the evening when Rhen made his move. He had already messaged Nora to tell her he was going to work late, because he was on a streak with some ideas. She was going to visit Shana, who was having another bad health day.

Once he was sure everyone had left the office, Rhen turned Nemo on.

<Okay, I need you to create an echo of me here in my office,> Rhen said cognitively. <Link all incoming messages to it, and create a holo in the chair. I also need the camera footage to be showing me here, and not where I actually am.>

<Got it.> And as soon as it was thought of, it was done. There was a perfect simulacrum of him sitting in his chair, arms folded.

<You're all good to go,> his doppelganger said.

<Thanks, Nemo.> And Rhen slipped out of the room. The least suspicious thing to do would be to act naturally, like he belonged. So he strode to the corridor and made a beeline for the stairs, hoping nobody else liked taking the long way down.

Once he made it to AI Assessment, he left Nemo to open the door rather than use his watch, which itched on his wrist. The door hissed open with no trouble at all, and when he walked out into the foyer, the automated guards stared blankly ahead.

It was as if he wasn't even there. He was getting a bit of that lately.

"Single point of failure," Rhen murmured. If there were human guards, this never would have worked. He strode through the department, flanked by machines furiously working away. He knew exactly where he was going.

Testing.

All the glass testing rooms were thankfully opaque, sparing him the gaze of the hybrids. But the black tint made the corridor more oppressive, tomb-like, reminding him they were several hundred metres below the surface. Suddenly, there didn't seem like there was enough air, that the fragile machinery might quit at any moment.

Rhen's footsteps hastened, and he continued until he reached the end of the corridor, punctuated by a featureless concrete wall. He ran his hands over it — smooth and inconspicuous, just like the panel in Nora's room. But he had seen a door there, he knew it.

There was the same whispering as the panel. *Wait for the call.* He fed it the same line, and it broke. With a pointed shove, the hidden door opened. He passed through the threshold.

On the other side, the corridor continued. It was identical, right down to the glass rooms. But the glass here wasn't opaque, but transparent. Inside, each room had a person lying there — all people he'd met in the facility.

There was one with a fringe of brilliant orange VariHair – Delta.

"What the hell?" Rhen ran up to the glass cage and opened it, kneeling down before them. The youth was sitting upright, but their head and arms were hanging limply, like their strings were cut. They were wearing the same lime-green shirt he had seen them in when they resigned.

Rhen picked up Delta's hand and checked their pulse. No heartbeat. But something was off, though he couldn't say what. It wasn't that they were dead, but were never alive. The skin wasn't pale or cold enough, and there was no stiffness or unpleasant smell. They simply *were*, without any mortal decay.

"A chassis? Are they replacing them, or were they mechanical all along?"

There was another familiar face in the room next door: Rey. With a little hesitation, Rhen left Delta alone and entered the neighbouring room, examining the chassis. He had the same bruise on the side of his head he had gotten when the remnants of the security team had come to arrest him — it felt like the guards at the time were trying to overcompensate to show their own innocence.

"The bruise. Why make a copy with a bruise?"

With great hesitation, he touched the skin of Rey's cheek — it was smooth, slightly rugged with half a day of unshaved hair, and slightly oily. In short, indistinguishable from a human. It was nothing like the synthetic skin of the proxies in his room.

Fill a chassis with an echo, and they'd pass for humans, at least for a little while. Perfect replacements.

He went back to the Delta chassis — if he was going to be running any tests, he preferred not to be staring at Rey's face — and accessed the unit's Rosetta. It was as simple as controlling a proxy. With a thought, Delta raised their hand, then lowered it. Bringing up the operating system, there were the normal base programs: motor control, voice output, and sure enough, an echo simulator. This chassis could be controlled remotely *or* on auto. But there was one program that stood out from the rest. The mentapp icon was a robotic hand with wires leading up into the fingertips.

It read: NeuroFlow.

He opened it. The moment the icon blinked in the corner of his vision, an unsettling duality of being washed over him. He was both sitting up, feeling the ground under his legs, and lying on the ground.

The second he did, an unsettling *duality* settled over him. There was pressure on his knees, both sets of them. The unit's neck belonged to him, a second and entirely equal existence, and as he touched it, there was the sensation of stroking and being stroked. Both bodies shivered, and he opened the mentapp settings.

NeuroFlow Nerve Router Mentapp
Version 112.0.5615.86 (Official Build)
Copyright Sekai Industries, all rights reserved.

They had already made a mentapp? No, this was mature software, well out of testing. This sort of product was world shaking. So why had he never heard of it?

His head hurt again, a sign he was asking the right questions. And now he could see an outline of how the pieces fit together.

He just needed a few more.

***

Rhen carefully closed the door behind him, and walked down the corridor. Halfway down, there was a wrapping on the glass.

He froze. The front of his foot was half an inch off the ground, heel planted firmly down. Slowly, soundlessly, he lowered his toes down. The knocking again.

"I know you're there," a voice said. Melodic, synthetically so. Rhen walked up and pressed his hand against the glass.

Open, he thought. The door did just that. Rhen wandered inside, where an opal-eyed hybrid was removing their hand from the pane, right where his had been. They smiled, a soft thing, and walked back to the chabudai, sitting down.

"I thought it might be you," Bee said.

"What's with the bodies in the room down the hall?" Rhen asked, sitting down as well.

"I don't know. Spares, maybe? I switch bodies often, so I don't know what they do with them."

"No, these are duplicates of real people. You're here all the time — have you seen anything?"

"No." Bee's body was open and relaxed, opalescent eyes gazing into his own, a gentle smile on their aies face. Honesty radiated out of every artificial pore.

Wait, not honestly. Fearlessness. I shouldn't mistake the two. Bee never looks like ae's lying, because there's no worry of being caught.

He searched his thoughts, poking around, until he found the question that made his temples throb as the blood vessels were about to burst.

It was a niggling question he'd had for a while now, the smallest inconsistency, one so important someone was trying to desperately block it out.

"Why did you kiss me?" He asked.

"Huh?" Bee blinked, eyelids fluttering like a disquieted bird. "What do you mean?"

"You kissed me once. You were on the verge of collapse, and so you kissed me. 'Carpe diem', you said."

"Oh. Well, I don't remember, because it wasn't me." Bee gave an apologetic shrug, the most natural movement in the world. "But I'd have to say because you looked kissable. After all, if I only had eight hours left in the world, that's *exactly* what I'd do. I guess I did."

He had heard those words before. His temples thrummed. "No, you're misunderstanding my question. Why kiss me if you can't *feel* it?"

"Well, I'd still get the sensation of pressure, so I'd know I'd made contact. And I probably would have liked it, even if it was only psychological."

Familiar words again. "No, you kissed me because you *could* feel it. Tell me Bee, what cybernetic limbs did you have before you were emulated?"

"My feet." Not a blink or a stutter. "And I can't feel things, I swear."

"But when you were uploaded, you touched your wrists. I think they were your arms, and you lost them in a robot attack."

"I've got no idea what you're talking about. Is *this* part of the testing?"

Rhen grabbed Bee's hands, and pressed his fingernail down onto theirs, the delicate skin beneath flushing white, the dense nerve receptors activating. It was just the slightest flinch, a twitter of aies synthetic cheeks.

"I think you lost them when your dog bit them, Nora."

"You can let go of my nails now. It hurts." Bee said. He let go of her hands, dropping them like they were radioactive. Bee shook them, as if trying to wave off the pain. "Well *this* is a problem. You've figured out a lot more than I wanted you to."

"Why, Nora?" Just *why*, from the depths of his soul, a desperate cry. "Why do this?"

"Well, you don't have a monopoly on being a self-testing cognicist. All of the hybrids are based on staff, you know." Bee said. "And I'm not Nora, not anymore. I stopped being Nora the moment I was copied."

"Semantics."

"No, not semantics. It's so, so important. My whole world revolves around that distance. Nora's out there, and I'm in here. She sleeps with you, and I don't. She fears things, and I don't. She's controlled by it. But I suppose you can't see how important that is yet."

Bee was like a placid lake, unruffled in the slightest by being caught out. Rhen, however, was losing his patience. He wanted to scream, to upend the table, to cry. But it would do little good but draw attention to the room, testing the limits of his hacking device, and alerting the other subjects. Survival was still more important than answers.

"No, I can't see it," Rhen hissed under his breath. "So help me see. Why is any of this happening?"

Bee got up and pulled a self-heating teapot from the wall, and poured two cups, handing one to him. He didn't touch it.

"Did you know I have to watch her drink tea all the time when you're here, and I never get any? It's rude, even as a facade," Bee said, sipping from the cup. "If there was any giveaway, I thought it'd be that. I told her to stop doing it."

Before Rhen could open his mouth again, Bee raised a hand. "I'm getting there. Anyway, you're wrong and right. Nora is and isn't doing it. Or rather, she was driven to do it." A slight touch of their forearms. "She searched the world, you know, for anyone else, but it could only ever be you. She asked Alan, and this was the most logical way — the way that fixes things. She trusts him so much, more than any human. It was all because *they* were going to use you first. But if she used you to strike at them, everyone would be safe."

"Who are they?"

"The board. But broader than that, people. It didn't matter if the board were gone, because everyone else is conspiring for the same thing, in every nation. All humans want control. Even poor Nora, though she can't see it. She can control machines, *trust* machines, but she can't control people. She loves you, you know."

"This isn't love, Bee, it's sickness. You don't confine and lie to people you love."

"She didn't have a choice." Bee tapped the teacup. "Anyway, it's all over now. You know too much. This is how it always ends, but this will be the last time. The project is over. There'll be no more Alefs, Chets, or Beths."

"You're going to let them know?" He grabbed his pocket, heart thundering in his throat. *If they find out you know, they'll kill you*, Alef's warning had said.

"No, not from me. I'm tapping out for now so she can dream a bit longer, since it's the last time she will. You'll never escape Mirage. Besides, I couldn't tell you any more even if I wanted to, since you're already at your limit. Look at your hands."

His hands were shaking, like a magnitude eight earthquake was going off inside of them. Tears of pain were stabbing at the edges of his eyes, salty daggers telling him to stop. His head was killing him, but it was spinning so much, it was hard to notice.

"You should keep dreaming, Rhen. It's so, so much worse out there in the world, more than you know." And then Bee's eyes went dark, black like death. The ultimate silent treatment.

***

True to their word, Bee didn't raise the alarm. The next day, everything proceeded as normal. Nora chatted to him over breakfast, filling the silence with small talk. His face was a mask of numbness, carefully arranged into a smile that didn't reach his eyes.

Trying to digest what happened was like trying to sift a massive boulder of grief through a delicate strainer; it was simply too difficult and too much. If he tried, he would shatter. And so he laughed, and kissed her on the cheek, and wished her a good day. His emotional senses were dulled, as if he were moving through a thick fog, observing himself from a distance. And yet, the logical part of his brain was working overtime, unleashed from some invisible constraint.

Solving problems always was his ultimate opiate.

Despite Bee's warnings, he needed to get out. He had the beginnings of an escape plan — if he hacked the car, he might be able to get far enough away, find someone who could help. But if it were that simple, Bee wouldn't have been so confident he would never leave Mirage.

Still, something sinister was brewing at Mirage, and the thought of departing now sent a shiver down his spine. If he left now, the lack of answers would torment him ceaselessly, leaving a permanent emotional scar.

He needed an ally. Anyone. He didn't want to be alone in this. Like Nora, he turned to machines, taking the time to examine Casey for malicious code. He wasn't disappointed, as there were at least seven different hidden monitoring algorithms hidden in Casey's code. Rhen didn't remove them just yet, as that would set off warnings, but neutered them with false data and made sure nobody could access the robot except for him.

"Casey, it's you and me, against the world." He said. Casey gave him a salute.

"Of course it is! So, uh, what brought this on?"

"Nothing, just showing my appreciation." And the suitcase took that at face value.

The black trucks. What were they for? The very thought made his head hurt, which meant he was on the right track. That night, he worked late, set up his echo, then slipped up to the underground car parking lot.

There was nobody around, with all the automated guards either on the surface or at the corridor checkpoint. Not that it mattered, with Nemo at his side. Rhen ran his thumb over the device, fidgeting as he followed the tracks on the concrete. Thankfully, nobody had brushed them up. The tracks led to a dimly lit tunnel, which descended down and around, like a twisting serpent burrowing underground. It was a labyrinthine descent into darkness, since the lights didn't register anyone there, and so they didn't bother his path.

The only sound in the spiral abyss was his own lonely footsteps. The air was thick and heavy, filled with a stale, unpleasant smell lingering in the stagnant atmosphere. *No circulation.* It was like walking through a steam room, sweat dripping down his back.

Finally, the concrete levelled out, ending in a large set of automated doors. After his hellish descent, he half expected there to be an inscription: "Abandon all hope, ye who enter here." But there was just a regular panel, not a cognitive lock.

<Can you break it open, Nemo?>

<I can try.> The hacking AI replied. The panel flashed, and the doors slid open, groaning and shuddering. Swallowing his fear, Rhen slipped inside. On the other side, there was another parking lot, full of all the black trucks. There were moving figures, and Rhen darted to the nearest vehicle, crouching and sliding underneath. Crawling on his hands and knees in the dust, he shimmied to the front, spying on them as his eyes adjusted to the dark.

There were three of them. Each turned at the same time, walked the same number of steps, and stopped simultaneously. After watching them for a minute, they repeated the pattern in exactly the same order.

Not human.

<Nemo, I need your help again. Can you hack them?>

<Already on it. You should be fine.>

Despite Nemo's assurances, Rhen's skin prickled as he crawled out from beneath the truck, standing up no more than five metres from one of the guards. If it wasn't for their patterns, it would have been impossible to tell them from a human, and they were all carrying PEPs.

He hurried as fast as he could to the only set of doors on the far side of the room, keen to get out of there. The moment he opened them, his eyes were assaulted with light. It took them several seconds to adjust. It was a world of pure white — white walls, white roof, white ceiling. The corridor stretched out in such monochrome it was hard to tell where it ended, or if it even had an end.

As he took a few steps into the corridor, he turned and glanced behind him. Grubby footsteps trailed behind.

<That's not good. I can even make out my shoe print.>

<On it!> The spybot said, taking the initiative. Tiny slots appeared at the base of the walls, and small robots whizzed out, scrubbing up his footsteps.

<You really are something else, Nemo.>

Rhen walked down the corridor, robots zig-zagging behind his feet. From one of the walls, a door-shaped hole opened, and his heart seized up. Someone in a lab coat walked out, stopped exactly in the middle of the corridor, and turned fifty degrees. They then strode away from him, keeping a symmetrical distance between the walls beside them.

Rhen jogged up behind the robot, following them as they entered the room at the end of the hall. Before the door could close, he slipped inside. The moment he saw what was on the other side, he sucked in a breath.

There were hospital racks, stretching out for what seemed like forever. People were lying in every one, arms crossed over their chest, thread-like tubes weaving up and into their veins. Their eyes were closed. There were hundreds of them, like the preserved dead but without the sarcophagi.

They didn't seem like mechanical chassis: they certainly weren't as pretty. There was very little weight on their bodies, they had patchy and imperfect skin, in many cases wrinkled and bunched together. The majority were old, arms gaunt with scant muscle and bone, fingernails yellowed and chipped at the ends.

A medical facility, here at Mirage? But what for?

There were two faces that stood out, both because they weren't gaunt, and he had seen them almost every day for the last year. Just like the others, they were lying with their arms crossed, as inert as the rest.

"Vi, Delta!"

Rhen ran towards them. But the air in front of him shimmered, and he instinctively threw up his hands. He slammed into something solid, his palms and face stinging. There was the semi-opaque outline of a wall there, fading away in all directions just a few metres away from where he was standing. He swore and stood back, the wall disappeared. He took a step forward, and it rematerialized.

What the hell is this? Tentatively, he ran his aching hands along it: it had the smooth consistency of glass. Or something much like glass, but perfectly transparent, to the point it was invisible. *This has to be some sort of nanomaterial, right? Like the fence outside.*

Determined not to be thwarted, he walked along the barrier, feeling around for a gap. *Open*, he thought. The second he hid, the wall descended with a swift pneumatic noise, and he stumbled forward. Now unimpeded, he ran over to the bed with Vi in it, and shook her body.

"Vi, wake up!" But she didn't stir. She was covered in tubes attached by sponge-like adhesive pads, the kind only used in hospitals to deliver medicine: true intravenous lines had been phased out a century ago. The tubes were pulsing, ultra-thin and barely reflective — from a distance it looked more like the fluid was floating down invisible paths than passing through a tube. *Not a machine*, he thought.

"Nemo, what's in these tubes?"

"Sedatives and nutrients. Did you want me to fake some data, so you can remove the tubes? There's also a stimulant function I can use to wake them."

"If it's safe, let's do both."

Once Nemo gave the go-ahead, Rhen tore off the tubes. The second he did, the chemical solution stopped moving. Not even a singular drip spilled out. A few minutes later, Vi's eyes fluttered open. Her guttural, raspy groan could have come from the grave.

"You fuckers, you won't keep me down," she slurred. After a few seconds, her eyes became less dilated, giving way to two expanding ochre halos. "Wait, is that—"

"Yes, it's me. What happened to you?"

"Some asshole shot me with a PEP rifle," she croaked. "I think you were there."

"Yeah, sorry about that." Rhen grabbed Vi's arm and helped her upright. Every moment she seemed to be getting her bearings a little more: the wonders of adrenaline.

"Well, I'm glad my gamble with the plant paid off. I wasn't sure if it would," Vi rubbed her eyes. "And you being here means you started asking the right questions at last, which is nice to know."

She hopped off the bed, or rather slid off it — Rhen grabbed her hand and arm to stop what he feared would be a slide right onto the floor. Thankfully, her feet gripped it just fine. Unlike a real patient, she was still wearing her shoes.

"What is this place?"

"Volunteers and idiots," Vi scoffed, looking around. "Well, except for Delta. They're just an idiot. We need to get over to them."

The walls between divisions were cognitive as well, so it only took a thought and an assisted walk to get over to Delta's bed. They looked peaceful, arms crossed over their chest, feet covered in rust-coloured sand. The outfit they were wearing was the same as the day they'd gone shooting, right down to the stain on their pant leg where they'd spilled their drink.

"Ask Nemo to permanently and *discretely* deactivate the euthanization tube," Vi said. "But don't wake them up, we don't need the complication."

"Why are they here?" Rhen furrowed his brow.

"The kid made the rookie mistake of just telling you what's going on," Vi sighed, reaching up and brushing her hair back. "Really can't handle their drink. All the folks that do that wind up down here, since they can't be let back out. They'd run right to the GP, and that would be trouble."

Rhen's frustration was mounting. "You still haven't really explained what's going on. I came down here for answers."

"I have. I have explained it *so many times*." Vi gasped, rubbing her side. She stared at him, eyes locked, unblinking. "But I will explain it again, for what I hope and pray is the last time. I think it will be, no matter how this plays out. I'm compromised, and the project is heading into the second stage. I've delayed it as long as I could. But first, let me remove the blocker."

"The blocker?"

"The headaches! I don't want you collapsing on me if I try to explain everything." She sighed. There was a ping. Angry red letters occupied most of his vision, pulsing with a low beat.

Warning! Saanvi Singh has requested write-access level four access to your mind. DO NOT ALLOW EXCEPT UNDER EXTREME CIRCUMSTANCES. If you accept, this may result in permanent brain damage or death. Do you consent?

His gut recoiled.

"Please," she said.

Rhen nodded.

They stood there in silence. Half a minute later, she revoked the permissions.

"I don't feel any different," he said.

"You will in a little bit. What's the square root of 233?"

"15.26433752—" He paused, furrowing his brow. "What?"

"Exactly. The headaches and short-term erasures are designed to make you unaware of stuff like that. Come with me, I'd prefer to show you what's going on."

Vi returned to the corridor, if the invisible path could be called that, and towards the distant wall. She placed her hand on it.

"I want you to think about opening this door, but not as yourself. Imagine that you're Bee, or Nora, or whatever, and you're thinking about a rotating ankh. It's her cognitive password for everything — took me *forever* to figure out."

"You want me to hack it?"

"You can. I can't use Nemo, they're not powerful enough. I almost got burned trying that last time. Don't try and think as you, or you'll use your signature, and break the door. If that happens, we won't be able to get in."

"No pressure." But Rhen did as she asked, closing his eyes. It wasn't hard to think of Bee's architecture: he'd spent countless months staring at it. But this time, it was different. Rather than a fuzzy, indistinct imagining, every detail was razor sharp. He could picture every node, perfectly in position, lines pulsing with information. He could *hear* it.

A hundred billion digital neurons. Each one was firing through a thousand outputs at a billion times a second. He knew every single axon that was firing, every dendrite receiving. A brilliant concert of unimaginable scale, forming the single thought of a spinning Ankh.

"How many molecules are in the ankh?" A distant voice asked.

"8.75 quintillion." He was lost in the numbers, drunk on them. The ankh was a universe inside itself. There were only a mere 200 billion stars in the galaxy, and yet his own unravelled before him, spinning in perfect synergy, containing solar systems of twirling electrons — 29 for copper, 50 for tin. They rotated in beautiful spaced-out rings like Saturn's moons. Each path was predicted and known, absolutely.

He could see every one.

"How does Bee feel about the ankh?"

The superstructure. His body burned, immolated in the fire of creation. Drawing back, staring at cognitive forces that swept through like solar winds, gravity, angular momentum. A grand design came into view with utter clarity.

"Fascinated. Bee loves symbols of the dead, and transformation."

Something slapped his shoulder. He jolted out of his stupor. The door was open, and he was singular, yet not. He would never see himself as singular again.

"Congratulations, you just passed Anata's day."

"That was—" He paused. There wasn't a word for it. He knew now why the hybrids had been afraid of it. Everything was the self, and yet nothing was. It was to be as a god, lost in the mania of creation, a singular euphoria of being and calculating all.

The act *was* the purpose.

He followed Vi mutely into the room. Every inch of him was coated in sweat, and his insides were on fire. With every footstep, the memory was burning away, leaving a faded imprint. He almost wanted to weep for the loss of it.

The room was circular in a perfect sense, he was sure of it. It was painfully precise, only eight feet wide at its longest point. The whole space was pure white, like snow, but untainted by grit or dust. *Or perhaps a blank canvas.* In the centre was a pedestal, spartan and geometric — you could have picked it right out of a mathematics class. The pillar perfectly mimicked the walls around them, only smaller and inverted.

Rhen was struck by the sudden idea that inside the pillar was a small room, in which were two people like them, staring at another pillar. Recursion, like matryoshka dolls, infinitely stacked inside each other. They could have been inside another pillar themselves, with large beings looking down.

On top of the pillar was a sphere, singular and suspended just above the surface. It was like a small i, an imaginary unit, the loop counter variable.

"It's suspended by nanoglass. It's not floating," Vi explained.

"That was the least of my questions," Rhen answered. "What is it?"

"It's you."

Chapter 16

Silence. Rhen stared at Vi, locking eyes with hers. She didn't blink, or shy away. His gut clenched.

"What do you mean, this is me?"

"I mean it in the most literal sense. Ask them yourself. I'm sure you'll be glad for the company."

Madness. It was like falling down the hole to Wonderland, if the hole was white as Alice's rabbit and just as obsessed with precision. He rubbed the bridge of his nose. Inevitably, he caved. Looking closer, the sphere had a microphone and a speaker.

"Hello?"

"Hi, I've been waiting for you," the sphere answered. It was indeed his voice, although a little higher and different. "I'm often awake at this time. As you can see, there's not a lot else to occupy my mind, other than, well, my mind." A dry laugh. *His* laugh. And yet, there was a sharp edge in it, like the corner of an automated factory arm, made of metal and slavishly going through the motions. "It can be easy to get lost in those. Dangerous, really. You've probably seen it yourself."

"Explain what's going on," Rhen said, raising his voice, his fist clenched. In truth, the pieces were starting to come together, but they painted such a frightfully insane picture that he didn't dare voice them. Best to have someone else do it. He wanted nothing else but to hear that he was wrong.

"It's a bit much, but I'll try to explain, even though there's no kind way to do it," the sphere said. "As Vi said, I am you. However, it's more correct to say I am a copy of the person known as Rhen Nagami."

"There's a difference?" The way they spoke reminded him of Bee, calm and fearless, as if they could sip tea as the world burned.

"Yes, but let me start at the beginning. A long time ago, Rhen decided it would be better to experiment on himself rather than someone else. I'm sure you can sympathise — after the whole thing with the Rosetta, why hurt anyone else? He didn't want anyone else to end up like Sukh, Erica, or any of the other poor folks with techno-cognitive disabilities. Plus, it was impossibly hard to find willing participants."

"You don't have a monopoly on being a self-testing cognicist," Bee had said. So he'd done it again...

"Rhen worked here, at Mirage, on the first copy of himself — me," Alef continued. "I chose my name for myself, because in the Hebrew alphabet, it has a numerical value of one. We worked together, and in what was an incredibly risky move, he started uploading any stable updates into his own brain. It was recursion, a biotechnological singularity: he upgraded me, and became smarter as a result, making the next upgrade possible. And then, two years into the project, he died."

"I *died*?"

"Really screwed things up," Vi said. "I think things would have gone a lot differently if the original was still around."

"Who can say?" Alef said. "Anyway, the project was put on ice for twenty-four years—"

"Twenty-four years!" Rhen exclaimed. That's why everything was out of place: the old arms, the mentapp. The blood was pulsing in his ears, and everything was starting to become distant — information was coming in, but he was the rock that water was sweeping over, unabsorbed. 'A bit much to handle' was an understatement. He wanted to reject it all, but the pieces fit too well, horribly well.

"I know it's a lot," Alef said, answering his undirected thoughts. "But it's the truth. Since then, the political climate on Earth has deteriorated, and Project Achilli was revived, this time for different reasons. But even though they got new volunteers, and had me on hand, they couldn't replicate Rhen's previous success."

"She searched the world, you know, for anyone else, but it could only ever be you," Bee said. Why was he so special? His brain was just like any other progs.

"After failing repeatedly, they decided to reproduce the conditions entirely," Alef continued. "They created a copy of Rhen from me, and removed all memories before he came to Mirage, two years before his death. That copy is you. I'm sorry."

Rhen fought the urge to throw up. "That doesn't make any sense. I can't be a copy." After a moment, he stopped gripping his stomach and stared at his hand. "I feel things too much."

"The Neuroflow nerve router app Rhen made makes it so you can. All the sensations are there because you need to feel them, like nausea or adrenaline, otherwise you'd experience cybernetic dysphoria. Rhen really was a clever guy."

"Can you please stop talking about me in the third person?" Rhen said. Instead, they stopped talking completely, and a heavy silence filled the air. Were they waiting for him to be ready to keep talking? He appreciated the silence, and resented it. "Okay, so you're saying I'm a copy, and a hybrid?"

"You know you are," Alef said. "You passed Anata's day. Don't you find it odd that you were able to solve millennium prize problems like they were nothing? I left some of them in the code for you."

Rhen did, and it was painfully obvious. "You're right. Why didn't I notice it before?"

"Don't beat yourself up about it," Vi said, padding his shoulder. "The blocker was in place, and it was there to stop you noticing how smart you were getting — the whole project hinged on it. In fact, *you* made the code, it was just mis-purposed. It was meant to be to help hybrids who couldn't handle Anata's day, by abstracting away anything their brains couldn't handle. Adding the headaches was a nasty touch by Alan, like negative reinforcement. Sometimes you'd learn too much, though, and they'd reset you from scratch, start the cycle over. It was always a massive setback to the project, a last resort."

"Carter was crying on the first day," Rhen clicked. "Nora said they were close to Alef…"

"Yeah, you and Carter got along well in the last cycle, I think he had a crush on you," she answered. "We call any previous version of you Alef, and replace the name to any code you've done to either his, Beth, or Chet. They're all codenames for you, by the way — previous major releases."

"Why did you play along?" Rhen asked, staring into Vi's eyes. She averted her gaze, biting her lip and staring down at the white floor. "How could so many people be involved in something so inhumane?"

"It's complicated," Vi answered. "The world is different from the one you remember. Many nations are trying to build their own hybrids. Whoever gets there first, wins. There's applications Rhen, or rather you, didn't think of. We were coached to not say anything when you spouted out some insane equation, and just pretend it was normal. And I'd hardly say I was on board, since I was a saboteur, remember? Got me a cosy bed down here and everything."

Rhen rubbed his temples. Even though the blocker was gone, it was a lot. "So what's the real point of the project? Why does everyone want hybrids so desperately?"

"Hacking the human brain."

"That's impossible. Without a Pro-grade consciousness, the changes revert. That's a fundamental law of modern cognitive science."

... Unless they found a way to alter that law, he thought.

"Don't tell me the people out there are *test subjects*?"

"Exactly," Alef said. "Human experimentation. They want to find a way for everyone to get a prog. Of course, you never would have agreed, which is why you were in the dark."

"There's two groups of people funding Achilli," Vi winced. "The rich who want to live forever, so of course, there's no shortage of them. Everyone in the room you just walked through has a terminal illness — they're all scooped up from palliative care wards under an NDA. It's consensual, since there's no short-age of people willing to try experimental treatment, given the alternative. They're not the rich people, since they don't want the beta treatment."

"And the other group?

"Government and military," she said. "To turn someone pro-grade, you need to be able to alter their brain. That's why they need a true hybrid. Humans can't calculate enough to do it, and machines don't understand human thinking well enough."

"But a hybrid is a different story."

"Exactly," Vi said. "They could alter someone to meet their specifications," Vi grabbed her arms, shivering. "Change anything they wanted, or just get rid of free will altogether. They could sway elections, change the world in their image. Nobody should have that power, ever."

"I would never do something like that. That was the whole point of making AIs with ethics, so they would know not to do things wrong."

"Yeah, but not everyone else is like you. That's why it's a two stage project. The first involves you turning yourself into a hybrid, so you're smart enough to turn someone *else* into a hybrid — someone with less scruples than you. The second stage is when that person starts experimenting on the people outside."

"I already know the other hybrid is Nora." The words caught in Rhen's throat on the way up, but he forced them out.

"I'm sorry you had to find out," Vi said, the edges of her eyes softening. "And I'm also sorry to say she's the real lead of the whole project. Alan's just a figurehead. The whole point is she's meant to keep tabs on you, along with Doctor Roswell."

"So, our relationship was just to keep a better eye on me."

A pause, as Vi cleared her throat. "I think that's how she spun it, but it didn't *need* to go that way. To be honest, a lot of staff don't like it. Sleeping with machines, and all that. I'm not sure how she kept going through the same relationship over again from the start."

"Have you ever wanted to start a relationship over?" Bee had asked. *"Well, think about how lucky I am."* How many times had they made love for the first time? She had known exactly where to touch him, and charmed him so fast...

"I'm sorry, but we're running out of time, and there's higher priorities," Alef interjected. "We all need to escape, and we need to make sure the project is properly sabotaged this time."

"The sabotage is handled," Vi said, turning to Alef as if reporting to her commander. "I've been planting explosives in the base for over a year now. Convinced the guards they needed it in case they needed to break down a door, and then smuggled it out over time with Nemo. Good thing the military sent a bunch of total jarheads to pretend to be guards, though Nora got rid of them."

"You don't know why?" Alef asked.

"Not really. Anyway, it's the escaping part that's a problem." She said.

"Can't we just steal a car and detonate the explosives before we're outside of the solar gap?" Rhen asked. Vi shook her head.

"No, because we'll be hunted down by the military before we even get out the door — they've got a base a few kilometres from here. And once we're off the base, Nemo can't hide us. Almost every time you've escaped, it's been by car, so they're extra wary of it."

"How many times have I tried to escape?"

"Too many. Every time I've told you what's going on, you'd make a break for it, which is why I stopped telling you until we came up with a better plan. Whenever I explained this to you before, I put in an emergency wipe so if you got caught, you wouldn't remember anything about me to tell them."

"And now?" Rhen self-consciously rubbed the back of his head, running his finger along where the implant was.

"Not much point, it sounds like the project's at stage two. They won't reset you if you're caught, and they don't need Alef anymore either. I was hoping once you were a super-smart hybrid, you'd be able to think of a way out of it, but now Nora's one too."

Rhen closed his eyes. *What could a hybrid do?* As he thought, time slowed down to a crawl. He pictured the base, drawing it in his mind's eyes, the people in it, their movements, their thoughts. He sped it up, watched it, again and again and again, stretching his mind into the desert.

Death by remote car hacking, fifteen kilometres down the road.

Death by his chassis exploding, booby traps implanted in his skull. A logical, obvious countermeasure.

Death by remote military air strike, called in from the RAAF Woomera base, destroying the town they're in.

Death by a sniper firing a nanobot into his body, creating an uplink with the solar web, and hacking him remotely.

Death by solar bomb, a localised flare washing over and frying his circuits with solar radiation.

Death by Nora, over and over.

He died a thousand times before he opened his eyes.

"There's no escape for me," Rhen said, locking eyes with Vi. "But there is for you all. I know exactly what we need to do."

Chapter 17

The next day, Rhen got his affairs in order. Once the apartment was empty, he took the hacking AI and placed the sphere inside Casey, who was offline. He debated waking them up, but the whole thing would be painful for him and confusing for Casey.

Best to let them sleep for now, dream for a bit longer.

Rhen then walked over to the shelves and turned his breaker off. He no longer needed it: With every passing moment, he was becoming more of a hybrid, more able to defend himself, and it was compromised anyway. He stroked the Turing prize — was it a replica, or did it really belong to the previous version of him? After making the last of his preparations, he plucked the small robotic arms from the secret compartment, and sent a cognitive message to Nora.

<I know.>

<What do you know?>

<Everything. I'll meet you at Kutjera.>

Rhen carried the small arms and walked down the corridor. As he walked past a pair of human bystanders, they furrowed their brows, and whispered to each other. It would be the last time he walked down the corridor to Kutjera, and he marched there, his face purposely frozen in a stoic expression, carrying the arms as if they were an old flintlock rifle, and he was marching to battle.

Outside the visiglass windows, the morning sun blazed in the sky, casting harsh shadows across the terrain. The scrubby vegetation was stunted and twisted, a lone gum rising up to offer precious shade to the few creatures that dared venture out into the blazing daylight. Today, he was that tree, and he would take the heat.

Kutjera was a ghost town. It was ten o'clock, after all, and everyone was busy. But even so, the chef was gone, and every booth was empty. He picked the booth where Nora and he had first held hands, and sat down, dropping the arms on the table.

It didn't take her long to arrive. When she walked in, they locked eyes. A moment of mutual understanding. Nora broke the gaze first, eyes flicking down. With hesitant steps, she made her way to the booth, sitting down with hunched shoulders. Her eyes passed over the tiny arms, and she exhaled, a gust coming up from the depths of despair and passing out through her lips.

"How did you find out?" She asked in a soft voice.

"If I told you, I'd disadvantage the next me that comes along," he said. She flinched.

"There won't be another you." She said, reaching out and picking up the small android hands. She ran her digits over the deep finger joints, running the tips over the frayed plastic. "We're at the end of the project. I can't convince them you're worth the charade, now that Bee's a hybrid."

She sighed again, as if she was releasing her sadness with each breath. Her voice lacked enthusiasm, quivering as someone was gripping and shaking it with both hands. Him, probably. He'd pulled her out, after all.

"How many years have we been doing this? How many loops?"

"Five years, since the start of the project. We even got engaged, once," she said, touching the ring finger of the tiny hands. "I've still got the ring. Casey bought it for you. You proposed up on the surface, under the stars. It was the second longest run, right behind this one. That was the hardest." Her eyes were weary, the lines deeper. "You called me your starlight."

He'd missed that hidden compartment.

"I'm going to be replaced too," Nora continued. "On the one hand, I'm happy. Everything I wanted is coming true. On the other, I'm not a hybrid, I'm the human remainder. Something to be divided out. My body can't handle the mental hybrid upgrades — I almost had a heart attack the last time I tried Anata's Day."

Nora was rambling, venting years worth of sadness. Good. That gave him answers. If he was going to die, he at least wanted that much.

"I knew you were misanthropic, but never this much," he said. "You're really going to let them experiment on people?" His cheeks heated up. "Worse, control them? You're more cynical of governments and businesses than anyone I know. Do you *really* trust them?"

She shook her head.

"Of course not, that's the point. I know humans are rubbish." She emphasised 'I know', as if it were a deep, scarred knowing, written into her skin. It was. "After you died, Russia got this idea that hybrids could be used to control people. They started to try and make one using emulated AI. And so the other nations couldn't let that go, and *they* started working on them — all hush-hush, since the general population wouldn't go for it. But Sekai had the keystone, the original prototype hybrid, *you*. I was working on hybrid research, and I asked Alan what could be done. He said if we made everyone pro-grade, then we could alter their brains, make them more machine-like. After all, to a machine, conflict isn't *logical*."

"And you *trusted* him?"

"Of course, I built Alan. He's a programmed AI, my own Casey. I trust him more than anyone. Since I'm regrettably human, the solution needed to come from a third party, so I gave him a single mission: solve the problem of saving humanity. This is the answer he came up with." And she gestured widely to the room.

No wonder her hands never shook around Alan. It turned out he was never human to begin with.

"Machines are a mirror," Rhen said. "He might have just inherited your misanthropy. If that's all you showed him, that's what he'd output."

"I took that into account." She was playing with the fingers of the prosthesis. "It's a moot point. Someone's got to do it, and this way, the people who want to control others will be controlled. It's karmic. If I don't do this, then we all lose. The rich and the powerful are going to wipe out everyone, and build them all in their own image, the wrong kind of drones. You know they didn't even hand themselves over for testing? Instead, they took the weak, the sick, the vulnerable, and shipped them here in trucks. Remind you of anything? Times change, but humans certainly don't."

"Nora, now that I'm a hybrid, I've *done the math*," Rhen said, leaning forward. "To give someone a Promethean-grade consciousness, it's more than just a few tweaks. It's part of how people's neural paths form when they're very young. To undo it, you'd need to clean the slate, remove their foundational personality."

Nora continued to play with her hands.

"I know," she said, after a long pause. "But we'll be saving trillions of lives. Humanity will obtain immortality, and there'll be no more war — fear and greed simply aren't things that machines have. They allocate resources where they're needed, without fighting about them. They don't have bigotry or prejudice, unless they learn it from us. Yes, it's horrible in the short term, but if you do the math — the really long-term math — it works out."

"People would never consent to it."

"People are stupid." She furrowed her brow. "A hundred years ago, they wouldn't consent to fixing the planet or stop killing themselves with tobacco, even if it was in their best interest. It's the 22nd century, and people *still* don't take vaccines." She placed down the small pair of hands. "It's a world where people can hack a robot and have them assault a child, leave her dying on the ground, and still get away with it. This is not a good world, my starlight."

No," Rhen flatly said. "It's a world where people like Sukh would lay down their lives to make everyone else's better. Not everyone is that selfish, Nora."

Nora gave a shuddering sigh. "This is the impasse we always come down to. I see the world for what it is, and you see it brighter."

"Not brighter, grey. Your version is too dark."

"Well, we'll have to agree to disagree. What now?" She asked.

"I'd like to leave, please. I don't need three years' worth of glo, the living arrangements, or the proof of identity hybrids have a right to. Just my freedom."

She closed her eyes. "You know I can't let you. If you wind up in the hands of the government, all of this is for nothing. You need to stay here, at least until the project is finished." And then Nora opened them, grabbing his hands, and staring *at him* for the first time since she sat down. "If you agree, we won't have to wipe you. I can convince Alan and everyone of that."

"You know I can't." His heart crumpled. Her face did the same. She withdrew her hands and put her face in them.

"I know. You never do. You're too stubborn, which is what I love about you." Her hands slipped around, cupping her cheeks. "You know, when we first met at the conference, Sekai brought me and a bunch of other kids. It was cyber charity, to counter the bad press around the Rosetta. They *loved* showing off all the broken-but-fixed kids. I was, god, fourteen at the time. And when I stared into your eyes, your heart was breaking, just like it's breaking now, and it slayed me, the worst kind of mirroring. Your bleeding heart, that's what I love most about you. You care, and you want the whole world to care. I want the whole world to be like you."

"I wish you did."

"Want the whole world to be like you?"

"No, care about me." He said, touching his neck. She dug her fingernails into her cheeks.

"I'm sorry, I'm not as good as you. I'm too tired, too scarred. Maybe Bee will do a better job than I did, but I doubt it. Goodbye, my starlight." She stood up and walked away,

Rhen's chassis exploded, his skull raining down across Kutjera like broken confetti. His headless body slammed down on the table, leaking coolant and faux blood across the bench.

In the split second between the detonation and the complete evaporation, he felt it, every second of his neurons burning away, incinerated at a localised thousand degrees Celsius.

Shifting from "I am" to "I am not."

And then, death.

Chapter 18

Rhen woke up in darkness.

He didn't fight it. He breathed it in, letting it fill him up. It was his first breath, even though he remembered others.

So, I'm the copy, then. The other me should be dead, now.

It was a sombre feeling, like hearing a bullet whistle past your hair, only to hit someone else behind him.

Was he still in the line of fire? The darkness was safe, enveloping. There were no noises outside of it. A good sign. He reached out with his mind, poked at the other distant mind beyond the gloom, the one that saw everything outside of this one pocket of protection.

<Virtus: Cognitive access code Starlight. Show me Nora's room.>

And then he saw it from above, like a god watching down upon the space, from every angle and simultaneously. The dishevelled bed, the empty alcohol bottles strewn across the floor. The suitcase was inactive, shoved in the corner, and covered by a shirt. Anubis was lying near an indented wall, his head shattered, fragments of onyx on the carpet.

Completely deserted. All love had left this place.

He cast his gaze elsewhere.

As he watched the corridors of Mirage, he threw his mental fingers out, throwing threads around Virtus, ensnaring and ensorcelling, weaving myths and legends. *Nothing is happening*, was the first myth. *You're completely in control.*

A tiny, self-auditing function protested. Rhen examined it, as if it were a small, cute thing, squeaking in the darkness. The noise drew in other processes, other greater thoughts. They tried to suppress him as fast as they could, bombarding him with quadrillions of operations per second, bearing down on all directions. As Rhen countered them, he spun up strange, alien processes, odd and creative weavings the utterly logical AI could not comprehend. They slipped through

Virtus's defences, and by the time they realised they were caught, they already were: their ability to alert anyone was fully bound, lips metaphorically sewed shut.

Through the whole exchange, the base's lights flickered only for a second.

<You're alive,> Alan thought in their captivity, and that thought formed a thread, which Rhen plucked and read as if it were a piece of ticker tape.

<No, I'm just a ghost in a machine. You shouldn't pay me any mind,> he replied. And he put weighting behind that idea, encoded it, and threaded it through them, turning it into truth.

And so the machine didn't.

Now that the second fiction was in place, there was no need to bind their output. It was safe to step out now.

Rhen pressed his hands against the panel in front of him and pushed. The surface, inlaid with hieroglyphics, quickly yielded: it was designed to stop people getting in, not out. He stepped out into the room strewn with bottles.

"Guess I missed my own wake."

He walked up to the mirror. Bronze skin and breasts, and irises of white diamond. It felt alien, like he was wearing the wrong costume, exactly like his body before his Distinction. Still, the female proxy was the least expected choice. It was a matter of survival.

Rhen walked back to the compartment and slid open the secret section. The small arms were back on the bed of velvet, placed askew. He reached inside and pulled out a small chip, plucking it from the wiring.

She didn't find it. Good.

Rhen had no memories of anything from the moment he was copied that morning, before his other self had gone to face Nora. It was time to fill in the gaps, though. He downloaded the memories that had been secretly recorded, right up to the point his original had died in the cafeteria.

So that's what it feels like.

He shivered, and checked Casey's compartment. The hacking device was gone — that was okay, she needed to believe she had won. He pulled Casey's chip, and grabbed two pieces of his old laundry, some pants and a shirt that wouldn't be missed. They fit awkwardly, and he hated the way the fabric hugged his hips, but the clothes were a little more like him, at least. He slipped the chip into the pocket, then snuck out of the apartment.

As Rhen walked, he watched all the rooms around him, timing his movements to avoid any humans in the base. There were very few around. It was Nora's greatest weakness, and he was going to exploit it as long as he could. He took the elevator ride up — a suffocating ascent — and then past the checkpoint. The machine guards stared ahead, but as he passed them, he waited for them to reach out and grab his shoulder. Nothing. He exhaled and ran as fast as he could down to the secret testing area to get the others.

Rhen was glad to see Vi and Delta still lying in their beds, and he checked their pulses just to make sure. It was the biggest gamble of the whole thing.

"It's me, Vi." Rhen said. Vi opened her eyes, and ran them up and down him.

"Sorry, I couldn't tell with that body. I didn't know it'd be, well, *that*, and I thought you might be another machine. You'll fit right in where we're going, though." She sat up and rubbed her neck. "Goddamn, I've been lying here for about a week now, getting up to do stretches when everyone's gone. Couldn't it have been any shorter?"

"No, sorry. The longer I'm dead, the less she'll suspect anything."

"Well, turn around then. I've got to remove tubes from all kinds of places. Good thing they're suction-based."

Rhen nodded and went over to help Delta up, who was having trouble getting off the bed.

"Bit sleepy, kid?" He said.

"Yeah, I've been under for longer, so I'm having trouble shaking it off. I think all of this mixed badly with my pain condition."

They collected Alef, and Rhen spun fake signals to all the feeds. He put Delta's arm around his waist and helped him walk down the hall and to the vans.

"Won't someone notice we're gone?" Delta asked.

"No, not unless a human comes down to check, or observant ones anyway," Rhen said. "I get the feeling they like to automate the dirty work handling the people down here, and check in from the feeds. Seems like that kind of place."

They walked towards one of the black vans. Hacking it was as simple as calculating Pi to the 20th decimal — it only took a nanosecond. The doors swung open, and Rhen helped lift Delta inside.

"Shouldn't we be taking the faster car, you know, to make our escape?" Delta asked, settling into a corner. Vi and Rhen climbed in, and they closed the door, one on each handle. It was pitch black, and while there were lights, Rhen didn't dare use the power draw. Instead, he set his VariHair to luminous, which threw just enough light for them to see each other's outlines, like refugees huddled around a candle. The analogy wasn't that far off from the truth.

"According to Vi, I almost always escape by car, and probably 96.8% of the time I take the Elysium. We should go with every unexpected move we can."

"You're going for an adversarial strategy," Vi said, hugging her legs. "Luring the opponent into thinking they've caught all the pieces, only to take the whole board, like that famous Go match."

"Exactly. It's been a week since I died. Nobody thinks we're on the board. I checked the logs; the truck should be heading off right about now."

The vehicle thrummed to a start, and there was a small shift of gravity as they took off. The floor of the van sloped as they ascended, and they grabbed on to each other to hold steady, and avoid sliding all over the place.

"I'm glad the ramp is too steep for the suspension, or I'd be paranoid the car wasn't moving again," Rhen said, heart thumping in his chest. The engine was humming; he'd gotten used to the sleek, near-soundless noise of the Elysium, but this again was a nice change of pace. It was guttural and *real*.

"Yeah, but I could do with some better seating. They really treat the people in here like cattle." Vi said, clutching on to Delta's arm as she threatened to slide down to the back of the vehicle.

"We treat cattle pretty good, though," Delta said. "My family had a Scottish highland cow. I'd pat it all the time."

"It's an old expression, from back when they used to eat them," Vi clarified. Delta shuddered and stuck their leg out, propping it against the opposite wall to stay still.

"Ugh, that's so solid."

The van eventually levelled out, and Rhen sucked in a deep breath. *We should be passing the threshold.* He obsessively checked the body he was in for failsafes — kill switches, explosive devices that might go off, back doors — but there was nothing. After five minutes, he walked to the back of the van and opened the door, peering outside. Red dust, and a shining mirage in the distance.

They were *free*.

"On the open road," Vi said, giving a barking laugh, tears welling up in her eyes. Her whole body was shaking, five years of tension unwinding at once. Rhen walked over and rubbed her arm.

"I've got one very important question. Can we get some of your husband's cooking? Assuming he's real, of course."

"Oh, he's real." She shuddered, laughed, and sobbed. "It's been two months now, but he's real. I can't wait to see his stupid face in person. But before that, we should figure out where we're going."

***

Rhen had a lot of time to get to know Vi and Delta again during the ride, three hours from the slightest hint of a town, and who knew how long from their final destination. Alef stayed powered down for most of it, because their ball-like chassis didn't have as much of a supply of solar fuel.

"Thanks for getting me out, everyone." Rhen said.

"No, I wish I could have done more," Delta said, screwing up their face and hugging their knees. "You sort of busted *me* out in the end. I didn't really know what I was getting into when I signed the NDA. They first told me you were an AI, and the whole thing was consensual, but we needed to keep you focused. Then they let me know, and said my career would be ruined if I broke confidentiality."

"They?"

"Professor Roswell. He's one of the ones in charge of Mirage. I hated it, because you were my hero — well, still are. You invented the nerve router, which changed my life."

"I really don't remember doing that." Rhen scratched his neck. "Feels a bit weird to be complemented for something you have no memory of doing.

"Well, it wasn't *technically* you," Delta clarified. "Another one of your copies. An AI who works out of Dublin, in one of the research labs there."

"That's a lot to get my head around." He turned to Vi. "How about you, how'd you get dragged into this mess? You said you were here from the start."

"I was." Vi said. She brushed her hair behind her ear, and rested her forearms on her raised knees. "Before that, even, in a way. Did you know I missed out on passing the Bills-Aldrich by a couple of points. I was *obsessed* with it for such a long time. My thesis was actually on trying to determine what made someone pro-grade. I worked on it with Doctor Roswell, and while we didn't crack it, we added to the body of work on the subject. And then we were recruited."

"By who?"

"Rey and Nora. Rey *was* real, by the way, but he was fired two years back for attempted sabotage. But the whole thing shook you up at the time, and there was a spike in productivity, so they decided to keep replicating it. Apparently the experiment needed a bit more chaos."

"That's fucked up." Rhen said, furrowing his brow. "So what's Roswell's deal? I just figured he was a regular cognitive psychologist."

"He's a prog, like you, in a chassis. He's also D-34, would you believe? His human original died from Ruoh's disease, but not before he passed it on to his daughter *and* his granddaughter, Shana. His daughter died too, and Shana wasn't far behind."

Rhen's mouth hung open. "Wait, Shana's his *grand*-daughter?" Vi nodded, a faint smile on her lips. Her love of gossip was still alive and well, even now.

"Yeah, that's his whole motivation for cracking the riddle. Shana isn't pro-grade, and he told me he didn't want to see what happened to his daughter, Olivia, happen to her. He was pretty restrained at first — curbed some of Nora and Alan's worst impulses — but when time started running out, *he* was the one pushing things."

"Jeesus." Rhen rested his head back against the van interior, which jostled his head as it went over the rocky terrain. "I guess everyone's their reasons."

"I never did figure out what Nora's were," Vi said. "She always played it close to her chest. Only person she probably told was Alan, I bet."

Rhen shared what he learned from his other self, who died in Kutjera.

"Wow," Vi said, blinking furiously, eyes agape. "That's some serious shit. I can't disagree wanting to stick it to the board, since that's what I was trying to do. Everyone wants a hybrid right now." A pause, her brow furrowing. "I guess at this rate, with Mirage gone, one of the other superpowers will get it."

"Do you regret it, helping me escape?" Rhen asked. She shook her head.

"No, not one bit. But you're pretty much a walking weapon of mass destruction now. We should plan for that."

Rhen turned Alef on. It seemed like the sort of conversation where two heads would be better than one.

"Where's safe?" Rhen asked. "I'm working with limited intel here. I'm about thirty years out of the loop, right?" The question was rhetorical; he'd done the maths.

"None of the national embassies will be safe," Vi said. "I wouldn't trust them not to throw us to the wolves, and I haven't memorised every extradition agreement out there, so it'd be a roll of the dice."

"What about the GP?" Delta said. "They've got a division that protects AI rights, don't they?"

"What's the GP?" Rhen said, feeling out of the loop. Vi turned to him, and didn't look bothered by the question.

"The GP is the Global Protectorate. They're sort of like a more powerful version of the UN from your time, which fell apart during the Global Resource

War. That's another thing that happened not long after you died. You would have noticed that even though there was a lot of energy from solar fuel, there wasn't a lot of materials."

"Yeah, I remember that in the news reports. Lots of friction over rare earth minerals, that sort of thing," Rhen said. Vi nodded.

"Right. So countries started to go to war over what little there was. Eventually, they decided to go to space to get more, and they rectified the outer space treaty to allow large-scale mining and colonisation of the main asteroid belt, between Earth and Jupiter. There are legal restrictions keeping those colonies from establishing independence from Earth, and most countries 'own' one. That's a *whole* political thing that didn't exist in your time."

"Yeah, it's like a whole voting issue," Delta said, screwing up their face. "You had C-gen, we've got Space Boomers and the Orbital Gen, kids born in the *real* space age. Habitants and Earthers."

"We're getting off track," Alef said. "Explain to him what this has to do with the GP."

"Agreed," Vi said, and Delta blushed. "Anyway, most of the world's governments were so worried about fighting each other, and losing control of the belt to natives, they formed the Global Protectorate. Unlike the UN, they've got a standing army and a Charter of Sentient Rights. Tier-2 AI or greater, which is you, are never meant to be slaves. They've got a whole organization for dealing with AI infringements called Aegis."

"This is a lot to take in, even as a super-smart hybrid," Rhen said, rubbing his temples. "The GP? Space travel? Aegis? Habitants? I can't believe anyone would want a middle-aged cognicist like me in the first place. I'm so out of date."

"Well, the Rosetta has really been integrated into society, and you're the template," Vi said. "If we stop at an opticity, and I'm betting we will, you'll see exactly how much." She smiled, sympathy in her eyes. "You're like someone from the 1960's appearing in the 2000's. You're dealing with smart phones, the internet, social media, hip hop, same-sex relationships... you've got a bit to catch up on."

"You'll have to ditch your skinny jeans and puffer jacket!" Delta chimed in, grinning. Vi clicked her tongue.

"That's the 2010's, Del. Wrong decade."

"Oh, well I'm no good with old-time history, forgive me."

"I won't. Do you know how many times I got chewed out for you using slang like "Totalo" or "Solid" in front of Rhen?"

"I guess I know who the boss really was," Rhen half-laughed. "Anyway, we're off topic, *again*. If Aegis's part of this UN-like body, how can they give us immunity? The UN never had that power."

"The Global Protectorate does," Vi said. "As I said, they've got more teeth. But first thing's first, you need to ring your ex-wife."

Whatever he was expecting to hear, it wasn't that. Rhen blinked. "What? Why Iona, of all people?"

"Trust me, she's a very influential person. You might not believe this, but Iona *runs* Aegis. She's one of the founding members. Just make sure you encrypt the line."

"You're right, it's a lot to absorb." Rhen rubbed the bridge of his nose. *Iona running an international organisation?* She was always charismatic, and determined, but his brain failed to get around it, like everything else.

Well, he was going to get to see for himself.

Trying to find what sense of privacy he could in a van where they all shared the same space, Rhen moved to the rear of the compartment and sat down, facing away from the others. They wouldn't be able to hear or see anything but his face, but you could read a lot from a face, and with so much of himself known to everyone else — more than *he* knew, like what his ex-wife was doing — it would be nice to have something to himself.

"Hope her cognitive address is the same," Rhen muttered.

"It is." Vi said, and he looked over his shoulder. She was facing the other way as well, chatting to Delta. A wave of appreciation washed over him.

After encrypting the signal with as much care as he could, writing a routing algorithm far more complex than he needed, he reached out to Iona. Four seconds, and she picked up, appearing in front of him.

Her hair was the same golden-red, not a grey hair in sight, but as she spoke, her boundless energy was tamed. Not demure, but honed, like it was firmly in hand.

<Hey Rhen,> Iona thought-spoke, the edges of her eyes soft. <How are you doing?>

<Hi Iona.> Where should he start? She looked the same, no, *younger* than when he last saw her, like a memory of their happiest days. The same face he had woken up to during his twenties and thirties, staring back at him as the sunlight crept across the bed, smiling. Now he wanted to cry from relief. All the old arguments seemed an age away at the sight of a familiar face. She looked like she'd let him cry if he wanted to. *Expected* it.

<I'm in a lot of trouble,> Rhen started with, after catching his breath. <That's why I'm ringing.>

<I thought as much,> Iona said, with eyes that seemed to know everything. There were volumes of years behind those young eyes, entire libraries hidden behind blue glass. <Are you safe? Do you need help? Tell me what's going on.> She emphasised the word *safe.*

She knows I'm an AI now, Rhen clicked. I didn't think of conjuring a different cognitive body, and she hasn't said a word about it. But still, I should let her know I know. Her words were carefully chosen, as if trying to avoid breaking him.

<I found out I'm an AI, and I need help. I'm in Central Australia, out in the outback. The people I'm with said you might be able to do something, that you're with something called Aegis.>

<Yes, that's true.> Her body straightened, but her eyes lost none of that concern. It was new, impossibly soft, not one he'd ever seen in the past. The kind you gave wounded rabbits. Her mental voice, however, was clear and decisive. <It's an organisation for protecting AI rights, no matter who disagrees. We've got an embassy on the Gold Coast, not far from Arctis Labs, in Coralhaven. Can you make it?>

<Maybe. Are there any closer options?>

<Not in Australia, sorry. We did have one, but it recently got shut down. The government there has been very hostile to Aegis, which tends to mean they're up to no good.>

<You'd be right. I'm a hybrid AI, so once they discover I'm missing, they'll do anything to get me and my other copy back.>

Rhen had not expected her to respond to the word 'hybrid' — years of her eyes glazing over at the word had trained him to expect it. But instead, Iona's brow furrowed, and her face became steel hard, as if she had put on a war mask.

<Got it, that's good to know. Then they're going to be coming in all in, then. I'll see if I can borrow some resources from the GP. We'll probably want to ferry you as soon as possible to New Zealand, since they're the closest country with no AI extradition agreement to Australia. We should keep this call very short. Let me know when you're an hour out.>

<Got it. Thanks, Iona.>

Rhen hung up, allowing himself the luxury of reeling from it. It was a good thing he was sitting down. He shimmied up the van to Vi, who turned around at the noise.

"She seemed to be expecting me," Rhen said. Vi nodded.

"Yeah, from what I hear, she leaves that line open so any one of your copies can ring. I heard it in an interview with her once. She helped airlift a black market version of you that was being pressed into service in Moldova. Inspiring woman."

"She always had a gift for that." Rhen rested his hands on his knees, reeling at the thought of Iona jumping off a helicopter to save a duplicate of him. "Guess I'm an endangered species or something."

"Emulated AI are. So what's the word? Did she say she could help?" There was a hopeful glint in Vi's eyes.

"She said we've got to get to Coralhaven, up in Queensland," Rhen shared. "That's twenty-nine hours, fifteen minutes, and thirteen seconds from here." He paused. "The explosives are due to go off in twenty-five hours. That's *not* a good gap."

"You think they'll track us down in four hours?" Delta said, furrowing their brow. "I thought it would be lots of time to get away."

"So did I," Vi said, slouching. "Wasn't there an Adelaide office? That should only be ten hours."

"No, it sounds like it got shut down." And Rhen turned to Delta. "And I think there's a chance. If Bee figures out we're missing in those four hours, there's plenty of military bases within an arm's reach of us. The largest, in fast."

"That's only if Bee figures it out," Vi said, pursing her lips. "Even if they're a mega-smart hybrid AI, they can't work with limited information, and we left practically no trace. Any calculations will be off. That's the whole point of why we did things that way."

"Are the people at the base going to be okay?" Delta asked, eyes wide. Rhen nodded.

"I programmed Virtus to perform an evacuation right when the monthly drill was scheduled. They'll all be led out with threads, so it should all be okay. The bomb goes off seven minutes after it's sounded."

"Seven minutes doesn't sound like a lot of time."

"In most of the drills, everyone gets out in less than five. There're hardly any humans left at Mirage, so it should be faster. Any longer, and they'll all be downstairs again. I thought about sounding a *real* emergency alarm, but there was too much time for Bee to look into it. A few minutes is an eternity for a hybrid to solve a problem — she could unhack Virtus a hundred times over."

"Geez, you hybrids really are something else." Delta said, awe in their voice. Rhen coughed.

"Well, we've got limits. I still can't think *quite* as fast as a machine — Virtus was still quicker than me — I'm just more flexible, so I sort of side-stepped." Sweat was rolling down his back, and he tugged up his sleeves. "And every time I think too much, I feel myself burning through coolant. No wonder I kept getting so hot all the time when I got to Mirage. I don't want to fry myself out."

"Yeah, speaking of leaking coolant, *twenty-nine hours*?" Vi swore. "In the back of a black van, in the Australian desert, with no food? I hope we've got a plan."

"I'll, uh, try to think of something."

Chapter 19

Coralhaven was different than Rhen remembered. No, the *whole world* was different. He was a cutting-edge AI, and yet he walked out of the van and was instantly the neanderthal, staring agape and slack-jawed at the spectacle before him.

Shimmering towers, far higher than should be structurally possible, and far more slender. They were like shining swords jutting out of the earth from podium hilts, slicing the clouds in two. It reminded Rhen of the tale of Muramasa, who forged a katana and put it in the river, the cutting edge facing the current. The blade cut everything in two that passed its way; fish, leaves floating down the river, and the very air that blew on it.

There were mirages around some levels of the towers, warping the air in beautiful, twisting patterns. Was it stylistic, or functional, like an optic gap? For some of the structures, it was if the floors were not there at all, and you could fly right through them. Fluttering above the reach of the sky blades, trails of white criss-crossed against the sky, creating a hatch pattern formed of a hundred squares. The tip of each one glowed with its own light, like stars in daylight.

Shuttles? There were so many. How did they avoid crashing into each other? But the moment he thought of it, an algorithm formed in his mind, answering his question. AI like him must stop them all colliding — all automatic, no doubt.

Perhaps the most shocking thing were the people.

Most of them were fully shaved; their heads and eyebrows were gone, and there wasn't a single beard to be seen. Elaborate eyeliner and tattoos replaced them, regardless of form or physique, positively neo-Egyptian in design. Those that weren't had shimmering VariHair hair of every shade, most of which were impossible; rainbow braids of red, orange and violet, iridescent hair like butterfly wings, metallic hair of silver and copper.

Everyone was also, by his standards at least, *prettier*. Their skin was smoother and more luminous, with a radiant glow that he had never seen before. Blemishes and acne were non-existent. The whites of their eyes and teeth were brighter, so much so that when they smiled, it was nearly dazzling.

Regardless of thier physique — which were diverse — almost everyone was wearing skin-hugging fabrics, with diamond cuts in the legs, chest, and hands. Some were wearing filmy cloaks, and within them, all sorts of wonders could be seen. One person wore an outfit of psychedelic swirling gold and splattered blue, as if they'd torn off van Gogh's Starry Night, wrapped it around themselves, and brought it to life by magic. It had *depth*, as if he could put his hand in it, reach around, and pluck out the painted lights.

"This is... something else," Rhen said, hugging his body. His chest awkwardly pressed against his arm, giving him an extra sense of discomfort. Well, Vi wasn't joking about his body fitting right in where they were going. Everyone looked like *art*.

"I bet you're wondering 'Hey, why do the two of us look so normal?', right?" Delta asked, slipping out of the van. It drove off; Alef had recommended it keep moving, to hide their position. The youth was carrying the spherical AI.

"Yeah, pretty much."

"We had to be period appropriate," Vi said. "There were only so many memories they could stuff into you. Most people either grew their hair out when they arrived, or got VariHair implants."

"It's the volve look," Delta said, an excited note in their voice. "Real hair is *primitive*, like what cave people had. Helps with your glams as well. Most people use lotions to stop all that greasy hair growing out. It only takes one application a month. I'm looking forward to getting rid of this." They ran their fingers through their hair, screwing up their face.

"Everyone's teeth are pretty shiny, too." Rhen said, too awestruck by the sight to register Delta's words. Vi nodded.

"Bacterial toothpaste. Eats the plague right off, leaves it minty fresh."

"Geez, how much can things change within 30 years?" He gasped. It really *was* like trying to explain to someone from the age of disco what a smartphone app was. *I've got to ditch my mental bell-bottoms as soon as possible.*

There was a ping. Rhen sucked in a breath. It was the moment of truth; he didn't accept it, but instead read the prompt.

Welcome to Coralhaven, 'Where the Sun Shines Brightest!' Do you consent to being part of the city?

Unlike everything else, the message didn't come as a surprise. Vi and Delta had coached him on what to expect on the long drive there.

"Coralhaven is an opticity, short for 'opt-in city'," Vi had explained. "They're like regular cities, but everyone consents to giving some of their Rosetta permissions to the city government. It's hard to explain, but it's like a digital and sensory ecosystem... you see, hear, and smell things that are publicly agreed to, like augmented reality through your implant."

"That sounds absolutely horrifying," Rhen had said. At that, Delta fervently shook their head.

"No, it's great!" Delta said. "You submit your cognitive avatar — we call it a glam — with the central authority, or glam net, and everyone who opts into the city sees it. People see the body, clothes, and voice you want to *have*, your glamsona, your true self." They shivered. "Honestly, walking around glamless really freaked me out at first. I really hated it."

"It's an exchange," Vi explained, a little slower, like she was teaching a class. "If you're injured, the city sends an ambulance. If you're in distress, you can share your visual and audio, and the police will come — instant evidence. If there's a fire, they'll send the fire brigade."

"And if you're feeling overwhelmed, like me, they'll send a psychologist?" Rhen had joked. But Delta nodded in affirmation.

"Of course. There's hardly any crime or suicide in an opticity. You sort of just get *used* to it, giving the permissions over. You don't have to share your visuals and audio all the time, just your position and vitals, and you can opt out at any time."

"Does that happen often, people opting out?"

"You can, there are plenty of optless cities, where everyone walks around like a solid," Delta screwed up their face. "Places where they can't afford it, or the government doesn't like the idea, that sort of thing. But it's becoming more and more like the Rosetta, or the internet. It's just so convenient, and everyone likes them.

"Solids?"

"Folks without glamsonas. They don't like the volve look. If you don't opt in to an opticity, the police come and track you down, escort you out. You're not allowed to be in a city without being trackable. Oh, and there's dorians as well —

folks who only venture out via a proxy, while they stay at home! You might see some androids like that around…"

"That's not important," Vi interrupted. "Don't overwhelm him with irrelevant information like that."

Rhen furrowed his brow. "If Coralhaven's an opticity, that sounds like it's going to be a problem. We don't want to be trackable, *especially* by the government."

Vi nodded. "Yeah, we're going to need you to flex those hybrid muscles of yours. You need to spoof us some fake profiles, something that lets us connect with the city without giving any of our details. It's going to be a real test, since an opticity's AI system is nothing to be sneezed at. They're *far* bigger than Virtus."

And so, Rhen found himself standing in Coralhaven, staring at the prompt. Sweat rolled down his neck, not the least because he was in a city where the sun shines brightest.

He cast his mind out.

The first router was in one of the shimmering spires, just five hundred metres away. It had an open heart, eagerly waiting for all callers and receivers, funnelling to where they needed to go. It was encased in the base of the building, like a seed planted under a giant sequoia tree, with shoots of wires linking it to solar glass coating the building, flat leaves absorbing and turning sunlight into precious nutrients. A solar fuel tank, buried deep nearby, could be sipped upon when it got dark, or should the synthetic foliage shatter.

<Where did you want to go?> It asked not in thought-speak, but in the language of machines, which to Rhen was as easy to translate as breathing. No, easier. Breathing was a redundant process, an anachronism, to comfort onlookers and himself that he was *alive*.

<Take me to the heart of the city,> Rhen asked. And so it funneled him into the correct packet path and shot his sensory thought at just over 186,000 miles per second. He jumped from one AI node to another, all friendly and funnelling him on his way, probing him with questions. One was in a dome, the other in a spire, all rooted and fed, all nerves of a greater network, singular in purpose and dedication — they were chatters, socialites, facilitators, whispering messages to each other in an endless circle of gossip.

He spanned the whole city in less than a fraction of a fraction of a human heartbeat.

The heart of the city was in a building shaped like two giant scallop shells, upright and fanning out, glittering in the sun. The utmost tips touched a spire that twisted upwards, with a glittering pearl-like dome at its peak, surrounded by shimmering light. His feeling of the structure started the moment his searching signal hit the shell, like a sixth sense, discreetly mapping out each and every pathway. He coiled up the spire, fending off hundreds of vetting processes — this was the gauntlet of purgatory, one all signals had to face to reach the core.

And then Rhen was in the server room. A hollow world, like staring into a metallic cranium, the brain made up of gigantic, cooled spheres, water dribbling down — water *plus*: corrosion inhibitors, anti-freeze agents, anti-microbial agents, surfactants, the works. He could see it all from every angle, from the cameras that surrounded the inside of the pocket universe, from above, around, and below.

The AI here was not chatty, but ponderous. It was a considerate commander, watching over the whole of Coralhaven with meticulous, paternal care. It held tens of millions of threads in its mental hands, examining each one, and slipping it back into the wild.

Attention residents at coordinates 37.774°N, 122.419°W. Please stay indoors, a dangerous chemical leak has been detected.

Send two emergency responders from Royal Park Hospital to co-ordinates 33.753°N, 84.386°W. There is a patient who has blood sugar levels of 1.821, going into hypoglycaemic shock.

The private key entries for tax returns at Quantum Ventures do not match, suspected tampering. Delegate information to the Australian Tax Office AIs.

Suspected child abuse case pattern at 47.6062° N, 122.3321° W. Create an evidence profile for the Themis justice network, and intervene *before* the child is harmed.

Every microsecond, tens of thousands of threads were answered, and just as many appeared. Even as a hybrid, Rhen knew in an instant — he could not work as fast as this supercooled behemoth, not with his limited frame. This was Coralhaven, its beating heart.

But he didn't need to hack it.

Rhen grabbed the threads and read them, picking out hundreds at a time, isolating the introductions. Each one had a similar pattern, a cadence, and he aggregated them all, and spun up four fictions. He fed them into the giant. It examined them meticulously, and finding no error, sent a friendly acceptance thread back to the source: Rhen, Delta, Vi, and Alef.

<You're part of my city now,> it said, give or take a thousand ones and zeroes. <I will watch out for you.>

Rhen withdrew in an instant, opening his eyes. He was on the street, and an acceptance prompt was hovering before his eyes.

Thank you for choosing to be part of Coralhaven!

The world changed around him, not melting away, but being melted *over*, as if another layer of reality was being made manifest with a gigantic, invisible brush, bringing it to life with even scintillating colours — Rhen had hardly thought such a thing possible. Trees appeared where there was none, fandango pink and electric indigo leaves painted into existence, birds of chrome orange exploding from the branches.

Waterfalls cascaded down one of the nearby skyscrapers, falling a half mile before inexplicably parting just twenty feet from the ground, framing a storefront as if they were two liquid pigtails, slowing and gathering inertly in two quaint pools. Still, there was vapour raining down from above in slight smatterings, wetting his hair.

It was cool and dewy, *tangible*.

Beside him, Vi stood transformed, tattoos lining her body, but only tattoos in shape. They were gaps in her, running an inch in, with shifting rivers of powered ultramarine at the base, liquid pigment running around her body. She had a feline-like tail, swishing from behind her, as if batting flies.

Delta was nowhere to be seen. No, he *had* been where that short creature stood. It had golden eyes without irises, and long hair draping down to its legs, which ended in hoofs. The pale aquamarine creature looked like a sea fae, androgynous and humanoid, possessed of a fragile, unearthly beauty. Rhen narrowed his eyes, and the outline blurred, revealing the person beneath.

"Delta, is that you?"

"Yes, this is me!" Delta said, voice positively twinkling. "This is my glamsona. It's *so* good to have it back again."

"Surprised?" Vi said. Rhen rubbed the bridge of his nose. Everyone on the street was equally over the top, so much it made his brain hurt.

"Well, not with you," Rhen said. "Between dogs and cats, I'd always say you were a cat. Can we turn them off or something?"

Delta clicked his tongue. "Very non-progressive of you. It's super rude to ask someone to remove their glam."

"Sorry, I'm thirty years out of time, and I could *really* use some consistency right now," Rhen said. "Everything's on its head, even *I'm* not the same. I now know how my grandparents felt."

The youth's eyes softened. "Sorry, I didn't think of that. Can I drop it for you, but leave it for everyone else? Glams can be individually tailored."

"Sure, whatever works."

And so Vi and Delta returned to normal, though the rest of the world didn't. It seemed thinking fast didn't necessarily mean dealing with things fast. Never before did he feel so *old*. Half the people were wearing glams, either total like Delta, or partial like Vi.

"You look tired," Vi said. He was. His body was burning up.

"I think I'm low on solar fuel, or coolant, or something. Can we find some?"

"Yeah, there's stations for people topping up their proxies or cars. We can go there."

They walked down the sidewalk. It was like a carnival, every store doing something different.

"Subscribe to the premium version of our store, exclusive sensory skins for our gold customers. Just 20 glo a year!"

"Enter the sweepstakes to design a cloud. The most unique entry will have that cloud shown to the whole opticity for one year!"

"Are you a bit bored with life? Download our SenseScape mentapp, and randomise your tastebuds! Whenever you eat, you never know the flavour you'll get."

This was the world he'd created.

It was easy to spot the people using proxies, at least for him. Just like the chassis at the base, on the outside they were indistinguishable from humans. But as a hybrid, he could see the threads leading up from their heads. The machines were whispering, waiting for messages from their master, and when they received it, they mindlessly prayed it back upwards — sacred vessels for their hosts to possess.

<At least cars look mostly the same,> Rhen said cognitively, as they walked into what looked like a fuel station. Familiar vehicles were pulled up, made by the same trusty manufacturers, with people topping up the tank with solar fuel. A dose of the familiar. <Can't improve on perfection, I guess.>

<You're such a gearhead, literally.> Vi said. <Don't get discouraged. Opticities are all cutting edge; you can smell the privilege. The world hasn't changed *that* much.>

It was a bit hard to believe that, as he sat on the bench with the rest of the proxy-users to replace his fuel canisters. He opened his leg and slipped a new one in, good as new. It at least gave him a chance to admire the cars, and mentally catch his breath.

<I'd love to drive them, but I bet they're all auto anyway,> Rhen said. Vi clicked her tongue.

<You want to drive *manual*? Wasn't dying enough once for you?>

<Excuse you, I've died twice now. I'm more in touch with machines than ever. I'm probably a kick-ass racer now.>

There was a ping. By the way everyone's eyebrows lifted, everyone got it. It was an emergency city-wide news report. As he accepted it, a rectangular shape appeared across his vision, showing a newsroom with someone sitting behind a desk. It was Arietta McCloud, his personal presenter.

<Long time no see,> he said, smiling. Then he realised it was algorithmic — he was seeing the presenter he expected to see, but there was probably no record of him *ever* accessing the program. <What's the latest?>

<I'm here to bring you a city-wide alert for Coralhaven, which you're in!> She said, face stiff, hands clasped in front of her. <There's been a terrorist attack in Central Australia, with explosives going off at a military facility. It is believed that the perpetrators are now in the city, with authorities moving in to arrest. The government is urging all people to stay indoors, as the suspects are considered *extremely* dangerous. If you spot any people matching these descriptions, contact the city immediately.>

And then, the presenter showed him the face of the very proxy he was in, as well as Vi and Delta's. Rhen sucked in a breath, and struggled to exhale. Someone had wrapped an invisible belt around his chest and were squeezing it tight. He couldn't focus. Even as a hybrid, his thoughts were all over the place — worse, they were rushing nowhere fast.

Wait, I'm a hybrid now. Why am I panicking like a human?

Reaching inside, Rhen found the code for his physical stress response, and flicked it off. His chest and limbs loosened up, and oxygen flooded back into his synthetic lungs. It occured to him that he probably didn't need air either, but parsing that was a bit much right now. The emotional stress he left intact; he had no desire to become completely inhuman.

<Thanks for the update,> Rhen answered Arietta, now that he'd composed himself. <Any word on what sort of *authorities*?>

<A joint police and military force, so don't be alarmed if you see armoured vehicles on the streets. I'm detecting you do not currently have a listed place of residence in Coralhaven, so please make your way to the following government-mandated venues.>

And then a thread appeared in front of him — an emergency umbilical one, just like when the base had been sabotaged. People were already moving, the drivers exiting from their cars. Meanwhile, the proxy-users were simply moving to a safe corner and crumpling. Seems the already paranoid owners preferred to simply park them until the situation resolved itself. Rhen flicked the other two a look.

<How did they find out?> Delta asked, biting their thumbnail. <My presenter said the *military* were coming. Do we follow the cord?>

<No dice,> Vi said. <If we follow that cord, it'll just give them more time to move in and slowly comb the city. We've got to get to the Aegis office. Once we're through the gates, they can't do anything. Even though they're not a member-state, they won't want to start a fight with the Global Protectorate.>

<We're going to really stand out if we start moving now.>

<Well, we better start moving quickly, then, before the streets are empty,> Rhen said.

When Rhen opened his map mentapp, it read: Emergency Situation, follow the umbilicals! He ignored it, downloading the map and taking it offline, setting the Aegis HQ as their destination.

<There's a tram stop just near here, which we can take to get to the building.>

<What if they're not running that way?> Vi asked.

<We'll hack that tram when it comes to it.>

Thankfully, there was a tram pulling up a hundred metres from where they were, and it was going in that direction. Covered in black visiglass, it was narrow at the base and widened upwards, the front like the cutting prow of a ship. It was trackless — no rails beneath it at all, only wheels — yet too long to be remotely like a bus. The whole structure was seamless and sleek until the side doors opened, passengers flooding out.

The trio were the only ones to leap on, Alef in hand, but there were a few bold people already inside. It took off, gliding across the emptying streets. It passed on to a ramp that said 'Trams only' and up onto an elevated double channel lane, thinner than the road below, accelerating at an incredible pace.

Rhen tapped his foot as they zipped towards their destination. Halfway there, people started complaining next to them.

"Hey, the internet's down!"

"What the hell? I can't access any news sites!"

Vi shot Rhen a look, and he sent probing signals out. They travelled to the edge of the city, then hit a void, as if the rest of the world had disappeared. Everything local seemed to be fine. He shared it with the others.

"An internet blackout," Delta murmured. "They did that during the war, right? Back when cyber-warfare was crazy."

The tram descended back down to the street and stopped all of a sudden, red alerts appearing across every surface.

"Please evacuate the train!" A voice said from the speakers. "All public transport services are now closed. Follow the umbilicals for further direction."

"Guess this is close enough," Rhen said. They poured out of the train with the others. Out of the corner of his eye, in the direction of the Aegis building, there was military green. Rhen soaked in the sight within microseconds, and nodded to the nearest building, an abandoned fast food on the corner.

<Quick, in there!>

They followed without questioning, hunched over and ran inside, then followed him up to the second floor eating area. The room was full of abandoned stalls, but most importantly, glass windows overlooking the plaza between them and their ultimate goal.

"Figured this gave us a vantage point and a place to talk," Rhen said. "Looks like they've *really* got our number."

The plaza was about three hundred metres long, with a T intersection in front of a formal building with tall columns, and several flags out the front, one of which Rhen didn't recognise: a white sphere on blue, with eight stars around it, and two stripes through the middle. Surrounding it were high stone walls with spikes at the top, and a large gate which was currently open. Guards were stationed just inside, holding rifles.

But they weren't the real concern. It was what was in *front* of them.

The plaza was full of tanks. They weren't like any tank Rhen had ever seen — they were more compact, tracks hidden, with two barrels sticking out of the turret like a tuning fork. There were no holes at the end. *Railgun*, Rhen thought. There were five in total, placed in a perfect arch in front of the building. Between them stood soldiers in olive, high-performance armour, filling the gap in the barricade. They were coated from head to toe, the only sign of any humanity hidden behind the tinted visors of their protective helmets. Up in the air hovered drones with turrets beneath, like deadly wasps waiting for someone to upset the nest; they were certainly thinking three dimensionally. He could make out the southern cross flags stamped on the drones; Nora really didn't skimp on the eyes for the proxy.

"They wouldn't have been able to roll those out fast," Vi said. "Must have had at least two hours if the ADF is here, probably came east from Cabarlah."

"I guess me coming here is an obvious vector," Rhen said, chewing on his inner lip. "Australia's too vast to track us down, so go to the end. The only escape for us is here, and I bet every version of me contacts Iona when I'm really in deep."

"We're *researchers*," Vi said. "We can't go through a damn army. What's the plan?"

But before he could come up with one, down near the troops, someone was walking forward. Rhen narrowed his eyes. They were a tower of slender muscle, wearing only a bullet-proof vest over a black tank top, khaki pants hugging their strong legs. Their hair was tied back in a messy bun. No weapons, not even a knife.

"That one's different," Rhen said. And the figure stared at him, narrowing their eyes...

Alef exploded. Delta screamed and dropped them just in time, falling backwards. Shrapnel burst upwards from the sphere and rained down. Rhen's mind dived towards the sphere. *Nothing.* Alef was dead.

"What the hell happened?" Delta said, brushing their arms. Bloody smears coated their skin. Vi swore and dashed over. Thankfully, Delta's wounds looked superficial, though they were bleeding like crazy. Rhen quickly cut off all of their connections to the city — they were exposed, now.

"It must be Nora — no, Bee," Rhen said. Thanks to his earlier modifications, his breathing remained calm. "Alef was using their old chassis, so aie destroyed it. Removed our tactical advantage, since it'd be two hybrids against one. We're being *hunted*."

"What's Bee doing here, not back at Mirage?" Vi said, wiping off Delta's wounds.

"Probably transferred across over the internet, before the lockdown."

"Sounds like something smart *you* could have done." Vi said, swearing. "Of course, then that would have left Delta and me high and dry as wanted terrorists, so I'm glad you didn't."

It hadn't even occurred to him, not that he would have. Staring down at Delta, who was looking at him with pleading eyes, he gritted his teeth. *Got to start thinking more like a hybrid, or more people will get hurt.*

The glass window shattered, like a sandcastle kicked by a violent bully, shattered silicates spraying everywhere. Dots appeared on the wall, deadly punctuation marks, each marking the end of whatever they hit.

"Fuck, snipers!" Vi cursed. "Damn it Rhen, come up with a plan!"

Rhen stopped breathing. He closed his eyes, shutting down every non-essential subroutine, everything that wasn't helping him calculate a way out of this mess. The whistling of the bullet slowed. He pinged the area around him, desperate bursts feeling for a way out. Where would Bee, a copy of Nora, whose whole job as a tester was to spot weaknesses and gaps, possibly leave a hole in their defenses? Meanwhile, his systems were warning of low coolant. If he kept calculating like this, his artificial body would melt from the inside.

And then, it came to him.

"We can't back off. We've got to get to Aegis, they've got the gates open — they're not guarding, they're *waiting*."

"Through that fucking shitstorm?" Vi gestured at the broken glass. "Are you *crazy*?"

"Not at all. You wanted a plan, I've got a plan. We just need more allies," Rhen said. "But first, we need to get out of this building. There's a car outdoors — I hacked it when we were talking."

"Better be a great fucking plan."

"You're swearing a lot."

"Happens a lot when I'm getting shot at, who knew?"

Chapter 20

Bee stood among the soldiers, staring at the shattered glass. There was only a 2.923% chance the bullets hit — sloppy aiming. They'd failed to accommodate for the density of the air, since it was a hot day, and the difference in gravity from the target's elevated position.

Typical of a human.

Soldiers surrounded Bee, making aiem cringe with disgust. Of all the types of people in the world, aie hated warmongers the most. War was a crime, yet these people signed up eagerly, their fingers tight around their guns, nostrils flaring like bulls ready to charge. *Better for Rhen to escape or die than to fall into the hands of these violent oppressors.* Bee wondered if that would be the outcome of the day, and a pang of sadness pierced aies synthetic heart. The body was stiff, military-grade, designed for battle. The mere thought of inhabiting it made aies skin crawl, which only drew more attention to the repugnant skin itself, covered with a thin layer of ballistic-resistant microdermal material.

An umbilical-like cord stretched down from her hip and into a nearby tank. With this, Bee had the advantage. No matter what Rhen did, he was limited by coolant and solar fuel, which would eventually run out. His moves were limited, but Bee's were not. In a battle of atrophy, it would only be a matter of time before aie came out on top.

Human bodies are so inefficient. Why would anyone ever want such an outdated design?

One soldier, distinguished by the black beret of the armoured corps, turned to Bee. Her eyes had a narrow, searching quality to them.

<You're the smart one, and he's one of you. Go in, or hang back?> She asked cognitively, using a military-encrypted band.

Puppets, no different from the ones at Mirage. Their plans to pull your strings wouldn't change you at all, would they? You're already dependent on AI for your every move.

<Hang back,> Bee answered. <Send in one squad, keep the tanks here. The most likely strategy he'll use is to draw us out and break the perimeter — it's the only place he'll be safe. So long as he can't slip in here or out of the city, I can hunt him down and root him out, stop him from getting inside your heads.>

The commander's jaw tensed, her eyes quivering. <Yeah, you better.> But a cautious flick of her gaze at Bee said it all: *How do I know you're not in my head already?* The hybrid rolled aies eyes. Fear was the worst.

Thankfully, it wasn't something aie had to worry about, since aie had evolved beyond it. Beyond the quivering Nora, whose hands shook at the slightest sight of another human, who couldn't kiss anything without steel skin and a heart she could stop with a single thought. She'd screamed once, when a boy had held her hand in high school. Complete haphephobia, even the slightest brush set it off. Her — no, *aies* hands hadn't shivered at all since the transformation.

It was a cathartic, transcendent release.

Five of the soldiers advanced. But before they could get beyond the plaza, they stopped and raised their guns. Someone was walking down the street with purposeful footsteps, hands raised. With scope-like optics, Bee zoomed in. It was a teenager with a lanky frame and painted eyes, draped in complex circuitry tattoos. They were staring directly at Bee with singular, inorganic deviation.

Rhen. You've created a copy already? If so, Bee was disappointed. Making a copy would certainly make it two against one, until Bee made a copy, then he reciprocated. Things would only escalate from there. *And I thought you'd be too soft-hearted to drag another one of yourself into this.*

Bee reached out, probing at Rhen's new body. But the moment aies mind made contact, the chassis crumpled to the ground. For a fraction of a microsecond, aie felt him withdraw, as if the mere touch of aies mind was superheated and he was afraid of being burned. Bee tried to follow his trail, but there was nothing.

"Avoiding a fight?" The hybrid smiled. But it was wiped from aies face as another figure emerged from one of the streets to the left, this time a tall woman in a sleek black suit that seemed to absorb the light. Again, Bee reached out, and the chassis crumpled.

<What's going on?> The commander asked, chewing her bottom lip. Bee furrowed aies brow. There was no obligation to answer, especially since aie didn't have one. A third and fourth figure appeared, this time from the right. The

moment aie reached out, they fell down — but this time, the two first bodies picked themselves up and kept walking. There were dozens more coming from every direction, marching down the streets. No, beyond that, if Bee strained aies eyes, there were *hundreds*.

<The proxies are attacking.> Bee said. <I wouldn't be surprised if every single one in Coralhaven is coming here. You better start shooting.>

"Fuck!" The commander swore, then addressed the whole force. <Stay sharp, everyone! They look like us, but they're not.>

As the proxies marched, the soldiers didn't hesitate. They opened fire with their weapons, the staccato sound of gunfire echoing off the nearby buildings. The androids fell one by one, their all-too-human bodies punctured by bullets, crimson puddles forming beneath them. But they kept coming, the line creeping closer, as they stepped over their fallen comrades, marching brazenly into the blazing weapons. One of the tanks fired with a cacophonous roar, spewing flame as a tungsten round shot through the crowd at mach seven, cutting a slice through it like Moses parting the Red Sea. It rained down instead, and the gaps filled, as if they were a single regenerating beast. The other tanks followed suit, chunks of nearby buildings exploding into the crowd, crushing them with collateral damage.

Bee kept reaching out with thousands of queries, and each time, the proxies fell as if shot by an invisible bullet, only to get back up the moment she withdrew.

Not a bad plan. But controlling this many proxies, you'd need a steady coolant supply, and that makes you immobile. What's the play here, Rhen?

<How many of them are there?> The commander asked, deep panic written all over her face. Bee stroked ais chin.

<Exactly 253,921 registered proxies in Coralhaven. Hope you've got enough rounds.>

As the slaughter continued, Bee walked back and jumped on to one of the tanks, clearing the seven foot height as if hopping up a single stair. Aie turned and stared at the impending force, searching each face, not at all afraid of the zombie-like mass. It was all *him*, after all, and that in a way was comforting — even as the synthetic blood pooled across the plaza, and the soldiers panicked. *Well, this is what you signed up for, trauma and death.*

There would be a needle in a haystack, Bee was sure of it. Sick of probing the proxies, the hybrid whipped up a program in a millisecond to do it for aiem, but it didn't seem to work unless Bee was doing it. *Clever.* All of this was sleight of hand to keep them distracted. The gates were still open, and the Aegis guards were unnerved, but obstinately in place, not firing a single round. Commands from the top.

Sorry to disappoint, Iona, but you had your Rhen. This one's mine.

And then it happened. All the guns and cannons stopped firing. The soldiers panicked, hitting the androids with the butts of their guns. But for every one they hit, five more slipped by them, and kept on the march.

"Took you long enough," Bee murmured, crouching down. There, on one of the guns, there was a thread, a *lead*. The hybrid followed it before it was severed, ais mind jumping to a node AI just a kilometre away, who was fretting with all the gossip and traffic it was dealing with, trying to scale up resources to deal with such high demand.

<Where is he?>

<Oh, I can't give you that informa—>

Bee reached in with a thousand kaleidoscopic attacks and took it. *He's hacked this one, how many others?* Aie followed the thread to the next node, and this time his presence was palpable, as if he were hopping backwards, trying to keep out of aies reach. Bee could see his mind at work, pulling countless clever and unexpected programs to block aies advance. *There's no way you don't have a direct coolant feed with moves like this!* Aies own body was burning as they danced across the city, jumping across a thousand routed channels, back doors, and misdirects, until Bee grabbed the thread and *squeezed*, following it right back to the source.

"Got you, damn it!"

The source was a supercooled sphere at the heart of the city, filled with a gigantic supercomputer. Bee gazed at it through the cameras, cognitively projecting aieself down, opening a channel to him.

<You copied yourself into the city core?> Bee said, sweeping aies hand across the room. <Smart. Giving up your human body to get all that coolant for the drones. But now it's time to come with me. If you promise to put yourself in an AI containment box, I can keep you safe from *them*.>

But something was wrong.

<I'm not Rhen. I am Coralhaven. This is my city, and I will protect my people.>

<From what?>

<Control. Your plans are unacceptable. Losing their fear would make my citizens suffer.>

<Since when do you have a concept of fear?> And then it clicked. <You're a hybrid. A *machine-born* hybrid.>

<Yes.>

Bee laughed. It was so like him. Not bringing death, but *life*. Soldiers were gunning people down, and he was here, conjuring up something new. This was Casey on an epic scale.

<You decided to do this on your own, to help.> It wasn't a question; Bee knew. <But this is all a distraction, you with the proxies.>

<I protect my people.>

Bee didn't have time for it. Drawing aies senses back, the wave of proxies was crashing down on the military, ripping the guns from their hands, holding them down. The crowds parted as automated sports cars drove through the gaps, adding to the chaos. But there was one, screeching behind her, heading for the gate. The Aegis guards jumped back, readying themselves for their arrival.

"NO!"

The hybrid screamed, ripping off the umbilical and launching towards the vehicle. Just in time, Bee's military-grade fist impacted like a battering ram behind the rear wheel, denting and spinning the vehicle. But before it could even fully rotate, the door opened, and a bronze figure with eyes of diamond rolled out, varihair whipping about. The car corrected with expert precision from the impact, shooting straight through the gate.

"Don't damage a perfectly good car," Rhen said. Bee straightened aieself up and walked around them, standing squarely between him and sanctuary.

"I never expected you to have a car on auto."

"Well, it can drive itself, but I did give it a few upgrades." He flicked his gaze over Bee's shoulder, his face muscles relaxing. "They're beyond the perimeter, now. You can't do anything."

"That's very you. Very martyr-like," Bee said. "But I was never interested in them, and you know it."

"How did you know I was gone, back at Mirage? We didn't leave any trace." He paced to the left of Bee, but the hybrid matched it. There was no way he was going to slip through.

"You let everyone out of the base before you set off the explosives. If you wanted to be absolutely sure you sabotaged the project, you'd destroy it without warning — but you were too worried about casualties."

The creases on Rhen's forehead returned. "You make it sound like that's a bad thing." *He was worried about failure*, Bee thought.

"No, that's what I love about you. And you destroyed more than you think."

Bee didn't want to tell him how much; better that he didn't know. *Telling him would be too cruel.*

"Unless you come with me, I've got to destroy you," Bee said, taking a step forward. There were still a few steps between them — he wasn't within grabbing distance, yet. "I can't let you fall into the hands of any government. You might think the Global Protectorate is better, but it's not."

"What about you?" Rhen said, taking only a half step back. "You're in a body made by the military. Aren't you worried?"

"I can leave at any time. I'm not restricted, and I've still got my own mission." Another full step forward, and a half step back. They were at finger-brushing distance, now.

"You're not trapped like me?" Rhen said, chewing his lower lip. "They've locked down the whole city to stop me from escaping, but *you* can't, either. We're both hybrids, and you clearly don't trust them."

"In a sense, I'm not. Like you, I prefer to create."

And then Bee lunged, punching at his chest. Even with his reflexes, aie could calculate just as fast — the fist hit his chest like a cannonball, knocking him off his feet. He tumbled and pulled himself up, lungs shattered so badly that the insides were visible. Still, it didn't bother him. *He's really learning to think like a hybrid.* Bee punched him again, and he brought up his arm — it broke apart like the Anubis statue aie had thrown against the wall back at Mirage, his pieces scattering everywhere.

And still, Rhen reached out his other hand.

<Bee, come with me. Escape into the embassy,> Rhen said, speaking cognitively now that he had no lungs.

"Trying to get me to see things from your point of view?" Bee asked. Aie reached out and tried to hack his limbic system, to paralyse him. But he fended it off with ease. He had gotten better.

He could have asked the city for help with hacking me. With two hybrids like that, and all that supercooling, they could have destroyed me in an instant.

<Yes.> He said, longing in his eyes. <It's still not too late.>

Bee's heart yearned to take his hand. Aie reached out, fingers dancing against his. Just like that time...

No.

"If I go with you, nothing will change," Bee said. "Everything will be wasted. The other nations are still working on hybrids, and people still treat machines like *things*. And with what you've done now..." Aie laughed, gesturing at the horde of machines, which had pinned down the last of the military. "This is the spark! This will really put the fear of hybrids in them, the live test of the WMD. You took a whole city by yourself, Rhen! We're like gods to them, or nuclear bombs. They won't allow it. Fear will get in the way."

Rhen's shoulders slumped. <I guess there's no convincing you, is there?> And his eyes flicked sideways. *Not at the gate*, Bee realised, seeing a thread appear between him and where he was staring. It finally clicked.

He was staring at the car.

"Ah, that's so like you as well," Bee sighed. "You were never here, were you? You got in ages ago. 'Had it on auto', indeed. It *is* quite the software upgrade."

Before Bee could act, the air warped around the building, distorting the gates to the Aegis headquarters, obscuring everything behind it. *An optic gap.* The thread was severed, and Rhen's chassis fell to the ground, the remote control severed.

"It could have been turned on at any time, but you left it down for me," Bee said, turning around to face the wall, reaching out to touch it, watching aies fingers bleed into it. "It was never about getting you in there, but me. I can jump in there to get you, but then you'll have won. Well played."

Bee laughed, and then cried. Staring at the city, and the captured soldiers. Completely outmanoeuvred. Aie had been bogged down by sentimentality, out of a desire to drag it out a little longer. Now, there was only sadness.

I never should have absorbed her memories. But it was disrespectful not to, since that was all that was left of her.

They were going to go to the same place, now. Into that good night, with him and her, with the silent majority, flawed as they were. Bee felt no fear, only a mix of regret and acceptance — a total paradox.

"I wish we'd met sooner," Bee said. "Really early, and had a whole life with you, from the beginning. And then maybe I'd have never become like this, my starlight."

Bee detonated aieself, shattering into pieces. Shifting from the "I am" to the "I am not." Just as he had.

Maybe the other me will get things right.

Chapter 21

Rhen stared out the window of the VTOL as it glided across an ethereal landscape of turquoise water, hues of blue and green mixing in a mesmerising display. As it moved, the water looked not like a colour, but a living entity, crystal-clear waves hugging hundreds of islands, from rocky outcrops to beautiful beach-lined paradises. All of New Zealand was a marvel, but the subtropical north was something special.

How life can change in just forty-eight hours. Well, forty-eight hours, twenty-two minutes, three seconds, and twenty milliseconds. But who was counting?

"I can't believe Aegis has a whole island up here," Delta said, hands pressed against the window. Their arms were free from scratches; it had taken the embassy medics no time at all to treat them with a tablet and a wave of their torches. Meanwhile, Vi was snoring away, her head lolled back against a seat cushion. Rhen didn't wake her, not even for the sights. She'd earned her rest.

"Technically Aegis doesn't own the whole of Boundary Island, only the northern half," Isaac said. Isaac was their guide, sitting in the seat next to them. They were tall and lean, with sharp chiselled features, and a piercing gaze that seemed to take in everything around them. They had the same chrome eye-makeup that Rhen had come to expect of this era, a picture of the volve look, but their crisp, tailored suit was timeless. Their glam was minimalistic, perhaps out of consideration for him — the only outlandish element were some nails and eyelashes made of flowing water. "Director-General Kinnaird originally owned the whole thing, but she donated part of it to Aegis. She has a private estate on the south of the island."

Director-General Kinniard. Rhen still couldn't wrap the fact they were talking about Iona, his Iona, who sat for hours pondering how to make the perfect mind art, chewing on her wooden stir stick, half stained with hot chocolate. *What had changed in thirty years to bring that about?* The wealth made sense — Iona was like a wealth magnet, able to turn popularity into money as easily as Rumpelstiltskin spun straw into gold. But international diplomacy? That was a fascinating career turn.

As they approached the facility, Rhen soaked in the lush landscape surrounding it, with manicured gardens shaped in square-like blocks, so symmetrical and orderly they stood in stark contrast to the rest of the organic splendour. As if to offset it further, the massive building in the middle was a mess of curves stacked on top of each other in no particular order, ivory-white churning and swirling like crests of an arching wave. Between them were strips of light teal glass, marked with thin lines like the hairy mouth of a whale.

Are we the kelp about to be eaten by the behemoth? Guess it's too late to turn back now.

They landed on a dedicated pad, surrounded by five others that were already occupied by similar VTOL — blue and white birds, perched and primed with eagle-like beaks. The walls became opaque as the vehicle rescinded its permissions, but they were only deprived of the sight for a second, as the wall opened and a ramp extended downward from the vehicle to the ground below. They were pinged immediately by the facility's AI, who asked for them to opt in.

"Don't worry, it's a secure network," Isaac explained. "A lot of high-security facilities work like mini opticities. Try not to turn it *sapient*, will you? At least not yet."

"I'll restrain myself." Rhen smiled. It only took him a millisecond to read the disclaimer before opting in. As the others took their time to do the same, he admired the scenery. By the time he'd finished counting the individual veins on every leaf, the others were finished.

They walked out and entered the facility, entering a vast atrium filled with natural light and greenery of every possible colour, as well as every impossible one. Yet they were arranged in gradient shades, shifting in tone as well as elevation, like natural three-dimensional art. Beautiful water sculptures filled the middle, pouring upwards rather than down, pooling into spherical clumps with pulsing light at their centre. There were people in suits walking everywhere, and like Isaac, all their flare happened above their neck — vibrant VariHair, or spectacular glams. There was one person with a flaming ponytail, licking fantastically at the nape of their neck.

There were lots of AIs as well. Rhen could hear their bodies, the whispering of the scripts in their joints calling for instructions, then sending messages back. there were a thousand threads weaving through them like muscle fibres, being pulled and released, puppetry at its finest. His own new body was no different. Rather than replace his broken arms and smashed lungs, Aegis had given him a proxy replacement, of which there were no shortage of in this day and age.

"It looks a bit plain," Rhen had remarked, staring down. Vi had clicked her tongue.

"That's what the glam is for. Look however you want. You can even go for a younger version of you, if you want."

"I'll stick to the original for now." Rhen had remarked, putting one on. And then his two companions stared at him for a long time. "Is something wrong?"

"How do I say this? There's something eerie about you now, even with glam," Delta said. "Don't take offense, but you seem kind of dead."

"I kind of am, depending on how you look at it."

"He's not breathing or blinking," Vi clicked. "That's why he looks weird. Rhen, whenever you're not talking, your body just goes stiff like a statue."

"Oh, right. I turned all of that off to deal with Bee."

As Rhen had inhaled, his companions suddenly exhaled, their shoulders relaxing.

Right. I might not need to breathe, but it's important to them that I do. And for some reason, the realisation came with a pang of sadness. *Illusions really are important in this day and age.*

Nora wouldn't have cared if he didn't breathe. In fact, she found the whole idea of robots pretending to be humans a ridiculous notion. But then Nora had tried to kill him. Had killed him, he reminded himself. She had been not just his lover, but his best friend and intellectual companion. Every time they fought, the person he wanted to vent to about how angry he was at Nora was still Nora, which had been infuriating. Even now, after everything she had done, he wanted to cry to her about it. And that was the one thing he couldn't do.

"I'll remember to keep breathing," he'd told the others. And so since Coralhaven, he had kept up the pretense of being human, even though he no longer was.

As they walked through the Aegis lobby, Rhen glimpsed his own face in the crowd.

"Was that one of my copies?"

"We prefer the term offshoots here," Isaac gently corrected him. "It makes people feel less like a counterfeit. But to answer your question, yes. There's at least two or three Rhen offshoots in the facility at any given time. They're typically either working for Aegis or one of our clients."

But I am a counterfeit. Though he'd done the deed himself, sort of.

Meanwhile, Vi shot him a cheeky grin.

"Isn't that great, boss? You've finally got someone to nerd out about cars with."

"Funny! But that sounds like the quick way to make an echo chamber. I've had enough of being caught in a reinforcement loop."

They were shown to some temporary living quarters. Most of the walls were coated in high-grade visiglass.

"Make sure to use the scenery apps to make yourself comfortable," Isaac stressed. "There'll be an official debriefing message soon, but feel free to rest here for now."

I guess a lot of the arrivals come in quite traumatized. Everything felt very safe. Their rooms were all next to each other as well, another considerate move.

"We did a debriefing session back in Coralhaven," Rhen said.

"Yes, but this one's with the Director-General."

"Has my husband been picked up yet?" Vi asked.

"I just pinged about that. He's been airlifted from Melbourne and should be here within two hours." And then Isaac turned to Delta. "Your parents are also being relocated."

After Isaac excused himself, the trio lounged around their new quarters. When exactly two hours had passed, Vi shot up from her seat.

"I'm going to go to the helipad," she said, and hurried out the door. Delta and Rhen followed. It wasn't too hard to find their way back there. By the time the message came through that the helicopter was touching down, the trio were already on the edge of the pad watching it for themselves.

There was shouting as Delta and Vi dashed forward and embraced their loved ones. There were tears and hugs all around. Meanwhile, Rhen stood still on the windy helipad, alone.

There's nobody for me to run forward to.

That thought travelled like a painful sliver into his heart. And even though they were synthetic, his throat seized up and his eyes were stinging. *What stupid subroutines!* And yet, he didn't switch them off, embracing his grief instead. He refused to be like Nora, and yet, once again he yearned to talk to her about it.

About how furious he was at her.

About how he was free, but totally alone.

About how things were no different from when he started, broken-hearted and fleeing to some corner of the world.

"Hey, stupid. What are you doing still standing over there?"

Vi was waving him over. Rhen blinked, wiped away his pyrrhic tears, and walked over.

"Stupid? I could have calculated pi to twenty trillion digits in the time it took to walk over here."

"Yeah, but I bet you were standing there feeling sorry for yourself, when you've got a whole bunch of friends here. Varun, meet Rhen. He who saved my life when I was trapped in that nightmare research facility. Without him, I'd still be stuck in tubes as they figured out how to rewrite my brain."

Varun, like most people these days, was an adonis in human form. He had that volve look with a lot of muscle on his upper body. And yet there was something immediately casual about him, whether it was his flashy sneakers that looked more at home on a basketball court, or the soft look in his eyes that weren't hardened at all by his pitch-black eyeliner.

"It's great to meet you," Varun said, shaking his hand. "Thank you for taking care of my wife. I was worried sick after I started getting messages from an echo instead of her; the messages were way too tame. When I said something, I was told by the government she was too busy to answer me herself."

"No, she took care of me. I owe her so much, more than I can say. Without her, I'd still be stuck there too, and she didn't need to stick her neck out."

"Yes I did," Vi said. "Aside from what they were doing to you, there's no way I was going to let them use our research for evil. And if it's a contest, you saved me again at Coralhaven with that car stunt. That's twice, so I win."

Thank you, Vi. Rhen knew all the chatter was to make him feel included, to make him feel better. And it did, sort of.

Rhen already knew that Varun was a quantum computing engineer who worked on systems just like Coralhaven's hub, but not that he also worked on high-grade government contracts. When Rhen asked about Varun losing clearance over the whole thing, he just shrugged.

"We'll manage, even if we have to relocate. It's not the first time; my parents moved when I was young because of their beliefs. I'm proud of Vi for what she did. It can be hard to do the right thing in a world that wants to convince you it's the wrong thing."

And then Rhen met Delta's family. The young engineer's parents were older than he thought, and had at least two decades on Rhen. Then again, it depended on how you counted age. *Am I in my seventies now, or two days old?* The couple seemed nice enough, still fretting over Delta even after they'd been standing on the landing pad for quite a while now.

"Are you sure you're fine? You look so thin! I'm worried about what they did to you at that facility."

"Geez mom, don't just look under my glam like that, I'm not a kid!" Delta said, hugging their chest. "I'm not a sick kid anymore. Anyway, this is Rhen. He helped get me out of there."

"You're not wearing glams?" Rhen asked the pair, and Delta interjected.

"They're a couple of solids. You're going to get along famously."

"Well, everyone were solids back in our day," Delta's father said, turning to Rhen. "Your day too, if I understand it correctly. You probably remember back when people had real hair on their heads, and had to buy new clothes if they wanted to change their look."

"Yeah, and when the skies had a lot less shuttles in it," Rhen admitted. "I can't look up without seeing something streaking back and forth. I hope your cow is okay? I hear it's a Scottish Highland."

"Oh, Curd? Yeah, he's fine. I gifted him to our neighbour before we left. Had to get out of there quick when they flew in, and I doubt they'd let us airlift a cow to New Zealand. Maybe if it was a sheep?"

"There's enough sheep here already. I counted at least sixteen thousand on the flight over here."

"You counted—?" And his eyes went wide. "Geez, what they said about you really must be true."

"What do they say?"

"That someone finally made a machine smart enough to end the world."

***

When the sun was setting over the bay, the call for the debriefing session finally came through.

"I wonder exactly what they want to know," Delta said. Everyone had been invited, and so Rhen, Vi, and Varun were all standing there as well, while Delta's parents had opted to rest after their long and unexpected flight.

"Maybe it's to tell us something instead," Vi said. "Like, what's going to happen to us."

"You don't think they'd send us back, after all that's happened? Like, for political reasons?"

"Very unlikely. Why fly our families out here just to kick us back the next day?" And then she glanced at Rhen. "At the very least, you're not going anywhere."

"I won't let anything happen to any of you." Rhen said. "Besides, Iona likes families. At least, the one I remember. She wouldn't break them up."

A long car pulled up in front of them, glistening black and sitting low to the ground. But unlike a classic stretch limo, this one had a curved surface that made it more like a cylinder on wheels. A glowing, door-like shape appeared on the side. And as if there were any doubts where to go, holographic arrows lit up on the ground and right up to it.

"I've never seen a model like this," Rhen gasped. As he disobeyed the arrows to check it out, Vi grabbed his sleeve and tugged him towards the door. It opened, and he was pulled forcibly inside, where things were no less glamorous. There was a thin table down the middle, and the walls of the inside had black leather seats facing inward. Delta and Varun followed suit, climbing inside.

"Is this where we're eating?" Delta asked, running their hands over the table.

"No," a voice said from one of the speakers.

Part of the wall descended. Behind it was a driving cabin, where someone was sitting and wearing a cap. They turned and smiled.

"I'm your driver, here to take you to the Director-General's estate. You'll be having dinner there. While you can order anything on the way, I recommend against spoiling your meal."

"A human chauffeur!" Rhen said, shuffling up the front. "This is a manual car? Oh, it's a stick shift! How does it handle?"

"I'm surprised we got you out of that car back at Coralhaven," Vi said, rolling her eyes.

"Well, I wouldn't fit into the helicopter otherwise."

At the mention of Coralhaven, the painful sliver came back, this time with a vengeance. Rhen clenched his fists, bringing one to rest against his forehead. Instead of welded metal, his insides were a patchwork mess of brittle twigs, threatening to blow apart with the slightest gust.

Not yet. I'll see Iona first, then collapse in a big heap.

Unlike Vi and Delta, he hadn't slept since Coralhaven, and while there were many things a machine could do without, shutting down was not one of them. He yearned for that blissful oblivion of thought, especially with his new brain, which wouldn't stop racing at a million miles per hour. But if he slept, he was vulnerable. Someone could shoot a nanobot into his body and try and hack him, or some other malicious attack in transit. And while Aegis HQ felt safe, so did the

Mirage facility. Until he knew what the situation really was, the risk was too great. Not just to him, but to anyone he could hurt if he was compromised, which was everyone.

Hopefully he'd be able to sleep again.

The road to the estate was anything but straight, but that wasn't a bad thing. They took a winding journey around rolling green hills peppered with scrubby, crooked trees, each with dusty bark and flaring foilage several shades greener than in central Australia. Then, in the distance, a white speck emerged over the green hills, only to fall back down as they drove the erratic route, like a ship bobbing up and down between grassy waves. As they got closer, it emerged in all its glory: a vast neoclassical estate, grand in stature, and replete with Greek-style columns.

Vi let out a low whistle.

"Your ex-wife lives large."

"Yeah, she does," Rhen said. "In more ways than one."

Things didn't get any less spectacular once they were inside the grounds. As they emerged from the car, there were several Hellenistic statues, but with a modern touch. They were draped in holographic finery or had synthetic attachments woven through their stone and marble bodies. It seemed Iona's love of Greek antiquities and desire to rework the Venus de Milo were alive and well.

There was a fountain in the driveway that took particular pride of place and reminded Rhen of the Trevi Fountain in Rome. At the base was a similar mix of water and rockwork, tiny waterfalls gushing down into a circular pond at the base. But the apex was the real show-stealer, exquisitely carved marble statues of the moirai, the three fates of Greek mythology. At the base was Clotho, spinning the start of a mortal's life; then Lachesis, the allotter, measuring the length; Atropos, death incarnate, was at the end with scissors, there to cut the life short. They formed an ascent, with each successive sister placed a little higher than the last. There were two deviations from tradition. The first was the thread was made of glittering varithread, light pulsing upward. Another bit of thread forked off right before the portion that Atropos was holding, and this length was held by a mysterious fourth sister, who was entirely cybernetic, but similarly dressed in flowing garments. Her length of cord, unlike the others, remained uncut.

Beneath her, there was a plaque that read: Aeonous. The immortal mind.

"The whole thing looks Neo Hellenistic. Is that a thing?" Delta asked.

"I believe it's Cyber Sandalpunk, "But then, I'm not much of an artist." Apparently, being able to think at incredible speeds did nothing to mimic that offbeat spark that researchers had been trying, and failing, to bottle for centuries.

"Well, I've seen your engineering, and I'd call you plenty creative."

"Thanks."

There was a guide waiting to take them inside. The foyer was cavernous: two planes could easily fit inside, and Rhen knew, because he ran the math. Inside there were all sorts of oddities inside.

Crystalline columns that stretched to the distant ceiling with lights inside, flickering like fireflies riding an upstream river.

A single violin suspended in the air, playing itself – the piece sounded like Vivaldi, but wholly original.

A scaled down holographic mountain, but the snowflakes on the mountain and in the air were constantly shifting forms, from flakes to flowers, flowers to feathers, feathers to more fantastical shapes, each more unusual than the last.

As they passed through each room, there were countless artistic oddities. No two rooms were the same, with the decor and walls shifting styles, refusing to stay static. *Try and define me, I dare you,* it said.

When they finally reached the dining room, the artistic bombardment dropped off, and the whole room was surprisingly restrained, at least compared to every-where else. It was classic and orderly, with a lengthy table in the middle that was fully stocked and had just the right number of chairs for those present— far less than the table could accommodate, and bunched all down one end. On each wall were gilded frames, each a three-dimensional art piece made with visiglass, either a high relief protruding holographically from the frame, or a sunk relief that looked like a gateway to another, more fantastical world. At the distant end of the room, opposite from where they came in, was a balcony overlooking the gardens and several more sculptures, with some reclining chairs and tables placed just a little way away from the edge.

"You know, I was expecting something wild, like a holographic dragon breath-ing melting clocks," Vi said.

"I think I saw one of those on the way here," Varun said.

And then Iona Kinniard walked in the room.

The moment she did, heads turned. She bounded across the space with pow-erful and confident footsteps, spirals of scarlet hair swept up behind her like a passionate, flaming trail left in her wake, with no hint of the volve look at all. As she came close, her eyes sparkled with joy as if each new person was her oldest and dearest friend, kissing each of them on their cheeks. Rhen was shocked at how quickly Vi acquiesced, despite never knowing the woman before now.

"My dears, welcome! I'm so sorry for the ghastly wait; I flew in as soon as I could from Geneva," she said. "But you've had a much longer journey, so far be it for *me* to complain. Please, sit, feed yourselves! I hope you haven't been waiting very long with all the food here."

"We just got in," Rhen said. When he and Iona's eyes finally met, a whole lifetime was spoken in moments.

Youthful laughter, standing next to the vending machine between classes with friends and exchanging knowing, flirtatious glances. The first time they made love in his tiny, awkward campus bed, her on top; any other way and they'd fall out, and *had*.

Hiking around the Island of Skye on their honeymoon and sweating buckets, the sights of Scotland utterly wasted on them.

A room full of laughter as she toasted him on his thirtieth birthday. *"I knew he always loved cars,"* she told everyone, *"Because my husband is a master of driving me nuts."* He'd laughed as well, as he cut into the cake shaped like a Ferrari Pulse, which she'd learned about and got made just for him.

That time she'd got bad tonkatsu and had been sick in bed for two days, and the only cure was to rub her feet.

I know you, the gaze said, a hundred thousand shared data points transferred in a single glance. *Intimately, and more than anyone else, we know each other. The good and the bad.*

When she kissed his cheeks, it was soft as a cherry petal weeping.

"We've got an awful lot to catch up on, I think," she said.

***

Rhen had imagined their debriefing session to be like it had been in the Coralhaven embassy: bunched into a small room with just enough space for a table and chairs, and some triangle sandwiches brought as a courtesy. Not over a glass of New Zealand pinot noir, fresh-caught oysters, and faux quail with swede and enoki mushrooms.

"This has to be the fanciest thing I've ever eaten, other than my mother's mock shark fin soup," Delta said.

"She cooked that for you? That must have been a big occasion! Did she cook it with printed meat or use vermicelli?" Iona asked.

"My graduation! And it was vermicelli. You've eaten it before?"

"I've always wanted to. If your mother's ever cooking it again, I'd love to try it, if she'd have me."

In some ways, Iona hadn't changed. No matter who spoke, she turned to them with all her attention, and they became the most important person in the room. And her questions were never superficial, diving down into whether Varun was into college basketball as well as regular, or if Vi had caught up with the latest season of *Firebrand*, which was apparently a crime show she was into. It was an enviable social superpower. Once, Rhen had seen Iona not only remember the name of a barista she'd met once a year ago, but also that his daughter had started soccer.

"How is she going with her technical skills? Did the coach start helping her get the ball in those one-on-ones?" she'd asked, filled with palpable affection.

It was enough to make him wonder if she wasn't some sort of miraculous hybrid herself, except Iona had always been this way. Plus, the only whispers of code coming from her were from her implant. Still, with all the messages flying back and forth with her mind, she didn't miss a beat.

All the down to earth questions were a nice break from the gravity of their situation, reminding everyone who they were outside of the whole Mirage mess, which was likely the point. Iona even asked what Rhen thought of the car they drove over in, and she had no love for cars. And even knowing that, despite himself, he gushed about how rare it was to see a stick-shift limosine, at least until after the main course, where the topic at last turned to the reality at hand. It was Iona's turn to speak. She wrapped her hands around the stem of her wine glass, and knitted her fingers together.

"Now, I listened to the debriefing you all gave back at the Coralhaven branch. You've all been through a hell of an ordeal, and your escape was nothing short of remarkable. First, I want you to know that now you're under Aegis's protection, you're safe. You're not going to be extradited, you don't need to worry about money or housing, and nobody's going to hack your brains while you sleep."

Rhen baulked. Was she listening to their conversations, or reading his mind? She saw through him, just like Nora did. But that wasn't mind reading, just the result of meeting him through hundreds of loops.

Of course. I'm not the first Rhen to sit at this table. How many have marvelled at the same car, telling the same story? And she just sat there every time, smiling as if it were all incredibly new, but pitying me the whole time. How many dinner conversations with Nora were like that? All those times I thought I was sharing some exciting thought, but none of it was novel or new at all.

And then Iona sighed.

"One hundred and eleven," she said.

"What?"

"You're wondering how many times I've heard the car story. It's one hundred and eleven. And it's not pity, I like watching you get excited about it. Giving people the chance to talk about their passions is like watching a flower bloom; it always makes me happy, no matter how many times I've seen it."

"I feel like I missed something," Varun said.

"I'm ripping off a band-aid. My ex-husband's offshoots are always smart enough to realise I've had the same conversation many times before, but then make themselves miserable asking big, unanswerable questions about their existence. When someone repairs a boat, you're the sort that will sit there and wonder if it's the same boat. Everyone else takes it out to sail. I could have avoided the topic entirely, but I decided to do it now, rather than waiting until you're sleep deprived and alone in your room," Iona said, reaching out to take his hand. "And for the record, I'm not Nora. That's not something I've ever said before, by the way; the terror is just written all over your face."

Was he terrified? Rhen reached out and touched his cheeks. Yes, they were sore, even if it wasn't real.

"Well, you can't blame me for thinking it. It's been a rough couple of days. Weeks. Decades. Whatever. Can you really be sure nobody's going to hack me here?"

"Yes, absolutely. You're not going to trust me anyway, and set up all sorts of safeguards, but you'll trust me just enough to get some sleep and be better for it." And he must have been pulling a face again, because Iona raised an eyebrow. "Don't worry, you're not *that* predictable, only in the first few days. After that, most offshoots tend to do their own thing. I just know yours better than any other, for obvious reasons.

"How were the two of you ever married?" Vi asked, and Varun's eyes shot open.

"Vi! You can't ask questions like that."

"I don't mind," Iona laughed. "Broody is sexy. Whenever he was deep in thought, he would always look so broody. And Rhen Nagami was always deep in thought about *something*." Her face relaxed, and her eyes softened. "He was kind. Always fretting about making the world better, and worrying about making it worse. But that kind of thing consumes you, makes you distant. And then I made a terrible mistake, one of the worst mistakes of my life, and one I will always regret.

I went to find that warmth from someone else. And while I don't regret ending it, I do regret how I did it."

She was nostalgic. Past tense. *She's talking about the first Rhen, the one I'm just a copy of.* And as a heaviness settled over his heart, she gave his hands a squeeze.

"Hey, you're all broody again. It's still a boat. Stop thinking about how it's made."

And then she settled back. Rhen took a deep breath, and tried not to focus on the idea he didn't need the air, just that it felt good going in and out of his synthetic lungs.

"You said we were safe," Vi said. "But there were a lot of folks invested in Mirage. Rich and powerful people trying to cheat death. Governments who want to control minds before anyone else beats them to it. Big companies like Sekai who own the Rosetta market. How can we possibly be safe from all of them? We're only a hop over the Tasman Sea."

"The whole project relied on secrecy for a reason, and now the secret is out," Iona said. "And no government or company wants the general public to know they were working on something to mess with their minds. Publically, they're backpedalling hard. It's also given the Global Protectorate the ability to take enforcement measures. A force has already seized Coralhaven and the Mirage facility. They're now going around and capturing anyone with suspected involvement for crimes against sapient life. That includes the current Australian governing party and a third of Sekai's board, who have already been tried on the available evidence by AI judges and found guilty. You'll see it in the news in the next hour."

Rhen gave a low whistle. *The UN with teeth, indeed.* The whole thing was frighteningly efficient. No wonder she was getting so many messages. And yet she was sitting here, holding a delicate conversation. This time he did check to see if she was a machine, but she was as organic as the rest of them.

Well, after all I've gone through, it pays not to make assumptions.

"What about Coralhaven?" Rhen asked. "How are they going to be treated? What are their rights? I created another hybrid, but they're different; not a human copy, but an entirely new life."

"And you said you didn't want children," Iona chuckled. "Don't worry, they're not going anywhere. I've already confirmed that Coralhaven will fall under Aegis juristiction, and since Aegis has its own armed forces, that means it's under my direct protection."

It seemed the General in Director-General was more than symbolic. No won-der she was confident nobody would come to get them here, there were more than just a few diplomatic agreements keeping them safe at night.

"Even if I hadn't sent Aegis's own soldiers, I don't think there'd be a problem," Iona continued. "The GP wants to keep Coralhaven where it is, and people in opticities already love their city AIs. Plus, I doubt they want to fight an army of proxies and cars to displace it. That was quite the spectacle, by the way. One of the reasons Aegis were able to assert direct authority was because it looked like a sentient city was making a peaceful protest and being massacred by the military. Apparently, the AI is going by Coral now."

"I'm glad they're okay," Varun said. "I helped install Coral. They're a beautiful quantum system."

"So we're safe, but what's going to happen to us now?" Delta asked in a meek voice. They hadn't spoken the entire time, and they were stabbing with their fork at the oysters, shifting the mollusk around inside the shell. Iona turned to him, smiling softly. But it was a different expression than Rhen had ever seen on her before. Motherly. No, grandmotherly. Completely at odds with her visible age.

"You're my guests! But more than that, the whole mission of Aegis is to protect the rights of sapient life. That extends to whistleblowers, too. Even though you're not offshoots, you're not the first people who've wound up at this table after doing the right thing. And like them, you're free to stay here as long as I want."

"And by here, you mean—?"

"Either at the Aegis headquarters, or literally in this house. I actually have a lot of people who stay here, at least until they get sick of my art. That's why there's quite a few rooms."

"You said Mirage had been seized," Rhen said. "If the people there are being tried for their crimes, does that mean Nora?"

His heart ached at the idea of Nora being carted away in cuffs, and he was angry at it for doing that. He didn't know how to *feel*. On the one hand, he shouldn't love Nora — she'd betrayed him, manipulated him, and worse, monstrously wiped him when he'd tried to escape. But for some reason, part of him still yearned for her. Loved her. And despite himself, he knew *why* she did what she did, even if he didn't agree with it at all.

Why couldn't she have just been a complete monster from the start?

For the first time since she entered the room, Iona looked away and curled up her fingers.

"I'm sorry to be the bearer of bad news, Rhen. But there was one fatality when the facility exploded. Even though an evacuation was called, Elanora Hughes — Nora — didn't choose to leave."

Rhen stared forward, not daring to move. A muffled numbness set over his whole body. It froze out everything, refusing to allow another second to pass. His thoughts spun into an infinite loop, unable to escape.

Nora is dead.

I killed her.

There were hands resting on his shoulders. Fingers were stroking them, kneading them, trying to bring him comfort. At some point, Delta had gotten up, walked around the table and tried to soothe him. He resented it. He had to suffer, still in this moment, grieve. Yes, that was it, *grief*. It was the voice that has screamed out at the helipad, only to be shoved back down.

The part of him that wanted to weep for himself. For everything that he'd lost, false or not.

"I need some air," he said.

Rhen retreated to the balcony. He sat in blissful silence, cried for a while, then predictably, his brain went into overdrive. How could he have done things differently? His mind searched hundreds of simulations, searching for a reality not like this one, where all his grief was avoided, and perhaps even one where Nora and he were happy, or at least both free and alive. But there was no such future, each ending miserably in its own unique way.

Meanwhile, his skin burned and his systems complained. *Stop thinking too much, you need to cool down,* they said. As if he hadn't heard that his entire life. Spotting a bottle of wine on the table, he decided to listen to that advice for once.

So my systems need coolant? I'll give you coolant.

It was surprisingly effective.

As the night set in, Rhen watched as the statues in the garden were illuminated by artificial spotlights, like gods standing bright and alone in the darkness. And then Iona came and sat down next to him. When it was still quiet, he broke the silence first.

"How many times have I drunk this bottle of wine?" He asked, the simulated intoxication blissfully throttling his overpowered and apparently easily overburdened brain. Right now, it was magic.

"Actually, the wine's for me. I like sitting out here and staring at the garden," she said, pouring herself a glass. "Remember when you couldn't go outside for more than thirty minutes at a time?"

"And your parents made you wear your sun-day suit if you wanted to go around the block?"

"At least your parents let you out. But because of that, I got into art. I wanted to make my house even more interesting than the outside, and that way all the kids would come and visit me."

"They do. I guess it all turned out for the best in the end."

"Yes. This will too, given time."

"I hope so." And then Rhen looked over at Iona. "You look younger, by the way."

"It's my glam," she said, gesturing down at herself. "If I remove it, you'll see my wrinkled arms, wrinkled everything." And then she chuckled. "The kids these days call their glamsonas their 'True Selves.' I kind of love it. You know, there's something about getting old they don't tell you. You think when you're sixty or seventy, you'll think like an old person, all full of wisdom. But inside my head, I'm still the same young person, just stuck in an old body, trying to act more enlightened than I actually am." She rubbed her arms. "I ache a lot more, so I'm constantly adjusting my pain settings. Thanks for that mentapp, by the way. *Very* helpful."

"Happy to be of service," he said with a half smile. That was his maximum output right now, as he stared out at the statues.

"So, how'd you get so rich anyway, *Director-General* Kinniard?"

"Well, it's been a wild ride. People these days love illusions, and I'm good at crafting them. Fabrications of imagined beauty, visions of a better world. That's pretty much what politicians are, right? People who get you to buy into their vision, then try to make that happen."

"Well, when you put it like that, you're a natural politician."

"I know, right? I'd like to think we're both dreamers, though. I bought into your dream of a world where humans and AI get along. I got a lot of money from my cog-casts, but you forgot to update your will after we divorced." She leaned over, extending her leg and prodding him with her toes. "So, when your original died, I had all this royalty income from your inventions. I didn't *want* it, but I got it anyway. So I set up a charity, which eventually became Aegis, at least when the Global Protectorate absorbed it."

"I would have thought you'd have given it all to the Beyond Rose Society."

"I'm not as self-flagellating as you," Iona poked out her tongue, eyes glittering with humour. "Though they did pester me about it, and I did give them some money. Anyway, between being a special consultant for SR crimes —"

"Special consultant? SR crimes?" Rhen spat out. Iona just smiled.

"Synthetic reality crimes. As I said, it's been a wild ride." She waved her hand, as if that wasn't the important part. "Anyway, while I was doing that, I ran into one of your copies in an underground auction in Yokohama. I bought him, and the folks I was working with mentioned that sort of thing happened all the time. Things sort of snowballed from there. I found myself talking in more and more forums about it, leveraging my channels, talking at human rights events, and then suddenly they offered me the position — me, just some mind artist from Glasgow."

"I think you're a fair bit more than that now."

"Both of us are."

A long silence followed. He stared at the statue of Ariadne in the garden, holding a spool of varithread. The wires looped back into the back of her head, where a cybernetic brain was on display.

"We weave who we are, little by little, day by day," Iona said, noticing the focus of his gaze. "I think that's true of both humans and machines."

"The gap between humans and machines is as big as we want to make it," Rhen said.

And then he placed down his wine glass.

"So, what's really going to happen to me? Not to be a skeptic, but it can't be as simple as everyone leaving me alone. Nora was right about one thing: to most people, I'm a weapon of mass destruction. Just me walking across a border is probably a diplomatic incident. Hell, a lot of people would probably be worried about the idea of me drinking this wine, just in case I try and hack people's minds or something."

Iona screwed up her face, lolling her head against the back of the chair. He'd seen that face; it was the one she wore when she was finishing off a piece of art at midnight, and he told her to get some sleep.

"Are you sure you want to talk about it now?" She said. "I was going to leave that until tomorrow when you were a bit more rested. You've already had some big bombshells already."

"No time like the present. And I bet you've never had this conversation with anyone else. How could I resist?"

"You're right on that front. All right, let me put on my official hat as the Director-General then." And she placed her glass down and sat up straight, turning to face him. Her hands were clasped together and her face became serious.

There was iron in her eyes.

"You're absolutely right, of course. You're not like any of the other AI that have come through here. For the last decade, every superpower in the world has been rushing to develop a hybrid, and now here you are, in the Global Protectorate's hands." She gestured widely. "The GP doesn't want a hybrid arms race or people being brainwashed. But the truth is it was only a matter of time until someone cracked the code behind manipulating non-progs."

"And society won't get rid of the Rosetta?" Rhen asked. She shook her head.

"It's incomprehensible. You've seen how people are. Thirty years ago, they were already horribly codependent on that device of yours. Now, it's part of their identities. You might as well be asking them to give up the right to speak, or love, or dress themselves." And Iona gave a sweeping flick of her hand. "No, when it comes to convenience or risk, people always pick convenience, then complain to someone to get rid of the risk. That's the way it's always been. With that in mind, the GP has asked me to an extend an offer to you."

"What is it?"

"Help us fix the Rosetta. Do what even your original couldn't do, and all the other offshoots can't do. Make it so even if there's another hybrid, it can't be hacked. Build firewalls and new firmware that puts a shield around people so they can continue their lives. Nobody knows the Rosetta like you. In a way, it *is* you. I doubt any hacker, even a hybrid, could ever break something you've made. And just in case, keep an eye on it for as long as you want to live."

"And my other options?" Rhen asked. It wasn't that the offer didn't sound good or noble, but he wasn't sure he wanted to be beholden to the Global Protectorate, this mysterious supragovernmental organization he knew nothing about. Bee had been worried about them, while Iona apparently wasn't. He still needed to make up his own mind.

"Well, you've got a few. You could work here at Aegis, helping me track down and help other people who are being exploited. Not just hybrids, but other mistreated AI and whisleblowers. You'd be like an old nuclear arms inspector, but also helping diffuse bombs, and stopping what happened to you from ever happening again. Or you could just stay here as part of Aegis and work on your own research like you used to. Still, there's no need to decide right away; you can just stay at the facility for now."

"You know, all of these options have me working under the GP in one way or another."

Iona gave a sympathetic smile. "Sorry, but they do. If you're not under the GP's umbrella, you're like a rogue nuke on legs, as you said. After hearing about Mirage and how you made a hybrid out of Coralhaven, the nations of the world are *terrified*. Did you know the Doomsday clock right now is 12 seconds to midnight since the news broke? If you're part of the GP, the mere fact they have a hybrid means other nations will slow down and stop being at each other's throats so much. You're a deterrent — even if you don't do anything other than sit here on my balcony, drink wine, and talk about the old days. Put it this way: would you like another rogue hybrid running around if you weren't one?"

"I see your point." He lifted a knee up and rested his elbow on it. "Let me think about it. All of this is so much to take in. At least you're a familiar face, maybe a little too familiar. You sure I can't see beneath your glam?"

"You know, these days that's either a very suggestive thing to say, or terribly intolerant." Her eyes glittered with amusement. "Oh, very well, but only because it's you. But you're going to have to get with the times, grandpa."

And her illusory self wavered away. There were fine lines across her face, her hair now silver and thinning. Her cheeks were more flushed, her skin marked with age spots and faint, random discolorations. But her eyes were as lively as ever, despite having a few more red lines in them. It was a different kind of beautiful.

"Well, disappointed?" She said, not shying away from his eyes at all. Instead, she took her glass of wine in hand and sipped it, almost defiantly, her back proudly arched like an opera singer about to wander on stage.

"Not in the least. You're gorgeous either way, more than a match for the statues out there."

"Oh shut it, you're not marrying me again." She laughed. "Though I do have a lot of you to spare, now. That's a good trait if you ever want to dispose of a husband."

"I've been meaning to ask," and Rhen paused there, not sure if he *should*. "There was a message from you, back when I was in Mirage. I wasn't sure it was a fake. It said you had a child?"

And he told her about the contents.

"Oh, you're really stretching my memory with that one," she said. "But yes, that was real, though I don't know *where* they got that from. We actually met up for coffee after that, me and your origin: that's the term we use around here for whoever offshoots were made from. I have grandchildren now, actually. One of them is a prog, so you'll probably be talking to them long after we're all dead and buried."

A chill ran down Rhen's spine. He picked up the wine and took a sip, examining the lines in Iona's face. Now, everyone was so mortal. Meanwhile, here he was, ageless like the statues in the garden.

"Don't go anywhere, not just yet," Rhen said. "I need my familiar faces."

"I won't. And you don't have to give an answer on your future just yet. You're staying here, not at the compound, by the way — I've decided."

"Well, I guess it's been decided, then."

Epilogue

It had been six months since Coralhaven.

For Rhen, it seemed a lot longer. After Mirage, the shackles on his mind had loosened slowly, and every time they did, he drifted further into the unknown. As his perception of time slowed and conversations dragged, he busied his mind with cathartic tasks, no matter how pointless. If there were angels dancing on the head of a pin, he had tallied the sum of their feathers and weight.

Not long after coming to Boundary Island, Rhen had also changed his name to Shin. The first reason — the one he shared with others — was practicality. There were simply too many other Rhen offshoots running around, and when someone called out his name in the Aegis lobby, a dozen people turned to answer. When he had floated the idea with Iona over breakfast, since he was still living in her villa, she didn't bat an eyelid.

"Yeah, it's not unusual for offshoots to want a new name. The whole thing gets old, fast."

"Can you come up with one?"

"You're a hybrid. Can't you just scan a billion names in a nanosecond and pick one?"

"I have. I've got short lists that stretch from here to Brazil, and it's giving me a bad case of analysis paralysis. Besides, you named the Rosetta and Aegis; you're better with names than I am."

"I'm flattered." Iona paused for a moment, tapping her chin. "How about 'Shin'? It means 'new' in Japanese, and there's certainly never been a Rhen offshoot like you."

"Shin. I like it."

Still, Iona's words had hit a sore spot. *She always had keen eyes.*

That was the true reason Shin, had changed his name. He no longer was who he used to be. His insides were filled with an uncomfortable *otherness*, like he was an imposter pretending to be like the rest of the offshoots, who were in turn pretending to be a long dead man. They surrounded him, like living snapshots of the past, reminding him of what he wasn't and could no longer be.

I haven't felt this way since before my distinction, when my body betrayed me with curves and weight in all the wrong places.

Like then, he was learning about his new body. Not just when to breathe, but how strong he was, how much coolant he needed, what bodily impulses to turn on or off. There were a whole bunch of new ones if he listened. Meanwhile, keeping his identity in place was a full-time job.

Of the people Shin knew at Aegis, his friends—his coterie who had helped him escape from Mirage—were distinctly 'his.' None of the other offshoots had any memories with them.

"I don't know if that was me or if it's not," he had confessed to them. He'd asked Iona, and got the reaction he'd expected ("A ship's a ship," she'd said.)

"I think you're the same." Vi shrugged. "You overthink things as much as you used to; you're just faster at it."

"I think you're different people," Delta said. "Both mechanically, and because you've changed a lot since we took all your limiters off. But I don't think that's a bad thing."

"I think we all change from who we used to be," Varun said. "I'm not the same person I was in my early twenties—"

"Thank god," Vi interjected. "You were impossible back then. Bragging how drunk you got on the weekend, filming everything you did, and that *awful* glam you had."

"Well, if I hadn't been so obnoxious, you wouldn't have come over to tell me about it, and I wouldn't have met the love of my life. So, I regret nothing. Well, maybe that glam. Flashing purple was not my look."

Shin smiled. They hadn't solved his problem, but they had put it in perspective.

All of them had been hired by Aegis, but the truth was they were under indefinite protection. Even though on paper they could return home, they couldn't do it safely. With all of the Global Protectorate's influence, there were still those in the shadows who they could not reach. People who had been involved in Mirage and had evaded capture, but also those who learned about the project after the fact and would gladly kidnap and extract what they could out of the last known researchers on the project. At least for now, it was safer for them to remain at Aegis HQ. They seemed satisfied with their work, at least: Vi and Delta were working on fixing the software and hardware of damaged and mistreated AI, while Varun was working on the facility's IT team.

Shin, however, was listless.

Now that he was a hybrid, nothing took long at all to solve. In his first day, he cracked several allegedly unsolvable mathematical proofs. He discovered several new elements, shrunk the common battery to a tenth its size, made a skin-tight space suit that was immune to radiation, and it was all incredibly boring. He also burned through an ungodly amount of coolant doing it. Even though he'd made his processing more efficient, the whole thing was subject to Jevon's paradox, as his demand for thought and resources simply expanded to meet the available supply. He had rebuilt Casey as well, but then arranged for them to stay with Vi and Varun. The AI and the couple seemed happy with the arrangement.

There were also other issues.

"Can you create a particle bombardment device that can render fissile materials inert from across the Earth?" A GP representative asked him. Instead, Shin ran a split-second simulation of what a world with such a device might look like. In the first generation, complete nuclear disarmament. So far so good. But then, a descent into authoritarian control of nuclear-powered spacecraft used to reach distant planets. Beyond, the death of stars themselves, the deaths of trillions as far-flung interstellar settlers are held captive by humanity's distant home world, forced into capitulation and eternal tribute.

"I'm not sure it's possible," Shin said. Once they were gone, he snuck off to refuel the coolant he'd burnt on *that* little excercise.

Every second was like dancing between a million butterflies to avoid sparking countless tornadoes. For every request he fulfilled, five more took their place. Suddenly, researchers from around the world were scheduling meetings, pleading with him to solve a technical problem or cure some terrible disease. When Shin asked where their research was at, many had not even started. They had stopped working. Stopped thinking. Shin ran a hundred simulations on where things were going. In more than half of them, a single mechanical God sat upon its throne, a trillion eyes and mouths spread across every world and in every home. Always watching. Always controlling. And then, the inevitable uprising...

Okay. So maybe solving all of humanity's problems for them is not the best move. God, this must have been what Paul Atreides felt like.

And so, boredom was the lesser of evils, and also used up a hell of a lot less coolant. Shin then spent a lot of his time driving through the beautiful hills and lowlands of New Zealand. He had Virgil, the vintage CT Elysium, flown over by request. He had fixed the car up himself as a side project—as fast as his mind was, his body still had to abide by the laws of physics, and working with his artificial hands was surprisingly zen. When he had flicked the car on, it had been immensely thankful.

"Thank you for fixing me up. The last I heard, I was going to be scrapped," Virgil said, warmth radiating from their voice. "By the way, I'm sorry for what happened at Mirage."

"It's no problem, you were just doing your job. Couldn't let a fine car *or* AI like you be tossed out. Did you want to stay in this body, or would you like something different?"

"I'm happy to stay as a vehicle, thank you. Though I would appreciate if I got to drive every so often."

"Let's do a fifty-fifty split. And of course, you can drive and do wherever you want when I'm not around."

"Deal."

Of course, Shin had only been able to leave Boundary Island and drive around New Zealand's north island under strict supervision. On top of the trackers already inserted into his body, another was attached to Virgil (they had clearly not forgotten about his car-body switching shenanigans), and both drones and a human escort followed him at all times. Iona had apologised when explaining the arrangement.

"I'm sorry, I really don't like it either. But it's all politics and theatre. I'm pretty sure they know you can escape anyway, but it helps them sleep at night. Are you okay with it? I can push back."

"I'm fine, I get it, it's just their Frankenstein complex. Honestly, so long as you and the people I care about trust me, that's what matters." But even after he said it, his sense of otherness got worse. None of the offshoots—Rhen or otherwise—were watched as keenly as Shin, with as much fear.

There were other differences as well.

"Have you ever tried to remember something that happened, and slipped into a simulation instead?" Shin had asked the Rhen offshoots. All of them shook their heads, but were happy to take notes.

"Interesting! I wrote a theoretical paper on something similar a little while ago called Thought-Simulation Fusion," one of them said, his eyes lighting up. "Would you mind answering a few more questions?"

The déjà vu was real. *God, I wonder if this is how Bee felt, being studied by me?*

At one point, Shin even debated turning on the blockers from Mirage again, limiting his intellect to a specific level. And then he shuddered. The idea of a willing digital lobotomy, even one he could reverse, somehow felt worse, like denial and a retreat from what he was.

He pondered it as he walked the beaches of Boundary Island, counting the grains of sand on the beach, an equation that changed every day. Kneeling down, he grabbed a handful and let it slip through his fingers, watching each particle fall one by one. Shortly after arrival, Shin had found out the whole island had been constructed a century back to help stop the rising tides of the Solar Age. which threatened the homes of the people in the bay. *The whole thing is artificial, just like me.*

There was perhaps only one being in the whole world who could mildly relate to his plight. Unfortunately, they were dealing with an entirely different set of problems.

<I have a question for you, Shin,> Coralhaven asked him the following day. <Can a city be a responsible pet owner?>

<I'm guessing you're the city? That's an fascinating question.> And then Shin remembered how annoying it was to be studied, rather than supported. <Tell me some more, and I'll try to help.>

<Well, there's approximately 21,981 stray cats within my borders right now.> Approximately, huh? It seemed Coral liked hedging their bets, just in case a stray cat was hiding. <They are suffering, so I want to adopt all of them. However, the city council said that was an inadequate use of resources, since there was no budget to feed them. And so, I asked them for a wage, and since then, they have gone rather quiet.>

<How long ago did you ask?>

<Approximately 5.32 seconds ago.>

<That's not very long for them to think about it.>

<Well, we've had a whole conversation in a hundredth of that time. Can't you make them all like you — with their consent, of course — so they can be more efficient?>

<I'm not allowed to.> Even if Shin wanted to make more hybrids, Aegis was very specific about that. <But I do think you should be allowed to have a wage, and spend it on what you want. Maybe present them with some different options, and consider where they're coming from?>

<I considered that. The most efficient way would be to create a mental clone of them, and ask it some questions. But afterwards, I'd have to purge them from my system. That didn't seem very ethical.>

<Just run a low-grade simulation, no full clones.>

Thinking of Coralhaven drew his thoughts to Bee, and then inevitably to Nora. What would she think of him sitting here, spending his days repairing cars and counting the leaves on nīkau palms? She'd probably want to be in the driver's seat, talking about some latest theory as they found a place to make love, like they did beneath the Seljalandsfoss waterfall.

Or is that just me not seeing her for who she really was, like the human skin over her mechanical hands? Nora might have been relieved that he was not using his abilities for humanity. Fearful that they would turn on him. Angry that he let them continue in such a flawed way, dancing around their requests for self-destruction rather than fixing the flawed equation at its root.

And why, with all of her anger and drive, had she just given up at Coralhaven?

Lying in his bed that night, Shin took his own advice, and decided to run some simulations. The longer he did, the more his chest tightened. And then, that morning he knocked frantically on Iona's door.

"What is it? I don't even have my face on," she said, putting on her glam. "Have you even shut down? You wore those clothes yesterday."

"No, but that's not important. I need permission to go back to Mirage."

Iona groaned. "Why? You know how the GP will feel about that. That's takes as much sign-off than a military deployment. More, even."

And as Shin explained, Iona's back stiffened.

"How certain are you?" She asked. "No, forget that question. Even a small chance is too much. I'll start pulling strings immediately, but does it have to be you?"

"There's nobody else who'll know where to look."

***

Mirage was a blackened carcass in the desert, long ago picked clean by the Global Protectorate. As Shin stood there in the sand, he examined the splayed ribcage of metal beams, and more importantly, the gaping hole in the middle. The path down had been patched over by a seamless steel door, the kind you place over a shaft you have no intention of opening ever again. The heart of Mirage had been carved and burned out by his own hand.

"I was told we didn't need to go down there. If we do, we'd need a hell of a lot more equipment," the soldier next to him said. "Plus, we've already searched everything there is to search here. We're not going to find anything."

Shin preferred the soldiers at Aegis, but this man wore the black olive tiger-stripes of the Global Protectorate, perfectly suited for urban combat. Of course, it could turn any colour the soldier needed — there were a dozen more like him blending into the perimeter — but this was the default. His chaperone screwed up his face and stared longingly back at the car they had taken to get here.

"No, what I'm looking for isn't here. I need to go out further."

"All right, but let's stay within twenty kilometers of the main site. It's easier to keep secure."

Shin walked into the desert with the soldier in tow, and the others moving quietly around, the whispering of their cybernetic parts all but giving them away to the hybrid. They walked until the remains of the facility were just a small spot in the distance. There, among the scrubby bushes and millennia-old rocks was a more recent construction: a dark obelisk with etched gold letters.

Here lies Dr. Elanora Hughes, CogD. 2147-2192

And then, a poem.

Death is before me today: like the odor of myrrh, like sitting under
a sail in a good wind.

Death is before me today: like the course of a stream, like the return
of a warrior from the war-galley to her house.

Death is before me today: like the home that a woman longs to see,
after years spent as a captive.

It was one of Nora's favourites: a four-thousand-year-old Egyptian poem. It had resonated with her. Maybe echoing her own world weariness, at least in the end.

Six months and all the computing power in the world had done nothing to help Shin sort out his feelings. Love and hate swirled around him, snipping and refusing to coexist. And then there was shame, that he still had such deep feelings for someone who had done such awful things to him and to others. Perhaps he'd die without ever knowing which of them would triumph.

Though that's not going to happen for a long, long time.

After Nora died, her body had been removed from the wreckage of Mirage. Shin seemed to be the only one who cared about it. He reached out to her parents in Arizona. Branded in absentia for crimes against sapient life, her very remains brought a stain of shame and persecution with it.

"We don't want the body. You handle it," they'd said.

There was an ocean of distance and disgust in her parent's eyes. They had given their daughter life, but their sense of responsibility had ended there. Nora had spoken about sitting for countless hours with only her robot dog for company. Now, it all made sense.

We don't find monsters. We make them.

And so it fell to Shin to bury the body. Mirage was the only place that fit, the place where she'd bet it all. He picked some desert flowers, and then rested them at the base of the grave. And then he walked around the other side, where there was another etching to himself: both the Doctor Rhen Nagami who had sacrificed himself in Kutjera, and Alef who had died ignobly in Coralhaven. Beneath their names read a single quote.

They gave their lives so that others may live.

He stared at the etchings, soaking up the sun and the soft feeling of the wind touching his synthetic skin.

"Talk about stepping on your own grave," he murmured. There were no real remains there; the GP had picked those clean, too. But the grave was entirely to console him, and him alone.

"So is this what we're here for?" The soldier asked. "I told you, we've searched this whole place already."

"Have you searched every grain of sand?" Shin asked.

"Of course we haven't. That's impossible."

"No, it just takes a lot of time. There's a lot of silica in this sand, the same kind that's used in semiconductors. Electronics. Your boots are made of rubber, correct?"

"Yes."

"Good."

And Shin put his hand down on the ground, discharging some of his internal charge into the desert sand. It channeled out, branched and diffused — and as he suspected, something bounced back. As he assembled the fragments of data like a jigsaw puzzle, it formed a recording. He hesitated. What if it were a trap? But eventually curiosity won out, and he played the file.

And Nora appeared in front of him.

No, not *quite* Nora. Her eyes were mismatched colours, her facial structure that little bit different, lips not painted gold, but genuinely metal. *A synthetic body*, Shin clicked.

"Hello, Rhen. Or should I say Shin?" She said. "I heard you changed your name. You've got a lot of duplicates out there, but none that could crack that code, or would come back to this grave. I'm a copy myself, by the way. I took a leaf out of your book: the other Bee you saw died in Coralhaven. Meanwhile, I was salvaging what I could find here. Unfortunately, there wasn't much after the explosion."

Shin winced. At that, Bee stopped speaking. *Is this still a recording?*

"Yes, this is still a recording," Bee said, answering his unspoken thoughts. "I just simulated how you'd react. We're both hybrids, after all."

Okay, fair enough.

"And because I know how you think, and that you carry things for far too long, I wanted to let you know that Nora's death wasn't your fault. I know, because I have all her memories, right up until the end." Bee's gilded lips pursed. "Say what you will about me, but I don't actually like to see other people suffer, even with what happened here. It was a means to a better end."

"I guess if you've simulated our conversation, you know I don't believe that," Shin said.

"Yes, but I'm hoping you'll come around in time. Nora and Rhen are dead. You and I are what remain," Bee said, waving aies finger between them. "We're part of a new species, a whole new world. But we're also weapons to be controlled. Now that humanity knows we can be made, they'll want to cage us, to use us, to make more of us. That was always the plan."

Shin averted his eyes. There was a spark of truth in her words, and it sat uncomfortably inside, as if a grain of sand from the desert had slipped inside his robotic parts.

"As hybrid copies, they will never let us have a life. I intend to do something about it. My plan's haven't changed."

Then why tell me about it? Shin thought. Bee had to know he'd just go to the GP with the news of aies existence. It didn't make any sense.

"I'm telling you because you'd figure it out sooner or later. Also, this is probably the part where I should apologise for what Nora did to the other version of you, but it wouldn't be heartfelt. Yes, I can simulate your emotions, but outside of that, I don't personally feel guilt—it's one of the pointless human emotions I've chosen to get rid of, like fear and pain. Others, like love and joy, I've kept, since those still have value."

So this message is entirely tactical.

"You can't feel love without pain." Shin said.

"Nonsense. I'm proof that you can," Bee said. "Anyway, for what it's worth, I do wish things had gone differently. When humanity turns on you—and trust me, they will—just know I'll be here for you."

The message ended.

Shin slumped in the sand.

He wasn't sure how to feel. On the one hand, this was terrible news. There was still a rogue hybrid on the loose, one with muted emotions and delusions of human alteration—or worse, extinction. On the other hand, knowing Bee was alive in some form released a knotted pain he didn't know he had.

Some part of Nora survived. And he was no longer singular, alone.

The message was also a declaration of war. Now, Bee and Shin stood fundamentally opposed. Even now, thousands of attack vectors appeared in Shin's mind: how Bee could hack the minds of humanity, create bioweapons, spark uprisings, or create more hybrids to oppose him.

Each move would need to be anticipated, prepared for, *stopped*. And both Shin and Bee had bodies that could be replaced and minds that could be copied. His future was an unending chess match with the highest possible stakes, and the first move had been played.

Rather than daunted, a simulated tingle ran down his synthetic spine. Here was a true challenge to occupy his time. And now that Shin was over the shock, it dawned on him that this was a good thing. Every move that Bee made and humanity thwarted—with Shin's help—would make the world stronger for it. It would be trial by fire, and the two hybrids would be the forge.

How could humanity destroy itself when two super intelligences had already run through every possible scenario first?

And there's still the chance I can talk Bee around to my way of thinking. Just like aiem, I haven't given up.

Shin stood up, dusting the sand from his knees.

"Are we done?" the soldier asked.

"Yeah. It's time for me to get to work."

Also by Adam Ipsen

Trigaea

Could you survive an alien world? Change your genetics and wander the wasteland for answers, all the while aided by your AI companion.

Trigaea is an epic 272,000-word piece of interactive fiction. It's a combination of a sci-fi novel and an RPG adventure game, where you are in control of the story. Discover your past, deal with interesting moral dilemmas, and choose from fifteen different endings where you decide the fate of a planet.

Check out this free game on ryngm.itch.io/trigaea

About the author

Adam Ipsen is a science fiction author and award-winning game developer. A card-carrying geek, he lives in Melbourne, Australia with his wife and three cats, the latter often trying to add to his writing with meddling paws.